SHATTERED PILLARS

TOR BOOKS BY ELIZABETH BEAR

A Companion to Wolves (with Sarah Monette)
The Tempering of Men (with Sarah Monette)
All the Windwracked Stars
By the Mountain Bound
The Sea Thy Mistress
Range of Ghosts
Shattered Pillars

SHATTERED PILLARS

ELIZABETH BEAR

TOR®

A TOM DOHERTY ASSOCIATES BOOK

NEW YORK

SHATTERED PILLARS

Copyright © 2013 by Elizabeth Bear

All rights reserved.

Map by Ellisa Mitchell

A Tor Book
Published by Tom Doherty Associates, LLC
175 Fifth Avenue
New York, NY 10010

www.tor-forge.com

Tor® is a registered trademark of Tom Doherty Associates, LLC.

Library of Congress Cataloging-in-Publication Data

Bear, Elizabeth.
    Shattered pillars / Elizabeth Bear.—1st ed.
        p. cm.—(Eternal sky ; bk. 2)
    "A Tom Doherty Associates book."
    ISBN 978-0-7653-2755-0 (hardcover)
    ISBN 978-1-4299-4777-0 (e-book)
    1. Fantasy fiction.   I. Title.
PS3602.E2475S53 2013
813'.6—dc23

                                        2012038826

First Edition: March 2013

Printed in the United States of America

0 9 8 7 6 5 4 3 2 1

For Robin David and Lillian Mai Evans

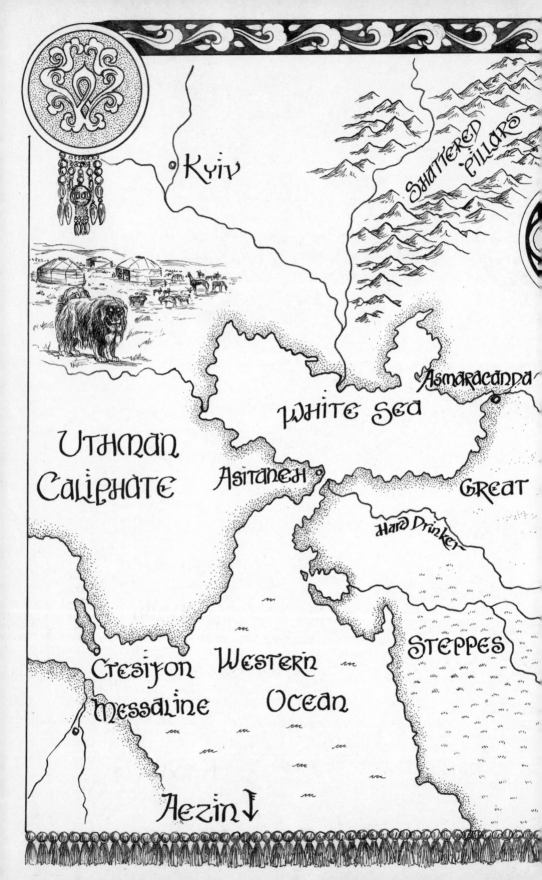

Kyiv

SHATTERED PILLARS

Asmaracanda

WHITE SEA

UTHMAN
CALIPHATE

Asitaneh

GREAT

Hard Drinker

STEPPES

Ctesifon

Western

Messaline

Ocean

Aezin ↓

SHATTERED PILLARS

 1

THE DESERT WRITHED WITH POISON LIFE. A RUSTLING CARPET SURROUNDED Edene on every side. Barbed tails curving over scuttling carapaces that were patterned sand-colored or stone-colored, glossy or dull, rust or taupe or black or brown.

Tireless, escorted by scorpions, she walked through day and night, through the hazy scent of baked stone. Light and darkness had no meaning to what Edene had become. Unpunctuated by sleep, the days joined seamlessly. She could not have said how many had passed when a sunset found her, light-footed and easy, climbing a rocky trail leading into a valley that cut a low sweep of hills. Mountains rose before her, one tier beyond another. She did not recognize the range, but they could not stop her.

Always east. She must move east.

There were ruins here, the remnants of a stone-and-daub house huddled like a mud wasp's nest against a great boulder. This was the first sign of habitation that Edene had seen breaking the desolate Rahazeen outlands since she escaped Ala-Din, the rocky clifftop fortress of the cult of Nameless assassins. Only her wits and the magic of the hammered green-gold ring weighting her left hand had won her free.

Edene paused, contemplating the winding path before her, the slumped carcass of the little house so alien in this landscape. The hills must be wetter than the plateau she had just walked across: their grim line against the evening sky was softened like a man's ill-shaven cheek by a thorny fuzz of shrubs.

Dust turned the sunset yellow behind those hills—east, still east. She was not out of Rahazeen territory yet. But perhaps if she walked the night through, the sun would rise in the same place come morning, and she would know by the changing skies that she was one nation closer to home.

She pressed a hand against her belly. The babe had quickened savagely since she fled Ala-Din, and now she endured a spate of blows that felt like dried rice fire-puffing inside her. It did not pass swiftly, but she was growing accustomed to the child's ferocity.

While she waited out the assault, her eye fell again on the tumbledown lodging. Curiosity drew her off her eastward path for the first time. The hut's walls were standing and roof collapsed, as if someone had carefully stepped in the center. She wondered who had lived here, and a few moments to explore would cost her little in light of the length of the journey still before her.

Her escort of scorpions broke away from her footfalls. A scurrying wave crested and crept, lapping the bottoms of stone walls and mounting crumbling mortar to whisper over the sills of deep, narrow windows. The hut had no remaining door, but a cracked stone lintel still bridged a narrow gap. Edene turned to pass beneath it—

And drew up short.

Within the hut velvet blackness puddled; without lay blue, quiet gloaming. Framed within the door, outlined against that interior darkness, stood an inhuman creature as gray-blue as the twilight hour and as velvety as the dark. It had a long face with a wrinkled muzzle, mobile ears that focused on her brightly, and the huge soft eyes of a night predator. Even in the evening's shadow, its pupils had contracted to pinpricks in the green-gold watered silk of its irises.

"Mistress of Secrets," it said, in a language that hurt her ears but that she nevertheless understood, despite never having heard it before. A thick tongue showed behind chipped, yellowed fangs. "Far we have traveled to find you. I am Besha Ghul. I have come to bring you home to old Erem."

"Erem?" She'd heard of the dead empire, as who had not? But it lay beyond the Western Ocean and the Uthman Caliphate—and no ruined city could serve her now, when she needed to win home to her clan, to her people, and to the father of her child.

For the whole duration of her captivity, she had restrained herself from brooding on Temur—where he was, if he was safe. If he was seeking her, as she suspected he must be. But now she was free, and the itch to return to him was the only fire close to as strong as the curling certainty that had risen in her since she escaped Ala-Din: that she would go home to the steppe and arise a queen.

"Erem," said the Besha Ghul, its ears flicking to and fro. "You wear its ring upon your finger, Mistress of Secrets, Lady of Ruins, Queen of the Broken Places. You walk half within its veil already. It is deep time; its nights and twilights speed like quicksilver to hurry you through the shallow days of this insubstantial modern world. You have more time than the world, my Queen."

She considered that. She considered the blur of days—had they been days at all, then? Nights? Or something else, some shape of time passing that her experience had not yet prepared her for?

"You call me by many titles," Edene said. "But I am not those things. I am Tsareg Edene, not your Queen of Ruins."

Besha Ghul bowed low from the hips, legs bent back to counterbalance arms and torso that swept the dust. Edene saw gray hide stretched gaunt over the shadows between ribs, in bony buttocks. It had no tail.

"You wear the Green Ring," it said, voice muffled by the dust.

Edene glanced down at the plain green-gold band upon her finger. "Rise," she said, recollecting some of the gravitas of the matriarch of her clan. "And explain yourself."

Besha Ghul straightened up as if the depth of its bow were no inconvenience, brushing a little yellow dust from its jowls with clawed fingertips. "You wear the Green Ring," it repeated, as if reciting a refrain. "The beasts of the desert that crawl and sting are yours to command. Yours is the domain of what is broken and what lies in ruins. Yours is jurisdiction over secrets and mysteries and those things intentionally forgotten."

"I see," said Edene. And perhaps she did: in response to Besha Ghul's words, the ring on her hand burned with a wintry chill. It seemed desperately heavy. The babe kicked and kicked again.

Besha Ghul smiled once more, or at least skinned back its flews. "It is I who am charged to teach you how to wield these things. To teach you the power you must employ, when you are Queen. Will you come to Erem with me and meet your army?"

"If I am your Queen," Edene said, "then I would have you guide me to my consort."

Besha Ghul smiled, gray soft lips drawing back from dry yellow teeth meant for tearing flesh. "First you must be crowned, your majesty. Erem is real. It is the true empire, and all khans and kings and caliphs that follow it are insignificant before its memory. How much more insignificant shall they be before its rebirth? When you wear its crown, Lady of Ruins, all the world will bow before you."

When I am Queen. She pictured Temur at her side. Her clan safe. Her child in her arms. Mares and cattle grazing peacefully to the horizon.

Edene felt strong and certain. Her mouth curved in a beneficent smile. She said, "I will come with you to Erem."

MUKHTAR AI-IDOJ, AL-SEPEHR OF THE NAMELESS SECT OF THE RAHAZEEN, knelt in contemplation before a plain, unornamented human skull. Paperdry and brown with age, it lay upon a low table in a room whose every wall was serried with unlit lamps. The skull reflected in the table's gilt and red-enameled surface as if it lay mirrored on blood.

Other than being relict of a dead man, it seemed quite ordinary and inoffensive in the dim evening light.

It was the skull of Danupati, the ancient warrior-emperor of the Lizard Folk. To al-Sepehr's honed *otherwise* senses, it reeked of the ancient knotworks of curse that bound it—and bound every land over which Danupati, once God-Emperor, had held sway.

Al-Sepehr had lowered his indigo veil, letting the night air cool his face. He was not praying. As the high priest of the Nameless and a priest of the Scholar-God, he did not pray to idols, to relics, or to ancestors. He prayed by preserving knowledge, for that was his God's glory—and his own. Nor was he incanting, precisely, for he had no intention of casting spells with the essence of the dead emperor.

He was contemplating, that was all. Allowing the possibilities of the future to fill up the room, his mind, his awareness.

Al-Sepehr was now a man of middle years, his eyesight not so keen as it once had been, and his joints ached from contact with the hard stone floor. He could have fetched a rug—or had one of his wives or servants fetch it—but for the time discomfort suited him. If he meant to watch the night through and give this dead man a proper vigil, the pain would help him stay awake.

Privation kept a man hardened.

The sun finished setting while he watched the skull, his hands folded, his eyes blinking only slowly. Shadows spilled from the corners of the room. The brass lamps—each tidy beside the next, handles and wicks militarily aligned—at first gleamed dully, then lost their luster as darkness grew absolute. The room should have reeked of lamp fuel—or the herbs steeped in oil to sweeten it—but instead it smelled dusty, dry. The lamps stood empty.

Al-Sepehr reached out one hand—the left one—and laid it on the crown of Danupati's skull as if gentling a child. He could see nothing, but he knew exactly the distance and the reach of his arm.

"So, ancient king," he murmured. "Where is the war you vowed would greet any attempt to move your bones?"

Silence followed, long and thin, until it was broken by the papery, powdery whir of insect wings. Not one or two, but thousands, filling the air with the scent of dust and mustiness: the flutter of ten thousand butterflies, then silence as they settled.

Swiftly but individually, the empty brass lamps in their ranks lit themselves, revealing in their own increasing light that each wick was briefly touched by a butterfly before each butterfly vanished into fire. A ripple of light and warmth ran around the room. A ripple that expanded outward, through al-Sepehr, through the walls of the chamber, through the wide rooms of the world.

*　　*　　*

THERE WAS NO COOLNESS IN THE PREDAWN DARK TO WHICH TEMUR AWAK-ened. He lay in yet another unfamiliar sort of bed—he'd learned so much about how the foreigners slept on this journey! This one was a mattress on the floor stuffed firmly with what, by its spring, might be bats of wool. The coverlet was cotton, woven with an open hand, but even that was too warm on such a night and he'd kicked it away.

The air was warm too, if not still. It moved softly beyond the stone-latticed window. The stone walls re-radiated the heat of the day, and the leaves in the garden beyond rustled. A whisper of light fell inside, from the foreign stars and from the city beyond the garden walls: enough that his dark-adapted eyes could pick out the curve of warm flesh in the darkness, the line of shadow below a shoulder blade, dark and sharp as if drawn with a pen.

A woman lay in the bed beside him, her hair drifting across his arm, starlight pooled in the cup of her palm. He knew he should have felt frustration, impatience with the slow grindings of Uthman politeness in this foreign city of Asitaneh when another woman for whom he cared needed his help—but it was hard, at just this instant, after so much fear and exhaustion, to do more than lie in the dark and fill himself with the scent of the person he rested beside.

In the morning, he thought. *I will make my grandfather help me find Edene. In the morning.*

We can have this one night.

The woman breathed softly—but not with the slow regularity of one asleep. As he lifted his head, he could see the gloss of light across dark irises.

"Samarkar," he breathed.

"You felt it?" she asked, speculation altering the contours of her face as it had when he admitted sometimes dreaming true.

He shook his head. "I was asleep."

"I wasn't." The Wizard Samarkar turned in the covers, and that starlight spilled from her hand, running across the bed to thin and vanish. The room was darker than before; now he could see her only as a dim outline of greater darkness against the night. He heard the faint consternation in her voice, but she made herself say, "I wanted to remember this."

He might be younger than she, but he wasn't so young he couldn't read all the pain of her loveless marriage and early widowhood in her words. He opened his mouth to soothe her and shut it again. Given everything they were hunting—the lord of the Rahazeen cult called the Nameless, Temur's stolen lover, vengeance for his slaughtered brother and hers—and everything that was hunting them—his uncle, her surviving brother, assorted murder cults, the dread memory of an ancient sorcerer—he could not promise much.

"I'm at your side," he said at last. "And I will remain there so long as fate permits. Sleep; there will be other nights to remember."

She kissed him in answer, a foreign custom for which he was developing a taste. Then she pulled back and said, "I think I shall not be sleeping in any case. Something cold and chill has passed across the world this night; I think I would have felt it even in my dreams."

"Cold and chill? Something sorcerous?"

"Only as your blood vow in Tsarepheth was sorcerous." Her shape moved against lesser darkness as she stood. Her hair swept his face again, full of the scent of the sea. "A true word from a man or woman of power has the strength to change the world, so the sages say. If you did not feel it, what wakened you?"

"I don't know. Perhaps just your breathing—" He cast from side to side, listening in the night. "No," he said. "Wait. No birds."

She cocked her head, a hand to her ear. But Temur did not need the confirmation. There *were* birds, heralding the first paling of sky before an incipient sun—but not outside the window. Birds in the city. But no birds in the garden.

Silently, Temur found his feet. Samarkar slid into a pair of breeches she'd discarded. Temur grasped his knife, which was laid against a bolster beside his bed—on Samarkar's side, but he had not been planning to share the couch when he retired.

He pulled on his clout, holding his knife between his teeth. She struggled into a tunic and found her own knife—a much shorter, square-pommeled one, meant for chores and not fighting. All Rasans seemed to carry the like. "Follow me," she said.

He did without hesitation. Samarkar had grown to adulthood in the terraced cities of Rasa and Song. She could find her way around a permanent dwelling place as Temur could not. But *he* could guide them across a steppe that would seem featureless to the uninitiated.

Barefoot, padding on blood-hot stone, she brought them to a door beside which paced one of the household guards, broad-shouldered and stocky beneath a robe of dark browns that blended into the shadows.

"Hail," she said.

The guard must have heard them coming, because he turned quietly in the gloom. Temur could only tell that his hand rested on the hilt of his scimitar by the outline of his silhouette.

"Who passes?" he asked in the Uthman language.

Temur's use of it was still raw, but he managed to say, "The guests of Ato Tesefahun," without choking on his tongue.

"To what purpose do you creep in the dark?" Though the guard's tone was suspicious, no scrape of steel on sheath revealed him to have loosened his sword.

"Someone's in the garden," Samarkar said. "We thought we'd go and see who."

Her sarcasm—Temur could see the raised eyebrows and one-sided smile that went with it in his mind, if not through the dark—seemed to ease the guard. "I shall raise the alarm—"

"Wait," said Temur. "Just wait a moment, is all, and watch us from the door."

He stepped up to it, allowing the guard to check suspiciously through the peephole before pulling the door aside. The guard kept it chained at top and bottom, so Temur and Samarkar had to sidle through a narrow gap to pass one by one into the garden.

Outside, the starlight less filtered, Temur's eyesight showed him a stark world of blues and silvers outlined in shadows that could have been cut from black silk. The graded paths of the courtyard seemed treacherously uneven, the plantations along their edges shrouds of vegetation over some bottomless pitfall. Temur's breath came fast and light, his hands cold with anticipation and his heart whirring like a chariot wheel. A motion beyond the screen of pomegranates caught Temur's gaze; pale light sliding on pale cloth. He watched for a moment, some of the anticipatory tension falling out of his shoulders and the weight from off his heart.

It was Brother Hsiung, the sworn-to-silence monk of Song. He stood in a clear patch of the central court, practicing the strikes and parries of his weaponless war form, moving with a fluidity no less impressive for the force with which he threw each kick or punch.

He must have heard Temur's or Samarkar's tread upon the path as they approached, though, because he let his hands fall to his sides and his flurrying feet rest on the gravel.

"What woke you?" Samarkar asked as they came up behind him.

Temur knew she wasn't really expecting an answer, not until they were inside and Hsiung could reach ink and paper. But Brother Hsiung turned, light on his feet for all the bulk of his barrel body, and Temur—hardened to war and death since his eighth summer—took a quick step back.

The monk's eyes blazed poison-bright as green glass held before a fire. The flickering light cast Temur's and Samarkar's shadows out long behind them, like coils of rope unreeling.

"Well," Temur said, in his own language. "That's not a good sign."

BROTHER HSIUNG HELD UP HIS HANDS AS SAMARKAR STEPPED FORWARD. She heard the crunch of footsteps behind them—the door guard coming at a run—but she reached out to Brother Hsiung as if there were no hurry in the world. Her own hands were blurred by a dim azure glow as she—reflexively—called her power. Hsiung backed away slowly, head shaking, holding eye contact the entire time. He did not seem ensorcelled—well, no, of *course* he seemed ensorcelled, Samarkar corrected herself—but he seemed in control of his faculties. So she paused where she was and lowered her hands to her sides, sweeping Temur and the guard back with the left one as it fell.

It was eerie to hold Hsiung's gaze while his eyes crawled with radiance, but she did it, watching for a glance or an expression that might offer a clue to what he wished of her. Brilliant green sparks chased one another through the space between his iris and the surface of his eye—a membrane that should have been transparent but by daylight would show the blue clouds of incipient blindness. Samarkar could see them now, lit from beneath. Her stomach tossed, her long muscles weak with fear. She thought it ought to subside when she reminded herself that she was a trained Wizard of Tsarepheth, who should be observing this both as sorcery and natural history.

Perhaps it ought to—but it didn't. It didn't matter; she forced herself to focus anyway.

She was leaning forward for a better look when Temur, beside her, caught her hand.

She squeezed his fingers and did not let him draw her back. "Wait."

The man-at-arms brought up a lantern from within the door. Samarkar did not see how he lit it, but it gleamed suddenly, flaring and then dimming, casting a natural light across the scene.

"Go," Samarkar said. "If you must raise the alarm, pray do it quietly. But above all, I bid you bring the master of this house."

He hesitated; she did not turn to see if he obeyed. She still had the voice and manner of a princess of Rasa. The man-at-arms left the lantern on a plinth and ran.

From the edge of her eye she saw Temur shift his weight, but he hesitated—dagger in his hand, to be sure, and balanced on the balls of his feet—but not yet stepping forward. She released his hand. From the way his head tilted, she understood that he would have given her a grateful glance for not fouling his line of attack, except no mortal power could have shifted his eyes from the monk.

Brother Hsiung stepped back into the courtyard, claiming his space. He resettled into his stance—balanced, fluid—and began to move again. Simple forms, meditations, building rapidly to more complicated and focused ones. Samarkar, who had practiced with him across the wastes of salt and sand, watched for a moment or two.

Then she walked forward, onto the flags of the open court, and faced him. She thought Temur would reach for her. Perhaps he did, but if so he paused before his hand made contact and let her pass unimpeded.

The early forms were easy. Samarkar kept pace at first. She thought she understood what Hsiung was doing—using the forms to control whatever sorcery raged beneath his skin—and she was determined to mirror his concentration. To offer him support.

That green light behind his eyes twisted and flickered, but they did focus on her briefly before his expression turned inward again. Sweat collected on his brow, first a skin of it and then beads, rivulets. It splashed from his nose and spiked his eyelashes, and still they moved in echoes.

He soon outstripped her skill and continued—at first ever more elaborate, then deceptively simple and with snakelike speed. But she paced him, falling into her own routines—a silent ally, if nothing else. And she watched his eyes.

The lines of concentration on his forehead smoothed as he found his rhythm, to be replaced by serenity. The crawling fire that burned within his irises began to dim, until it was like looking at the last veil of flame surrounding a red-hot coal before it gutters to an ember. He continued, hands stroking the air with conviction and certainty now, feet moving fluidly from one stance to the next. She had lost her focus on Temur and only with the dimming of the glow infecting Brother Hsiung did she become aware that the lamp still burned over her shoulder.

Samarkar might not have known when the light died entirely, except the crawling shadows died too. Hsiung did not cease, however, until his forms were complete—and so Samarkar perforce kept pace with him. Their martial dance was a spell, now, and she would not risk breaking it.

Eventually he came to rest, facing Samarkar, his broad chest rising and falling slowly, but strongly enough to be visible in the firelight. His hands hung relaxed at his thighs. His clothing hung too, sand-worn and sweat-soaked, clinging to his skin. He bowed his head to her, and when he raised it again his eyes were wide and brown and faintly cloudy.

A male voice—full and controlled, worn smooth by years—spoke over Samarkar's shoulder in tones of mild surprise and satisfaction. "Edifying. Perhaps we should take this inside, where the tea is waiting."

Ato Tesefahun, Temur's grandfather and their host, had arrived.

Aто Tesefahun—*Grandfather*, as Temur was still trying to learn to think of him—was a small, spare man whose brown skin bore a scatter of even darker spots across both cheeks. He dismissed the man-at-arms back to his post and led the remaining three into a house that now glowed with the light of dozens of lamps. Having closed the door, he gestured them to seats on jewel-colored cushions arrayed around a low tea table. He provided a robe to cover Temur's near nudity. Temur was glad to slip the cool cotton on and settle himself cobbler-fashion on the tiled floor. He glanced around the room as he adjusted the cushion under his hips. It was a fighter's impulse—assets and liabilities—which he smiled slightly to recognize in himself.

This was a large chamber, red-walled in stone and clay like most houses in Asitaneh. But in this house the stone was worked with every contrivance of the mason's art. A counter-relief of vines wriggled up alongside each of the many narrow windows, intaglio flowers picked out in pigments so brilliant as to be visible even by lamplight. The room held little furniture—just a second low table in addition to the one around which Ato Tesefahun seated them. It bore a laden tea tray and four glasses. Ato Tesefahun fetched those himself and brought them back.

The black-and-red enamel of the tray was protected from the heat by a folded towel. Steam coiled from the chased silver pot as Ato Tesefahun lifted and poured through a long spout into each glass. His motion drew Temur's attention to the small roll of paper and the brush and the well of western-style ink beside it, but Ato Tesefahun made no gesture toward them when he set the pot down again and served the tea.

Only having done so did he seat himself beside Samarkar, with some fussing of old joints and drawing out of his striped kaftan to make room for his knees. For a moment, Temur was struck by the incongruity of it—the four of them, all sleep-mazed and half-dressed, their hair uncombed, preparing to sip tea. Ato Tesefahun raised his glass, and so did they all.

The tea was minty and sweet. It did a great deal to return Temur to calm wakefulness from his state of high alert.

No one spoke except for pleasantries until the first round of tea was drunk and the glasses refilled. Although their earlier conversation—nearly yesterday, now—had been marked by a stunning adherence to the social niceties and very little actual business, Temur was not yet accustomed to the stately procession of events demanded by Uthman polite custom. But on pain of being seen as a barbarian by his grandfather, he watched the old man's hands and face and waited for his cues. He watched Samarkar too, with his peripheral vision, aware that her court manners were second to none.

Hsiung drank his tea in predictable silence.

Finally, Ato Tesefahun turned his glass around with his fingertips and looked from each of them to the next. His impression of quiet expectation emboldened Temur, but Samarkar must have been biding her time, because she spoke first. "Has anyone seen Hrahima, I wonder?"

That was Uthman politeness too, that indirectness.

Ato Tesefahun refilled the tea. "Who can keep a cat in at night?"

But he winked, leading Temur to understand that the Cho-tse scout might be on some mission for the old man. When Tesefahun smiled, his strong, worn teeth were revealed. They had bands of brown and amber color like tortoiseshell; Temur's mother's teeth had been similarly stained, and he had never seen it otherwise.

Temur shivered with unaccustomed nostalgia. To shake it off, he leaned into the table, his hands in his lap, the edge pressing his arms. Ato Tesefahun met his regard for a moment before looking away and nodding.

"Perhaps," he said, "it is time to address the issue of the Nameless after all. Although I fear that at this point, it's bound to ruin all our breakfasts."

"One meal or another." Samarkar looked drawn from their long journey, her bones showing too strongly through the fine flesh of her face. Temur wondered if he'd ever see her face round and plump as a ripe fruit. "That was not a Rahazeen spell."

Ato Tesefahun, a wizard in his own right, though of a different tradition than Samarkar's, shook his head. "No."

"What was it?"

With uncharacteristic directness, he turned to Hsiung, who sat— hands folded—and gave them all a face as deceptionless as an egg.

"You have read from a book of Erem," Ato Tesefahun said in the language of Song. "It is the reason you are going blind, Brother Hsiung, is it not?"

Hsiung's air of relaxation seemed not all that different from his air of deliberate readiness—until one saw him shift states suddenly. He pulled his hands into his chest, steepling the fingers together. Slowly, twice, he nodded.

Samarkar began, "How did you know—" but Ato Tesefahun's raised, tipped hand made her rein herself in.

He said, "Is it the reason you took a vow of silence?"

Again, the nod, although this time with a head tilt that Temur took to mean *somewhat, but not exactly.* It was accompanied by an incremental softening of Hsiung's shoulders, as if he began to set down some load.

Temur wondered what—in a book—might lead to such a vow.

Ato Tesefahun poured tea again, and each of them drank it—even Hsiung, though Temur could see his hands shaking as he raised the glass to his mouth. He swallowed, or Temur presumed he did. In the lamplight, there was no chance of seeing that bull's neck ripple.

"Was it the glass book?" asked Temur's grandfather.

No, said Hsiung's gesture.

"Not the Black Book of Erem?" said Ato Tesefahun.

Again, the headshake. Whatever the Black Book of Erem might be or might presage, Temur almost feared to know, because the relief that softened Ato Tesefahun's face was powerfully unmistakable. "A minor text, then. That's a small mercy."

He poured more tea, sipped, and continued. "What we witnessed tonight was an effect of the rekindling of some deep magic of old Erem."

Temur felt Samarkar sit straighter. "Danupati," she said, her knuckles whitening, fingers pinkening as she knotted her hands together.

Ato Tesefahun tipped his head, suspicious as an old wolf. "Pray," he said. "Continue."

"We would have told you last night," Samarkar said. "But—"

But for Uthman custom inviolable as law that said a guest must not speak of evil things before a night had passed. It was Ato Tesefahun himself who had kept the conversation to trivialities and diverted any attempt to redirect it. He could scarcely complain now.

He just nodded, and wound his right hand in a spooling motion.

Samarkar looked at Temur. "It's your story."

Even if he was not the sort to have a lot of comfort in telling it. He breathed in once and sighed it out again. Slowly, in spare but precise detail—recounting the story as he once would have reported the outcome of a raid to his now-dead brother Qulan—Temur told Ato Tesefahun how he had been barricaded into Danupati's tomb by a rebel faction among the People of the Dragon Banner, and how he had discovered while there that the tomb had been desecrated.

Remembering now, Temur felt the chill fear that had crushed him then rising once more. *You survived it*, he told himself. *It cannot hurt you now.*

When he had finished—with Samarkar and his bay mare, Bansh, riding to his rescue, and the following attack by the Nameless Rahazeen—he paused and waited for Ato Tesefahun to refill his glass. The teapot was empty, however, and so Temur's grandfather pulled a woven silken cord that hung beside the door.

Temur heard the chime of a distant bell.

When Ato Tesefahun turned back, the lines of concern on his forehead had graven themselves even deeper. "I think," he said, "given the timing of the assault, we have to assume that al-Sepehr is in possession of the skull of Danupati. And that possibly what we felt, what caused Brother Hsiung's reaction"—he bowed slightly, and Brother Hsiung returned the courtesy—"was al-Sepehr calling upon the legacy of Danupati's curse. For Danupati conquered Erem, and knew well its powers . . . and the powers of Erem are a sort of contagion—"

"Like plague?" Temur asked, thinking of Hsiung's stories of the far east and how sickness might be sweeping west along the Celadon Highway even now.

"War," Samarkar said. "That is Danupati's curse, anyway."

Ato Tesefahun kissed the air like a grandmother. "The two are not . . . mutually exclusive."

"There's more," Temur said, but was interrupted by the scrape of slippers in the corridor.

He bent his head, studying his knuckles while a servant whisked the old tea tray away—with the unused ink and paper, as Hsiung had not required them—and supplied a new one. In addition to tea, this one contained pastries—some laced with jam, some jellied rosewater—the smell of which made Temur's stomach grumble anxiously.

Ato Tesefahun waved the servant away and slid a plate of pastries in front of Samarkar. As he served Hsiung and Temur, he said, "Continue."

"There is a woman I care about," Temur said. "She was captured by the Nameless, stolen away by the blood ghosts they command. Her name is Tsareg Edene, and I have reason to believe that she is still alive and captive."

Ato Tesefahun, who had just placed a fragment of pastry in his mouth, chewed thoughtfully. Temur took the opportunity to eat as well. He and Hsiung and Samarkar had not yet recovered from the privation of their long journey. Flakes crumbled in his mouth, releasing richness, the sweetness of glaze, the pungency of rose petals.

He imagined the pastry was good; the truth was, he was too hungry to have noticed if it wasn't.

Ato Tesefahun rinsed his mouth with tea and swallowed. "They will have taken her to Ala-Din," he said. "If they wish to hold her securely . . .

they call it the Rock. And the Rock has never been taken. Not even by the Khagan, your grandfather."

My other grandfather, Temur thought. He said, "How do I get there?"

"Getting *there* is the easy part," said Tesefahun. "Getting *in* will be trickier."

"I see," said Samarkar. "So how shall we get in, then?"

Ato Tesefahun showed his brown teeth in a narrow grin. "Magic, Wizard Samarkar. Magic shall see you within. The magic of *architecture.*"

3

IN THE RED-AND-WHITE CITADEL OF TSAREPHETH, IN THE RASAN IMPERIAL second city of the same ancient name, the Wizard Hong leaned aching hands on time-smoothed white stone battlements, his head fallen below his shoulders. His exhaustion weighed on him like old heartbreak, like everything and everyone he had left behind when he fled Song. When he found the strength to lift his face, his gaze fell down the long misty river valley toward the summer palace of the Bstangpo—the Emperor Song-tsan, forty-second of that name.

And perhaps, Hong-la thought, the last to bear it—given the plague that had come to Tsarepheth. Not from the west, through the Range of Ghosts and the Steles of the Sky along the Celadon Highway—for that fabled route was all but closed with the civil war that had raged between would-be Khagans of the Qersnyk people of the steppe—but from the east, overland from Song and through the capital, Rasa.

It was like no plague that Hong-la—who had once been a bondsman in the southern principalities and who was now a surgeon deemed skillful even among those legendary healers, the Wizards of Tsarepheth—had seen before. The news riding in advance of the illness had called it the Black Bloat, and some of the symptoms were similar. But Black Bloat it was not.

Whether it *killed* like the Black Bloat still remained to be seen.

Hong-la stroked the sun-warmed stone, feeling its age and substance with the layered awareness of a trained wizard. Generations of master stonemasons and master wizards had devoted their lives to the construction of the Citadel. They had built it from the exhumed bones of the earth, its foundations intertwined deep with those of the mountains whose flanks it bridged. And all the strength of their lives and knowledge and intention, and all the strength of those mountains, was still set in its blocks. That was strength a wizard could use.

In addition, the sacred river Tsarethi forged through channels beneath the Citadel, its stream bearing the blessings wrought by wizards down through all of Rasa—and several other kingdoms—until it reached the sea. This close to its headwaters, the Tsarethi still ran with distinct currents: some warm from the sulfurous hot springs that trickled from the roots of the volcano called the Cold Fire; some frigid with ice melt from the heights of the Steles of the Sky. There was power in that too—both in the sources and the mingling.

Hong-la opened himself to the stone and let the strength it contained trickle into the emptiness of his exhaustion. It started with a fingertip tickle, the sensation of running one's hands across a boar's-bristle brush. The feeling of pins and needles crept up his fingers joint by joint, pushing the bone-tired ache before it so a band of soreness ringed his wrists, then his forearms, then his upper arms. Behind the pain and the tingling came fresh strength, vitality, a sense of new life as seductive as water to a man worked dry.

It wanted to be a cataract, a wall of energy that could have slammed the Wizard Hong up against the walls of himself, splashed him aside and crushed him under its roil. To tap the reserves of the Citadel was not a thing done lightly: Tsarepheth's was an antique and weighty strength, and sipping its flow was not unlike dipping into the flood with a drinking goblet without being swept away.

Hong-la constricted the eager push of energy to a thread and let the new strength push his elongated frame upright. His black wizard's coat was limp with too-long wearing, stained with sweat and worse things. It hung on his already spare, square frame with new space against the ribs and underarms. The jade-paneled wizard's collar had worn galls on his clavicles. His hands no longer ached with exhaustion, because the counterfeit strength of his borrowed vitality concealed it, but the skin was raw and peeling from constant bathing in antiseptic chemicals, which had begun to bleach out the cloth of his rolled-up sleeves. He knew he stank of those antiseptics, and also of old sweat and sickrooms, and he wished he had time to adjourn to the bathing chambers below and come back to his patients with a fresh body and fresh will.

Like sleep, it would have to wait.

His hands wanted to clench, to clutch at the wall and keep the flow of energy coming until it burst him like a blown-up bladder. It was so *good* simply not to be tired that it took all a wizard's discipline to control the desire for more. The power, given its own devices, would use him as a conduit: he would blaze with it, burn like a candle, and it would flood through him to equalize from the great storage cell of the Citadel into the cold mountain air beyond. He'd incandesce before he died.

He pulled his hands away. The borrowed strength filled him like rough wine. He stepped back from the battlement, and as he turned—

He startled. A small man stood there, skinny rather than slender, perhaps half Hong-la's weight even haggard as the surgeon had become. A gray moustache trailed down sunken cheeks to brush the chest of the old man's plain black cotton coat. Though it was worn shiny at the elbows, it could not disguise his air of authority. Yet he had waited for Hong-la with silent patience.

"Yongten-la," the Wizard Hong said, bowing carefully. The strength buzzing in him made him dizzy.

The master of Hong-la's order needed no pretensions, no marks of ceremony to set him apart. Among those with the wit to recognize it, his learning cloaked him in all the majesty he could desire—and to those who could not recognize the truth of what he was, greatest wizard among the Wizards of Tsarepheth, it was just as well he pass unremarked.

Now he studied Hong-la's countenance, and Hong-la knew what he saw: the too-bright eyes of recharged exhaustion, the healthy color like an ink wash over sallow fatigue, the cropped hair grown long enough to stick out in sweaty spikes around his ears and nape. Completing his inspection, Yongten-la frowned, but he nodded. "You'll do."

"I'd better," Hong-la replied. "You didn't run for me yourself because you were out of novices."

It got a tired smile, at least. Yongten-la turned; Hong-la fell in step beside him.

"You were on your way back to the wards?"

Hong-la inclined his head. "Will you accompany me, Old Master?"

"If it will not be an inconvenience," said the Wizard Yongten, exactly as if he were merely someone's curious uncle.

Whatever sound escaped Hong-la, it must have reflected his incredulity, because Yongten-la's smile widened and grew crooked. "Very well," Yongten-la said. "We will offer what comfort we can."

"It won't be long now," Hong-la said. "Unless we discover something miraculous."

They descended.

The great stairways of the Citadel were dished from the passage of thousands of feet and hundreds of years. The steps cupped Hong-la's feet through the flexible soles of his split boots—he'd never gotten used to the Rasan toe-box, and so he had his shoes made specially in the eastern style—and the steps made him feel he was walking in the grasp of hard, unyielding hands.

The plague wards were not within the Citadel itself but under canopies at its base, where the waters of the wild Tsarethi would carry the taint of illness away and pound it against stones like soiled linens until the currents licked it clean. Hong-la and Yongten-la paused by the entrance, where a row of newly arrived patients rested on litters, awaiting triage. The wizards allowed the novices staffing the makeshift gates to drape them in protective canvas coats that could be boiled when they were shed and to wrap their feet in linen pouches. It wasn't enough, Hong-la knew, but it was better than taking no precautions at all. What puzzled him was that quarantine and isolation seemed to be having no effect in slowing the spread of the plague. It was as if it actually *were* carried on the fog, or by evil spirits of the night air, as any superstitious merchant or noble might insist.

The disease that sickened the plague patients in these pavilioned wards always followed the same course, and the wizards who tended them were keeping them separated by its stage of progress. The outer wards—where

most of the triage patients would soon be admitted, the worst-affected having already been found by the litter crews and brought into quarantine—
were full of people well enough to sit up, whose breath rasped and wheezed
through constricted air passages and whose bodies burned hot with the
fervor of their life force fighting the pestilence.

They were tended by novices and a few of the less experienced wizards,
but Hong-la made a point of moving among them as well—feeling the foreheads and palpating the auras of men and women in the first stages of the
disease. It was possible—even likely—that if a clue toward successful treatment could be found, it might be found in those not yet sick unto death.

In this ward the novices had made an effort to separate tradesmen and
minor nobility—anyone, even a prince, who sought the care of the wizards must come into quarantine—but there was still a certain amount of
interpersonal friction. The patients felt well enough to squabble: here a
prostitute who did not think she should be bedded beside a slave woman,
here a farmer's wife looked upon with scorn by the wife of a cobbler.

Hong-la and Yongten-la moved from pallet to pallet, crouching to
examine the patients and rising up again. Hong-la found nothing new: in
this early stage, the sick showed signs of weakening life processes—but
something else, something contradictory. Over their chests, front and back,
the aura of strength and health grew slowly stronger. Stronger, but blacker,
so that Hong-la wondered if it was the life processes of the *infection* that
made his fingertips tingle.

He'd tried drawing off that excess before, and the patients he'd attempted it with had rapidly worsened and begun to choke like asthmat-
ics. So he did not attempt that now but instead stood and bent almost
double to bring his head close to Yongten-la's for a private consultation.

"It feels like a curse, not an illness," said Yongten-la against his ear.
"Something that draws the life processes of the patient to feed itself. I'd
say it was worth looking inside, but . . . I have not your skill in surgery."

"If it were the abdomen, and not the heart and lungs, I would look for
a volunteer to let me open them," said Hong-la. He had neutered enough
female wizards in his life to be confident in poking around inside a living
human belly. Surgery on the pump and bellows that sustained immediate
life, however—

He shook his head.

"We are waiting for someone to die," said Yongten-la.

No treatment had worked—not magic, not herbs, not fungus. Not the arts of manipulation of the life force at which the Wizards of Tsarepheth excelled.

Hong-la said, "We are waiting to perform an autopsy, yes."

They stepped apart a hand's breadth, moving toward the inner ward now.

"There's a minor blessing of this illness," Yongten-la said bitterly, his voice still far too low to carry. "It's forced the Bstangpo to seek reconciliation."

Hong-la was too tired to pretend shock at his master's ruthlessness. The Bstangpo—the Emperor Songtsan—was not best pleased that the Citadel had chosen to protect the Wizard Samarkar—his sister, once-princess—when she had spirited away Payma, an imperial wife pregnant with the child of the emperor's younger brother Tsansong, who was to be executed for treason. But Songtsan could not manage an outbreak on this scale without the wizards and their healing skills.

He had not so much come to them cap in hand as offered, magnanimously, not to arrest the Citadel's litter-bearing novices and healing wizards on sight if they ventured out into the city to tend the sick and enforce quarantine. It was a first step, and Hong-la knew that a warming trend in political relations was easier to maintain once established than to create from scratch.

The air grew gray and chill. The sun was setting, and wizard-lit globes were brought from within the Citadel and hung about the pavilions by robed, hurrying servants. Hong-la was still contemplating what he might have said in response to Yongten-la when a novice—masked in gauze and gowned in that same boiled canvas—staggered up, clumsy in her linen foot shields. "Hong-la," she said, bowing low.

Hong-la could see the thrust against her mask as she pushed out her tongue in a sign of respect. He would have to break her of that; it was unsafe when confronted with contagion. But even with the power of the Citadel humming numbingly in his fingertips, he was too tired to remonstrate with her now. She cast her eyes at Yongten-la's feet but managed to restrain herself and address Hong-la here in his area of expertise, despite the daunting presence of the master.

That was good. It showed discipline.

"Wizard Hong," she said. "Come, hurry. The tinker Pemba is—"

She hesitated.

"Dying?" Hong-la suggested.

"I did not presume to know his fate," said the novice, whose name was Sengemo. Her eyes stayed determinedly fixed on the ground between the wizards. "But Master—I would hurry."

"Lead us," Hong-la said.

Hong-la suspected that Pemba had brought the illness to Tsarepheth with him. A traveling tradesman, he had been the very first person in the city to sicken; it seemed entirely too tidy that he should also be the first to pass. But that was this disease in all ways—unnaturally tidy, unnaturally uniform in its course and speed of progression.

The Wizards Hong and Yongten chased the hurrying novice as she wound through the wards of sicker women and men. These patients were not well enough to fuss overmuch about whom they had been set beside—or even notice—and merchants lay beside beggars, all whistling each breath out as if through reeds. Their arms and legs were swaddled, their chests bared to ease the painful heat that grew within. Some were dosed with poppy; some had chosen instead to bear the agony, or were far enough gone in delirium that wizards had made the difficult decision to husband scarce resources for those who would benefit more.

Black and violet shadows grew between their ribs, beneath the breasts of the women and across the pectoral muscles of the men. Hong-la thought that bruising was a sign of internal bleeding, perhaps the rupture or dissolution of the lung tissue. Once it began, the faces of the victims grew yellow-gray beneath the varied pigments of their skins, their lips and nail beds the color tale-tellers called blue, which was in truth a horrid bruised purple-gray. That fetid life process burned strongly near the hearts of these patients, while their own strength ebbed from their limbs and minds like that of a man who drowns.

The victims grew worse and worse, the course of the disease more and more advanced, until the wizards and their guiding novice reached the bedside of Pemba the tinker. Another wizard—Anil-la, who was young but skilled—had crouched there, one hand laid flat on Pemba's sweat-slicked crown. A cup and pipette were set nearby: someone had been trickling honey water into the sick man's mouth.

Hong-la hunkered beside Anil-la. The patient's breath—or breathlessness—had moved beyond wheezing and into a teakettle whistle like nothing the wizard and surgeon had heard before. Pemba's chest rose and fell like a bellows. When Hong-la laid a hand against his nostrils, he could feel the suck and push of air in the spaces between his fingers with each desperate gasp.

But the air he was finally moving seemed to do Pemba no good: his lips gleamed the color of pewter; his protruding tongue was like rotten meat. Hong-la pinched Pemba's fingertips and poked his gums. Where Hong-la had pressed they whitened and stayed pale. Pemba's lids lay nigh closed. Through the clotted lashes, Hong-la saw dull slits of eye. When he drew a lid back with his thumb, though, a tremor shook Pemba's body, and his pupil contracted like a flinch. He was conscious, but too weak for want of air to curl a finger or blink an eye.

That moved Hong-la to more pity than anything else.

"Poppy," he said, and Anil-la reached for a vial at his belt. He added a drop or two of tincture to that cup and stirred with the pipette. When he held the pipette over Pemba's mouth and let the water flow in, it trickled back out the corners.

"Rub the tincture on his gums," Hong-la said. The blood was flowing so poorly—Pemba's pulse thready and so fast Hong-la could not count the individual heartbeats—it still might have no effect. But Hong-la could imagine, too vividly, the patient's panic and distress and utter helplessness. He could not do nothing.

And so Hong-la told himself until, with the sound of cracking cartilage, Pemba's breath stopped—just stopped, though Hong-la could see the contraction of his abdomen as his diaphragm struggled—and his throat began to swell.

Even the Wizard Yongten, standing aside to give the surgeons room to practice, made a noise of dismay.

Black blood and crimson blood—threaded through slick, shiny mucous with stinking strands of yellow-green pus or phlegm—welled up Pemba's windpipe and slid gelatinously from the corners of his mouth, bubbling from a slack jaw as Anil-la snatched his hands back. Pemba thrashed, his body arching from feet to shoulders, hips lifted and arms flung limp at his sides. His jaw gaped—not drooping, now, but thrust wide by the force of the matter welling from his mouth as if from some spring in the Song hells of Hong-la's childhood stories. The stench of putrescence made Hong-la's mouth water and his belly clench.

Hong-la would have recoiled—his muscles shivered with the desire to scramble back—but he had seen the foulness of burst appendixes and suppurating wounds. This was not so much worse.

Not so much.

He grasped Pemba's jaw in his left hand, levered a wooden wedge from his belt into the hinge of it, and dug with frantic claws into the rising tide of slime. Ropes of mucus broke around his fingers, stretching and slick—until he brushed something hard and moving—*rattling*—in Pemba's distended throat. He grabbed for it as he would grab the slick skull of a half-born child, trying to find a place to hook a fingertip—

It slid into his palms. Black, glistening. Draped in membranous webs of mucus and blood and stinking phlegm. A jointed, chitinous thing that blinked slime-veiled eyes and snapped ragged needle teeth at Hong-la's face.

He should have held it. He should have grasped its ankles and swung it against the tentpole, against a nearby stone. He should have crushed its skull, the glaring yellow eyes it turned on him, and dissected the remains.

He recoiled, tumbling backward. It kicked off from his palms, needlepoint talons pinpricking his hands—and launched itself into the air and was gone.

What welled from the sides of Pemba's wedged jaw now was clean blood, thick and dark from lack of air. As Hong-la rolled to his knees, holding his pus-smeared hands wide, he watched the tide stem to a trickle, then fail.

Mercifully, Pemba was dead when the second demonspawn followed its clutchmate into the sky.

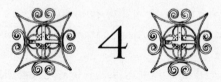

4

BESHA GHUL WAS QUICK AND QUIET, ITS LONG HEAD HUNKERING BETWEEN angular shoulders on a long, thick neck. It paced like sidling smoke on the pads of thick-clawed paws, heels or hocks moving high, like levers, as it led Edene into the shadows of the derelict hut. A smell of carrion reached her as she ducked the cracked and slanted lintel—the ghul's supper? Or the remains of a nest left by some temporary inhabitant?

The rich, rotten smell did not nauseate her as it once would have, though her child struggled in her belly as if in response.

Inside the crumbled hut, her eyes adapted quickly to shadows. She stepped carefully, ducking to avoid the spindled timbers that slanted from wall to hearth like so much carelessly tossed kindling. Somebody had brought those timbers here, Edene thought, at great effort or great expense. Somebody had hauled them from whatever wet hollow grew trees—even slight, contorted trees—in this desert.

Somebody, no matter how poor, had thought this a place worth living in.

The walls were daubed stones piled course on course. The floor was earth only. It slanted back to a well dug in the rear corner of the hut, which they found by skirting the edges of the ruin. The walls still bore up the outer end of the roof timbers, making a passage where a ghul and a woman who crouched down upon her heels could creep through.

Edene had no problem seeing in the dark. The well was edged in stones, a pavement set into the earth for an arm span around it. You might build your house over your water, in the desert, to protect it from heat and from wanderers—but no one would want the earth of their floor made mud every time they needed to haul up a drink. Edene crouched beside the ragged semicircle of the pit, staring down into a darkness even her eyes could not pierce.

"Water?" she asked Besha Ghul, when it crouched beside her.

"There is no water in this well," it said. "It drained into the tunnels long ago. We claimed it."

Edene stayed where she hunkered, and stayed silent. The curve of her belly pressed the tops of her thighs, hard and yet resilient, like a drumhead. She considered the ghul, the well, the cramped angle under the collapsed roof, and the daubed stone beyond.

"You want me to climb down."

The ghul blinked at Edene, round-pupiled eyes no longer lambent in this close darkness—though she could make them out, still. "It's an easy climb."

She let her left palm rest on her belly, highlighting the arch of it under her stained robes. The ghul had no problem in seeing her: she watched its eyes focus. But it seemed to attach no significance to the gesture.

"How easy?"

Besha Ghul shrugged and showed her hooked fingers, long claws. "A scamper."

She touched the edge of the well. The stone was rough, lipped. She could hook fingertips behind its edge, brace her palms against the roughness. Her shoes were little more than soft-soled slippers, laced tight, meant for scuffing about the fortress Ala-Din in pursuit of the duties a captive had been assigned. Edene's nose wrinkled involuntarily as she remembered the ammonia reek of guano, the slick sound of primary feathers, each as tall as she was, as hard as steel and as light as spider silk, sliding against one another.

It was irrelevant.

The shoes would serve.

"You first," she said, and waved Besha Ghul forward.

*   *   *

EDENE HAD NO DIFFICULTY IN CLIMBING DOWN; HER TOES FOUND LEDGES AND her fingers holds as if she had come this way a thousand times. And in truth, it was little more of a scramble than she had managed all the years of her youth among the broken slates and granite of the foothills of the Steles of the Sky.

In those days, her belly hadn't pressed her hips away from the cliff and her center of balance hadn't seemed to slosh precariously from side to side with every incautious movement—not to mention changing with each passing day. She knew she climbed clumsily, awkwardly, clinging and panting in a manner that shamed her. But she did it nonetheless, and despite her awkwardness found her strength and agility burgeoning. Sand rasped between her fingertips and the stone beneath, scattered and pattered beneath her when her kilted robes brushed the wall.

It was a long climb, some seven or eight times her own height, and Edene found herself admiring whoever had dug so tenaciously to scrape water from this desert soil. But when she was twice her height from the bottom, her eyes pierced the darkness enough to see earth and stone below.

A voice seemed to speak to her from the darkness. *Leap.*

Leap, if you would be Queen.

That wasn't so hard. Easier than it had been to sling her leg over the stone lip of the well and lower herself into penetrable darkness. Edene uncurled her fingertips from their surprisingly solid grip and kicked off the ledge. The fall whipped brief wind through her hair, and when the bottom of the well stung her soles, the shock traveled pleasantly up her body. She bounced on her toes, vitality and joy suffusing her until she raised her arms and twirled for the sheer pleasure of it.

A moment later, Besha Ghul landed gently beside her.

"Come, mistress," it said, lightly flicking dust from one velvet shoulder. "We have far to go."

IN THE DARKNESS, IN THE TUNNELS, THEY PASSED BY SECRET WAYS. SECRET, THAT is, except to Edene. At first, the ghul led her, but soon Edene realized that she could feel the tunnels spread out around her in a convoluted labyrinth.

Besha Ghul and others of its kind moved through them, and Edene could sense them all. They were like fish moving through a weir, shadowy—translucent. Edene did not see them with her eyes but sensed in some other fashion, as if she were a spider and the passages were her web.

She laid her fingertips on the wall and felt it—not moist, gritting stone. Or rather, yes: stone, and chill, and damp . . . but somehow simultaneously giving the sense of something soft and alive, as if she touched a loved one's shoulder at the same time she touched the labyrinth wall. It welcomed her. It leaned into her.

She leaned back as if into the embrace of a friend.

She thought of all the suns she had seen or heard of—the changing moons of the Qersnyk night, the backward flight of the Nameless sun.

"You have your own gods here," she said, understanding. "And your sky is stone."

"It is the realm of my kin," the ghul answered. "As the steppe is the realm of yours."

Edene let her fingers trail across that strange, cool, welcoming stone. "And would you spread your stone sky over all of us?"

Besha Ghul, padding silent as a piece of the dark beside her, paused long enough that she knew it was considering carefully what next to say. Her own footsteps, no matter how light and careful, echoed down tunnels that also murmured with ceaseless chiming, trickling, the hushing of water falling and flowing against stone. Echoes built and layered, an intoxicating and alien music with her own heartbeat, the ineluctable rhythm around which it all wound.

The air that filled Edene's throat and lungs and the spaces in her skull with each breath was moist and cool. She would have called it odorless, except she had not realized before now that rock and pure water had odors of their own, when concentrated in such a confined space. She knew the metal-and-mold scent of rain on dry ground, of an oasis carried over an arid landscape. This was different: less . . . dusty, somehow, no matter how strange it was that water should smell dusty. More like the spirit or essence of the thing.

The truth of water and stone lay in that smell as if it were a name.

At last, Besha Ghul drew an audible, echoing breath and answered,

"We have held empires, and served them, and lost them. Now we mind our sunless realm, and live safe here. If we come forth again to conquer, it will be in service of the ring you bear and not our own ends."

That ring swung chill and heavy on her finger. "You are thrall to it?"

"Those who built the wizard ways of Erem care little for the desires of things that live and breathe," Besha Ghul answered. "We—the ghulim—are children in an ancient universe, Mistress of Secrets. And your race is even younger. We may seem very different, your folk and mine. But we have this in common: we are warm, and we must eat, and we must create our children alive and fragile and pulsing with the hot blood that is so easy, so terribly easy to spill."

It paused, leaving Edene with a breathless sense of this antique race, surviving, burrowing, hunched against the weight of torchlit centuries. Then it continued, in a tone that might be awe or fear or—worse—reverence. "There are powers and sentiences so old, and alien, and terrible, that to them we are of less significance than an infestation of insects would be to us."

Edene touched the ring with her thumb and said, "And yet we bind these ancient powers."

Another silence followed, not so long this time. At the end of it, the ghul simply sighed, and said: "Do we?"

ONE NIGHT, TEMUR HAD PROMISED HIMSELF. A SINGLE NIGHT TO GIVE EN-tirely to Samarkar, to the exploration—no, the *affirmation*—of the affection they had discovered between them.

They would not have it, and he felt selfish and small that he mourned it bitterly.

The tea was drunk, the pastries devoured before the flat yellow Uthman sun found the edge of the flat turquoise Uthman sky. The council done—at least for now—Samarkar, Hsiung, Ato Tesefahun, and Temur each re-turned to their own chamber to prepare for the day. In predawn chill, Temur washed himself with a rag and cool water, thinking that at least for now the smell of Samarkar lingered in the tight bends of his braided queue.

Temur's grandfather's servants had laundered the clothes from his saddlebags, including the ones Temur had preserved by avoiding wearing them. He dressed himself now in breeches and a shirt, sparing himself the padded coat that was self-mortification in the heat of Asitaneh at the end of summer. His felted boots were worn almost through at the soles and across the arches where the stirrup pressed, but his grandfather's people had left him some sort of shoes composed, like open-work baskets, of a weave of leather straps fixed to soles. Temur took some time to work out how they fastened, and the straps felt strange between his toes . . . but they would be unimaginably better than boots once the sun rose.

A foot scraped in the hall, presaging an eastern-style scratch against the frame. When the bead-weighted curtains of his room were pushed aside by a woman's broken-nailed hand, Temur was already on his feet—but not because he anticipated a threat. Instead, as Samarkar permitted the hangings to drift closed behind her, he put an arm around her shoulders and pulled her into an embrace.

She—steel-spined, spire-straight once-princess and Wizard of Tsarepheth—buried her face against his neck for a moment, a gesture that made his heart swell against his ribs until he would have sworn he could feel each one like a brand. She breathed in deep and out again—just once, stirring his beard at the corner of his jaw—before he felt her body firm in his arms.

She stepped back.

He had a moment to look at her in the dim but steady lamplight. She too had dressed in her own clothes, the silk of her best six-petal wizard's coat only slightly frayed and faded but folded by the belt where she had cinched in a waist that now floated around her. Her hair floated too—clean, and slept on damp and loose after their exertions, and brushed out without oil, it waved and crinkled and drifted to the tops of her thighs. He'd never seen it all clean and unbound and in good light before. Her wizard's collar might have been lost in it if she hadn't tossed the mass behind her shoulders. Instead, her hair made a black, silken backdrop for the figured panels of translucent jade that encased her throat, hinged and framed with gold and bordered with the baroque silvery twists of river pearls.

Someday, Temur thought, he would have to ask her to explain the delicate carvings on those panels—impossibly proportioned women in sweeping robes, dancing skeletons, flames or clouds, a writhing dragon and a twisting qoroos, all intertwined or counterpointed with symbols he knew were words but that he could not read. But not now, when she was looking at him intently, seriously, beneath a conscientious frown.

"Edene," she said.

He might have flinched. He thought he limited it to a quick, tight press of his lips. The careful words he'd thought about the night before deserted him, and rather than stand there stammering he said, "I care for you—"

She nodded.

"I care for *her* too. And I owe her safety, a rescue if I can manage it—"

"Re Temur," she said, not needing to raise her voice to silence him as utterly as if she'd drawn a knife across his vocal cords. "I cannot bear your heirs. I cannot be your queen—or even one of your queens. I am the Wizard Samarkar, though, and you would not be the first emperor to keep a Wizard of Tsarepheth as consort and confidant."

She paused. His mouth gaped, but whatever he had meant to say was utterly lost. If ever he had thought to look upon a queen, a khatun, an empress—on the image of his own imperial mother, in spirit though not the least in form—this was she, strong and stern and viciously pragmatic.

Her expression broke into the faintest curve of smile. "Do not think I begrudge you Edene. Or any of the other women you will marry, if we do not die. Re Temur, I am Samarkar, and I will win you back your queen, and I will set you in a golden saddle as Temur Khagan, and I will see your brother avenged and this al-Sepehr of the Nameless put down in your name."

The moment stretched, tore, spilt. She looked away, pride still in every line of her shoulders and throat. Her hair drifted across her face and hid it now. With her eyes off him, suddenly he could speak again.

The saddle is not gold. But this was not the time for petty corrections.

"Samarkar," he said. "I know what you are. And I am not the only one with a brother in need of avenging. But I . . . I cannot marry *anyone*."

She blinked at him, and he wondered if he had jolted her out of her martyrdom. "I don't understand."

"Anyone," he said. "You, Edene. Any woman of the clans. My family is dead. I have no mother, no sister, no brother to whisper my true name to a wife and make us family."

"You cannot tell her yourself?" Samarkar asked, with that slow care that told him how deep her incomprehension truly was.

"I do not know it," Temur said helplessly. "If I knew it, the demons could use it to trick me with."

She glanced back, and the conquering wizard was gone, fallen into a proud woman with drawn cheeks and a sun squint beginning at the corners of her eyes.

"It is true," she allowed. "You have got a problem." Then, conversationally: "Empires are filthy things, you know."

He knew. He had grown up in the war camps and on the borders of one. And he knew, too, what happened when empires fell. "But are they so filthy as the lack of them?"

She tipped her head. Acquiescence. Or at least acceptance of a valid question. "Better you than my brother Songtsan," she said. "Better you than this al-Sepehr."

He touched her shoulder. "Can we fail?" he asked her.

Uncertainty flickered across her expression, but her lips grew tight. And what she said was, "Being what we are? Not if there is any substance to the stuff of legends, sir."

"WE WILL NEED ALLIES," ATO TESEFAHUN SAID, AS SUNRISE ANGLED ACROSS the open top of the courtyard and steam rose from eggshell cups of thick, bitter coffee, its surface gilded with iridescent oils. "Your uncle will not be dislodged by righteousness or harsh language, and if he has allied himself with the Nameless, then there is every reason to see him out of the Padparadscha Seat with all haste."

Temur pushed unleavened bread through salted oil, but hesitated with the dripping scrap poised over his plate. "You want to go before the caliph."

Ato Tesefahun sipped coffee and made a satisfied noise. "Uthman Caliph is not without political liabilities of his own. It's possible we could sell him a war as a solution to some of them. Especially if we can come up with an elaborate moral justification. As much as I hate to say it... blood ghosts *will* help."

"The destruction of Kashe," Samarkar said.

Ato Tesefahun nodded. His eyes flicked to the drawn, livid scar on Temur's neck. "Which you have seen with your own eyes. And it will not hurt our case—excuse me, Temur—that my grandson bears the marks of hard fighting. You being a woman will present some difficulties, Samarkar-la, but you are a foreigner and a wizard. You will not be expected to behave as would a daughter of the Scholar-God. Still, we must consider our strategies."

"I will wear a veil if I must," said Samarkar. "It is not the first time I have made such concessions."

Ato Tesefahun tipped his head at her. "Oh," he said. "Not a veil, I think."

No, NOT A VEIL.

What Ato Tesefahun produced from some deep of his storehouses was the battle armor of a Wizard of Tsarepheth—a coat of boiled leather dyed black as ink, the six-petaled skirt laid over chain mail that rustled and rang with each stride. It had been made for a man, but Samarkar was a large woman, and it did not fit too poorly—though the leather creaked with the expansion of her bosom at each breath. Samarkar felt like a martial wizard indeed, with the armored boots laced up to her thighs. But Ato Tesefahun's true genius was apparent in the helm—black leather over steel, with a lacquered faceplate like the face of a snarling cat.

It hid everything but her eyes, which glared unnervingly from the shadows below the brim of the helm as she regarded herself in a looking glass bigger than any she'd seen outside a palace.

Ato Tesefahun, who had been adjusting the laces of her shoulder plates with his own hands, peered around her head for a look at the reflection. "There," he said, smugly satisfied. "That will serve modesty."

"Yes." The helm made her voice echo with portent. And it hid it when Samarkar smiled with pleasure at the effect. "I dare say modesty will be served."

IT WAS A MEASURE OF ATO TESEFAHUN'S STATUS IN THE COURT OF UTHMAN Caliph, fourteenth of that dynastic name—not all of them related by blood—that he had sent the messenger requesting an audience with sunrise and that reply returned before he, Temur, Samarkar, and Hsiung had finished lunch. It happened to return simultaneously with Hrahima, Ato Tesefahun's Cho-tse ally who had accompanied Samarkar and Temur from Tsarepheth.

The Temur of the previous winter would not have believed he could feel so relieved—so encouraged—to see a doorway filled upright to upright with the massive shoulders of a tiger who went on two legs. But he had come to rely on Hrahima, to trust her—and her absence had been more of a worry than he'd realized until she returned.

She had let the messenger with his note enter first. Now, while Ato Tesefahun read it, she paused in the shade of the awning beyond the door and, with a damp cloth brought to her by one of Ato Tesefahun's men, sponged away the red road dust obscuring the char-colored stripes on her feet and lower legs.

Temur rose to meet her, glancing at his grandfather for permission before filling a drinking bowl with water.

"You're a Khagan in waiting," Ato Tesefahun said.

Temur could not miss the paternal warmth in his tone. It sparked a heartache that Temur, fatherless, did not know how to control.

"And you are my grandson. The hospitality of my house is yours to share. Especially when you're sharing it with my friend."

Hrahima, ducking beneath the lintel, chuffed: a tiger's laugh, laying her whiskers along the sides of her muzzle and revealing streaked, yellowed teeth.

"Employee," she argued, accepting the water.

Temur wanted to ask where she had been, and on what errand—but if Ato Tesefahun would not share the information, Hrahima was unlikely to undermine him.

She drank from the cup like a woman, except she curled up her lip and poured the water into herself rather than sipping. When it was empty, she handed it back to Temur with a nod. "Samarkar, Temur, Hsiung—well met. What news?"

Her gesture took in the scroll ribboned in the Uthman Caliph's personal and imperial colors of crimson and indigo that Ato Tesefahun was carefully cracking open with his thumbs.

"We are invited to present ourselves before Uthman Caliph in the third hour after sunrise, tomorrow," he said. "We are advised that this will be a private rather than an open court."

"That doesn't actually mean private," Samarkar said, as Temur re-seated himself beside her. "Not in the sense somebody who wasn't caliph might use the term. It just means that only his closest advisors and current favorites will be present, not every minor functionary and courtier who wants to demonstrate an obligation or allegiance to the court."

"Fewer favor curriers," Temur said. Power was power, the world around. Though the trappings differed, the politics were the same.

"The important point," said Ato Tesefahun, "is that Uthman's war-band will not be present in force, although I doubt if we can avoid having to placate them entirely."

Temur tapped his fingertips against one another. "Are relations so ... uneasy between the caliph and his war leaders?"

"Where power is shared," said Ato Tesefahun, "there is always tension. Uthman will no doubt use our quest—and the prospect of your future allegiance, Temur Khanzadeh and Samarkar-la—to solidify his authority."

"Your human politics," said Hrahima, prospecting through a plate of lamb in sharp-smelling sauce with her claw tips. She selected a nugget and pushed it into her mouth, wrinkling her nose at the spices. "Is not your caliph a priest-king of the Scholar-God? And yet his position is so precarious?"

Samarkar looked up first, the opportunity to discourse on politics too much for her. While Ato Tesefahun waved a servant to the kitchens—for raw meat for the Cho-tse, Temur presumed—the wizard smiled tightly and began. "The caliph is, indeed, a sort of priest-king. He is elected from the priesthood by the men who serve the Scholar-God, and often the courses of these elections follow bloodlines and dynasties. But the men who may compete for the role raise warlord-bands, like any would-be Khagan"—Samarkar raised her eyebrows at Temur, and he swallowed hastily; better get to work on that—"and they must keep the will of those warlord-bands behind them, or ... the usual repercussions follow."

"Civil war," said Hrahima.

"Regime change," said Ato Tesefahun.

Samarkar said, "Sometimes the elections do little more than confirm the outcome of the fighting."

"And if they do not?" Temur asked.

Samarkar's smile was tight. "More fighting."

5

AL-SEPEHR'S YOUNGEST WIFE READ ALOUD WHILE AL-SEPEHR SAT IN CLOSE-lidded contemplation. Through the discomfort of hearing the words, he focused on their meaning—hands folded, head tipped back—until a sense of presence roused him.

Someone watched from the doorway. Al-Sepehr thought at first that he was seeing a ghost. Not one of the Qersnyk blood ghosts, but a proper Uthman haunt, a soul rejected by the Scholar-God and yet unable to find its way to Hell.

Just within the door stood a slender figure in breeches and a sashed knee-length robe woven in the dusty colors of hard-baked desert. Two wheel-lock pistols were thrust through the sash, the long chased barrels angled carefully down and away from the body. They shared space with a scimitar and a dagger.

The figure's face was obscured by the wraps of an indigo veil, but even from across the room, even with his own failing eyesight, al-Sepehr could see the striking lightness of the eyes that fabric framed.

Shahruz: that was the name al-Sepehr's lips framed—but Shahruz was dead, head caved in by a Qersnyk war mare as he had been about to finish that steppe-born boy nuisance Re Temur for good and all.

Al-Sepehr's youngest wife had ceased reading. In the silence, al-Sepehr glanced around the chamber, seeing its empty spaces, few cushions, heavy lap desk resting on short legs propped on the golden stone floor. His wife was looking up at him from behind it; seeing his gaze upon her, she quickly and demurely ducked her head. Her eyes were still clear brown. She had not yet begun to stumble over the ancient words. That was good. It meant a while yet before al-Sepehr must again remarry.

It was then that he realized that he was standing, and that she had stopped reading because he had come to his feet. "Go, beloved," he said to her, with an encouraging smile. He did not wish her to think she had displeased him.

Head still bowed, her robes twisting in the wind of her passage, she scuttled for the door. The figure in desert garb and the indigo cowl of the Nameless stepped aside fluidly to give her room. Now that his startlement had passed, and as he moved a step or two closer, al-Sepehr could see that the flare of hip and swell of bosom outlined under the man's garb were anything but masculine and that the figure was some inches shorter than Shahruz. The cuffs of the trousers had been skillfully hemmed up. The cuffs of the sleeves were rolled.

Al-Sepehr stopped a man's height from the figure: close enough to speak without shouting—a bit immodestly close, in fact—but not so close as to be an immediate affront to a woman. Or at least, not any more immediate affront than merely being in her presence must be, but that was beyond helping, and it was far from the first time for that sin.

"Saadet," he said, averting his eyes. As if she had been forcing herself to look forward against some inexorable weight, her gaze dropped, her neck twisted: her cheek pushed almost to her shoulder. In the gaps of her veil, her skin flamed burnt umber with shame.

She did not answer. Of course she would not; he must speak. It was his burden as a man, no matter how uncomfortable.

"Saadet," he said again, making his voice gentle. Children and women were easy to frighten. "I know you mourn your brother, my sweet. But it is not modest to dress in his clothing."

The flush was fading from around her eyes, leaving her skin its more usual almond color. Her fingers, long and tidy and so slender al-Sepehr sometimes found it hard to believe she belonged to the same species he did, fretted the edge of one cuff, rolling and unrolling it to flash the back and fingers of the opposite hand.

"Master," she said.

He did not recoil, but that was because he was al-Sepehr and had long since trained himself away from any such outward evidence of human frailty. He had grown accustomed to hearing Shahruz's tones layered over his sister's. Now, though—

"Shahruz," he said. "Saadet, you said that what he is—persists." He had thought she meant that she retained his memories, his experiences. The remnants of that unity of mind that al-Sepehr himself had forged between the twins. He had not understood that she meant Shahruz had not passed into the libraries of paradise and the presence of the Scholar-God.

"He is with me," she said, in her own voice. "He will not leave me. Not until we can go on together. Al-Sepehr..."

Al-Sepehr waited.

It was Shahruz who finished the sentence—or rather, who began it again and this time chased it to the end. "Al-Sepehr, give me leave to train this body, that I may serve you again as one of the Nameless."

"You are a woman!" al-Sepehr said with force. "Would you profane the Scholar-God's semblance?"

"That is only the form," said Shahruz. "Only the shell. Return me to your councils." He raised his eyes, and in the set of his shoulders, the lift of his chin behind the veil, al-Sepehr could see no hint now of the self-effacing female. The stiffness of his posture betrayed great discomfort, however, to find himself clothed in a woman's sacred flesh. "Al-Sepehr. You have not the strength to accomplish our liberation alone. Saadet and I have both seen how your wreakings in the service of the Nameless have exhausted you. The Nameless need you; without you we shall never escape the oppression under which we've toiled these centuries."

"I have the ghosts," said al-Sepehr. "They will feed me."

"They will feed you until you must send them to fight again. And then they will draw the life from you until you are even less than they— a wraith!"

Al-Sepehr's lips pressed thin with amusement; here indeed was his old friend Shahruz, lecturing him on taking care of himself and his priest-hood. It was love, and it warmed al-Sepehr more than he could express.

"Not until Tsarepheth has fallen to the plague, in any case." The ghosts could not directly attack the Rasan city, protected as it was by great beds of rock salt layered through the mountains. The wizards had chosen the site of their Citadel with more than earthly defense in mind. "And by then, perhaps the wars will be raging without our direct assistance. Then we can lie in wait, collecting power, ready to step in when all these self-styled kings and princelings have their reckonings."

Saadet nodded; al-Sepehr could still tell her gestures from Shahruz's, even when they used the same flesh.

He sighed. The twins were right.

"Go to Re Qori Buqa," he said. "Ride the wind. He is a heathen Qer-snyk, and will not care that you wear a woman's sacred shape. And when you are there, counsel him to war. Lead him against the Uthman Caliph-ate. Tell him . . . tell him that Re Temur is in Asitaneh, and that the ca-liph will no doubt lend him arms and men in exchange for a promise of allegiance and quiet borders—and that even if the caliph would not, the caliph's war-band will press the issue. Tell Qori Buqa that if he wishes to maintain his grandfather's empire, he must do as a Khagan does—and conquer anew."

Saadet bowed like a man—not to al-Sepehr, but to the will of the Scholar-God. She did not ask how he knew where Re Temur had escaped to. When she spoke it was in her own voice. "And if he wishes to consolidate our allegiance, al-Sepehr? If he wishes arms and men and more sorcery and science?"

Al-Sepehr shrugged. "Offer him a marriage," he said. "That should satisfy him for a while."

"And if I must go through with it?"

"Then that makes you his queen, does it not?" Al-Sepehr paused, and smiled suddenly. "It's not as if you shall be married long."

Shahruz—or perhaps Saadet—must have caught his change of mood. They flinched, and one of them said, unhappily, "Master?"

"Actually," he said, savoring the simple elegance of the idea that had come to him so suddenly, inspiration a gift of the Scholar-God, "you can run an errand for me along the way."

"Shall we speak to the rukh, Master?"

"Yes," said he. "Let us speak with the rukh, my Shahruz."

AFTER THE FIRST DEATH AND . . . HATCHING, OTHERS FOLLOWED. AT FIRST A few, scattered, like the plink of mustard seeds popping in a covered pan. But then, like those seeds, more followed—drifts and spates, crescendos and finales. And Hong-la could do nothing.

He and Yongten-la both immediately, hopelessly thought of killing the victims, to spare them—at least—the suffering of the spawn's emergence. But then the third victim, a city whore with two fingers amputated for thieving, survived the hatching—horribly, Hong-la thought, more horribly than if she had died—and the wizards realized that if the emergence was survivable, granting mercy to the infected was untenable.

Hong-la thought perhaps they could poison the demons in the lungs, and started those most recently infected on a course of inhaled caustic vapors. Not kind, and he wondered if—even if it worked—he was merely condemning any possible survivors to a death by sepsis as the spawn rotted inside their lungs. He was certainly condemning them to scarred lungs and invalidity.

To other victims, the Wizard Hong fed poisons, as he would to treat any parasite. Arsenic, quicksilver—in limited quantities, that might poison the spawn and preserve the host. Cinnabar powdered and blown into the lungs of those who could still manage to inhale. He tried tracheotomy, opening a gap in the victim's throat for the demons to squeeze through in the hopes that it would be more likely to preserve life if they did not have to force their way up through the base of the skull and the jaw. He instructed wizards and lay surgeons both to save the doses of poppy and whiskey to the very end, so at least the sufferers need not be wholly sensible when the beasts were ripping their way free.

It was Anil-la who came up with the idea of channeling fire into the spawn while they still lay within the lungs of their victims. But these subjects died as well: delicate lung tissue could not stand exposure to the

controlled heat that the wizards brought to bear on the monsters gestat-
ing within them. Those who endured a day or two, coughing up burned
husks and shreds of twisted demon flesh, eventually drowned in the fluids of their own insulted lungs.

Yongten-la devised a means for trapping the demons as they emerged:
an apparatus strapped over the patients' face, giving the spawn no route
of escape except to crawl through a narrow tube into a glass jar, which
could then be corked—the demons died of suffocation, just like any
beast—or filled with boiling water or spirits of wine.

Some of the trapped ones pissed fire, which ran back down the apparatus and peeled the flesh from the face of one—Hong-la thanked his
ancestors—already-dead sufferer. After that, he rigged up a flexible tube
that could be forced into a U-bend once the demon has passed the halfway point.

Days passed, nights, sharping to nightmare. As one horror piled
upon another, Hong-la kept expecting to awaken. The plague—or
infestation—was too precise a hideousness to seem credible, even when
he stood in the reek of unburned bodies and suppurating wounds and
the burned-hair acridness that was the smell—alive or dead—of the
demonspawn.

Hong-la and Yongten-la kept a few demonspawn alive for research.
The hunched, gaunt little things sat balefully in their jade cages, wings
twisted, the mottled, membranous skin over their torsos stretching to
tautness and collapsing in hollows between starveling ribs with every
desperate, air-thirsty breath.

"They're starving for air," Yongten-la said as he sealed a particularly
bruise-colored yellow-and-purple one into the carved stone cage. Originally intended for songbirds, they were a snug fit around the demonspawn. Hong-la did not feel too bad for them.

In his blood-and-phlegm-crusted smock, Hong-la kept working to
stem the flow of blood from this latest victim. He thought this one might
live—speechless, tongue torn and voice box crushed, jaw unhinged by
the fury of the spawn's emergence.

Hong-la's hands moved as if of their own will. He had not slept in
days. The energy he drew from the Citadel was a constant blurry buzz in

his veins, in his head. He could feel his heart skipping beats occasionally, or accelerating beyond any safe level. His own breath came pained and sore, as if somebody had been scrubbing *his* lungs out. It was secondhand exposure to the caustics, despite the mask he now wore habitually—but it was also exhaustion, and the price for wearing his body and soul down to the warp and relying on the Citadel to keep him on his feet.

It would kill him if he continued. But where were the choices?

He sent Anil-la and several of the others—full-collared wizards, including the redoubtable Wizard Tsering, who had never manifested powers but who had a mind for theory the match of any wizard in the Citadel—out among the city with heralds to cry the protocols. Since the victims—so long as speech did not desert them—reported awakening with the cough and fever, Hong-la hypothesized that whatever infected them came at night. He and Yongten-la recommended that everyone sleep indoors, windows barred, faces masked. Chimneys must be stuffed with rags and sealed as best as possible. Everyone who had the resources must sleep under netting and signs of ward.

Hong-la tried not to think too much of the slaves and indigents of Tsarepheth, who might be lucky to sleep under a scrap of wood and hide angled to keep off the rain.

No one of the Citadel and no one in the Black Palace had sickened yet, which made Hong-la fairly certain that the wards and prayer flags and incised stones, the ancient blessings and geomantic protections upon those strongholds held. Yongten-la freed himself and some of the elder wizards, ones who *had* found their power, from the duty of nursemaiding the sick. It did not take a wizard to blow cinnabar dust into a dying man's lungs through a quill.

These wizards would pick their way among the sigil-incised boulders through which the Tsarethi crashed and tossed as it passed beneath the Citadel, renewing blessings. Some of them would finish and dedicate a new wardstone, a great jade boulder housed in the depths of the Citadel, and—eventually—roll it into the water as well, where its blessings could be tumbled downstream through the plague-wracked city and to the suffering lands of Rasa and Song and the Hundred-Times-Hundred Kingdoms of the Lotus below. That would take months, though, perhaps longer.

Yongten-la sent regular missives to the Bstangpo—the Emperor—recommending that a shaman and a wizard bless every dwelling under imperial edict and that sheltered housing be provided for the indigent. Emperor Songtsan issued commands, and inasmuch as possible these things were carried out . . . but so many were ill, and a wizard caring for the dying was not carving protective sigils upon doors and over windows.

In the meantime, mostly, the contagion raged. And mostly, Hong-la toiled, and waited for word from the emperor.

THOUGH ACOLYTES AND WOMEN CLEANED THE ROCK SHELF WHERE THE RUKHS nested, the taint of ammonia still reached the heights of Ala-Din's five towers. The twins and their master stood atop the nearest, the thumb of the fortress that had once been called the Hand on the Rock.

Centuries had truncated the name, though not the towers. *Ala-Din* meant only *the Rock.*

The twins had folded their hands in the sleeves of their coat. A hot, rustling wind scarfed their veils in long banners; below, the rukhs huddled in their nest. The female had just returned with a meal for her mate and offspring: two camels with necks broken, which she carried as a hawk might carry a shrew, served whole—along with whatever awful chunks the giant bird could regurgitate from her own breakfast. Of what creature those bits might be the mortal remains, the twins did not inquire.

Smaller birds swarmed the pile. They were eagle-sized or slightly larger, miniatures of the great rukhs with their white and scarlet crests and long necks: the grayer female and her brassier mate. The male's chain rattled as he stretched for the first camel. As with most birds of prey, the female was larger. Her body partially blocked his from view, but as he fanned his wings and gulped the camel down whole, tossing his head—again like a hawk with a shrew—the twins saw the rule-straight edge of brassy pinions, the flash of a creamy belly. Steel scraped on stone when he moved—though he was chained and his wings were clipped, he fluttered vigorously, exercising.

The female fluffed and settled herself. While her family dined, she busied herself rearranging the stones and twigs of her nest: boulders and uprooted trees as thick as the twins' thigh. She turned a rock as large as a sofa dreamily, with the edge of her recurved beak.

When al-Sepehr clucked, she lifted her head slowly and shot him an unmistakable glare.

"Come, my lovely," said al-Sepehr, while the gray-gold wall of her hatred broke against him like the sea around a pillar. "As you love your family, it is time for you to fly for me again."

WHEN THE SUMMONS CAME, IT DID NOT COME FROM THE BSTANGPO. HONG-LA in his exhaustion, hands dripping brown streamers of blood into the bowl of water he washed with, blinked in surprise at the messenger clad in imperial blues who had just prostrated himself before the wizard.

Exquisitely aware of his state of crusted filth and exhaustion, Hong-la nevertheless tried to attain—and project—the serene peace expected of a wizard. "Say that again?"

The messenger raised his head, eyes downcast. "The empress, Yangchen-tsa, commands your attendance, Wizard Hong."

YANGCHEN PACED. THE BABE WOULD NOT STOP CRYING. SHE GAVE IT HER breast, but though it mumbled and fussed with the nipple it would not latch. She jiggled and coddled it. She gave it to the nurse to be burped and diapered and reswaddled and returned.

All this, and the babe, Namri—her son, her husband Songtsan's heir, the child whose birth had made her first wife to the Bstangpo and the Empress of Rasa—would not stop crying. It wailed like a peacock. It shrieked like a tiger. It threw fits in circles and spirals and explosive vortexes of noise.

There is something about the sound of a crying baby—a truly inconsolable crying baby, not a merely fussy one—that brings a form of madness to otherwise calm and settled adults. Yangchen-tsa, at nineteen, considered herself very adult indeed: an empress, and one whose mastery of the viperous politics of the Rasan court had put her husband on the throne in advance of his majority.

It was she who had removed her husband's dowager mother from the center of the web where she had sat like a bloated spider so long, controlling

Songtsan and Yangchen both. It was she who had managed to cast the blame for that removal on the doorstep of her husband's brother, thus requiring the new—and premature—emperor to condemn his sibling to death. Unkind, and ruthless—but Yangchen-tsa's father had cautioned her when he sent her to marry Songtsan and Tsansong that if she wished to survive the imperial court, she must be subtle and unrestrained by compassion. What she did, she told herself, was for her son.

It was she who had ascertained that the child she would bear would be a son, and that *her* son would be born first among all the children of her sister-wives. She was not the empress by blood or birth; Yangchen had been born to a minor wife of a noble family of Song, the third living daughter and fourteenth child of her father. She had been traded away to Rasa because her father was notable, not because she was.

And yet it was by her own hand that Yangchen-tsa was Empress of Rasa, and though history and her husband would never know it, still the victory should have been sweet, so sweet, as secret and sweet as stolen honey on her tongue. So her father had assured her—that the sweetness of power paid for everything.

But the execution of Prince Tsansong would be carried out by burning this very day. And a plague as horrific as anything out of the bad old tales that Yangchen loved so dearly and so desperately raged across her empire. And as she gave the babe back to his nurse again so that her women could dress her for the arrival of the surgeon-wizard Hong-la, Yangchen entertained a momentary fantasy that the bitterness of her own acts had soured her milk and her son would *never* stop crying now.

What a ridiculous superstition, she told herself, and dropped her dressing gown. *You might as well suppose that your own honored father could have offered poor advice.*

The clothing and coifing she had to endure was elaborate, but it commenced, at least, with a hot and scented bath. On another day, Yangchen would have managed to relax as she leaned her head on the steep side of the neck-deep cedarwood tub. She would have felt the pain in her muscles subside as one of her women worked to ease the cramping brought on by elaborate hairstyles and elegant posture—not to mention the workings of a guilty conscience. Today, though, any sensual pleasure she might have felt was lost to the weight of her distraction. She scarcely noticed that the water had begun to cool around her until her women helped her to stand.

Yangchen waited on a cedarwood grating beside a brazier stocked with aromatic coals while the women scraped lingering droplets from her with sandalwood paddles, then softened her body with sandalwood-scented oil. The tub was emptied halfway and carried out. Yangchen—swathed now in a soft robe to give her skin time to absorb the oil—took a seat before the brazier. She perched on an elevated stool so her hair could be combed out without brushing the carpeted stone of the floor. Her women, as drilled as any military unit, moved on and off stepping stools so they could comb the whole length of each strand.

In the next room, Namri was still wailing. Ridiculous superstition or not, Yangchen shifted uncomfortably. If it were her milk souring, the babe would not fuss so when presented with the nurse's breast.

At last her hair was dressed, her face painted. She stood to let her ladies fold and drape layers of silk and cloth of gold around her body. At first, the over-robe they provided was one in white and crimson, the colors of bone and blood for mourning. But Yangchen sent it away. The ladies might have raised their eyebrows, but they brought her another, this one in deep violets and indigos.

As they twisted the sash around her middle, she thought that soon she would be ready to wean Namri—or at least give him over to his nurse completely. Which meant that soon, she would be bearing again. She still had a supply of the herbs the foreign sorcerer had given her to ensure conceiving a son.

Now that Yangchen's youngest sister-wife, Payma, had fled court to protect the baby *she* carried, a baby that was most likely the child of Songtsan's condemned brother Tsansong, it would be Yangchen who gave Songtsan his second heir as well as the first.

She found herself to be dressed. While she took her place on her chair—her privilege as senior wife was not to crouch on cushions now that the Dowager Empress was dead—and her calligraphy, the ladies uncovered the windows to let in the light and air. The brazier that had been necessary to warm the damp from the air when the chamber was closed up and Yangchen was nude was carried out by the same brawny servants that had handled the bathtub and water. Songtsan's other wife, Tsechen, and the ladies of the court began to arrive, each with a subsidiary lady bearing her calligraphy, or reading, or embroidery. If they came in neat order of precedence and began filtering in as soon as the doors opened for the removal of the brazier, that was only because each of them kept a servant stationed in the hall from sunrise onward.

Tsechen wore crimson and snow white, egret feathers dazzling against the glossy blackness of her hair. She, like Yangchen, was also the wife of condemned Tsansong. She, like Yangchen's body servants, took in Yangchen's choice of garb with an impassivity that could only hide condemnation. Yangchen met her silent outrage with a smile, hiding how she might otherwise have quailed before it.

Yangchen had done what she had done, and she was pleased with the outcomes. Whatever hard and ruthless choices she had made to ensure her victory... they were the price of protecting the empire and her emperor—and her children, not only Namri but also those she had yet to bear.

One who did not deal by heartlessness in the arena of politics did not live long enough to see one's lofty ideals lead inevitably to the ruin of nations.

Tsechen had no child, and Yangchen would see to it that she stayed barren. As long as that was so—as long as Tsechen's blood remained unmingled with that of the emperor—Yangchen did not fear Tsechen, and so Tsechen did not need to fear Yangchen. Of course, it might be safer to remove her entirely—but Yangchen preferred to be merciful where she could. And there would inevitably be other wives, as time passed. Such was the course of empire.

Even if Yangchen could find the stomach to remove them all, the pattern would inevitably become noticeable.

The ladies breakfasted within the hour. For some time after that, they sewed and practiced their painting and read aloud by turns. Namri was brought to Yangchen again so she might nurse him—this time, comfortingly, he cooperated—and before the midday meal she excused herself for her appointment with the wizard.

Another day, she might have waited for the doorkeeper to bring her word that Hong-la had arrived. But she had seen a large strange bird, gray and long-necked like a heron but with a raptor's beak, beat heavily past the window. So she required that rarest of commodities for a royal person: a few moments completely alone.

A series of painted screens concealed the corner in which Yangchen slept from the rest of her chamber, where the ladies gathered. She rounded the flimsy barrier on some pretext—a fan or scent, she wasn't even quite sure herself what she said. But she had to wave two of her ladies back to their cushions when she stood in order to fetch it herself. Unable even for the moment to dispense with her awareness of politics, she wondered if her independence would increase her legend or serve to remove some of the awe of her under which her subjects should rightfully toil.

Whatever the effect, she would have to adapt it to her needs. This was not a task she could safely abandon to any hands but her own, nor one she could perform under watchful eyes.

The brassy-gray bird perched on the window ledge beside Yangchen's bed, peering suspiciously this way and that. Papery eyelids blinked and opened with each turn of its crested head.

A bit of indigo ribbon bound a copper-bright capsule to its ankle. Her swift, short strides constrained by the whisking hem of her robe, Yangchen crossed to the window. Her fingers fumbled the capsule at first, but she managed to twist it open. The note within—on western-style paper—was ciphered, but by now Yangchen could read those symbols as easily as the syllabary sigils of Song.

It was brief.

I will visit you. Await another letter.

She read it three times, all a courtier's trained memory required, before sliding it between her painted lips and chewing quickly, grimly, until the paper and bitter ink collapsed into a paste that she could swallow.

Upon his arrival at the Black Palace, Hong-la had expected to be shown into the empress's reception chamber and offered a cushion on the floor among her ladies. It was the accepted means of doing such things, and avoided any hint of scandal. Instead, she met him alone, in an opulently paneled and carpeted chamber divided down the middle by an openwork ivory screen and otherwise completely devoid of furnishings.

Hong-la wondered how many spyholes and niches were concealed in the elaborate, elephant-carved, coffered paneling, and if any of them were occupied.

She was waiting for him when he entered, the pierced screen rendering her indigo-clad form into something more akin to a flock of birds or a swarm of bees.

"Empress," he said, performing the ritual obeisance. The hem and the draped sleeve of her robes twitched as she beckoned him forward. In the situation of a formal audience, even a Wizard of Tsarepheth advanced upon the emperor's wife with his head bowed and his eyes averted. He scuttled up with humility largely unpracticed since his time in Song, amused despite himself by how far he had to hunch to get his head below the level of hers. Hong-la was taller than most men, and broad-shouldered, and even after the birth of a prince the empress remained a porcelain doll of a woman.

He dropped to his knees before the screen, relieved to ease the strain in his thighs. The carpets absorbed the impact; he landed with only a faint thud, despite the lack of grace engendered by middle years and a chronic lack of exercise.

"Empress," he said again. "I accept my duty to serve you with great pleasure."

He wondered if she would bring up the flight of Samarkar-la and the escaped princess, Payma. Surely, that had been adequately hashed over through official channels—Hong-la had not been privy to the discussions between Yongten-la and the emperor, but he had heard enough about them from Yongten-la to have an idea of how hard the bargaining had been and what concessions had been made by the wizards to avoid reprisals. And it was not as if either the empress or Hong-la had the authority to gainsay their respective masters. So it must be something else.

He had time to muse on what, because she kept him waiting. Formulating her response or stretching out his hoped-for discomfort, he was not sure . . . but then, nor was he particularly uncomfortable. Hong-la was unusual in that he had been a eunuch before he became a Wizard of Tsarepheth. He had come into his adulthood as a civil servant in Song, and it was there he had acquired his skills as an archivist and administrator.

The Rasan dynasty was replete with canny politicians and ruthless manipulators. But the Rasan emperors had been eliminating rival branches of the bloodline for centuries, and compared with the intrigues of the so-called Ten-Thousand-Princes of Song . . . there just weren't enough nobles in Rasa to make things *really* interesting.

So her silence gave him no great pause. What she said when she finally spoke, though, brought his eyes up quickly in a reaction too startled to hide.

"Rise, Hong-la," she said. "I cannot speak to the top of your head at this time."

He realized he was staring and averted his gaze, but not before he had glimpsed the strain creasing the maquillage that should have rendered her face an expressionless oval. He stood, his attention fixed on the bottom edge of the screen between them. It had been carved in panels of cherry trees in blossom, homey and familiar to Hong-la, and he wondered if the empress had brought it with her, or if it had been part of the once-princess Samarkar's bride-price when she in her turn had been sold to one of Song's Ten-Thousand.

He thrust his tongue out in respect, and though he stood, he continued to bow low. Her inviting him to stand in her imperial presence did answer one of his questions, however: if there were any watchers in the walls, Empress Yangchen did not know of them.

She said, "I have drawn you from your duty to the victims of the pestilence, and for that I apologize."

"I am not sure," Hong-la said carefully, "that we may call it— precisely—a pestilence any longer. Not with precision, anyway. An affliction, certainly. An infestation . . ."

He was, he understood with detached rationality, taking refuge in scholarly babble. With an effort, he silenced his tongue. He drew a breath, pained on his own behalf, and continued. "That is to say, if by my duty to the empress I may serve the empire, I am at her disposal."

Through the screen, out of the corner of his eye, he saw her smile. That too disturbed her paint. "We both have a duty to the empire, Hong-la. And to Tsarepheth. How is it, do you think, that these demons have managed to enter within the sweep of the city's blessings and the prayers that guard it? And how is it that the Citadel and the palace remain unsullied by their presence?"

"Something has corrupted the city's blessings," Hong-la said. "And those on the temples are beginning to fail, I fear. Priests now are sickening as well. We—the Citadel—we have begun the process of checking and renewing the prayers all around Tsarepheth, but as you must be able to imagine, great empress, this is not a simple process, nor a swift one, and we are so very busy with the sick."

"And anyway," she said, "the demons have already come within."

"It is so."

"But previously—someone, somehow, must have given them permission to enter."

"It is so," he said again. "Or, at least, somehow abrogated the protections against their entering."

Cold danced along his spine as he said it. *Who can give such permission? The master of a house. Or the master of an empire.*

Hong-la, veteran of two courts and a college of wizards, was glad for the moment that the woman he stood before was an empress, and that he could not be expected to meet her gaze. *But why would an emperor invite demon spawn into his own realm? Unless he were somehow tricked into it?*

"Empress," he said, when the silence had stretched long, and he was too aware of her painted gaze on him through the lattice of the screen, "is there more? My patients—"

Silk slicked against silk as she shifted. "We are burning my younger husband at sunset," she said. "You must stay to witness the execution."

6

A LINE OF GOLD LIKE THE EDGE OF A PAPER SET ALIGHT CRAWLED THE EASTern horizon when Temur led his liver-bay mare from her stall, and even the desert was mild. Not cool, precisely—but not dangerous.

He watered Bansh well, stroked her fetlocks and pasterns, felt her flesh firm and cool and sound wherever his hand touched. She had been brushed and was gleaming, her tack cleaned meticulously, restitched where it was worn and hung beside her door. Someone had replaced her threadbare saddle blanket. Temur felt a pang of discontent with himself; it was he who should have seen to those repairs, and while he had visited Bansh daily, it was he who should have seen to her care. No matter how competent Ato Tesefahun's grooms were.

She seemed happy to see him now, though, and—her owner-notched, black-tipped mahogany ears pricked, her tail switching—she also seemed pleased at the prospect of exercise. She nibbled his shoulder while he saddled her and grabbed for the bit so eagerly Temur had to defend his fingers. He liked the spring in her step, the sparkle of well-rested spiritedness that attended her. He liked the way she pranced a step as he swung up into the saddle—and he liked his own response too: the strength of adequate food and sleep seemed to throb from his fingertips, and all the tension of worry and conspiracy crackled through him, lending nervous energy.

The sun was rolling along the horizon by then, orange rays broken by buildings striping the world into dark and gold bands like the hide of a Cho-tse. A vulture lazed upon the sky, flexed pinions clearly visible. Temur entertained the fancy that it supported itself by its fingertips against some invisible wall.

As if his thought had summoned her, Hrahima's tiger-great silhouette slipped from the side yard as he and Bansh passed. Bansh rose into a trot. Hrahima jogged gently alongside, keeping pace with swinging, easy strides. Her harness lay smooth and clean over her fur, supporting her knives; a slender rope bounced at her hip and a flap-covered wallet rode the other. Temur had never seen her with more gear.

"Out for a run?" she asked, ever so casually.

"I guess we both are," he answered.

Mare and cat jogged a few strides companionably before Hrahima raised a retracted claw to the sky. "That's a steppe vulture," she said. "They don't usually come so far west."

"Maybe it followed us."

Warming, Bansh stretched out, and Hrahima's breath and strides came faster. Still without strain, however. When Temur stole a glance at her sideways, her whiskers pricked forward. In her relaxed, ragged ears, the gold rings jingled.

They reached the earth-paved street and were no longer alone. They had continued out the back of Ato Tesefahun's property, moving farther from the docks and more toward the periphery of Asitaneh. This street was dominated by a glassworks—the roar of the ovens could be heard from the road, even though the building itself was set well back from other structures for safety—and men with carts and little clots of veiled women with market baskets and bags were beginning to make their way through the outskirts of town.

With a shift of weight, Temur slowed his mare. Bansh wanted to run, and at a walk she placed each foot fussily, kicking it high and snorting as she set it down again. Temur and Hrahima—and Bansh, no doubt, with her clean steppe lines and rangy, nearly maneless build—attracted quick glances and a few outright stares.

They edged around a knot of men that crowded the street in front of a coffee seller's. The conversation in the queue was mostly local politics—the aging caliph's reputation in contrast to that of one of his popular lieutenants, as near as Temur could gather with his fractured Uthman. Most of these men seemed to be partisans of the charismatic up-and-comer, but one—Temur guessed from his leather apron that he was an employee or the proprietor of the glassworks—was defending the caliph at length, and another appeared to be preaching anarchy.

Temur snorted to himself. So it was the world over: Asitaneh no different from Qarash. Nevertheless, he slowed to listen . . . and for his trouble heard little more, except a torrent of abuse heaped by two men who seemed to belong to the dominant Falzeen sect upon one whom Temur assumed to be Rahazeen. It broke off, however, as soon as the men noticed the Cho-tse jogging past and listening.

Temur and Bansh and Hrahima won their way through with only a little delay and exited a lightly guarded gate, which seemed to have stood wide overnight. People came and went; there were villages without the walls and farmers were arriving with loads of chickens, of eggs, of melons and dates and other such produce as could be coaxed to grow in the dry plain and rubbled hills behind the city. The angled light showed details in the landscape that Temur had not previously noticed. He was used to glimpsing these hills from the windows and yard of Ato Tesefahun's house and seeing them baked flat by the fierceness of afternoon. Slanted illumination and shadows revealed textures to the landscape that he had never suspected—wrinkles, gullies, and ridges in sharp relief.

Temur, Bansh, and Hrahima veered off the road after a few strides so they could stretch out and run.

Temur wished Samarkar were with them. He wished they could just keep going until they reached the horizon and then choose another horizon and run some more.

He wouldn't. He would choose to face the tasks that fate had set him. But he couldn't make himself not want to run.

✳   ✳   ✳

As they entered the court of the caliph, Samarkar was greeted by the ethereal scent of frankincense and the equally ethereal sound of a soprano voice, floating unaccompanied upon the fan-stirred breeze. The armor, no matter how impressive, restricted her field of vision. She glanced from side to side, but though the motion reassured her of the exact locations of Ato Tesefahun, Hrahima, Temur, and Brother Hsiung, she could not locate the source of the singing.

Those glimpses *did* encourage her to slow her stride and take in the design of the caliph's palace. The once-princess Samarkar had seen many a royal dwelling, and resided in not a few of them—in Rasa and in Song—but this was like something out of a traveler's book. She tipped her head back as subtly as she could manage, permitting herself to be all but swayed on her feet by the grandeur of the domed and vaulted spaces above. She—who had seen the impossible span of the Wreaking in Tsarepheth, who had slept and worked within the white-and-crimson walls of its impossible Citadel, who had lived as a prince's wife in one of the famed—and equally impossible—paper palaces of Song—even she, the once-princess Samarkar, was overawed.

The walls of the palace were massive blocks of gold-chased lapis lazuli, a blue so fine and true as to defy description. There were no skies in all the civilized world that color. Graceful words—passages of the Scholar-God's scripture—carved fingertip-deep in the walls seemed cut from black shadows, while the walls themselves glowed in the light that fell through glass-finished windows taller than three men standing on one another's shoulders. The stone filigree holding the glass cast articulated shadows across the cream marble floor as if flowers of light were strewn by giant's handfuls for any foot to tread upon. Overhead, a lofty chain of vaults and domes seemed to hover, higher and finer than anything Samarkar had even envisioned in dreams. More script adorned it: words everywhere, even worked in gold into the marble underfoot. Even cast by the shadows through the ranks of windows. Even drifting in the air through that unbelievable, acoustically perfect space.

Samarkar noticed that Temur, who tended to hunch uncomfortably under a stone roof, was leaning back and staring about himself in wonder.

"It's not so humble," Ato Tesefahun said effacingly. "But it is for the glory of the Scholar-God."

"Who was the architect?" Samarkar marveled aloud.

Ato Tesefahun looked down at his feet. Samarkar blinked at him from behind her helm's slatted mask and winced when Hrahima cuffed—gently, by a Cho-tse's standards—the old man.

"Not so humble," the tiger scoffed. "Yes, so says a great wizard of Aezin. Not so humble, indeed."

Samarkar stumbled on the smooth stone. "This was built . . . in your lifetime?"

He smiled. "In yours, granddaughter, if I estimate your age accurately."

Samarkar was too stunned by the courtesy he did her—*granddaughter?*—to fill the pause he left her. She knew Aezin folk used family endearments as a sign of respect to unrelated friends—but she also knew they never did it casually.

After a moment, he continued. "Though the thought behind it commenced some fifty years ago, when I was a very young, very conceited man. Knowing what I know now, I might not plot quite so boldly again."

Hrahima chuffed: her feline laughter. Samarkar noticed how many of the bustling slaves and functionaries who zipped from place to place across the beautiful atrium deviated from their line long enough to nod to Ato Tesefahun in his threadbare, expensive robes—though none of them paused to pass a word, and neither did he seem so inclined.

"I thought—" She glanced from side to side, and lowered her voice, and spoke in the Qersnyk tongue. "I had been given to understand, Ato, that you were not a great supporter of the caliphate."

He looked at her, wide-eyed, guileless. A simple old man. "Because I am Aezin, or because I make my home in Ctesifon . . . when I have not been called to Asitaneh on business? Both Aezin and Ctesifon, as you know, are loyal vassals of the caliphate, rendering tribute *willingly* to the representative of the Scholar-God's hegemony on earth."

Samarkar heard Temur's foot scuff the floor like that of a chastened child. For was he not—had he not been?—the soldier of still another conqueror? Was not Samarkar the daughter of such a one? She met Ato Tesefahun's eyes through the slots of the helm, for a moment forgetting the modesty expected of a woman here. Ato Tesefahun winked into her regard.

It was Samarkar who looked down. In order to keep from shaking her head continually in amazement, she asked, "The singing. A eunuch?"

"A slave poetess," Ato Tesefahun said.

"But a woman—"

"Oh," he said, as if apprehending her confusion. As if the source of it were not new to him, and he had made this explanation many times before. "Women are reflections of the Scholar-God and Her Prophet, after all. They are to be encouraged to study the natural histories, or literature, or medicine. For them to do so is like holding a diamond before the lamplight of the Scholar-God's grace and glory."

Samarkar touched her mask. "But how can you study science—how can you exist as a colleague—when a man can't look upon your face? Or speak to you?" She gestured to the air. "How can this poet perform in a public place if she is forbidden to speak to men?"

"She sings from behind a screen," said Ato Tesefahun. "Or from within a veil. That is Ümmühan, one of the city's greatest slave poetesses. Is she not fine?"

"Ümmühan," Samarkar said dubiously. "'The Illiterate?'" Her voice was pure and powerful enough that Samarkar could have believed it to have belonged to a eunuch.

"Their performers," said Hrahima, "are given stage names by their patrons or owners, and the more humble the name—so as not to affront the Scholar-God—the more prestige usually attached to the performer."

"I see," said Samarkar finally, a little forlornly. The worst of it was, she did.

She tugged her helm down a little more snugly over the cushion of her hair and squared her shoulders as Ato Tesefahun led their little party across the word-wrought stones. They progressed toward an area beneath the great dome that was segregated from the common atrium by pierced stone screens and ranks of *kapikulu*, fanatical slave mercenary guards in skirted coats of cerulean blue.

The *kapikulu* were legendary for their loyalty and fierceness, and Samarkar knew they served all over the realms claimed by the Scholar-God. But they were not the only holy warriors sworn to the caliph's service. Arranged among the *kapikulu* were the royal guards, the so-called Dead Men, whose presence supplied another hint to the caliph's location.

They numbered a dozen. They stood arrayed in elaborate reproductions of Uthman grave robes wrought from rich fabrics, the wide sleeves decorated with artful, layered tatters of dust-colored linen and silk, the hoods dropped down their backs. Each robe was belted with a crimson sash through which was thrust a sword, but otherwise left to hang open-fronted over silver-bright mail. Like the robes, shaven heads and eyebrows indicated that these Dead Men no longer belonged to the world.

They had no families outside the caliph's household. They were chosen from among the orphans of the street, ceremonially beheaded and reborn into the caliph's family and raised up as warrior priests. The caliph's household provided everything for them: education (or perhaps *indoctrination* would be the better-chosen word), training, wives, wealth, care for their children, the assurance of Heaven. There were said to be no more pious, no more incorruptible swordsmen in the world. There were certainly few better trained, if the reports of Samarkar's father's intelligencers could be believed.

THE CALIPH WAS A MAN—NO LONGER YOUNG BUT NOT BY ANY MEANS FRAIL— whose dark eyes blazed out from bruised hollows. A few steel-colored hairs stippled his brows and beard, but a filet-bound linen cloth edged in indigo and crimson embroidery concealed his hair, so Samarkar could not see if the signs of age progressed further. Veins and tendons stood out in the backs of hands like saddle leather, incongruous as they cradled an eggshell-porcelain coffee cup.

Upon an elevated platform he sat, not enthroned but rather upon a sort of chair consisting of a brocade sling between crossed wooden supports. The richness of his raiment half-concealed it. At his right hand, a veiled and shrouded woman crouched upon cushions, motionless as if carved. She supported the tray from which the caliph must have lifted his coffee cup. Three well-dressed men, whom Samarkar assumed to be heralds or viziers or advisors of some sort, were arranged seated behind and below the caliph's chair.

The caliph looked up as Ato Tesefahun's little band was brought before him, but he did not speak. The slave poetess sang still.

She must be concealed in the louvered sandalwood box just big enough to comfortably enclose a standing woman that had been placed at the base of the caliph's dais. It must have been cunningly constructed to augment sound, because the poet's voice rang as clearly as if she stood at the focus of any amphitheater.

Samarkar could now make out most of the words of her chant, though the dialect was archaic and the diction formal. Still, that was the way of court language everywhere, and Samarkar had been raised and bred to it.

The poem was a young girl's plaint of grief, a plea for a husband gone to war to return safe and soon. It might have seemed simple, Samarkar thought—and on the surface it was. A ballad, with the end-rhyming lines that marked Uthman poetry—but the naïveté of the poem's construction and topic was underlain by darker threads. The poem might be written in the voice of a young girl, but it marked a mature woman's understanding of inevitability, and it was shot through with a sense of futility and loss and wasted youth that made Samarkar think that the robed silhouette visible only as flickers of movement through the slats of the blind was no girl, but a poet of experience and grief. Samarkar would have hoped that Temur's shaky Uthman was insufficient for him to understand the gist of the song, but a glance at his face disabused her. His eyes bright, his expression blank . . . she knew without asking that he was thinking of Edene.

The song dropped away to a whisper, a falling air of shadows undermining the narrator's lingering words of hope and loyalty. Only when the echoes had died did Samarkar, transfixed, notice that Hrahima too showed every sign of being in the grip of some tremendous emotion: ears forward and whiskers fluffed. Her claws had popped from their sheaths to draw creases in the striped fur of her thighs.

Samarkar laid the back of her hand against the Cho-tse's arm and leaned in close to whisper, "Does she speak for you too?"

Hrahima looked down at Samarkar. Tigers did not weep, but Samarkar did not think anyone could look into those mottled eyes, like heat-crazed tourmalines, and deny that a Cho-tse could grieve.

"The Sun Within links us all," Hrahima rumbled. "No cub or mate can ever truly be lost."

But you deny the Sun Within, Samarkar would have argued, had she not seen the amused, arch look the caliph turned on her and Hrahima. Thus did the Wizard Samarkar comprehend the genius of the interlocking sky of domes and Ato Tesefahun's unprecedented architecture. It was a whispering vault. The caliph could hear any word spoken in his audience chamber, no matter how low the voice was pitched.

And Samarkar and Hrahima had been muttering in Uthman.

Samarkar winced a quick apology before she remembered the helm that entirely concealed her face. Instead, she bowed low, boiled leather creaking, and heard the rustles and scrapes and rattles as her companions echoed the gesture.

A pointed silence dragged on while they waited for the caliph's acknowledgment. Samarkar heard the patter of bare feet moving with the lightest of steps over stone, the oiled slide of long poles through locks, as if someone shipped oars. *The sandalwood box,* she realized, a moment before bearers silently lifted it up—slave poetess and all—and bore it away.

Like a songbird in a cage. Samarkar wondered grimly if Ümmühan was ever suffered to leave it, and was grateful for her helm once again.

Her back ached with the depth of her obeisance and the weight of her armor before someone cleared his throat and said, "Grandfather architect! That is quite a menagerie you've captured."

"Your serene Excellency," said Ato Tesefahun, with the air of one sidestepping confrontation. "May I present Re Temur Khanzadeh. His father was Otgonbayar Khanzadeh. He is the grandson of Re Temusan Khagan. His traveling companions are Samarkar-la, a Wizard of Tsarepheth and sister to the Rasan emperor; Brother Hsiung, of the Wretched Mountain Temple Brotherhood; and Hrahima, a warrior of the Cho-tse. They have come with grave news from afar and to offer an alliance with your serene Excellency."

There was a pause, and then: "Rise," said a second man. "Approach."

Lifting her head, Samarkar was surprised to discover that the caliph—Uthman Caliph Fourteenth, Commander of the Faithful, Viceroy of the Scholar-God, Successor to the Prophet—had spoken himself. She would have expected one of the men surrounding his chair to serve as his voice—as, apparently, one had begun to. The disgruntled-looking one on his left, her right, most likely.

She advanced with the others, halting on an invisible demarcation a hand span or two behind Ato Tesefahun. When the Aezin wizard bowed again, so did she. And remained so until she noticed Temur straighten in response to some gesture she did not see around the restriction of her helm.

"Re Temur Khanzadeh," said the caliph. His tone was playful, light. It put Samarkar's guard up at once. "Your family has been a plague upon the borders of my nation since my great-grandfather's day. And now you come to me as a supplicant? I know your family wars against itself, and the moons fall from your sky. Why should I offer you assistance, princeling?"

Temur stood proud, his shoulders square and his hands at his sides in the posture Samarkar had seen him use to pray. From the rear, she could see that his head rode strangely on his neck. Sadly, sickeningly, contracting scar tissue was beginning to twist his posture out of true. Samarkar cursed herself for a poor wizard and a worse physicker—and a bad lover, most of all.

"My usurping uncle has allied himself with one of your own rebel warlords, your serene Excellency," Temur said. "They have resorted to carrion sorcery, the raising of blood ghosts, and perhaps more dire witchcraft yet. They have sent those ghosts against refugee trains and at least one city that had taken no part in the battles. Qeshqer is fallen, your serene Excellency, the city my grandfather took from Rasa, which is also called Kashe—"

Samarkar would not let herself bristle, not before this caliph who might yet prove an enemy. Temur was Qersnyk; it was natural he should use the Qersnyk name first. That he even thought of the conquered Rasan city's Rasan name was either a sign of more diplomacy than she'd expected from him or a concession to her sensibilities.

As once-princess, as wizard and as woman, she wasn't sure which she would have preferred. She turned her head aside and found Brother Hsiung's blue-shadowed gaze regarding her steadily. He tipped his head and winked. She bit back on the slightly hysterical chuckle that wanted to answer. Mute the monk might be, but half the time she thought he needed language less than did a dog.

"This rebel warlord," said Uthman Caliph. "Name him."

"Mukhtar ai-Idoj," said Ato Tesefahun. "Called al-Sepehr of the Rahazeen Nameless."

Samarkar saw the caliph glance to the left before he spoke, taking the temper of the man there—the man on her right who she thought had spoken those first, mocking words. She shifted her attention as well. The helm concealed her eyes: another unanticipated benefit.

He wore a blue kaftan sewn with stars, perhaps some mark of the caliph's favor. He was younger than she would have expected—fresh-faced and pretty, his beard as black as if drawn on with a pen and steadfastly refusing to cover the center of his chin. Samarkar imagined from the lift of his head that he thought well of himself. He met the caliph's gaze boldly, and while Samarkar would not hazard to guess what communication passed between them, she knew she had shared such gazes with her brothers on occasion—though never with her husband.

"Devotees of some medieval just-so story," the caliph said. "He has no armies. His cult clings to the caves and fortresses of the mountains because they dare not descend. And I should find them a threat? If you think me so weak, why would you even seek my patronage?"

"We do not think you weak," Temur began. "This al-Sepehr commands a rukh, great caliph, and the armies of the dead. I believe . . ."

The silence stretched heartbeats long. Samarkar was startled that no one filled it, but perhaps the shaking intensity in Temur's voice held even the caliph and his black-bearded advisor in thrall for those few moments.

Temur controlled his voice and continued. "I believe he may try to raise the Sorcerer-Prince himself."

This silence *rang*. Even the caliph leaned forward, expectantly—until the black-bearded advisor broke it with a muffled chuckle, quickly—perhaps ostentatiously—stifled.

No one glanced at him, because the caliph uncurled one hand from his untouched coffee cup and half-raised it. "What the Scholar-God put down, no man can raise up again."

Hrahima and Ato Tesefahun might have been shadows cast by the fall-ing radiance within the palace, for all the noise they made—but Samarkar heard Brother Hsiung's clothing whisk against itself as he shifted his weight, though his feet made no sound on the stone. She too winced in-wardly, though her face—she hoped—showed none of it.

Temur was inexperienced yet. But he was no fool; when the side of her gauntleted hand drifted to touch his, he seemed to realize he had come to a logical stopping place . . . and stopped there.

Samarkar said, "Great Caliph, I have seen the destruction of cities with my own eyes, and so has Temur Khanzadeh. The blood ghosts left naught of Qeshqer but heaps of sucked bones in the market square, neatly stripped and sorted. Those skulls will bleach there, your serene Excellency—the skulls of the toothless elderly side by side . . . heaped each upon each . . . with the skulls of newborns, equally toothless and no bigger than my fist. This is not just a war that can be waited out, with the hope that our neighbors will weaken each other and we can chip some land away from them. I believe your lands are in peril too, as are those of my brother."

"My caliphate is in peril if we lose the mandate of heaven," he an-swered, with another sidelong glance. The black-bearded man regarded him, simply expressionless now. "I rule by the will of the Scholar-God. The entrails speak of avoidance of war, Wizard Samarkar. Not rushing headlong to it. You speak as if you have some knowledge of politics?"

How astute, she thought, when Ato Tesefahun had told the caliph her family and her history.

"Some," she said, keeping from slipping into sarcasm mostly by dint of breath control. If her years as a political hostage in Song had given her nothing else, they had left her with the ability to control her tone.

"Then you know that the longer war rages on the steppe, the worse my trade situation becomes. A stable Khaganate benefits my cities."

"A Rahazeen rebellion will not benefit you, your serene Excellency."

To his credit, he looked her in the eye—or the general direction of it, given her helm—as he said, "The Rahazeen cannot feed their children. I am not afraid of any army they might raise."

"Serene Excellency," said Hrahima, the titles smooth on her rough cat's tongue, "you have the power to deny al-Sepehr the use of the Qersnyk army, whereas so long as Qori Buqa remains unopposed he serves as al-Sepehr's cat's-paw. No other power in the world can do this thing. You alone have the strength."

The caliph did not preen under the flattery. He regarded the Cho-tse from beneath brows drawn shrewdly together. "Cute," he said. "But no."

As they left the palace, the *kapikulu* and the Dead Men taking no more notice of them than they had on the way in, Samarkar heard music rising behind them once again. This time, the singer was a man.

"IF YOU WANT THE CALIPH'S TROOPS PUSHED OUT OF CTESIFON, WHY DID YOU build him a palace?" Temur whispered in his grandfather's ear as they left the building in question.

Ato Tesefahun sighed. "He paid," he said with a shrug. "And . . . he commanded. You noticed, of course, the man in the starry caftan?"

"Kara Mehmed," Hrahima said. *Black Mehmed.*

She swept them out onto the steps of the palace and into the bustle of the street. As they descended to join the throngs—of water sellers, of camel drivers, of hurrying, veiled women in groups, each clutching her market bags—she continued. "He's one of the faction leaders in the war-band."

"He's young." Temur was not quite able to ignore the irony of being the one to say so enough to get it out without stammering. When the others turned to him with dubious expressions, he clarified. "What I mean is, isn't he too young to have voted to install this caliph?"

"He'll install the next," said Hrahima. "If he lives."

Ato Tesefahun, the more patient teacher, explained: "His grandfather did. The position is hereditary."

Temur boggled. "But if there is no personal loyalty between war-band and leader—"

Hrahima interrupted. "Exactly. Uthman Caliph's not afraid of the Rahazeen," she mocked. "Just the political pressures of his war-band or anything that might restrict trade."

Samarkar pushed irritably at her helm. Her voice echoed eerily within. "Those are the same thing. Whose treasure houses do you suppose are furnished by the trade that passes along the Celadon Highway? By the oxcarts, the spindle weights, the glass beads, the saffron, the aloes, the myrrh? By the sandalwood, the dates, the silk, the porcelain? There were kilns along the road when we came in from the port—convenient to shipping, and at least a little out of the city traffic in the case of a disaster. The merchants trade cedar, malachite, electrum, jade . . . look here!"

She caught Temur's wrist and whirled him to face a shop. The awning was raised, and through the lattices Temur could see that it was a stone-worker's. Within, shelves and benches supported examples of the work of more than one artisan. There was eastern jade in several styles, including one reminiscent of the steppe, and soapstone carved after a manner that drew inspiration from the whimsical caricature animals of Song. The subjects, however, ranged the known world.

The rhinoceros was out of scale, wearing a flat Song saddle as if it were a chubby pony—but Temur had seen one in the menagerie at Qa-rash once, and he was impressed by the knobbled detail of its armored hide. The flirtatious look and curve of smile the artist had given it, how-ever, were pure fantasy.

"Trade," he said. "You're not telling me anything I didn't know, Wiz-ard Samarkar."

She spread her hands, asking for another moment to make her point. "But ask yourself who collects the taxes and the bribes. I think you'll find Black Mehmed's name fairly high upon the roll. So it's to his good—in the short term, anyway—to return the steppe to tranquility as soon as possible."

"Even if the long-term outcome is a wider war?"

"Empires," Ato Tesefahun put in, "have always sustained the Celadon Highway. It is the longest road in the world, and it has persisted and con-nected through the reigns of Erem, of Aezin, of the Lizard Folk, of Song, the caliphate, the Khaganate . . ." He shrugged. "The road feeds the kings and the kings feed the road."

"What if we convert the war-band?" Temur asked. "Bring them to our cause?"

Brother Hsiung shifted his weight, shaking his head so the sweat ran down his shaved scalp in rivulets.

"Figure out how," Hrahima said. "And you'll already be a better Khagan than your grandfather ever managed."

"LET ME LOOK AT THAT," SAMARKAR SAID, AS TEMUR STRIPPED HIS SHIRT OFF over his head.

He had turned his back on her, which she would have found charmingly, ridiculously shy if she had not been so intent on examining his scars before he blew the lamps out. She was reminded again of how young he was—by the way he hunched to hide the injury from her when she stood stripped to the trousers before him, her own scars evident in the flickering light. She should have sighed and shaken her head; instead, she found it charming.

"Pardon?" He turned over his shoulder, shirt clutched to his bosom as if he were a maiden. She saw that he turned to the left to regard her out of his eye corners, and it clawed at her. Yes, he compensated—but that was no excuse for her not noticing how the healing injury had begun to restrict him.

She wished Hong-la were here, or Tsering-la. But she was what she had, and so she would have to suffice.

"Your scar," she said. "I want to see it."

He said, "I don't think—"

And she answered, "I have saved your life once, Re Temur. Do you think my curiosity idle? Will you still think it so when you are too twisted to stand within a bow?"

He still held the crumpled linen clutched to his chest, but the expression on his face had changed. He was looking at her now—*at* her, regarding her, with a focused, transfixing awareness.

"Once?" he said.

"Excuse me?"

"You have saved my life *once*, Wizard Samarkar? Say rather you saved it at Qeshqer, and between the Steles of the Sky, and in the salt desert, and among the Lizard Folk of the woman-king Tzitzik—and eight more times besides. If it's life debt you'd claim, claim all of it."

She blinked at him. He stared at her. The lamplight cast sideways shadows across his face—soft beside the broad shallow bridge of his nose, sharp above the cheekbones. They did not move: the oil was too clean, the wick too trimmed for the lamp to flicker, and Samarkar realized that Temur was not breathing.

"Idiot," she said at last, when she'd finally managed to parse through what he was implying.

Then he turned to her. The lamp lay behind him and the shadows hid his face. "I'm sorry?"

"Idiot," she said again, fondly. She came to him and pushed the shirt aside. "I'm not claiming debt. I'm trying to prove I will not harm you. Lie down. Head toward the light. We have work to do, Re Temur."

He pushed her unbound hair—still kinked from the pressure of the helm—behind her shoulder bemusedly, but obeyed her order. He composed himself upon the pallet like a corpse upon a bier—hands crossed at his belly, spine as straight as the scar would allow.

She knelt on the floor behind him and placed her hands upon his shoulders. They made lighter silhouettes against the brown of his flesh. She let herself pause there, feeling the warmth of his body press against her palms.

She leaned down and kissed his forehead.

"Is that something all your patients have to look forward to, Wizard Samarkar?"

"Only the sarcastic ones." She let her hands touch his neck. "Since somebody already tried the obvious remedy—"

It got a laugh, albeit a grim one. When her hands began to move, the laugh became a sigh. Temur fitted his fingers over hers. Gently, she pushed them away. "You cannot defend yourself from this. Not if it is to help you. You must resist the urge to protect the injury, even though that urge is perfectly natural."

He forced his hands away. "My mistress commands."

That was a defense too, but for the time being she let it stand. "This will hurt," she said.

She carried emollients in her kit, oil of coconut and other things. And she would use them before the night was through. But at first, she just outlined the scar with her fingertips, pressing under the edges, feeling adhesions and the way it bound up the skin, the way it drew tight into it-self like badly cured leather. She should have been doing this all along, keeping it supple and flexible . . . but like badly cured leather it was not completely beyond repair. It would never be as soft as if she'd been treating it properly since they left Tsarepheth but that was just one more minor failure she—and Temur—would have to live with.

She went to work. He bore the prodding stoically. She limited the amount of pressure she brought to bear, but it was on his throat—and you could break a man's collarbone with your thumbs. She knew she was hurting him.

"Without the caliph's help," she said, "it will be best if we find ways to spread the word that you will be returning to claim the Padparadscha Seat among your people."

"Rumors?" he asked.

"A promise," she replied. She laid her palm flat against his cheek and turned his face, stretching against the contraction of the scar. He gri-maced but made no protest. "So they know Qori Buqa is opposed. So they know there is a choice, and those who would oppose him have a banner to rally toward. Just the—yes, rumor—of your return can con-jure support among your uncle's enemies."

"More war," he said. "More dead. More famines. More blood ghosts—"

"To do otherwise," said Samarkar, relentlessly, "is to allow him to consolidate his power."

A scowl pulled Temur's mouth crooked, but she felt his muscles move as he nodded, reluctantly. "If I tell the tribes where to meet to support me, I also tell my uncle where to bring his army."

"That is the flaw," she agreed.

He raised his hands again, this time reaching past her arms to touch her waist, cup the sides of her breasts.

"You're distracting me."

"I'm distracting myself," he replied. "I need it. Beside which, there *is* a topless woman leaning over me."

"An issue we can address later." She winked.

"I cannot be Khagan," he said, "or even Khan, if my partisans do not know where to meet to proclaim me. I must raise a banner if they are to flock to it."

She pushed and stretched him again. This time, his breath hissed between his teeth. "There are some old magics—I don't know them, but some of my masters would. Knowledge bindings. Perhaps we could find a way to knot the knowledge up so that only those sympathetic to your cause could understand it."

He pushed against her hand to look her in the eye then. "That's a mighty magic."

"It's one that's beyond me."

"I will need a shaman-rememberer. What one knows, they all know. They could spread the word."

Samarkar hesitated, considering. "What if a shaman-rememberer were among the blood ghosts?"

"I don't know," Temur said after a silence. "But one thing I cannot do is call for the support of the clans with foreign monks and sorcerers arrayed at my side and none of the shamans of my own folk."

"I shall efface my—"

"You shall do no such thing," he said sternly. This time he touched her face, upside down, cupping her cheek and holding her gaze through the dim light. "Are my people not famed across the width of the world for having no concern for which gods a man—or a woman—worships, so long as their skills are of use and they live under law? It is just that for my own people, I must be seen to have the mandate of the Eternal Sky."

"You believe you do?"

A curious expression crossed his face—faraway, swiftly flitting. "I do."

She nodded, and left off his neck for the time being, turning to fit herself by his side. He opened his arms to pull her close and she settled into his warmth with a sigh.

Before him—without him—she never would have known this comfort of skin on skin. The enormity of it silenced her for a moment. They lay in the lamplight, breathing together, until she recovered herself enough to say, "One thing wizards know, Temur Khanzadeh, is the power of words. To say a thing is to make it so."

"Princes know that too," he said.

Samarkar, once-princess, snorted in the most indelicate manner imaginable. "Wizarding and kinging are not such disparate trades." She paused, her silence hard-edged enough that Temur stirred against her.

"What?"

"The caliph," she said. "He may not give you men or arms. But it would cost him very little indeed to offer you something almost as valuable."

She felt him still again. "Yes," he said. "Of course. Recognition. His war-band won't like it, if you and Hrahima are right."

"I shall see him tomorrow," she said.

"Will he see you?"

"I am a Wizard of Tsarepheth," she scoffed. "He'll see what I tell him to."

She paused; she saw him considering her silence. He said, "Whatever brilliance is upon you, Wizard Samarkar, pray share it."

"Is there a . . ." She didn't know the Uthman term. "An empress dowager, a valide sultan? The mother of the caliph? If I could infiltrate the harem—"

"Cocky." His tone shifted along with hers: what had been hushed and serious became banter, flirtation. "But then you'd be stuck in the harem, and what if you could not gain the sympathy of the valide sultan?"

Samarkar sighed, frustrated. Despite that, she was startled anew by just how *easy* it was, lying here in the arms of someone who cheered and comforted her.

She turned her face to his and breathed in his breath, let him breathe hers. He leaned his forehead against hers and smiled at her. "Stay out of the harem. They'd keep you if they got you, and I wouldn't trade you for eight good mares, Samarkar."

"So show me again," she said, gazing deeply into his eyes, "what you've learned in the saddle, Re Temur."

He drew in a breath and held onto it, fighting giggles. Until she poked him in the ribs and he collapsed into laughter in her arms.

That laughter—and their pleasure in it—was a little frantic, uncertain in her ears: a shine off a bitter edge. Edene still lost, their allies fragile and scattered, an army at their face but no army at their backs . . . and yet. Samarkar touched Temur's face in the shifting dark, his downy beard snagging her travel-rough fingertips. The skin of his shoulders, which never felt the sun or wind, was supple and soft. His breath tautened as she traced the line of the bone and turned her head to press her open lips to the soft hollow between his neck and collarbone. His scar was rough and hot—and slick with grease—against her cheek. He gasped; his thigh slid between hers. She felt the press of his sex through fabric, against her hip. His mouth passed over her eye and cheek to find her lips, his fingers beneath her chin to lift her face. The kiss was soft at first, nibbling. She did not bite, but caught his lip between her teeth so gently. His mouth opened. The slippery, velvet roughness of his tongue found hers for long moments before he broke it off and pulled back the width of her hand, panting.

"You see?" he said. "Very adaptable to your foreign customs, my folk."

She pulled him down to her again. His hand skimmed her breast, the softness of her belly, dimpling flesh as it slipped inside the waist of her trousers. Now she caught her breath and held it.

He paused, perhaps concerned. "Too soon?"

There had been blood, that first time. Not much, but enough for irony. She, widowed and barren, had offered up a virgin's sacrifice to the six merciful immortals of fertility. She'd laughed brutally at it then; he had been horrified he might have done her harm. And here he was, worried still.

She put her hand over his. "The surest way to expertise is practice."

He hesitated still but found her gaze with his own, and she made sure to hold it. Her tone, she thought, could have been more confident.

"I want you," she said, adjusting her tone to that of a wizard—or a princess—who gave orders meant to be followed even when her heart quailed with uncertainty and misgivings in her breast. At least there were no misgivings this time . . . and the only uncertainty was that of inexperience.

His, as well as hers, she thought, watching relief smooth the hesitation from his face. He had not said, but she thought his Edene had been his only lover. It made her like him better, and she already liked him very well.

If he needed her to be certain for him—she was Samarkar. She could seem as certain as anyone.

"Touch me," she urged, finding a smile for him that was fierce and sincere and more passionate than she herself would have believed she had the heart for, back in Tsarepheth. And he did, gently and slowly, until they both forgot themselves again and the awkward carefulness dissolved into a messier and more enthusiastic sort of awkwardness altogether.

 7

THE TWINS HUDDLED IN THEIR INSUFFICIENT COAT AND BOOTS, DIZZY WITH altitude and glad of the feathered warmth of the enormous bird whose neck they bestrode, glad too that the rukh was perched and not beating into the savage winds that had borne them this far. Though it was high summer below and beyond the Steles of the Sky, they had flown up into the depths of eternal winter. Only the rukh and the bar-headed goose could fly so high.

It could have been the whole world spread out before them, if the world were only a bruised ring of sunset swirled around the rim of a wasteland of iron-colored rock and pallid ice. Forbidding, shattered, the mountains receded from the summit upon which the twins perched with their mount, marching to the twilight horizon on every side—except where the Tsarethi broke from beneath the span of the Citadel, leaping from stone to stone the length of a narrow valley picked out in shimmering lights. Lamps burned below, and witchlights, and torches.

The twins shivered, and Saadet pulled the white-bleached lambskin close about their shoulders, fingers clumsy in unaccustomed kidskin. It still wasn't enough, though in fairness no coat *could* have proved sufficient. To keep out a cold such as this was beyond the technologies of men. The twins' lungs ached with cold as much as want of air.

Shahruz lifted the spyglass from the twins' saddle and raised it to their eye. Saadet saw what he saw: down at the far end of the valley, men and women were stepping out onto the balconies of the Black Palace, before which crouched an unlit pyre.

Three Nameless warriors had arrived on rukh-back with the twins. Those three warriors were infiltrating the city below in accordance with the long-term plans of al-Sepehr. The twins were alone now. Perhaps that aloneness contributed to a sense of unease, of being regarded. The twins glanced over their shoulder, where mist coiled in the caldera of a quiescent volcano. Saadet suppressed a hard shiver—fear, this time, rather than chill.

If it were mist-dragons, surely the eyes would give them away? Wasn't it most likely that what poured like water into a cauldron, to seethe and swirl, was merely clouds trapped by a trick of topography and colder air settling?

If it *was* mist-dragons . . . would even *they* dare to ambush a rukh?

"It's time," Shahruz said, their throat and lips stretching uncomfortably around his still-unfamiliar voice. "See to the Cold Fire, sister."

Saadet let herself smile. Al-Sepehr had entrusted her with the blood-soaked spell stones, the sacrifices meant to commence weakening the bonds that sealed the ancient fire-mountain and had since the reign of the Sorcerer-Prince. Now, she manipulated the long reins, directing the rukh down into those seething mists.

It moved uncertainly on the ground, for all its strength, picking its way blindly through fog to reach the bottom. Stones scattered from its talons as it waddled, chickenlike, down the slope. Here the air was warmer, almost comfortable. Heat soaking from the earth pushed the mists up, making it possible to see barren terrain.

When Saadet signaled it to stop, the rukh plucked hewn stone after hewn stone from the carrier pouches at its breast. It laid them one atop another to form a stone table. They had been carved and fitted according to the instructions found in grimoires of ancient Erem; the twins were not surprised to see that the rukh's beak grew friable and rotten where she touched them. Nor were the twins surprised that the slabs fell together perfectly: the masons who had made them were probably dead by now, but while they lasted they had wrought well.

Saadet let her brother feel her sense of satisfaction, rejoicing as he echoed it. She stretched into his approval, warmed, and gave him control of the reins. It was he who guided the rukh back to the crater's rim, though it scrabbled and fluttered the whole way. They paused there, overlooking the world, while their mist-damp hair froze in crackling serpent-strands about their face.

"For the Nameless," she said.

She knew what he answered, though the wind of their falling snatched his words away. Lifting his hands, urging the rukh to drop from the parapet into flight, he cried out, "For the world!"

It was not the Wizard Hong's first execution, nor even his first burning. But it was the first one where he had stood in wizard's weeds behind an empress, bearing witness to the execution of her junior husband, with her senior husband painstakingly expressionless beyond.

Flanked by attendants and guards, Emperor Songtsan wore the funeral white and crimson his senior wife had eschewed. The crown rested on his head, a latticework circlet carved from a single round of translucent green-gold crystals embedded in iron-gray matrix. Not just iron-gray, Hong-la knew: iron, most simply, studded as thickly as currants in a cake with peridot and olivine. The Bstangpo's crown was carved from a piece of a skystone, and between material and craftsmanship it hummed with enough hoarded *otherwise* strength to make a wizard's skin tingle.

The pyre had been raised in the square before the palace, constructed of seasoned sandalwood and cedar as befitted a prince of the empire. Beyond, spray rose above the tossing river as it leapt between stones. Hong-la had been hearing the noise of the emperor's subjects arriving to witness the execution for hours now. It rose into the windows of the Black Palace, mingling with the river's roar and hiss, while he wasted the afternoon dancing attendance upon the empress and her women—and seeing to their entertainments.

Now he stood above that crowd on a balcony with the family and executors of the condemned, and wondered how many of the commoners below came to rejoice in the suffering of one of the ruling class, for a change. Pestilence—or infestation—aside, there were hundreds in the square. There might have been thousands, were it not for the demonspawn.

Most of the crowd wore ghost white—or "white," anyway, some scrap of natural fabric bleached as pale as they could make it with stale urine or stranger concoctions—but Hong-la wasn't the sort to be fooled by a public face of mourning. Oh, some would feel pity for the doomed prince, he was sure. And some would feel kinship to him, no matter how wretched their own status, because if one thing about human nature was universally true, it was that there was always somebody who was willing to support an oligarch in contravention of his own best interests. But there were plenty in the crowd who bore the marks of the law's draconian intervention in their lives: a man with his lips severed there, a woman wearing a hook in place of her right hand here. And those—or at least many of those—would be here to watch a prince burn, and imagine for an afternoon that someday it might be all princes.

Barriers and soldiers kept the crowd at a distance that Hong-la estimated might be safe, once the flames rose; it would not be comfortable. He guessed he would feel the heat even here, on the palace balcony, and half-pitied the courtiers in their endless layers of robes.

And the emperor? Hong-la watched Songtsan-tsa from the corner of his eye, noticing the gray, set face and the lift of the emperor's chin.

A man who would burn his own brother might deserve to feel the heat of those flames. But given Songtsan's expression, Hong-la suddenly wondered if perhaps he actually believed his brother guilty of the murder of their mother. If that was so, it would mean that Songtsan had not, as Hong-la had assumed, poisoned the dowager himself and hung the frame around Tsansong.

And that . . . was politically interesting.

The empress, by contrast, appeared utterly cool and sorrowful in the colors of a gloaming sky, as if she had performed her mourning already. Either she believed in her junior husband's guilt or she was a consummate actress.

Among all that white splashed with red, she—and, Hong-la assumed, he himself—stood out like ravens in a crowd of doves.

She leaned sideways for a word against her senior husband's ear. The wizard turned away.

The sun had already drifted below the shoulders of the mountains, leaving the city below still brightly lit, though indirectly now. Within the embrace of the Steles of the Sky, twilight was a lingering affair. Hong-la could still make out the silhouettes of several hawks circling against the blue twilight. One soared high enough that the last rays of the sun illuminated its pale belly.

The imperial company had not been summoned to the balcony until preparations for the execution were complete. Hong-la did not have long to wait before a surge in the crowd below alerted him—and the others—that events were proceeding. Imperial guards with their splinted armor bound in white cords came forth from the palace courtyard, lining the route left open for them by the barricading soldiers with another rank of bodies, three deep. They must have nearly concealed the next cadre of guards from the eyes of the crowd, and though Hong-la's view from the high balcony was unobstructed, he could not imagine that anyone on the ground could clearly see the doomed prince.

Tsansong walked calmly in the midst of his killers, his head high and his hands unbound. He wore green, the shade of jade and early summer, a leafy iridescence visible even from this distance giving evidence of expensive imported silks. Cries rose from the crowd—jeering, an echoing hiss of half a thousand angry voices that rumbled in the cavity of Hong-la's belly like the wrath of dragons—but the prince did not respond. It could have been the smoke of the torches that left Hong-la's eyes burning. He thought rather it was exhaustion.

Tsansong's executioners paralleled him inside the hollow box of guardsmen. A common criminal mounting the scaffold would have been pelted with dung and rotten food, but the soldiers must have searched the crowd before allowing them to assemble. No foul missiles arched through the air now, and Tsansong-tsa reached the pyre unsullied.

The guards peeled away then, in precise formation and lockstep surrounding the square base of the latticed pyre. Tsansong did not check his step, though he ducked his head a little as he climbed. There must be steps built into the pyre, because he ascended smoothly, and the executioners followed.

The wood looked seasoned and dry. It would burn with little smoke to hasten the prince's end and ease his suffering. Hong-la wondered if Songtsan-tsa would have arranged for his brother to be garroted before the torches were applied.

Four guards followed Tsansong up the back of the pyre. While he had been accorded the dignity of walking to his execution, his wrists were now locked to a chain at his waist. Another chain trailed behind him, where it was controlled by two of the executioners. Anyone who faced burning might be expected to seek a cleaner death by fighting his guards—but Tsansong's composed dignity made Hong-la suspect either that he had been promised a garroting if he behaved or that he was determined to preserve as much face, dignity, and honor as possible.

The executioners backed him against the upright post and encircled him, winding the chain about his torso six times before securing it at the back. The prince bore it proudly, his eyes raised to the balcony upon which Hong-la and the imperial family stood. From the hushed tension in the crowd, the way they stood pressed together, their hands upraised to cushion their bodies from those of their neighbors, Hong-la guessed that it must have appeared from below as if Tsansong were staring at his brother. But Hong-la had the better vantage and could read more accurately the angle of Tsansong's gaze.

He was staring at the empress, his wife.

The executioners withdrew. They had not been unnecessarily rough, and one placed a hand on Tsansong's shoulder before he walked down the steps. A shaman passed them, ascending, the bells trimming his raiment shimmering with every movement. Hong-la swallowed to ease a dry throat, blinked to ease eyes dry with exhaustion. He might as well have dragged handfuls of sand across the tissues. It seemed there would be no mercy granted Tsansong after all.

The shaman blessed the prince; the prince did not acknowledge him, or the six small white stones daubed with red that he placed around the prince's feet. Or the joss sticks—trailing banners of scent that Hong-la could only detect at this distance because of those selfsame powers of suggestion so often useful to the manipulations of wizards—that he thrust into the bundled wood between them. That seemed an unwarranted cruelty to Hong-la—smoke in anticipation of the smoke to come—but this was not his tribe, and these were not his customs.

There was a moment when Tsansong might have spoken. He seemed from the lift of his shoulders to take a breath, though the distance was too great to be sure. Those same four executioners came forward with torches. They stood at attention, their stations each corner of the pyramidal pyre.

With a glance at Empress Yangchen, Emperor Songtsan raised his hand. The empress did not seem to notice his regard. She had eyes only for her younger husband, who stood like a blade in the spiral of his chains. Her hands tightened on the balcony railing, though her face smoothed—as expressionless as it had earlier failed to remain.

The emperor's hand fell.

As did the torches.

As did . . . a shadow, blurring from the height of mountaintops with the speed of a stooping falcon.

The pyre must have been soaked in a flammable fluid, because the flames caught instantly and leapt upward, whooshing over the surfaces in a reverse cataract. The blaze roared toward its apex—and then was knocked flat by the snapped-open downbeat of enormous wings, as something vast and dark filled the square below as if it had apparated in. The buffet of wind knocked Hong-la back a step. He had a confused perception of feathers, of a human-seeming figure entirely clothed in white except for an indigo head wrap perched between gigantic pinions, of the wave of sharply heated air that blew the petaled skirts of his black wizard's coat between his legs.

The feathers snapped down again and the bird was gone, lofted on heaving wingbeats. The flames of the pyre rebounded, higher and brighter, slamming closed over the space where the stake to which Tsansong was chained had stood and stood no more.

Faintly, Hong-la thought he heard a rising sound, blown away by the wind and the cries of the crowd—only now reacting. A sound that could have been laughter, or could have been a scream.

THE SNATCH WAS AS UNEXPECTED AND DEFT AS THE TWINS COULD HAVE wished, the rukh striking from above and lifting the stake—and the chained prince—clear of the flames in a fortuitous instant. Now he dangled by his shackles from the pole in the rukh's talons, the great bird laboring not at all. She could carry off an elephant—and her killing stoop could snap the spine of an Indrik-zver. The weight of two moderately sized people was nothing to her.

The rukh's wingtips brushed tile roofs; its long neck strained and bobbed like that of a rising goose. Its musculature surged beneath the saddle. The twins raised the third rein, urging the rukh into its steepest ascent. Saadet sang encouragement, aware of her brother's amusement that she would so cosset and chivvy a thing that had no choice but to serve. But would not even a slave work harder for a kind master?

Upon the thinning air they rose. The rukh labored now—not from exertion but from the suffocation of altitude. The twins felt the sting of cold, insufficient air in pained lungs. The chained prince, swinging below, must be gasping and freezing—but he had been born to the Steles, and the twins believed he would bear the deprivation well.

Tsarepheth was a sinuous line of shimmering lights behind them. The elegant cone of the Cold Fire rose to vanish in clouds that still caught a shadowy edge of day. The twins lofted into those concealing mists, lost except for the wingbeats of the rukh, the occasional creak of the twists of chain in which the prince hung.

They broke from clouds into twilight, the Cold Fire's sharp black rim rising like a stone circle from a misty sea. It was matched on the far side of a fog-filled chasm by the ragged peak of the Island-in-the-Mists, which dwarfed even the mighty volcano.

The twins guided their mount toward the Cold Fire, bringing the rukh down gently. It had been trained to land carefully with quarry—or passengers—in its claws. It settled between wing strokes that curled clouds at its feather tips, balancing at last on one foot as the other held the stake upright. The prince did not scream; it would be a pity if he had been killed in the rescue.

The twins uncoiled the saddle ladder and slid down it without touching the rungs.

Prince Tsansong dangled from the upright stake, chains around his waist and under his armpits, his hands pulled whitely against his belly by the shackles. He was wild-eyed, wild-haired . . . but unmistakably alive. He looked up, his face stilling, and observed their approach silently. There was still enough light in the sky to see by.

The twins reached over their shoulder as if drawing a blade from a back sheath and produced a pair of long-handled cutters. The prince watched carefully as they fitted the blades into the chains that bound his wrists and pushed the handles together. It was hard—Shahruz would have cursed in frustration at Saadet's body's limited strength, if he had not been so pious a man—but with a grunt and a heave they levered the arms shut. Metal parted with an unmelodious *spang*, but the chains still held the prince off his feet.

"Be ready," the twins said in Rasan.

The prince, watching their veiled face, nodded. When they snipped the long wrapped chain, he brought his hands up as he dropped to break his fall.

You did not often see the brother of a Bstangpo on his hands and knees among cinders. The twins paused for a moment to stow the cutters in their pack again before they reached to help him up.

But the prince was already pushing himself upright, blood dark on scraped palms and spotting the knees of his jade-colored breeches. He rose with the poise of a fit man, for all that the twins could see that he was disoriented—as who would not be?—and inclined his head to them.

"I am in your debt," he said in Uthman.

"You are," the twins responded. "Please, follow me."

HAVING LIT A LAMP, THE TWINS LED THE PRINCE AWAY FROM THE RUKH. THEY descended the obsidian- and pumice-strewn slope of the volcano's caldera more elegantly than the rukh had done, though the lantern's light got caught in the thick shrouds of mist and illuminated little besides the treacherous, rolling stones directly beneath their feet.

When they broke below the mists, their clothes and hair were drenched.

"We'll freeze when we leave," the prince said, his first words since the admission of debt owed.

"There are dry clothes on the rukh," said Shahruz, keeping their hand from the hilt of his sword. "Here, just ahead."

The twins pointed to the stone table, just visible now at the light's edge, atop a strange, circular rise. The prince glanced from their finger to the incongruous piece of furniture and back again. He cocked his head, reminding Saadet of the rukh when it was deciding whether it wanted to eat someone.

"Hmh," he said. He looked at her. "You know that what you have done—freeing me—will lead to war."

"It needn't have," said the twins. "But yes, now that your brother has declared your life forfeit, your survival guarantees it. Even if you were to vanish, to flee to another land, Prince Tsansong . . ."

The twins shrugged.

The prince smiled tightly. "I would not even need to raise a banner myself for partisans to flock to it. Others would do it in my name."

"Anyone with a grudge against the Bstangpo," the twins agreed. They bowed and extended an arm, indicating that the prince should precede them.

He stood his ground, however, and regarded them steadily. His nostrils flared, perhaps at the faint scent of sulfur that hung all around. "I begin to comprehend why it is exactly that a Rahazeen assassin comes to the rescue of a condemned second son."

The twins knew their smile showed around the veil—in the creases of their eyes, in the outlined shape of the face it hid. They had seen such smiles on one another's faces often enough in times gone by. Whether the prince could read it or not was an open question, but his expression did seem to ease.

The prince stepped forward, the twins following a few steps behind. "What is this?" he asked, gesturing. His tone was light, interested. Intrigued.

"An altar of ancient Erem, the City of Jackals," the twins answered. Saadet felt the handle of Shahruz's wheel lock smooth against their palm as the prince leaned forward slightly, toiling up the rise in the breathless air. "Carefully, your highness. Do not stare at it too long. It is said that the dead script can blind you, the inscriptions rot your animus within your form."

"And do not touch it, I suppose?" He crouched though, hands on knees, by the head of the table.

"Be very careful not to touch it," the twins said.

The pistol barely hissed on cloth as Shahruz drew it into the hand that did not hold the lamp. But the prince heard it, and turned, eyes widening—

The lead ball—carved with symbols of ancient Erem, just as the table was—took him through the temple. It exited behind his left ear, taking most of his brain out with it.

The prince fell across the table, shivered, and lay still. Saadet felt the trigger sharp against their finger.

"For the Nameless," said Shahruz.

"For the world," his sister answered, as her gorge heaved and rose and she kept their eyes focused on the lumpy red spray smoking softly where it had fallen across the black stone altar.

The hot earth cracked beneath their feet. The ground shook, hard, like a waking beast.

Clutching the pistol in their right hand, the twins turned without a word and ran.

8

Edene climbed.

Long had she paced through moist tunnels. First she followed Besha Ghul's bent shadow with eyes that pierced the dark as easily as if it were a night lit by ten dozen moons. As she gained confidence and felt the ring grow warm, felt the pull of ancient knowledge filling her blood and heart like it had always been there, *she* led the way through the labyrinth. In the end, as Edene had known they must, she and Besha Ghul found a stair, each riser low and narrow and worn from the passage of more feet than Edene could imagine.

The stairs might not go on so long as had the corridors, but it seemed while they climbed that they climbed them forever. Still Edene felt no fatigue: no hiss of tired breath, no ache of exerted muscles afflicted her. She climbed, that was all, as in a dream—and Besha Ghul climbed just behind her, nails of dry dog paws clicking on stone. Compounding the sense of dream, sometimes a faint thread of perfume came to her—resin incense, soured by ammonia in a way that made her think of Ala-Din.

At last, Edene rounded the corner of a landing and was dazzled. At her heels, Besha too blinked and snorted, ducking its head in dismay. "Suns-set," the ghul said. "We can outwait it safely here, but should climb no higher."

"Suns?" Even as she asked, the ring gave her the knowledge. The daylight was dangerous. Edene craned back her head, watching shadows move on the walls above. They were overlaid as if the light from several lanterns—or several moons—fell through an aperture. The effect was both strange and strangely familiar. She had long moments to examine it as she paused beside the ghul, waiting for the sense that it was safe to continue.

Erem had four suns, the nightsun and the three that ruled the day. The nightsun was a white pinpoint, as bright as four small moons. One of the daysuns was similar, and often ranged far ahead of or behind its companions. The other two danced closely with each other, neither bigger in the sky than a grain of barley. The larger was squashed and sullen and orange, twisted in a coil of flame like a dancer in her veils. That wreath made a streamer connecting the orange sun to its blue-hot companion.

The light of the blue star killed. It blistered flesh at a touch like dragon flame and whitened eyes until they were as blind as boiled eggs.

People had lived here once. But Erem was not a place for human gods.

At last the light above dimmed to indigo and Besha Ghul shifted restlessly. Edene climbed again. But only a few steps this time, just the length of one flight.

They emerged into a night such as Edene had never seen. They stood in the sandy belly of a canyon, cliff walls breaking the horizon on either side. The sky between them was a narrow torrent of indigo-violet, a textured deepness punctured by so many stars it was hard to see the color between them. There were three moons only—but such moons! The smallest—still bigger than any of the moons of the steppe and casting the light of ten such—was mottled ivory, sliding across the heavens so fast that Edene could stand and *watch* its forward edge eat the stars. Its next largest companion was a rust-hued monster, a wheel Edene thought she could stand inside, spread her arms and turn with—turn within—as it rolled through the sky.

The last and largest, though, was blacker than the night that lay behind it, visible only as a silhouette and a lazy gleam of opalescence. A semicircle loomed above the cliff edge, so heavy and present that Edene had to force her eyes down to counteract the fear that the swollen great thing would drop on her.

The green ring weighed warm and heavy on her hand. She touched it with the opposite fingers and wondered for a moment if she should pull it off, toss it away. But it was strength; it was power. It was her route to reclaim her family and her home.

Sand sifted across her worn slippers, filtered in through the holes. Her eyes adapted to this dark as well, and to the sharp, dueling shadows cast by moons and stars. When she looked up again she could see the dwellings carved into the tawny rock, the windows and doors black as the holes in a rank of skulls, the short sandy rise leading up to them. And she could see too the dozens or hundreds of gaunt shapes arrayed before those hollowed cliffs, standing not in ranks or lines but in ragged bunches, straggles, and clusters.

"Erem-of-the-Pillars," said Besha Ghul.

"An army," breathed Edene.

IT WAS EASY TO SLEEP IN SAMARKAR'S ARMS. TOO EASY, TEMUR THOUGHT, drifting, her fingers on his hair and the curve of her bosom pressing his cheek. He could *reach* the anxiety and outrage that had driven him this far, but he *had* to reach for them. They were somewhere else, at arm's length, and the warm ease and comfort of the woman breathing against his scalp was here, now, present and real. The scent of her warmth filled his awareness. Her sweat dried lightly on his skin.

Well, he thought, *at least you shall be rested.*

He wasn't sure why he fought the relaxation. His misery made nothing better for Edene in her durance—but in an obscure manner it comforted *him.* He thought Samarkar was asleep, but in his head he could hear her measured tones, the mountain accent with which she'd say *It comforts you because it comforts your grief, Re Temur. Your grief wants you to live for nothing else. Will you fight less hard for Edene if you do not allow it to cripple you?*

He thought, *I will fight harder.*

Ato Tesefahun must have ordered that lamps be hung in the courtyard tonight, because their light trickled through the louvers like dawn, golden and fragile, moving with each breath of wind that flipped the garden's leaves. Temur watched it play along Samarkar's hair that lay unbound and sleek across her shoulder and breast, watched the shine on the small hairs of his own forearm where it lay across her rib cage, lifted and dropped by the rhythm of her breath. Her head was toward the window; the gold light limned her silhouette: the downy edge of her cheek, the eggshell curve of an ear, her princess-stern face in shadow. No moist gleam of slitted eye suggested she was anything other than deeply asleep.

The glow from outside brightened. *Fire*, Temur thought, confusedly, but there was no tang of smoke, no crackle of burning. Had he slept after all, without knowing? Was he drifting awake again, the sun on the rise?

It was too silent for dawn. Where was the cacophony of birds and insects, the irrigated desert stirring awake? Where were the morning sounds of Asitaneh? All he could hear in the failing dark was the easy blur of his own breath, the more-and-more stentorian rasp of Samarkar's. If not for the unease tossing in his belly, Temur might have closed his eyes and smiled against her shoulder.

The once-princess was snoring.

Except the sounds grew sharper and harder, rising to a wheezing whistle, a rattle, that made Temur's fingers cold with fear. Her belly heaved, her body convulsing as if in a spasm of pleasure, and something rigid and smooth pushed her flesh against his arm. Temur recoiled, clutching at her shoulders as he rolled to his knees. He saw with horror the white foam at the corner of her mouth, the pregnant bulge of her abdomen that made her scars stretch shiny-taut in the daylight brightness. *She is the Wizard Samarkar*, he thought ridiculously. *She cannot get with child—*

She gasped, then, or tried to gasp—but no air filled her. She strained and strained, face gray, eyes bulging, her hands pressing clawed nails frantically to his chest below the collarbone. Sweat beaded on her skin and ran into her hair. He watched the blood vessels burst in the whites of her eyes.

Something heaved inside her. That hideous creaking sound, the sharp greenstick snapping—those were her ribs, bowed up by the struggling of something within.

They were not alone in the room. Someone was behind him, a shadow at his shoulder, looming over them. The certain cold of a stare pierced his shoulders, but he could not turn away from Samarkar.

He reached out to her, laying his hands against her chest. An unfamiliar pins-and-needles tingle numbed him fingertips to wrists, chill soaking his flesh as if the life and energy rushed from his body into Samarkar. He had a sudden, vivid memory of Mongke Khagan laying hands on a leper, of rotten flesh growing supple under the Khan of Khans touch—and of the Khagan, afterward, shaking his hands as if his fingers had been frozen or burned.

What made Temur think he should have this power over life and death? And why did the flow of strength out of his hands seem to confirm that something, indeed, was happening?

Whatever he was accomplishing, it wasn't enough, though he tried until the dark room spun.

Not until her struggles ceased and the first lank, slimed demonling undulated from her mouth in a well of blood and mucus did he turn away. Then, he could not turn fast enough. To his shame, he recoiled from the spatter across his face as the demonling fanned membranous wings and shook its head clean. Temur's head snapped to the side, Samarkar's blood unnaturally bitter upon his lips. He sobbed, but even clenching his eyes like fists did not remove the image of the skeletal, clawed thing drying its dark wings in the warm morning air. Temur thought the frail, bony limbs, the beaked and barbed head, the half-shuttered eyes would be with him until he died.

He groped for his knife, left beside the bed. When he raised his opened eyes again, Samarkar stood over him, gold-flecked hazel eyes too pale in a changed face. She seemed stretched, misaligned—as if the bones lay wrong beneath her skin. She reached out to him with a hand that was wrong, taloned, the fingers crooked and too long. She clucked, as if to a mare.

. . . not to Temur. To the demonling; it flew up with still-moist wingbeats, lofting itself to perch on her fingertips like a tame songbird with its long tail trailing behind. Behind it, a second hatchling began to drag itself from between Samarkar's fleshless jaws, and the thing standing over her—wearing her skin stitched tight with black cordage over alien bones—smiled in maternal delight.

Outside the window, Temur realized, a million more of the tiny monsters roosted, and the light had been dappled not by the turning of leaves but the movement of their gently fanning wings.

TEMUR WOKE IN WARM DARKNESS, A WOMAN'S BREASTS AGAINST HIS BACK, her arm around his waist, a press of lips to his nape that told him she lay awake. He was frozen at first, dream-locked, the horror of what he had seen still creeping up his spine and in his veins. For a moment, it was all he could do to breathe, in and then out again, and to curl his fingers around Samarkar's supporting arm.

"Sky and stars," he muttered when he could say anything at all, and he felt her pull him closer.

"Dreaming true?" she murmured.

He closed his eyes to better feel her breath against his ear. "I hope not. It was the Sorcerer-Prince again. Breeding an army of demons in the bodies of my friends."

"Ugh." She waited for him to continue, a gentle strength.

He leaned against her. "It wore a different skin this time."

She kissed his neck again, still breathing. "Yes?"

She must have known already, from the weight of his pause. But she waited nonetheless for him to get it out.

"Yours."

THE SCENT HAUNTED EDENE. AT STRAY MOMENTS, WHEN HER MIND WANdered, she would catch a hint of the smell of hot desert, of ammonia, of frankincense and bitter myrrh. It made her stomach clench as the babe had not, and made her wonder, each time, at her sanity. She could almost feel al-Sepehr at her shoulder—his cloying paternalism, his grotesque parodies of human emotion. Just the smell—remembered or imagined—was enough to bring paroxysms of loathing up in her.

She had been touring the storerooms with the tireless Besha Ghul—so many bolts of cloth, so many salvaged weapons of ancient Erem, so many barrels of meat too rancid and vile for anyone who was not a ghul to eat, all laid in readiness for war—when the sense of presence moved over her again. Sniffing, she turned—this was a storeroom, and it already smelled of putrid meat and resin; surely that was all—but she found that the scent followed her into the hall. She stood, sniffing, and the ghul was right behind her.

"I'm not crazy."

Besha Ghul gave her exactly the look anyone would give a crazy person, if anyone were a dog-snouted, velvet-gray monster. "You smell something unclean, my Queen?"

Besides the rotten meat? "I smell . . ." she hesitated. But she would not allow herself to be afraid to say his name. "I smell al-Sepehr. I mean, the man who—"

"We know of the al-Sepehrs," the ghul said, its normal air of obsequiousness lost with the force of the interruption. Its ears went flat against the wrinkled head, lips curling in a slight snarl. "We knew of their master."

Edene paused in surprise. "You don't approve?"

"He cared not for Erem," the ghul said. "Only for using its power against the other worlds." A flicking gesture of distaste and dismissal with a clawed hand. "You will be a better Queen."

The ring warm on her hand, Edene smiled. *I will be the best of queens.* But was not her own plan to use the ghulim to fight an outside war?

It was the curse, perhaps, of being commanded by a ring. Could she choose not to command them? Could—

She must. She *must* bring an army to Temur.

Her finger sweated under the warmth of the ring. The scent of frankincense suffused her senses. She closed her eyes, turned her head. *You are not real. You are not real.*

It was like pushing back the felted wall of a collapsing white-house: a muffling pressure that wanted to overwhelm her, smother her under softness and weight. She breathed deep—pulled in, pulled up. *I am free of you! I am Edene!*

The pressure broke. The stench of resin and guano faded.

Edene opened her eyes to see Besha Ghul. Its head cocked in concern.

"I'm fine," said Edene, and fainted against the wall.

*   *   *

AL-SEPEHR JERKED HIS HANDS FROM THE BROWNED, BURNISHED SURFACE OF a bone-dry skull and gasped as if he had been struck in the solar plexus. The image of a woman shivered in the air before him as if painted with smoke. When he breathed out, it blew to shred.

Rage washed him. *That a Qersnyk whore would oppose the Nameless!* But rage was a young man's weakness, and after a moment of contemplation he folded it and set it aside.

"So," he said. "Another way."

IN THE MORNING, SAMARKAR SOUGHT OUT HRAHIMA. SHE FOUND THE CHO-tse in the still-shady courtyard, lying on her back with her head pillowed in her arms. Samarkar settled beside her, legs folded and fingertips resting on her knees. Assuming the pose brought back a powerful sense memory of cold wet and darkness in the proving chambers in the belly of the Citadel, and, though the heat of the day was already rising, Samarkar had to fight back the dry warmth that wanted to crackle from her fingertips.

The silence she sought eluded her at first; her awareness churned and fretted, returning again and again to Temur's dreams, to the image of an army of demons bred in the bodies of the unsuspecting. Samarkar knew from practice that forcing her ill thoughts away would only bring them back increased in strength. Instead, she allowed the worries to enter her mind, acknowledged them, dismissed them. She came into a place where the heat could not trouble her, nor the press of responsibility, nor the threat of dire futures.

"Wizard," said the Cho-tse lazily, after some time.

"Hrahima," Samarkar answered, rising from the depths of a quieted mind. "I did not mean to disturb your rest."

She opened her eyes to find the Cho-tse unmoved, still lying sprawled, but now regarding Samarkar with an unnerving tourmaline stare.

"It was only rest after a fashion." Hrahima stood balanced on the pads of her hind feet before Samarkar had quite registered that she was rising. "A discipline of my tribe; the contemplation of the sun without and the Sun Within."

Samarkar thought about questioning Hrahima about the Sun Within—that deity the Cho-tse both denied and yet, seemingly, venerated. But Samarkar deemed it likely that questions would beget only eva-sions, yet again. The wizard rose less gracefully, but—she flattered herself—with sufficient nimbleness for a mere human.

"There's no sun here yet," she said with a smile.

Hrahima crouched again like a fall of water and laid one massive hand flat on the stone. "But there has been, and there will be again, and a little of the old warmth lingers." She looked up, whiskers flat against her cheeks. "Why do you seek me, Wizard Samarkar?"

"A favor," Samarkar said. "Will your travels take you anywhere near the caliph's palace this morning? If you are willing, I need you to be my messenger."

BUT IT TURNED OUT SHE DID NOT, AFTER ALL. BECAUSE THE MESSENGER FROM the palace arrived while Ato Tesefahun's household (and guests, and those who—like Temur—hovered somewhere between) were sitting to breakfast. Bidden enter, he approached Ato Tesefahun and bowed beside the Aezin wizard's seat. Ato Tesefahun acknowledged him immediately. Samarkar noticed that the messenger avoided even glancing in her direc-tion. An unveiled woman at the table with men! She comforted herself that no matter how far she traveled, no matter how changed her role, she was still and always would be a scandal.

The messenger did not rise but extended a folded and wax-sealed packet: rag paper, by the look of it, less rare here than from whence Samarkar hailed. Ato Tesefahun accepted it, flipped it, and read the ele-gant script aloud.

"Once-Princess Samarkar-la," he said, eyebrows rising. "Wizard of Tsarepheth."

Someone less schooled by years of court than Samarkar would have glanced at the messenger in confusion, or at least lowered her gaze. Sa-markar felt her own face grow still, the traces of amusement dropping from the corners of her mouth and eyes. It was almost a numbness, the creeping tingle of impassivity that she had learned so early and well.

She wondered if anyone—even Temur—could spot the way her pulse drummed so suddenly in her throat. He had been watching her differ-ently. She did not think it was only that they had become lovers: it was his dream and the aftermath of watching her die. It frightened her—not for herself but for the anticipatory grief she saw in his expression already.

One of us will *lose the other,* she told herself—once-princess, wizard, widow. *Possibly before the sun sets on us tonight.*

She extended her hand and accepted the letter as Ato Tesefahun excused the messenger. The paper was soft and thick, crisp along the folds. It smelled sweet. She examined the writing. Flipped the note over and tilted it to see the seal and that the seal had not been broken, or lifted off and reaffixed. It was cobalt wax over crimson and dusted with gold foil. The snarling head of a griffin regarded her from within a wreath comprised of a verse of the poetry of Ysmat of the Beads, Prophet of the Scholar-God.

The verse concerned itself with the duties of nobility. The whole seal was uncommonly fine work. Silken ribbons lay beneath it.

"That is the caliph's personal seal," said Ato Tesefahun. "It is used only on letters written in his own hand."

Samarkar looked at him through her lashes. She flipped the letter again and read the address, resting her wrist against the tabletop to hide how her hands were shaking. "He has an uncommonly fine hand."

"He does not write so many things himself that it degrades with haste." Ato Tesefahun placed his coffee cup down on the glass tabletop. It was piping hot, but in this arid climate it trailed no plume of white steam. "Are you going to open it?"

"It might be confidential." She set the letter facedown, appropriated a jam knife from Brother Hsiung's plate, then heated it against the chased silver side of the coffee service. When the dull blade was warm, she eased it under the seal and lifted.

The letter fell open in her hand when she picked it up again.

"*O lovely Samarkar,*" she read aloud, while Ato Tesefahun's eyebrows rose and Brother Hsiung stilled utterly, a bit of pastry and jam in his mouth. Across the table, Temur rocked back, forehead creased in a frown that did not reach his lips.

Watching him, Samarkar thought better of reciting the contents of the note verbatim. Instead, she scanned quickly—as quickly as she could, given the Uthman script—and set the note down before summarizing.

"He wants to meet with me. Alone. In his chambers."

Silence, except for Hrahima's faint chuff and the jingle of rings as she flicked her ears.

"That," said Ato Tesefahun, "would seem to be a romantic proposition."

"Would it?" Samarkar said. She flicked her left hand toward her face, skimmed it dismissively over the front of her body. Now Temur made a sound, but not an articulate one, and Samarkar could see his knuckles tighten where he gripped the table.

It's easier to be shared than to share, she thought half-cheerfully and waited for Ato Tesefahun to speak.

"So it would seem," he said, with a sideways glance toward the messenger—who was still regarding Ato Tesefahun, and not Samarkar at all. Which was all to the good, because it meant he didn't see her roll her eyes.

"Excellent," said Samarkar briskly. "Please tell his serene Excellency's messenger to inform his serene Excellency that I will be in attendance this noon, as he requests."

Ato Tesefahun did, and the messenger withdrew. Samarkar could still feel Temur's eyes upon her.

"It's a way of speaking to him in private." She returned her attention to her breakfast.

"Some will call you his concubine, just from that," Ato Tesefahun observed with the air of one pointing out that if someone does not eat the last slice of cake, it will go to waste.

"To name a thing is half of making it," Samarkar said.

Ato Tesefahun's lips quirked. "Only half, Wizard Samarkar?"

Whatever she might have replied was lost when Hsiung pushed away the remains of his meal and stood abruptly. He paused for a moment, fist clenched at his thighs. His eyes were downcast, but Samarkar could see the flicker of green light through his lashes. He turned away. She would have risen to support him, but he held up a palm to stay her. They watched as he made his way with clipped strides to the courtyard door and passed through it.

In the stretched silence that followed, Samarkar glanced at Temur, held his gaze. After a moment, he nodded and said, "I must see to the mare today," as if merely making conversation rather than offering a truce, and a sort of apology. "If we must be ready to travel on an instant, it will not go well should Bansh be unsound."

The others at the table busied themselves with their cups and plates, granting Samarkar and Temur a moment of privacy even in their midst. Samarkar could feel in that instant how something between Temur and her that might have stretched and snapped, otherwise, suddenly made itself solid and correct. A glorious, uneasy sensation rose up inside her. It could have been the feeling of the future rearranging itself a new pattern— but wasn't that moment long past?

"She's never unsound," Samarkar said, a peace offering of her own. In her head, she heard her father calling her his heir, a near son, telling her that as she had no brothers, she must learn to be a man in their place. All that had changed with the birth of Songtsan . . . and yet none of it had changed at all. *A wizard knows that to name a thing is half of making it. What you call someone . . . defines them.*

Samarkar took a breath, and—willing it to be prophecy—said, "That horse is an immortal, Temur Khan."

Temur hid his wince. Tightly, he nodded.

"So Samarkar is the first," said Hrahima, pushing a salted fish across her plate with a claw tip.

Samarkar had filled her nervous mouth with coffee, so it was Temur who asked, "The first?"

The Cho-tse puffed her whiskers. "The first to call you *King.*"

IT WAS TEMUR WHO CAME TO HELP SAMARKAR INTO HER WIZARD'S ARMOR, to tighten her buckles and check the corded lacings that held the armor skirts to the cuirass. He did not speak, and she did not ask him how he had persuaded Ato Tesefahun's omnipresent, self-effacing servants to allow him this role. She watched him in one of Ato Tesefahun's huge silvered mirrors while silently he attended her buckles, and silently he combed her hair and braided it—with fair facility—and coiled it around her skull . . . and silently he kissed the side of her throat before he set the helm over her head.

She might have spoken: she had a thousand things to say. But he didn't, and so she left her wistfulness silent too. Silent, she thought, but understood.

"I'll see you for dinner," he said when the helm was secure, his fingers gentle under her chin, still resting where he'd fastened the strap. He hadn't lowered the faceplate. She could still see her own eyes in the mirror. Not his; his face was lowered, his gaze turned away. A grayish color dusted his face along the hairline; the desert drying his skin. She made herself a promise to oil it for him when she got back.

"Though all the hells of Song bar the way." She craned her head to the side; he leaned around the helm to kiss her, wincing as the motion pulled his scar.

She brushed it lightly with her fingertips. This time, he didn't recoil. "And don't forget to stretch that while I'm gone."

"I'll use Bansh's liniment on it," he promised.

Imagining the sting and burn, she said, "Ow."

She could not have walked alone through Asitaneh in any other garb, and now Samarkar relished what might be a unique opportunity. Ato Tesefahun had offered her a retinue, bodyguards and a chaperone. Samarkar had turned him down, saying that if the caliph was intrigued by the exotic reality of a woman who wore armor and a wizard's weeds, she would only reinforce that with a show of independence. "And if he should decide to slay me or take me prisoner in his own house, what exactly could your guards do to prevent it?"

Ato Tesefahun had ducked his chin in agreement. Samarkar knew he was thinking, as did she, of the ranks of *kapikulu* and more—of the caliph's personal bodyguard of Dead Men. She was placing herself completely in his power, and the only defense she'd have was her own ability to convince the priest-prince of her authority.

As a sort of apology, Temur's grandfather had given her a map to memorize.

Now Samarkar walked alone through Asitaneh, head up and striving to remember everything. Once she left the hustling boulevards, the red stone streets were close and winding. Often, Samarkar could reach out and place a hand flat on either wall, and the leaning balconies kissed overhead. Asitaneh was not built on flat land, and more than a few of the streets were constructed as stairs—an architectural tactic familiar enough to her from the rugged terrain of Tsarepheth.

She had left Ato Tesefahun's house early enough to spend some time exploring the side streets near the palace, lest she need to escape her appointment with the caliph in haste. The maps were good—she didn't think Ato Tesefahun would tolerate a bad one—but a map was not the same thing as a city, and if Samarkar were to find herself running down alleyways with blind speed, she'd hate to suddenly fall over—or into— sewer repairs in progress.

And if she were truthful, the city itself fascinated her. The smells were so different, the texture of the mortared stone, the sounds of the voices. The way the crowd broke around her armored form: no one raised their eyes to her helm but the men strode past as if she were invisible and they had simply missed striking her fortuitously, the women scuttling by in groups with their eyes downcast behind their veils. Even the taste of the dust was strange.

At last, the city's many sweet-sounding bells tolling the half hour before her appointment with the caliph, Samarkar turned toward the palace. Finding herself alone in one of the narrower stair-alleys, she glanced over her left shoulder—back down the slope—and raised one hand to the wall. The gauntlets of the armor were designed to preserve a wizard's dexterity for magic in combat; they attached to the backs of the hands and fingers with straps, leaving the palms and pads bare—a design also used by archers. When she touched the red stone she was surprised at how it gritted, and at how some sand rubbed free beneath the pressure to roll between her fingertips and the wall.

The walls had been patched many times, with mortar and brick and newer stone, and reinforced with planks of bolted-on wood worn black by centuries in the desert heat that had nevertheless preserved them. She could just reach up and touch one such if she stood on the tips of her toes, which she did hastily, curiously, hesitant that someone might see. From the slick texture, she was not the first.

As she dropped her heels again, she caught a glimpse of movement from the corner of her eye, an indigo flash in a shade that left her with a crawling chill of recognition.

The Rahazeen assassin had just emerged from the cover provided by a kink in the street and was closing on her quickly. Not at a run, but with confident strides that flared his loose white trousers and left the ends of the sash through which his pistol and scimitar were thrust licking the air behind him. Samarkar glanced right—forward—*upward*—again.

Two more stood just before the next twist in the stair. Overhead, the balconies did not meet—the left wall showed a scaled scar where one had ripped away—and three more veiled faces peered from the rooftops over-head.

Six, then. And probably two or four more out of sight, if she ran.

All right, Wizard Samarkar. Wizard your way out of this one.

The assassin coming up the stairs behind her—the tallest and broadest of the ones she could get a good look at—was drawing the pistol from his belt. It was a flintlock, the striker held back on a pin curved like a swan's neck. He leveled it at Samarkar and tilted his head to aim.

"Put your hands up, Wizard Samarkar," he said in her mother tongue. "We'd rather have you alive."

One of Samarkar's hands was already raised, still stretching after that age-polished board she'd been investigating. The other was extended for balance, reaching toward the far wall.

She thanked the six merciful stalwarts that the Rahazeen had pistols rather than bows. If someone like Temur had been with them, Samarkar would have had the choice of surrender or death—unless she could have managed a very tricky bit of fire-summoning on very short notice. But this: she had options.

She kicked her right foot out to the far wall, hooked the toes of her left boot over the edge of a hewn stone that protruded from the mortar on the near wall, and pushed herself upward as fast as she could go. The left hand hooked the top of that board again: there was just enough pur-chase for her cantilevered fingertips to take her weight when she pressed hard to the right. That let her move the left foot up, using the opposition between the two facing walls—and she climbed half again her height before the assassins even realized they should be reacting.

Something to be said for their overexposure to cloistered Uthman harem girls, she thought. *They seem to forget that women can climb and fight.*

The helm impeded her vision; the fingertip overlap on the gauntlets scraped stone. Samarkar cursed them as she climbed, ignoring the shouts from above and below. The Rahazeen above were scrambling down to that one remaining balcony. She heard the scrape of a sulfur stick and caught the acrid scent as one lighted his matchlock, but she wasn't worried about the gunmen above. It was extremely hard to shoot at a sharp downward angle, or so she'd been told. They would only hit her by luck, and they'd be as likely to hit their friends below.

A moment later the explosion followed, deafening in the confined space. Her helm was some protection—not enough, her ears rang and the shouts of the Rahazeen seemed strangely muffled afterward—but more than they were getting from their veils. She glanced down; one leapt to try to catch her and she snatched her ankle up just in time. The biggest one was still tracking her with his flintlock, and *he* might have a chance of hitting—the range wasn't great—and now another had his scimitar out. She didn't think her climbing skills, honed in the crags of the Steles of the Sky, would avail her if somebody chopped her foot or hand off.

She had hoped the big one would flinch when his friend shot and missed, but he was too focused, too well trained. She pulled the idea of fire into her mind. There was fire in the powder in the gun and it wanted to come out: it would have been easy to make it simply burn. But if the gun were aimed at her, that was no help.

So now she coaxed the fire to stay itself, to wait. And she persuaded some of that warmth into the lead ball within the barrel of the gun. Warmth made things swell—with the exception of ice, which grew as it froze. But with a pistol, the ball must be a close fit to the barrel of the gun, so the expanding force of the black powder behind it could fire it out with great velocity, without too much of that pressure escaping. A hot ball was bigger than a cold one. If it fit as tight as it ought, it would catch in the barrel.

Samarkar could climb and work wizardry both at once, an indirect result of her masters' years of patient instruction. She didn't need to maintain her persuasion for long. As the assassin's finger flexed on his trigger, she allowed the fire in the powder to do what it would. The spark flared in the pan, the heated ball lodged within the barrel—

The gun exploded in his hand.

Sandstone gritty, abrading her fingertips, Samarkar was still climbing. She had glanced down, seeking a foothold and keeping an eye on those below. The big assassin dropped to his knees, clutching his wrist. There was blood; she could not see how much. Her hand found the edge and then the railing of the balcony.

She didn't trust it, but she hadn't much choice. Brother Hsiung might have vaulted the railing and come down among the enemy kicking. Samarkar had no such skills, and therefore no such luxury. The assassins seemed to have dispensed with their pistols—a wise choice when dealing with a wizard, it turned out—but there were still three of them, and they had short blades out. The better for such work at close quarters.

The two uninjured assassins climbed behind her, if not quite with her skill and facility. Now she was treed like a cat between hawks and hounds, and the hounds were closing the gap. Her breath raked her lungs; her heart beat a martial tattoo within her rib cage. Muscle and ligaments stretched painfully under the weight of her armor.

A hand clutched her boot, fingers scrabbling at the lacquered armor. She kicked it off her ankle and used the momentum to scramble upward. A Rahazeen stabbed at her hand on the balustrade; she found a drainpipe with the other hand and swung around it, a gyre of momentum. As if of its own will her foot lashed out and took one of the attackers in the face; she recognized a motion that Brother Hsiung had drilled into her over hands and hands of days, crossing the desert from Stone Steading.

So that's what that's for.

She followed the motion through, summoning her will into her hands. A blue blade no longer than the span of her palm shimmered at her fingers; she struck toward an assassin's face, but his flinch carried him clear. The magic that could open locks with keys made of intention could construct a dagger, too.

Her foot kicked off the balcony rail and she felt it settle slightly. Her fingers hooked the scar where the other balcony endured no longer. Her hands were busy, her focus sharp—but a wizard's will and sense of structure fanned around her, and the wooden joists beneath the balcony the Rahazeen stood on were old, weathered. Nearly petrified.

Samarkar grinned behind her helmet, her breath rasping through the faceplate, as she hauled herself atop the parapet opposite. A knife glanced off the stone beside her. Another punched her on the spine, but the armor protected her. Still she felt the blow like a kick and nearly went sprawling to the roof. Only a quick turn with the force of the blow and the reflexive curl of her fingers over the parapet edge saved her.

She perched like a vulture, her armor coat spread over her knees, her eyes on the Rahazeen who still held a knife poised to throw. She would twist as it left his fingers, she decided. She would protect her eyes and throat. Each heaving inhalation crushed her breasts and ribs against the inside of the armor, but she managed a calculated chuckle between gasps.

"Six Rahazeen chosen men," she mocked. "And yet no match for one Wizard of Tsarepheth."

The assassin threw. Samarkar dodged to the side and let the knife whisk past her, so close she thought for a moment she'd misjudged, but it was only the whistle of the blade that startled her.

There was fire in the old wood of the balcony, too. The stone it bore up shivered as she released that long-constrained energy. Even behind the veils, she could see the eyes of the Rahazeen widen. Their arms windmilled gracelessly. One tried to leap to the parapet. But the stone flags of the balcony poured away beneath them like sand through opened hands. The Rahazeen below did not shriek, but tried to leap away.

Samarkar did not linger to see if they succeeded.

The flat rooftops of Asitaneh were hardly uninhabited. Not only were there men and women working here, even under the blazing light of the sun, but there were tent cities, roof gardens, children playing tag from house to house. Samarkar got an unexpected glimpse of the inner courtyards as she trotted past, forcing feet and legs that felt coated in some heavy, rubbery substance to rise and fall with monotonous regularity.

SHATTERED PILLARS * 115

Sweat trickled between her breasts and shoulder blades. She felt herself the brunt of many stares, but did not return them.

When she came to the broad boulevard upon which the palace fronted, she found an exterior stair she could drop to and descended. She'd not be late: the fight had lasted a hundred heartbeats, no more. But she was in disarray—sweat-soaked under her cuirass and helm, the quilted cloth of her arming coat squishing unpleasantly with every movement. As she reached the street, Samarkar stole a glance at her palms: scraped, bloody, the fingertips chafed raw.

Well, if Uthman Caliph wanted a martial female dancing in attendance, that was what he'd get. And not the high-court version, perfumed and jeweled, either.

Samarkar stood for a moment, still breathing deeply. *Rahazeen. Here.* Temur was in danger, and Hrahima, and Brother Hsiung. And all of Ato Tesefahun's household too. Her feet itched, her body half-turned with the desire to run back to Ato Tesefahun's house and make sure that everyone was safe—to give them the warning. But private appointments with the caliph were not plucked in meadows. She carried paper and a stick of pigment. Perhaps she could disguise her voice enough to hire one of the loitering messengers near the palace doors to run a letter back to Brother Hsiung. If she wrote it in Song, the contents should be safe enough from casual prying.

No: she'd send the message from the palace. Surely they would accommodate her. Surely they would also read her letter, but being attacked by Rahazeen in the very streets of Asitaneh was nothing she needed to hide from the caliph in order to convince him that the threat was serious and Temur worthy of his support.

She strode up the boulevard, projecting every featherweight of boldness and bravado she could muster. People gave way before her again; she'd at least regained that much presence. She'd have to muster the rest before she reached the caliph's chambers.

It gave her something to focus on when her mind wanted to chase itself in circles of worry for Temur. *He can protect himself. And if he cannot, our companions* certainly *can.*

It didn't help.

She took the broad steps up to the palace gate at a jog, strips of lacquered wood rattling flatly with every bounce. A portico ostensibly protected the doorway, but it was high and at this hour the sun shone under
it, sweltering on the heads of a score of *kapikulu*. An enormous arched
doorframe loomed open overhead: Uthman Caliph had faith in the
peace of his city, or faith in the strength of his guards. Or he was simply
aware of the emotional power over his people that was offered by the
pose of strength and security. No weak king would leave his door standing wide.

That appearance of openness was abrogated by the stiff ritual posture
of the *kapikulu* who flanked it, cerulean coats brilliant on the pale stone as
patches of sky glimpsed through cloud. Samarkar found it effective nonetheless and noted it for her own applications, when a time and place
should be found. For now, she paused at the top of the steps, hands on
hips, and waited.

A doorkeeper lurked within the shaded arch, perched on a folding-
framed sling of natural canvas. He was a snarled-looking little man with
crooked, skinny legs and arms that seemed to stick out every which way,
but the wiry muscle knotted across his calves and shoulders bulged when
he scraped and made a courtesy. He wore nothing but a white loincloth,
and while Samarkar did not envy his horny bare feet the searing touch of
the stone steps and threshold, she would have given a great deal to be out
of the black oven of her armor.

Ungrateful, when it had saved her the bite of a thrown dagger. But if
she then roasted to death because of it, there would be little time for her
gratitude.

The doorkeeper looked up at her inquiringly.

"Samarkar," she said. "A Wizard of Tsarepheth. I am summoned to
an appointment with his serene Excellency, Uthman Caliph Fourteenth."

When he heard a woman's voice, the doorman did not react. *Kapikulu*
were raised from a young age to be stoic and impassive, and a caliph's
doorkeeper must certainly be able to maintain his composure in the face
of all things . . . but Samarkar suspected in this case he'd been warned
in advance. Perversely, this made her more uneasy—but if the caliph
wanted her visit to go unremarked, surely he would have had her present

herself at the servant's entrance rather than walking in the front door like a visiting queen, albeit one inexplicably shorn of her retinue.

"You are to be made welcome," the doorman said. He straightened at last from his obeisance—a good thing, as it had been inspiring Samarkar to sympathetic cramps in her thighs and calves to watch him. With a hooking gesture, he summoned a boy of middle years from the shadows behind the door. This bird-eyed brown child wore a linen tunic that fell halfway down his thighs. He went barefoot, his hair cropped short below his ears. The doorman laid a hand on the child's shoulder. "Show the Wizard Samarkar to the Chamber of Crocuses."

"Please follow me, sir," the boy said. He bowed low, leaving Samarkar chuckling and striding to keep up in his wake. Of course she was a *sir;* she was tall and wore armor and walked the street alone, and no matter that a woman's voice had issued from under the helm.

She considered for a few moments whether she was being led to the slaughter, but the room he left her in was a small, pleasant reception chamber. That did not preclude its becoming an abattoir, but Samarkar rather thought the caliph would have caused the silk rugs from Song and Rasa to be taken up if he intended to have her cut down in her blood. She requested a moment to scribe her note to Brother Hsiung, and the page promised to see it delivered. Then he left her with grapes and with wine and water— cold enough to chill the pricy glass goblet that it stood in—and an assurance that she would be shown to the caliph as soon as possible.

Samarkar raised the visor of her helm to drink—mostly water, and a little wine—and felt her dizziness and exhaustion recede almost as soon as the cup was lowered again. *The desert is waiting to kill you. Just as surely as the winter and the cold mountains are—or your brother the emperor, or the Rahazeen— though the mechanism may be different.*

One could forget that in the walled gardens of Ato Tesefahun. But it would not be prudent to allow one's self to forget it for long.

Predictably, some time elapsed. Now that her battle excitement was ebbing, Samarkar ached from her skinned hands to the bruise over her spine, and every muscle in her body was issuing a resounding protest of ill and unaccustomed use. She occupied herself waiting for her arming coat to dry upon her skin—or as much as it would, with the armor strapped on over it—and with drinking more water and examining the contents of the room. As she had noted upon first entering, the carpets were rich, and layered deeply so they formed an uneven surface for walking on, making Samarkar doubly glad that she had no plans to engage in a swordfight here.

Other than that, the furnishings were opulent and well maintained, if obviously somewhat worn. The windows were shaded by the louvered blinds that were so common here under the killing Uthman sun, but a warm breeze and slanted slats of light still eased through them. Two daybeds heaped with cushions and robes and furs were separated by the low table that had received the fruit and wine. They had been refinished and reupholstered, but Samarkar could make out marks of wear beneath the gilt on their wooden frames: rich, but old. The caliph was not the sort of person who had to buy his furniture.

After the climb and the running, her feet hurt too. She sat on the nearer divan and took a grape, rolling it firm and cool between her fingertips. She had just popped it into her mouth—a tiny explosion of crisp sweetness backed by the crunch of pips—when the door opened again, and a vigorous-seeming man with iron-colored streaks in his beard and hair entered. Bareheaded, he was clad in a simple white kaftan that fell open over his tunic and trousers. He came with no entourage and no fanfare.

Samarkar was not often taken aback by the dance of politics, but she spent a full three heartbeats blinking at the newcomer before slamming her visor closed, leaping to her feet, and immediately dropping to her knees again. She bowed her head and stammered.

"Your serene Excellency!"

He waited long enough for her knees to burn and her neck to ache. But Samarkar had the advantage of the helm, and if she stretched her eyes upward, she could glimpse his face through its visor.

The caliph was smiling.

At last he said, "Stand, Wizard Samarkar," and slid the bolt of the door behind himself.

She did, working to show none of the nervousness that made her heart race and her hands tremble. A fresh crop of sweat seeded itself throughout her already-itchy underthings. Now that they stood on the level, she could see she was of a height with the caliph: whether that was an advantage or would make him more aggressive, she did not yet know him well enough to say.

But not only was he confident enough in his own strength to leave his palace door open to the street . . . he was confident enough to bolt himself into a small room with a wizard. Or did he even think of her as a wizard? Perhaps he only imagined he had bolted himself into a boudoir with a woman, weak and mild.

Well, kings had also died in that manner.

He regarded her curiously, little threat in his expression. From this close—if they both reached out to the span of their arms they could have taken each other's hands—she could see the bushy, aggressive curve of his eyebrows, the way the wiry hair had been combed out to accentuate the chipped-looking edge on his nose.

"Raise your visor," he said. "Wizard Samarkar."

Swallowing, she hooked her thumbs under the edge and raised it. The cool air that rushed in allowed her to breathe more easily, but the constriction of her chest counteracted that.

The caliph looked at her frankly, curiously—but briefly, before averting his eyes. "If you would be more comfortable," he said, "you may remove the helm. I promise to respect your modesty."

"Excellency," Samarkar muttered. A suggestion from a king was no such thing, and so she lowered her chin and fumbled with the buckles that Temur had fastened for her. She lifted the helm off, feeling strands that had worked loose from her braid lift and pull with it. The bone-dry air that tickled her scalp was not cool, but it evaporated the lingering sweat enough to seem so. The caliph kept his eyes averted. Just as well; Samarkar had no illusions that she was currently impersonating a ravishing beauty.

He gestured to the daybeds. "Sit and drink with me."

Samarkar steeled herself—and if he did make a direct proposition, what then?—but he settled himself across from her, on the other divan. He indicated with a hand jeweled only by two tasteful rings that she should pour. She blinked; of course he would not serve her with his own hands.

But she had not been searched and could have any venom at all pressed between her fingers or slipped up her sleeve. The caliph was either exceedingly foolish or exceedingly brave, and foolish men did not usually live into their seventh decade—at a guess—still as reigning kings.

She poured the caliph his own wine, unwatered this time. She set a glass before him. He raised it, toasted her silently with his eyes still cast politely to one side, and drank a healthy swallow. He took a grape and popped it into his mouth, closing his eyes in pleasure as he chewed.

"There," he said, putting the glass down again precisely, turning it with his fingertips so the square-trimmed base aligned with the tiles of the tabletop. Samarkar had barely touched her lips with hers. "We have shared a meal, and you are a guest in my house. Does that assure you that you will come to no harm at my hands today, Wizard Samarkar?"

He was working to disarm her—and succeeding. But Samarkar bowed her head in something that could be interpreted as a complaisant nod.

The caliph said, "It would be best if your armor were in some disarray when you left, good wizard."

She felt her smile press the edge of the glass she had raised again to her lips as if enjoying the aroma of the wine. In truth it was very fine, but not fine enough to be worth letting her guard down. "So," she answered, discarding the glass on the low table, "this *is* a stratagem."

"We are who we are," the caliph answered. "Would it be possible for there to be anything else between us?"

Now she let him see the smile in full. "I doubt I would be to your taste," she said. "Not when you have your pick of perfumed harem girls."

"There is more to worthy womanhood than perfume," he replied, undaunted. He settled himself against the back of the divan and crossed one long leg over the other. "Ysmat of the Beads is not said to have been known for her beauty. And yet she is renowned above all women."

Samarkar turned her wineglass again. "Is that blasphemy, your serene Excellency?"

His teeth glittered in his beard. "Perhaps a little. But yes, this is a stratagem. My advisors will be certain of it, but—as in so many things—in this it is the appearance of the thing that matters."

"And so, wine in the afternoon and the *appearance* of an assignation."

"Drink deep," he said. "You should have it on your breath when you leave."

She obeyed. Three savoring swallows, and then she set the glass down again. She needed a clear head, not one wine-muddled.

"You sent us away."

"I did that."

"What if I could offer you Asmaracanda back? Not for troops, your Excellency, nor any monetary support. But merely in return for the acknowledgment of Re Temur as Temur Khan, as a rightful claimant to the Khaganate."

"Not even Temur Khagan?" the caliph asked. "Just Khan?"

"I thought I was pushing to get you past Khanzadeh," she admitted artlessly, with all her art behind it.

She must have hit the right note, because the caliph laughed. And then, with a canny look, he said, "Asmaracanda? Then you do not know that I have already taken it."

Samarkar had the experience to keep her face impassive, but there was nothing to be gained by trying to hide that he'd scored when he knew it already. "The news had not reached me."

"Or perhaps I should say that Asmaracanda has been retaken. By men sworn to Kara Mehmed, who is in turn sworn to me."

"It is very important to Kara Mehmed to reopen the trade routes," Samarkar observed impartially.

"Oh," said the caliph. "You *are* a delight."

She would not allow herself to be charmed. But it wouldn't hurt to let him wonder if he was succeeding. She sipped wine again and waited, wishing she'd already disarrayed her armor. Sitting on the lacquer skirts was less than comfortable.

"Kara Mehmed," the caliph said, "is of the opinion that trade would be *best* served if the caliphate's reach extended all the way to the openwater ports of Song, as well as west to Messaline."

"It would be advantageous to any prince who could control the length of the Celadon Highway. But the challenge of pacifying and stabilizing that much territory is immense . . . and that doesn't even consider the challenge of then administering it."

"I don't want to go to war with the steppe lords," the caliph said. "I have seen war. I have *waded* in it. But you understand the politics of the situation with Mehmed—"

Samarkar did. Any land Mehmed could reclaim from the Qersnyk host would bolster his image. And if, as the caliph intimated, Mehmed was eager to start a new war not just for the liberation of formerly caliphate lands now held by the Khaganate but for conquest of new lands, a civil war raging between Temur and his uncle Qori Buqa was an opportunity so perfect it might have been gem-polished and set before him in a cup like a soft-boiled egg.

She said, "You want to see the situation in Qarash settled as soon and as decisively as possible, I understand that. What if I tell you that Temur Khan will not *contest* your rights to Asmaracanda, whereas Qori Buqa will—of a certainty, once he is settled in his power—bring the war to you?"

"It's a small concession."

"So is what we ask of you. He'll sign a treaty to the effect."

"Sign it Temur Khan?" the caliph asked, mocking.

Samarkar let herself laugh. "Of course. How else would he have the power to agree to it?"

The caliph made no encouraging expression, but from the way his architectural brows drew together over the bridge of his nose, Samarkar thought he was considering it. "It's a long road from *Khan* to *Khagan*. A road drenched with the blood of family. Your young man . . ."

He shook his head. *Is he ruthless enough? Will he quail before the bloody work that is the building of empires?*

". . . he seems nice," the caliph finished. Samarkar did not think she imagined the bitter regret that soaked his tone.

She straightened her shoulders against the weight of the armor and said, "He has been raised in war camps since he was old enough to ride, your Excellency. His uncle killed his father, to whom Temur Khan never had the chance to speak. Qori Buqa killed his older brother, for whom Temur Khan had a younger brother's worshipful adoration. And Qori Buqa is allied with your own rebel warlord, as we have said—and that warlord has taken Temur Khan's woman as a hostage. So you can see, *al-Sepehr* thinks Temur Khan is a threat—enough a threat to take punitive action against him."

"His woman?" Surprise, at last. Real surprise, if only a little. "Are you not his woman?"

"A man may have more than one woman," Samarkar answered blandly. "As I am sure your serene Excellency has reason to know."

The caliph laughed. "He could do no better in you than if Ysmat herself stood at his right hand." And that *was* blasphemy. "How can he then fail?"

I don't know how we'll succeed.

"Temur . . ." The caliph hesitated, toying with whatever sat upon his tongue. Tasting it. "Temur *Khan* aside—your Rahazeen rebel seems to think highly enough of *you*, Wizard Samarkar, to send his assassins into my very door-court to have done with you."

Well, of course he knew. He was the caliph: it was his job to know everything, and he doubtless employed a great many people whose entire mandate was making sure he did so.

"They were only a little trouble," Samarkar lied.

Uthman Fourteenth smiled at her. He *winked*. "I imagine there is very little that you would admit to perceiving as a great trouble, once-princess." He gave her the Rasan title in a flawless accent. "Thank you for your time. I will think on what you have said—as you should think on what I have said as well."

"Thank you, your serene Excellency." Samarkar paused. "You said *Temur Khan*, just now."

"I did."

"Does that mean you will support us?"

"It means . . ." the caliph said. He rose to his feet, leaving his half-drunk wine. "I'll think about it."

Think quickly. Samarkar bit her tongue. She dropped to her knees again, her armor rattling around her.

"Stand," said the caliph, brushing a strand of hair away from her cheek. "We must disarray your armor."

As she complied, as his hands unknotted and then inexpertly reknotted her bindings, Samarkar stood stolid. But behind her unfocused eyes, their subterfuge was the last thing she considered. Instead, she could not help but wonder: *And who knew to send assassins, Uthman Caliph? Who knew I was coming here today?*

That night, Hong-la slept at last.

But not before the great wings had spanned the marketplace; the bird, enormous beyond imagining, had struck and vanished once again, leaving executioners and observers beating out sparks and chasing embers—and the emperor and empress standing dumbstruck, side by side but not touching one another until Songtsan abruptly, impulsively grabbed his wife's hand. Hong-la had seen Yangchen-tsa glance down in surprise and then, a long moment later, her fingers tighten over Songtsan's. She had stepped back then, pulling the emperor within. The guards and Songtsan's other wife had followed behind them, leaving Hong-la alone on the balcony.

It was a tactical mistake, and Hong-la could have eased it. He was not inexperienced in the arts of governance, and the thing he should have done—if he was of a mind to reinforce the emperor's political position—was step forward. He should have raised his hands, raised his voice, and found some words to soothe the crowd and cast Tsansong as a boogey-man, a threat now vanished into the night.

If he did not, morning would find Tsansong's escape well on its way to transmuting him into a folk hero.

Hong-la laid his hands on the balustrade and reached out with otherwise senses until he found the energy of the scattered fire below. Embers and sparks had fallen on stone, against brick—and flesh, in a few cases—and on more fertile soil. A thatched roof curled smoke. A wooden house seemed unharmed now, but Hong-la could feel the ember that glowed hungrily, patiently in a chink beside its door. Fire was a clever monster. It could wait.

But not if a Wizard of Tsarepheth called its strength to him, consumed it, transmuted it. The air around Hong-la grew warm; his tired head spun with new exhaustion. But down in the square the kindling fires died, the scattered pyre itself flickered low. He could see now that one executioner was dead or gravely injured, crushed under the fallen timbers and burned. And now, slowly, every eye below was turning back to the balcony, to Hong-la with his black coat and his height.

He should raise his hands, raise his voice, and find those words. He knew he should.

He let his hands fall from the balustrade. He stepped back from the edge, and with all the folk of Tsarepheth watching, he turned his back, the skirts of his coat swirling about him, and stiffly walked inside.

Within, all was hushed chaos. There was no sign of the royal family, but servants and guards and courtiers rushed from one place to another, their faces exactly as grim as if they were accomplishing something. Hong-la passed among them unremarked, one more striding figure with an intent expression. He straightened his spine, though the world swam with weariness. Whatever followed, besieged Tsarepheth could not afford to see a wizard weak.

Without, work went untended everywhere. Screens were rolled down over the windows of noodle and teahouses. Shops stood with closed doors. Hong-la strode through an unattended flock of the feathered, warm-blooded lizards that provided so much meat to the Rasan diet, scattering the brightly colored, hip-high creatures every which way in the street. Their attendant was nowhere to be seen.

So extreme was Hong-la's exhaustion that at first he did not understand why it was that the lanterns lining his route began to gutter as if shaken. There should have been more—every street in Tsarepheth should have been ablaze with light—but lamplighters were no more immune to the demon-spawn infestation than any other trade. The world pitched and yawed under his feet. The stones rose up and struck his soles, and he put a hand out to a wall and felt it shiver. *Have I been poisoned?*

But then he heard the rumble, the crack of thunder, the shuddering depth of sound that made his teeth feel loose in his jaw. The overcast glowed vermillion behind the Citadel, lit from within as if by a rising sun, until the clouds burned back. Like curtains drawn they revealed the tower of smoke behind them, the layered reds and oranges of the earth's deep fires cracking upward: questing, thrusting, twisting . . . breaking free.

The Cold Fire was cold no longer.

For a moment, Hong-la stood in stupor—half-bent, still, one hand on the wall that supported him. Distantly, he heard cries: alarm, wonder. They did not turn his head. He had eyes only for the column of smoke and fire mounting the night, wreathed in a coruscating lace of violet lightning, too bright to look at and too terrible to look away from. The thunder rumbled softer, higher overtones to the voice of the mountain.

He reached out with his *otherwise* senses and felt the fretwork of other wizards also reaching. Felt them organize around the familiar presence of Yongten-la, seeking, gentle fingertips of the spirit and will exploring the energy trapped within and leaking from the no-longer-dormant volcano. If this were the prelude to a violent eruption, some wizards would stay behind and control the volcano for as long as possible—mollify it, redirect its energies. Others would lead the evacuation, if evacuation there could be.

The energy Hong-la felt had a strange, vile flavor—acrid and awful. He'd never felt fire from the very belly of the earth before, but the heat that soaked the sulfurous waters from the depths of the Cold Fire was soothing, and this . . . felt as if it should shrivel flesh.

Hong-la released an easier breath when he sensed the direction and power of the flow. An eruption, yes—and the first flakes of ash began to brush his hair and face as he thought it—but not an apocalyptic one. One that could be contained, channeled. One within the powers of the wizards whose calling it was to soothe the volatile earth under Tsarepheth.

Blessed stones, there would not be an evacuation tonight.

Hong-la walked back to the Citadel breathing through the gaps between cupped fingers to filter out the ash that blew like snow on every side and gritted underfoot. Pride alone had kept him upright until he regained the Citadel and reported to Yongten-la.

He did not remember, later, falling asleep mid-sentence.

WHEN HE AWOKE, IT WAS ON HIS OWN BED, HIS COAT AND BOOTS REMOVED, his shirt and trousers loosened. Tsering-la, compact and moon-faced, her braids glistening with the first few strands of silver, sat cross-legged, waiting patiently while Hong-la rubbed at crusted eyes.

She pressed a warm, damp cloth into his hand. Any wizard knew what awakening from a long slumber was like.

As Hong-la cleaned his face, the thrush in the black cage beside the window chirruped sleepily. No one had covered him, and the lamps were keeping him awake. At least it seemed the novices had kept him fed and watered in Hong-la's incapacity.

"How long did I sleep?" Hong-la asked, dropping the used cloth in the basin that Tsering also presented.

"It's after moonset," she said. "You collapsed a day and a half ago."

He would have protested the term, but it was probably fair. He was lucky his heart hadn't simply stopped when the Citadel's borrowed energy ran out. He would not have been the first wizard to die that way. "Did I walk to bed?"

"Carried," she said.

He heaved himself onto his elbows and took the next thing she held out: a bowl of steaming broth and noodles, with scallions and shreds of ginger floating across the top. There was a brazier beside Tsering and sweat dewed her forehead—while he himself felt shaky with chill. He had exhausted himself past the point where his body could maintain its own warmth.

"Situation?" he asked, letting her steady the bowl as he raised it to his mouth. He had the strength for brief movements, but simply keeping his hands lifted made them tremble.

"Complex," she answered while he drank, and went on with details.

As he'd expected, the rumor of Tsansong's escape had spread wide, and while it wasn't precisely possible for it to grow in the telling, it had certainly become more detailed. Hong-la himself had apparently called down lightning, the better to defend the emperor when the great bird struck at him.

"I don't remember that," Hong-la said mildly, setting the soup bowl aside.

Tsering replaced it in his hands with a cup of salted, buttered tea. "There are plenty to remember it for you."

"Is there rioting yet? Have Tsansong's faction thought to claim that the bird's intervention is a sign of favor from the Six Thousand?"

She shook her head. "There is other news."

Strength seemed to be returning as fast as it had fled. He was warmer. His teeth did not chatter on the rim of the tea cup now. He managed it one-handed, and with the other gestured her to continue.

"Anil-la says the Cold Fire was awakened intentionally. He can read the signature of a sacrifice in its energy. And Yongten-la says the taste of Erem's poison magic is bitter through all its emanations."

Hong-la's mouth worked in memory of the acrid flavor he had not previously identified.

Watching him, Tsering-la continued, "The hatchlings . . ."

His throat closed; his stomach soured. He let the teacup drop to his knee.

She closed her eyes before she could continue. "The captive hatchlings *speak*, Hong-la."

He would have asked, *What do they say?* He would have made it easier on her. But he couldn't remember, for long moments, how to shape a word, how to push air from his lungs.

The Wizard Tsering was brave enough to get there on her own. "They speak of the Carrion King, of Sepehr al-Rachīd. They prophesy—" She shook her head. "I'll take you to hear for yourself. But there's . . . other evidence."

"Evidence more convincing than a city overrun by blood ghosts?"

Lamplight shone off her collar, the satin of her wizard's coat as her shoulders rose and fell. She had been there, seen silenced Kashe with her own eyes—albeit from a distance. Hong-la had merely taken her report, and that of Samarkar-la. "A skinned corpse," she said. "His head blown out. Fresh, and found above the Wreaking yesterday. It was . . . very neatly done."

As if by a practiced hand. "Left for carrion," he said.

She lifted the cast-iron teapot from the warming plate over the brazier, and despite the heat she was clearly feeling, poured her own strong cup of tea. "That is the name we gave to al-Rachīd in this land."

Hong-la held out his teacup for more. "Here's something else to work on. You're the best theorist I know—"

Tsering-la ducked her head and covered her face with her palms. Her jeweled collar pressed the flesh around her chin up oddly. "I cannot so much as light a candle!"

"Does that render your learning less valuable?"

She busied her hands with her own tea, avoiding his eyes and the answer. He continued, "As a theorist, Wizard Tsering—ask yourself this. How does a demon enter a warded house?"

"Someone who has the right to do so invites it," she said promptly. "Or is fooled into inviting it."

"So how does a demon enter a warded city?"

She stilled. Her hand did not tremble as—carefully, precisely—she set her cup down. "Someone who has the right to . . . invites it. Or is fooled into inviting it."

"Songtsan-tsa?" he asked, when she had been silent long enough. "Tsering, we must find the flaws in the wards."

"The demons are inside now. How do you get them out again? How do you revoke their permission to enter?"

"I thought," he said, "that you might know."

Her head stayed bowed, her hair hiding her expression. "The wardstones of Qeshqer had been intentionally defaced. If that had happened here, we would have found it now. There is a different source."

After a pause his answer did not fill, she changed the subject. "Yongten-la has been working to convince the emperor that he must evacuate Tsarepheth, that he must relocate to the winter capital early."

"And Songtsan is *against* this?"

She shook her head. "The emperor may not believe that the Citadel had nothing to do with his brother's escape. He may not believe that the awakening of the Cold Fire is . . . not our doing."

"Curse of the stones," Hong-la muttered in Song, watching Tsering's eyebrows rise in amusement. "So—let me guess—the emperor suspects that his own wizards are involved in a conspiracy to usurp him. So he's afraid that if he does the sensible thing and allows his people to leave the vicinity of *an active volcano,* he'll be handing us an advantage?"

"Your grasp of politics is nuanced," Tsering said dryly.

"My parroting of the obvious is pretty good even when I've just crawled out of a coma, you mean." He sighed. "Perhaps I can . . . talk to the empress."

She said, "There is also news that a refugee train is en route through the mountains from the steppe. Having found no succor in Kashe, they come to plead with Songtsan-tsa for asylum from the reign of Qori Buqa."

"They should not have come here."

"They had nowhere else to go."

"Songtsan will use them as cannon fodder," Hong-la said. "Human shields."

Tsering cupped her fingers downward, caging every side of the cast-iron cup. "Not before I interview them, he won't."

Tsering-la walked out of the postern gate at first light, flanked by novices and guardsmen, into a familiar landscape rendered unknowable. The white-and-red hulk of the Citadel of Tsarepheth curved behind her: gravity incarnate. The sacred river crashed in the gorge below. Bands of steam writhed from its surface where hot water and cold intermingled.

Those things had not changed—and those alone.

Gray ash lay like drifts of dirty snow across the road, across the high white arch of the Wreaking—that impossible bridge that spanned the impossible gulf where the headwaters of the Tsarethi tumbled from the glaciers of the Island-in-the-Mists—across the flanks of the mountains. It looked as soft as snow, but where Tsering wiped it from her cheek incautiously it drew blood and stung. She thought of it sifting down inside her boots, the mischief it could work with every step, and shuddered.

The Qersnyk refugees camped beyond the Wreaking had made no attempt to cross; they had merely stopped before the guarded bridge and waited. They had no more protection from the ash than their tents, and they would not huddle inside those when there was work to be done. As Tsering moved toward the bridge with her entourage, she saw people—mostly women and children—dusting the backs of livestock, hauling water, sweeping the ground and creating makeshift shelters where animals could eat clean fodder untainted by ash.

Her approach triggered a sudden bustle as one child—boy or girl, she could not tell—looked up from grooming and took off running back into the encampment. He (or she) vanished between tents while Tsering was cresting the Wreaking.

She paused at the bowed height of the bridge, like a vast white rib, and took a moment to enjoy the view of the river surging far below. She was stalling to give the Qersnyk leader time to prepare, but it was still valuable to fold her arms and lean on the waist-high wall, organizing her own thoughts.

After a stir among the tents, she straightened again and continued on.

She was met at the bottom of the bridge by two women. One was so old that her age had become indeterminate. She was a withered apple doll of a person, hunched in thick robes despite the summer's warmth. She leaned on a stick, but for all that she had moved nimbly across.

The other emissary was a surprise, physically speaking: a younger woman, but not young, compact and sturdy-seeming with motherly hips and the brown skin and broad nose of the Aezin nation. She rested one hand in the crook of the older woman's arm, though neither of them seemed to need the support.

She lifted her head as Tsering-la approached, and said in the Uthman tongue, "I don't suppose you speak Qersnyk?"

"I brought a translator," Tsering answered, gesturing to the novice on her left. They had stopped well back, and she made no move to close the distance. "But I am comfortable in this language. I am the Wizard Tsering. You have reached Tsarepheth, the white-and-scarlet Citadel. You may camp here, but you may not enter. There is plague within."

"This is Tsareg Altantsetseg," the Aezin woman said. There was a whistle on her breathing that sent a chill of unease across Tsering's chest. "She does not speak your tongue, or this one either. But I will translate for her." She paused, and did so—accurately, from the little Tsering could follow.

"What is your name?" Tsering asked in the pause that followed.

"I am Ashra," said the Aezin woman. Her teeth flashed when she spoke. They were banded like old ivory, shades of brown and bone. "This plague—"

Ashra looked at Tsareg Altantsetseg. She said something in Qersnyk. The old woman responded.

Ashra placed a hand upon her chest as if easing pressure within. Tsering felt the sickening drop of an unpleasant suspicion confirmed.

"We know it," Ashra said. "Some dozen or more have sickened, since we came into the mountains. Our shaman-rememberers and surgeons have no physic for it. We had hoped, with the fame of the Wizards of Tsarepheth—"

Tsering knew from the other women's expressions that she had failed to keep her dismay from coloring their own. "I'm sorry," she said. "We have studied the course of the disease..."

She could not continue. But if she had expected Ashra to let the silence stretch into awkwardness while Tsering struggled to express some futile sympathy, the Aezin woman surprised her.

"I see," Ashra said, queenly and unperturbed. "Then it is rather as I expected. My father was a wizard in Aezin, Tsering-la, and I know something of his strategies. Perhaps we can work together?"

Tsering found herself smiling in unwilling sympathy. Ashra's dignity and charisma were hard to resist. "That...might buy you asylum. If you can prove your expertise."

Ashra glanced at the clan-mother beside her. She said a few words. Tsareg Altantsetseg considered them—and nodded.

"Show me to a laboratory," Ashra said. "I will prove what I know."

THE WIZARDS ANIL AND HONG HAD CAUSED A SORT OF FIELD SHELTER TO BE built near the tent city of the infirmary. It was a structure such as might have housed the blacksmith's forge and anvils on a military campaign.

Open-sided, though tapestries had now been hung to keep the worst of the falling ash at bay, it was made of lashed timbers sunk in the earth and braced. The turf where it was erected had been peeled back and used to roof the structure, and within it were dissection slabs, a kiln, crucibles and chemicals, sand tables, alembics, flasks, mirrors (silver, brass, and glass), and glassware of more mysterious purpose and provenance. Mortars, pestles, racks of scalpels, tongs and forceps. Quicksilver, oil of vitriol, the fine dust of powdered sapphires, blocks of white salt and violet. And from their cages—each within a crystal dome that had been created open at the top to permit stale air to exchange with fresh—half a dozen demonspawn stared out with baleful intent.

It was here that Tsering brought Ashra, or—as Tsering was already thinking of her—Ata Ashra: the Wizard Ashra. Hong-la was at work here, looking less gray-faced for his enforced rest but not significantly less weary or frightened. He bent over a small wardstone with a hand lens. Tsering, having spent hours at the same work, could not locate any hope in herself that this time he would find the flaw.

He was surrounded by Anil-la and several other junior wizards, all bent over magnifiers or wax tablets to which necropsy specimens lay pinned. Anil-la, wearing a face shield and a butcher's apron, was using glass blades to vivisect a quivering demonspawn. Glass, Tsering knew, for its sharpness . . . and because the spawn's fluids would dissolve mere metal.

A flayed human body lay on one of the dissection tables, flesh red and raw. The whole corpse had been pared like a persimmon and the head lay against the table with unnatural flatness. Another, beside it, had been opened from collarbone to belly button, the ribs sectioned, the flesh peeled back in layers. One lung had been opened, and Tsering could see evidence of bruising in the swollen flesh. She suspected that the spawn pinned to Anil-la's dissection board had found its origins there.

Reassured though she was as to the strength of Ata Ashra's will and purpose, Tsering had nevertheless warned her of what she would find here, and what it meant. She had told Ashra that she could not be allowed within the Citadel itself, and why—and now she paused at the edge of the work space to let the Aezin woman take it in.

Ashra pressed a fist against her chest. Tsering heard the whistle of her breath going out, saw her nostrils flare with effort as she drew another in. Hong-la winched his great height up from where he had hunched over his workbench and hooked them toward him with a bony hand.

"Hong-la," Tsering said, and made her decision. In Uthman, she continued, "This is Ata Ashra, from the Qersnyk train. She has some ideas on how we can fight the plague."

Ashra gave her a sidelong glance. "It was my father who was the wizard, Tsering-la. I have not studied architecture or music, and what I know of tactics I learned from my husband and father-in-law, not in a college of wizardry."

Tsering had heard of the great Aezin universities and the scholars they trained. She opened her mouth to reply, but Hong-la beat her.

"If you have some insight into the infestation, you're wizard enough for me." He cocked his head. "Forgive my forwardness, Ata Ashra, but . . . I detect a hesitation in your breathing."

Her small smile tightened. "I am infected, yes. These are examples of the organism?"

Both Hong-la and Tsering-la turned at her gesture. Ashra might be facing her own horrific death—but her face and posture revealed curiosity and intensity of focus. She paced from glass bell to glass bell, leaning close to each cage. The skirts of her sleeveless fleece coat tapped at her ankles as the spawns' heads swiveled to follow her. Tsering expected them to break out into one of their choruses of poisonous prophecy, but they only stared. One mantled its wings like a threatened owl; one hissed with a flickering tongue and spat. Viscous, transparent, rust-colored venom smoked against the bars of the cage and trickled in strings down the glass.

Ashra straightened and turned her back on the beasts. "I assume the emergence is similarly hideous?"

"You've lost no one so far?" Hong-la asked.

"The first infections came only a few days ago." She wet her lips. "How long is the . . ."

"Incubation?"

"Gestation period?"

When the others hesitated, it was Anil-la who took a strengthening breath and said, "Without treatment? Fourteen days. Precisely."

Ashra nodded. "Not long enough, then. But I can at least get you started."

Anil-la glanced at his seniors as if seeking permission to go on. Hong-la tipped his head in acquiescence. Anil-la continued, "We believe some weakness has sundered the magical protections that kept demons from Tsarepheth."

"If the Khagan's rule can be said to metaphysically shelter the Qersnyk lands . . ." Ashra winced. "Well, that's in disarray. Has there been trouble in your royal family?"

The silence that greeted her—and Anil-la's frustrated scowl—must have been answer enough, because she hastened to change the subject. "Have you considered killing the spawn when the infection is new?"

"More than considered it." Hong-la came to her, his spine curling like a fern as he brought his face closer to her level. "But the patients died of gangrene and poisoned blood, from the creatures rotting inside them. We have a simple that can help—a mold—but it's better packed in wounds than consumed, and even having the patients inhale the spores was insufficient."

Ashra's jaw worked. Tsering has no wizardly powers, but she had enough common empathy that she could almost taste the vileness spilling across the back of her tongue.

"There's an Aezin brew," Ashra said, "a kind of millet beer—you know beer?—that is good against some fevers, though not all. But wound-fever and childbed-fever, these it can cure, if given in a timely manner and in sufficient quantity. Would you agree that the fever of a rot in the lungs is likely to be of a similar origin to wound-fever?"

Tsering saw Hong-la's head bob before she realized her own chin was nodding as well. Something filled her up—a startled ache inside her ribs, a peculiar lightheadedness as if from hunger. It was long seconds before she realized that what she felt was elation. It was *hope*, a sensation gone unfamiliar with disuse.

"If given to children, it stains the teeth." Ashra smiled self-consciously, revealing those odd bands of brown and yellow once again.

"Something like that," said Hong-la, "it would require a mother, wouldn't it? A culture from which to brew?"

Ashra reached into the keyhole collar of her tunic and hooked a thong, silk-soft by the way it folded. By contrast, the leather pouch she drew up was stiff and stained, an age-glossy, worn-shiny, unlovely thing. "I carried a mother from my father's house when I was given in marriage," she said. "But there was no brewing in the harem, and long before I was stolen from my first husband by Qersnyk tribesmen, it had died. My second husband traded this for me in Song; it can be had in certain markets along the Celadon Highway if you know what you are asking for and how to name it. We will need a brewery, of course—"

"And time," Tsering-la said, feeling the inevitability of it like a lead blade in her chest.

Ashra's forced smile flickered into something sadder and more honest. "It will take more than fourteen days."

WHILE HONG-LA WENT TO SPEAK TO YONGTEN-LA ABOUT REQUISITIONING A brewery and making arrangements with the palace for the refugees to stay, Tsering took Ashra to seek housing and a meal. They both ignored the reality that soon—too soon—she would be joining the patients in the vast tent wards sprawling below the Citadel.

For now, Tsering brought her to the temporary kitchens servicing the makeshift hospital, where volunteers greasy with exhaustion set bowls of soup and tea before them. The broth was thin, the noodles more salty than flavorful, but at the long tables and on the benches all around, heads were bowed over bowls. Wizards, novices, and volunteers ate not with the reverential contemplation tradition demanded, but with the determination of men stoking coal furnaces on a brutal winter night.

After a few sips of her soup, Ashra turned, pushed her cloud of hair behind her shoulder, and said, "I am looking for my son, who may have come this way."

Tsering's hands stilled on her tea bowl as she thought of the brown skin and broad features of the Qersnyk man she and Samarkar-la had rescued from the road near Qeshqer.

"He fought in the battle of Qarash, and so I had feared him dead. We rode out through the battlefield when we fled the city—" Ashra covered her eyes with her hand, as she had not when contemplating her own mutilation and death. "There were so many dead. The refugees of the city—the train wound past the horizon in both directions. Everyone fled, though I have heard that some are returning, that Qori . . . that the new Khan will rebuild, and reopen trade."

"We miss the trade," Tsering admitted. "But then, it seems likely that the lack of caravans is at least slowing the spread of plague."

Ashra snorted. " 'Even a hard frost helps the hunter.' As we traveled, in any case, I heard through the gossip of the refugee train that a Qersnyk warrior of Aezin descent had been seen with the Tsareg. I rode up the train to investigate and learned it was true, and that the warrior was my son Temur. And that he had gone on ahead to seek his woman, who had been stolen from him by the blood ghosts."

Certain now, Tsering said, "He seeks her still."

"He was here!"

"Here and left. In the company of one of our own, the Wizard Samarkar. And a Cho-tse warrior, and the breeding wife of the emperor's brother who had been condemned for treason. Which was the reason they fled in such a hurry . . . that, and Temur believed he had discovered a hint on where to find or perhaps avenge his woman. Edene, he called her."

"She is Tsareg Altantsetseg's descendant." Now Ashra drank her soup with better appetite, her eyes on Tsering's face. "The Tsareg clan have not held a Khanate in generations, but they have given wives to nearly all of them. There would be rewards, if Edene lives."

"I cannot tell you that," Tsering said. "But I can tell you that Temur was alive when he left here, and in strong company, and in good health as well—much better health, in fact, than when he arrived."

Ashra set her empty bowl aside. "Tell me all."

10

THE TWINS WALKED INTO QARASH OUT OF THE DUST OF A FADING SUMMER. They had sent the rukh away while still well out of sight and as they approached they were treated to a lingering review of the war-trammeled steppe.

The bodies of horses and men had not been burned or buried, but only dragged into heaps from which the reek of decomposition still rolled. There were paths to walk on by way of which one was not treading on the dead, though spilled blood blackened the dry earth between stems of green-gold straw. Insects and scavengers had done such work as they were able, as had the slow deliquescence of putrefaction, so the white bones showed through hide like swags of bronze-black leather, but even so it might be years beneath the Eternal Sky before the clean bones were bleached and scattered.

The twins promised themselves: for the Nameless, for the world—though it was a cleansing to be much desired, the Eternal Sky would not endure long enough to see the wind blow sweet across this steppe again. That would happen beneath a Rahazeen sun, with more men piled among these bones until it was made so.

A half day's march brought them to the former outskirts of the Qersnyk trade capital, and the company of others—travelers, herdsmen, men and women raking up the ashes of white-houses once sacked and burned and raising the felt walls of new white-houses on the earth already scraped for floors. The white-houses clustered around the breached walls of Qarash, and some enterprising subjects of the would-be Khagan had prised broken stones from the mud matrix of those and carried them off for shelters and fireplaces. Wagonloads of new stones stood here and there, guarded by Qersnyk warriors whose helms were surmounted by the three-tiered horsehair falls that were the crest of Qori Buqa. Stonemasons who obviously came from far east and west of the Qersnyk lands were raising scaffoldings at the gaps. Piles of burned timbers and other scrap scattered the countryside.

The twins entered the city before the improvised gates were closed for nightfall. The wrong-colored sun setting in the west never ceased to be unsettling, but the twins turned their back on it and joined the crowds of people moving through the comfortable avenues of the Khagan's city.

Coming through the westernmost gate, they saw stone houses under repair or demolition, turf and slate roofs replacing tents stretched against the weather. Reconstruction was clearly piecemeal, but it was also clearly well under way. Qori Buqa was consolidating his position.

Other than the stonemasons, there were few foreigners; the twins drew some attention. As darkness fell and the lantern bearers came out to stand on street corners, crying their escort services, Saadet and Shahruz chose to melt into the darkness, leaving the bustle of more traveled thoroughfares behind.

They came up on the palace by the postern gate—though they had no intention of using it—and streets less populated. Though fire-scarred, these walls were more intact—and just as heavily patrolled and guarded as those surrounding the city proper.

It was acceptable. There were shadowy corners, and Shahruz knew how to set a rope and climb, though the twins were still coming to terms with Saadet's untrained and womanish muscles. Many physical accomplishments were easier with a man's strength behind them, but what Saadet lacked in power the twins made up for in determination. And at least this body was lighter than that of Shahruz had been.

The wall was surmounted despite the physical strain, the patrols circumvented with ease. It could have been a challenge—perhaps, once, years ago, it would have been. Now, while it was an occasion for mindfulness and care, the twins achieved Qori Buqa Khan's chamber without misadventure. There was no ledge outside the narrow window. Shahruz tried to hide his exasperation behind chivalry as he crouched on the roof and placed knots along their silken climbing rope for Saadet, but Saadet knew him too well to be fooled. When the twins lowered themselves before the window, they could glimpse the shoulders of two Qersnyk tribesmen standing stolidly within, the visible right hand of one clutching a bannered spear. The more secure manner in which to guard would have been by facing out.

"Excuse me," said Shahruz in the Qersnyk tongue. "I am here to speak to the Khagan."

They turned reflexively, well-enough practiced that they did not foul one another when they thrust with their spears. The twins twisted on the rope, one foot to the wall, and grasped one spear below the horsetail tassel. A straight yank would have pulled the guard into the window frame, though probably not through it, as the aperture was narrow. But the twins gave it a twist instead, slamming the guard's hand against the wall. With a cry, he released the spear haft.

The twins choked up and reversed it, holding the other guard at bay with the point.

"I'm carrying a pair of pistols," Shahruz said, companionably. "If I'd wanted to kill you, I'd have just shot you. Now. The Khagan is expecting me. Please be so kind as to tell him I've arrived."

"Step inside," said the guard who was still armed, while the other stood dumbfounded. "Hand over your weapons. Have a seat. I'm sure we can come to some sort of an arrangement."

RE QORI BUQA WAS A BROAD MAN, STOCKY, FAIR-SKINNED FOR A QERSNYK, with a drooping moustache, drooping eyes, and leathery, acne-scarred cheeks that bespoke an entirely predictable life in the wind and sun and winter. He arrived with reasonable haste—his arrogance was not the sort that demanded he act with rudeness—and as the twins rose in respect, the Khan cleared the guards from his chamber. A servant beside him brought *airag*—fermented mare's milk—in a pitcher and fragile-seeming cups from Song. She set the tray on the floor on its folding legs and was then also directed out the door.

"Sit," the Khan said unceremoniously. "Drink. Tell me who you come from."

"Al-Sepehr sent me," the twins answered, pleased that, whatever else, Qori Buqa would not give away that information to one who did not already know it. They seated themselves again on a threadbare pillow, pushing the empty sheath at their belt aside. These might be the Khan's chambers, but the stone floors were bare other than a few carpets and cushions, the hangings on the bed smoke-stained. If this was the best of the salvaged furnishings, the sack of Qarash had been complete.

The Khan seated himself. He poured thick, sour-scented fluid into the cups and passed one to the twins. Saadet loosened her veil to slide the cup beneath it, so she could drink without revealing her features. The beverage was pungent, sour-silky, and refreshing.

The Khan watched the twins in amusement. The twins were unmoved by his regard. "So. The Rahazeen train girls as assassins now?"

"We serve the Scholar-God in whatever manner our gifts permit."

The corners of his moustache lifted. "Your hands are very clean."

The twins glanced down at their untattooed hands. "As you have so astutely noted, I am a woman."

"But maybe not a girl like *other* Uthman girls?" His eyebrows arched. It might have been a leer. It might as well have been teasing. Qersnyk girls ran wild, rode ponies like hoydens, whored as they pleased until they married. These barbarians thought a big belly on a bride to be was a point of pride to groom and girl alike.

When the twins did not respond, Qori Buqa shrugged and asked, "All right, Rahazeen warrior. What news do you bring me from my honored ally?"

"Our agent in Tsarepheth continues to work to weaken the Rasan empire, setting brother against brother." The twins folded their hands together. Saadet felt the sting of the pistol against her palm as if she had just fired into Prince Songtsan's head. What she said was not precisely a lie: that the empress thought she worked for the benefit of herself and her husband did not change the eventual outcome of her choices. "When you have dispensed with the last rebels against your rightful authority, Khagan, Rasa will be yours to conquer—a rightful vengeance for the massacre at Qeshqer. Their empire will flounder in political chaos. Your hand will hold the reins of lands even the Great Khagan could not master."

He knew it was flattery. His level look told her so. But she also saw the flicker of his mouth as he smoothed away a smile. "That is fine news indeed. And what of the caliphate?"

"Our agents are at work there too. Soon my master's men will depose Uthman Caliph; soon my master will bring his own army to support yours. And then who can stand before two great empires united, from the oceans beyond Song to the vast erg that bounds Messaline?"

"Easy to promise," Qori Buqa said.

The twins smoothed their veil. "He sends me also with an offer in marriage, Qori Buqa Khan, to cement our alliance and the friendship between our tribes."

Satisfyingly, that surprised him. "A marriage. That could be far more to his advantage than to mine. He has no empire. He does not sit in the Padparadscha Seat."

"An empire he helped you claim. A saddle he assisted in setting you in. Your magnanimity..." the twins hesitated carefully "...is wellknown, Qori Buqa Khagan."

"Hmph." The Khan sipped his drink. He cradled the cup with a surprisingly delicate grip. "With one of his children? A dutiful and terrified Rahazeen virgin? What heat would such a one bring to my marriage bed?"

"I am al-Sepehr's adopted daughter," the twins said. "Give me back my sword, and I will show you what heat I bring to a marriage bed."

THE CALIPH SENT SAMARKAR BACK TO ATO TESEFAHUN'S HOUSE IN A SEDAN chair, under guard—and this time she allowed it to happen. She disembarked in the courtyard, surrounded by oiled slaves in loincloths—each one broader and more beautifully muscled than the next. They stared straight ahead, proud and composed as carriage horses, effacing them-selves from her perceptions.

Once, she was uneasily aware, she would have taken no more notice of them than of the sedan chair itself. Possibly less, because she was forced to interact with the litter. But that was before she had come to know Hong-la and her husband's eunuch administrators. The princes of Song did not call their bureaucrats slaves and accorded them a kind of social status—but that didn't change the reality of a chattel relationship.

How many potential wizards, she wondered, had been lost among the illiterate ranks of collared laborers? And how would you run an empire without cheap, disposable labor? It was as impossible a question as how you would run one without conquest and expansion.

Irritated, she unfastened her helm, ripping it off as she strode toward the common rooms. She did not look back to see if the slaves broke their statuelike poise to avoid seeing her face, but she did pause to ask the doorman to see that they had water and were tipped before being sent back to the palace.

Hrahima and Brother Hsiung came hurrying out to meet her. "Pa-per," Samarkar said, tossing the helm to the monk. He tucked it under one arm, then pulled paper and an Uthman ink-pot from the wallet de-pendent from his sash.

Silently—how else?—he proffered them.

Stopping dead in her tracks, Samarkar smiled. "Brother Hsiung," she said. "The ever reliable. I don't suppose you have a pen or a brush in there too?"

SHE SAT CROSS-LEGGED BEFORE THE LOW TABLE IN HER UNDERWEAR. INK stained her fingertips black-brown. The gold tassels on the cushion scratched the back of her thighs. Her scrapes stung and itched. Sweat dried in white crusts on her forearms, around the collar of her chemise. It stuck escaped strands of her hair together. The armor and arming coat, discarded in a corner, had been removed by servants.

Hrahima and Brother Hsiung had cleared the room of others for her and then stayed, watching silently. She didn't know when the others arrived, but when she looked up again it was because Ato Tesefahun was lighting lamps against the failing day, and Temur had come and sat down beside her.

He set a cup of tea by her hand. "I see the princess now."

"Once-princess," she corrected. She set the pen on its stand and pushed the pages she'd covered with fine lines of characters toward him, trading for the tea. It was Song style, plain red, drifting with faintly floral steam. The splash of it into her empty stomach awakened a growl.

He glanced at her pages, careful of the liquid ink. "I don't read Uthman."

"May I?" Ato Tesefahun reached over Temur's shoulder; Temur allowed it. There was a pause while the Aezin wizard read; during it, Brother Hsiung somehow produced a plate of food and set it before Samarkar. She ate with her fingers, scooping up fowl, those minuscule wheat-flour dumplings, and steamed vegetables dressed in a richly spicy red paste.

She was still sucking the grease from her fingers when Ato Tesefahun looked up and said, "It is a treaty. Between Uthman Caliph and Temur Khan. In which you agree to relinquish all Qersnyk claim to Asmaracanda and he promises basically nothing."

"And I sign this . . . because?"

Samarkar swallowed, her belly almost unpleasantly tight. She still felt like she wanted to eat more. "Because you sign it as Temur Khan. And its mere existence, and the caliph's willingness to treat with you as a fellow sovereign, establishes your legitimacy in that role."

"Oh," Temur said. He looked over his shoulder at his grandfather. "Read it to me. Word for word." To Samarkar, he added, "And you—be prepared to answer questions."

She pressed her teacup to her mouth so he would not see her smile of approval.

No man could endure this. As Ümmühan was jostled in her sedan chair, the louvered windows offering no significant breeze or escape from the trapped, suffocating heat, she was certain of that as nothing else.

Trapped and suffocating herself, her silks adhered to her flesh by rank sweat, she gritted her teeth and told herself over and over again: no mere man could endure this.

Of course, no man would have tolerated it. If *she* were a man, she'd have climbed out herself and walked or ridden camel-back under a suspended canopy. Men did not have to tolerate such things. They used their physical strength to see to it.

In part, Ümmühan thought—wincing at a sharp jar through her hips through the cushioned seat as one of the bearers stumbled—men used their strength in that way because in all other ways they were pathetically fragile. What did physical prowess matter when spiritually, emotionally, they were weak?

Men must be protected from so many things: the sight of women's faces; the truth about God. The apparently crushing fear that a woman might judge them in relation to another man and find them wanting, if she had any standard of comparison.

Ümmühan sighed and lazily waved her fan. As it happened, she did have some standard of comparison. And as it happened, she did judge.

"Not too much farther, my flower," said a male voice from outside. A shadow fell across her louvers as Kara Mehmed leaned close, down out of the tasseled saddle of his gray gelding. "Be grateful you're sitting inside in the shade, not out here toiling over stones."

As if she had not been the one whose plots and counterplots and careful webs of alliances had brought them here.

But men were weak and must be permitted their illusions.

"My gratitude to you knows no bounds, O lion of the desert."

The slave poet pitched her voice low and sweet and gently teasing, resting the folded fan on the (sweaty) pillow of her abdomen. Her rings glittered dully in the filtered light. At least the sedan chair and its curtains kept most of the dust out, and she could lower her veils.

"Not 'lion of your heart'?" he responded, playfully hurt.

"That too, of course. Do you see the forked rock yet?" Surely, surely they must be in sight of it by now. Ümmühan sipped her carefully hoarded water.

"Not five hundred cubits off. Shall we pick up the pace, my flower?"

Ümmühan touched her golden collar, traced the words of the Prophet inscribed there: *Wise are the blossoms in a walled garden, for they shall know no want.*

"Not unless the gardener doesn't show up for work," she muttered, shaping the words without breath behind them. She knew how her sedan chair amplified every sound from within. From behind screens, she had collaborated with the wizard who had designed it for her.

"He will find us," she said. "Have no fear."

She let the lassitude of heat take her. Half a varst, five hundred cubits, another two finger-widths of the sun moving across the sky. Enough time for a brief rest. She was jolted from her reverie—a more romantic word than *stupor*—when the sedan chair was lowered. The bearers were skilled, but the ground was hard and uneven. The heat still oppressed, but no light fell through the louvers, and Ümmühan realized her chair stood in shade.

She heard Mehmed dismount. Someone shot the bolts on her sedan chair and drew the slatted door open. Dusty silk draperies lofted on the arid wind, and her robes and veils swirled around her as she allowed Mehmed to hand her out. She stood, breathing in relief, amazed that *this* air could seem cooler when it dried the sweat from her body in instants.

The bearer on the near front quarter stood with a canted ankle. It must have been he who stumbled. Red dust palled all of them to thighs bronzed dark as old metal; their sweat had dried too quickly to streak.

As Ümmühan straightened, pushing her fists into her back, Mehmed sent the bearers out of sight, around the spire of stone they had paused in the shadow of.

Nothing was in sight now except for Mehmed, his horse, the sedan chair, and the wasteland. The glittering-pale gelding nuzzled among stones with a dished black nose but found nothing. Ümmühan let her hand fall on Mehmed's arm as if she needed him to steady her. She turned to regard the desert. A line of hills separated them from Asitaneh and a view of the sea. In the other direction, a cracked plain swept to the foothills of haze-blurred mountains. They looked so close . . . but Ümmühan knew that she, Mehmed, and the horse would all die of thirst and the brutal sun before they walked halfway there. Distances in the desert were deceptive.

"Not long now, my lion," she assured Mehmed.

He lifted the fall of her head scarf and smoothed it over her shoulder. Her collar weighed on bones.

From those mountains, a shadow sailed up and swept closer. It seemed to come slowly, on ponderous wingbeats, but its speed must be tremendous to be seen to be moving at all. It grew—and impossibly grew—and grew once more until the shadow of its wings seemed to sweep from one horizon to the next. Not so, of course—but when it furled its wings, banked, and beat downward to a heavy, hunch-shouldered landing it was still so immense that Ümmühan imagined she must be entirely beneath its notice . . . unless it should deign to consume her like a date: in one juicy bite. Ümmühan's veils gusted about her, obscuring her vision until she caught them back. Mehmed's horse quivered, white-eyed, ears rolling. Mehmed stood with a hand on its reins, an arm draped over its withers: Ümmühan thought it only stood, even then, because it was hardened to cannons and to war.

The rukh lurched two steps, a red-crested head dragging its curved neck into jerky thrusts until it found its balance. Stone-gray wings flipped closed, concealing paler flanks. The hooked beak snapped with a keratinous *clack* and Ümmühan's breath of awe swelled her chest painfully. *Great is the God from whose studies such wonders arise!*

She would write a poem to the praise of this great bird and the man who had tamed it.

The ladder unrolled across the rukh's shoulders, and in a billow of white and indigo a figure slid down. His veil concealed everything about him except for eyes that must have been almost black once, before the blue of incipient blindness hazed them. He squinted, examining the man and woman who awaited him.

"Kara Mehmed," he said. "I am Mukhtar ai-Idoj, al-Sepehr and servant of the Scholar-God. I come at the summons of a woman who loves you."

He ignored Ümmühan utterly, as was polite—not even an acknowledging flick of his gaze. That did nothing to silence the thrill that rose up in her at the sound of his voice. She could not cling against Mehmed's side, not here where another man could see them. But she did step back as if she were lending her support, as if she were shrinking behind Mehmed for protection. It would have the same effect.

"I too come to the summons of a woman," Mehmed said. "Are these not strange days?"

Ümmühan bit her lip. The veils hid so many sins.

"Stranger than you may know, Black Mehmed. Shall I speak plainly?"

"If I have my way," Mehmed answered—a flash of humor that almost made Ümmühan like him, momentarily, when all the hours she had spent pretending to adore his earnest sweating atop her softness had only resulted in her despising him the more.

"Your caliph is weak," said al-Sepehr. "He is profane. He is no true follower of the Scholar-God and Ysmat of the Beads, Her Prophet."

"That is treason," said Mehmed, but he did not sound upset.

"The caliphate needs a new king."

"I see nothing in your words to disagree with."

"That king should be you, Kara Mehmed. A strong man, a pious man. A man with many allies among the war-band. A man who will restore trade and make the caliphate a great empire again."

"I am listening," Mehmed said. "Who are you to ensure such a thing?"

"I am the priest who leads all the Rahazeen. I am the recipient of all the secret knowledge of Sepehr al-Rachīd ibn Sepehr, whom the uninitiated call the Sorcerer-Prince. And trust me"—even behind his veil, Ümmühan could tell that al-Sepehr smiled—"his wizardry is a very great and holy wizardry indeed."

"And what do you gain?"

"An ally," said al-Sepehr. "An end to persecution for my tribe. Renewed trade and political stability. All the things I gain by also trading with the Khan of the horse tribes—oh, you have heard? Yes, Black Mehmed. I hide nothing from my allies." He leaned forward slightly and pulled the veil from his face.

Though her heart beat savagely in her chest, Ümmühan averted her eyes. But she could not close her ears to the roll of persuasion that filled his voice when he said, "Trust in me."

She thought she would have offered him her heart on the point of her knife if he'd asked—and not only for love.

Mehmed considered for a long while. And then he said, "Your blood on it."

Al-Sepehr drew a dagger from his sash and set the point against his wrist, above the border of the tattoos. He pressed down until the skin dented, and a red bead welled. "I have a few men—chosen from among the finest of the Nameless—in Asitaneh already. I can deliver the army: my priests have converted their leaders. All I need now is you, Mehmed Caliph."

The moment could have chimed like crystal. The wind fell away; the desert was as still as the moment after the last breath of a dying man.

Kara Mehmed nodded and Ümmühan allowed herself to breathe again.

"We must kill the bearer slaves," al-Sepehr said. "And in their blood I will write your destiny. With their entrails I will divine the path that will lead you there."

"The bearers," Mehmed said. "Who will bring my flower back to Asitaneh?"

"Kill them," said Ümmühan. "The rukh must eat." She showed her palm to the vast bird as if to a pony, smiling when it cocked its head to stare at her out of an eye she could have stood inside. "As for me? When we return to Asitaneh to claim your new city, my caliph, my lion? I shall ride the wind."

Mehmed grabbed her shoulder, clawed fingers bruising. The fabric of her robes bunched under his grip. Perhaps silk had not been the best choice for this day's activities. She turned to meet eyes narrowed with jealous rage and quickly downcast her own. Men were weak, so weak, contemptible.

Men, but not al-Sepehr.

"Alone with this one?!" Mehmed fumed.

"He is a priest!" she said. "And I am the woman who loves you. I have given my heart and my will over to only one man, my lion. Fear not that they will ever desert you."

Oh, she lied behind the veil. But when she smiled behind the veil, who could know it?

Not Kara Mehmed, blinded by his heart, his arrogance, and his-ambition. He looked away from her; his clutch at her shoulder became a caress the length of her arm.

"Very well. Sacrifice the bearers," he said.

"Have no fear of me, Kara Mehmed. Show me your weak caliph," the al-Sepehr said. "It is time a strong man ruled."

Ümmühan needed nothing in this moment, save to die. Thirty years a poet, twenty-five years a slave; lover of great men, weak men, men who aspired to neither; conspirator, visionary, secret priestess—nothing in her experience ever had or ever could rival this: winged flight.

The body of the rukh rose and fell between its toiling pinions. The head stayed steady, more or less, as the long neck compensated. Ümmühan bestrode a saddle just behind the crested skull, with straps and harnesses—and al-Sepehr's arm about her waist—to hold her in place.

She wouldn't have cared if he'd hurled her to her death, if this was the last thing she experienced. The hot wind tattered her veils. It blew them back against her face. The ground rushed below—she knew by the wind how it rushed—but it was so far beneath them it seemed to crawl. It was unwomanly, but she laughed and could not stop laughing. Though she felt the stiffness of al-Sepehr's disapproval in the grip of his hands, she threw her hands into the air and tried to grasp the wind.

Let him disapprove. Ümmühan was flying.

They swept over cragged and crenellated lands, spinning wide around the city to approach it from the sunset shadows of the east. Their shadow raced them to one side, an oblique smear cast by the last rays of the sun. A salt pan shone like a pool of blood in the sunset. Above it, the curls of a rising dust-devil rose in lazy spirals.

That was wrong. The sun was setting now, the air cooling and settling. Ümmühan was no wizard, but she had been the lover of a few, and she knew the desert weather well enough for metaphor.

When blue tongues of flame lashed through the rising vortex, she was sure. "Al-Sepehr," she said, returning her hands to the saddlebow. "Are you prepared to meet a djinni?"

"I see it."

The rukh dropped its tail like a hovering hawk and backbeat, throwing Ümmühan's shoulders into al-Sepehr's chest. He bore it stolidly, reaching around her to choke up on the rukh's reins as the whorl of fire whipped higher. Ümmühan felt the expansion of al-Sepehr's body, heard the rush of air as he drew and held a breath.

Out of the vortex rose a naked figure of an azure man, his ropy body wreathed in cerulean fire. He towered; he ascended; he folded hands more broad than the rukh's wings over lean forearms latticed with distended veins that might have been small rivers. His lower body rose in flame from the shadows of the rising twilight. The light cut a bright ascending line across his chest, like sunset chasing up the slope of a mountain. He tipped a head so wreathed in the haze of altitude and distance that his features blurred with it. Ümmühan could not be sure, but—craning her head back—she thought his eyes slitted against the sun, or perhaps in irritation.

The heat blasting from the djinn curled her eyelashes. She sensed the rukh's desire to withdraw, the force of will with which al-Sepehr held it steady.

A rumble like the earth cracking wide shook the air under the rukh's fluttering pinions. It was a moment before Ümmühan realized the djinn was speaking.

"MUKHTAR AI-IDOJ. YOU HAVE TRIED TO *TRICK ME*."

All that breath came back out of al-Sepehr in one long, liquid, convoluted, incantatory pronouncement.

"O Fy-m'shar-ala-easfh-ala-wtqe-shra-tw'qe-al-nar-ala-fasheer! Hail, prince of fire! Hail, prince of the air! . . . Actually, I rather think I *succeeded* in tricking you. But only because you thought to turn the trick on me."

Around and around the pillar of the djinn, the flames crawled higher. Ümmühan would have squeaked, perhaps even screamed, but she could not get a breath. The djinn's name rang through her head as if she had been struck like a gong and she hastened to memorize it—a poet's trained recollection a blessing now—as it had been all the times she snuck and spied. Mnemonics and images built upon each other as she built a room in her house of memories just for it, and for everything it might say. *In the path of the whirlwind, the moonlit desert lies afire.*

She expected the djinn to roar, to bellow. With a shock she realized that these thundering tones were its equivalent of mocking, furious sweetness. "THE BLOOD OF A WORLD STAINS YOUR HANDS, AL-SEPEHR."

Those hands—tattooed with geometric patterns in black on the backs, rust-colored on the palms—did not move on the great bird's reins. Al-Sepehr didn't seem to see the need to raise his voice either. He leaned over Ümmühan's shoulder, his breath hot on her ear, and said, "You were content enough to trigger war when you believed you were thwarting me. So you're here in wrath and fire because I won a wager you accepted willingly?"

The djinn settled back—Ümmühan would have said on his heels, but his heels were obscured by the vortex of the tornado of fire that he rose out of. "MY KIND WOULD REJOICE SHOULD YOUR WET, COLD LITTLE RACE BLOT ITSELF FROM BENEATH THE FOUR PILLARS OF THE SKY."

"But a war that serves my purposes, O Fy-m'shar-ala-easfh-ala-wtqe-shra-tw'qe-al-nar-ala-fasheer—that, you will have none of? That, you threaten and rage at me for? Tell me, Djinn—did you come here in the hopes that I would make some other error?"

The djinn looked crafty, and remained silent.

"So destroy me, then," cried al-Sepehr. "If you do not think I fooled you fairly! Destroy me, if you think the compact permits it! Destroy me, if you think your case would stand before the Justices Eternal!"

He was, Ümmühan thought, beyond magnificence.

The djinn crossed his arms and boomed, "WHERE IS YOUR GREEN RING NOW, AL-SEPEHR?"

"The Green Ring was stolen from me, O Djinn! Its curse lies on another head now! But the bargain was not that I should keep it." Though Ümmühan could feel him shaking, al-Sepehr stripped his veils from his face, tossed his head back, and laughed. "But it's true. I have bested you, and you admit it."

The djinn's expression could have been no blacker if he actually were ablaze. "I DO."

Al-Sepehr smiled. "Then you must serve me and seek redress, as the ancient pacts require. Is this not so?"

"YOU TOO ARE BOUND BY THOSE PACTS. I AM FORBIDDEN TO HARM AN-OTHER AT YOUR COMMAND."

"Fear not; I will not abrogate the ancient contracts." Al-Sepehr's voice rang with masculine calm and certainty.

"YOU WILL REGRET THIS CHOICE, AL-SEPEHR."

"I regret many things, O Djinn. After the manner of princes, I often do them anyway.

"Here are my commands. You will travel to ancient Erem, called Erem-of-the-Pillars, called City of Jackals and first of that epithet. You will seek there a woman known as Edene . . ."

11

In the court of Qori Buqa, the twins experienced a rough and unpredictable luxury. There might be only limited water for drinking and none for bathing—but the lack was made up by rich wines in golden goblets, by scented oils that could be slathered on the skin and scraped away again with implements of gold and mother-of-pearl. There might be no flour for bread, no oats for porridge—but there were potted meats from Song, rank in their complexity, and there were lychees preserved in syrup and fragrant cinnamon. There might be no blankets, but there were furs.

Two trading parties set out in the first five days after the twins' arrival—one east and one west, both heavily guarded by Qersnyk riders. Qori Buqa was attempting to reopen the Celadon Highway. No caravans arrived with fresh materials, though, and laborers and artisans conscripted from the very borders of the empire by Mongke Khagan or his father Temusan, Khagan before him, made do with what was available or could be salvaged as they attempted to rebuild.

In the meantime, Qori Buqa Khan—or Khagan, as he had begun to style himself with Saadet's encouragement—gave away riches to his men at every opportunity—horses and salt, goats and sheep, pelts cured supple as if they still graced a living animal.

In a fashion, the Khans were to be pitied. They did not wield the spiritual authority of an al-Sepehr and must ensure the loyalty of their tribesmen by providing plunder and through even more direct forms of bribery. It was a simple matter of appealing to the greed of men who had not yet come into wisdom, and spiritual adulthood, and the embrace of the Scholar-God.

The Khans led by acclaim rather than by birthright, and so the trade routes must be reopened if word was to spread of Qori Buqa's assumption of the Khaganate. He could not rule the wide-ranging people of the steppe unless they came to support and acknowledge him, and once they did he must be able to feast them and reward them. Which would mean the promise of new lands to conquer and new riches to pillage. Empires must grow to live, and there was only one way for an empire to grow.

It did not take long for the twins to identify the major powers among Qori Buqa's war-band. There was Hulegu, gray-templed and suspicious, the traditionalist—a role she wondered if he had fallen into because he was the youngest of Qori Buqa's inner council and wished to be taken seriously. And there was Gansukh, with a forked beard and a bald pate and a taste for coats dripping with gold embroidery. He was friendly to Saadet, which set her more on her guard than Hulegu's patent dislike.

Summers on the steppe were balmy by standards honed to the Rahazeen wastelands. When Qori Buqa summoned the twins to ride out with him hawking, Saadet's now-habitual wardrobe of trousers, robe, veil, boots, and weapons demanded no amendment. She simply rose from the couch where she and Shahruz had been reading, made sure her veil was well wrapped about her face, and followed the messenger through the doorway and down a hall contained between the inner and outer files of the keep's stone wall. It was narrow enough that even Saadet must turn her shoulders to pass from time to time—where stones made level on the exterior protruded less neatly into the passageway—and a ceiling too recently rebuilt to have yet garnered many smoke stains hunched close overhead.

Qersnyk tribesmen did not believe in stables, per se. The Khan's herds were guarded by boys and girls out on the plain that stretched in all directions around Qarash, and selected animals brought to the would-be Khagan for his use as required. By the time the twins attained the courtyard, six matched mares stood in readiness. Their white-dappled, steel-colored coats were brushed gleaming, their pale faces marked by expressions of alertness. They wore Qersnyk saddles—high-cantled, high-pommeled—with a bar at the front of each, padded thickly in leather. The horses' caparisons were inky black, appliquéd in golden curlicues and spirals. Women and men garbed in knee-length coats and fur-trimmed hats adorned with similar designs—the gold rose like stylized flames along the plackets and unfurled over the yokes—stood beside five of them. A boy held the reins of the sixth out to the twins.

"Her name is Khongordzol," the boy said.

Thistle. Well enough. The twins showed the mare the flat of their hand, and waited while she snuffed it. They wondered where Qori Buqa was—and, more immediately, his mount. But as the men and women in black and gold seemed to respond to some signal the twins did not recognize by assembling each beside their stirrup, the twins too moved to the ready position—and so, when five black-coated Qersnyk lofted as one into the saddle, the Rahazeen in white and indigo was only a half beat behind.

Those skirted coats did flare dramatically.

The mare—Thistle—sidled. Shahruz straightened her with a touch, then the twins settled a pistol more comfortably in their sash. Now younger boys—and one girl—also in the black-and-gold livery proceeded across the blue flagstones toward them, each one carrying an enormous bird on braced arms at shoulder height.

The twins had heard of the Qersnyk hunting eagles, but never seen one. These could be nothing else: the copper-black wings mantled over children's arms that trembled at their weight, the napes of feathered necks that shimmered in sunlight as if they had been bathed in gold dust, the great round amber eyes larger than a man's. Their beaks were black, and each hooked to a point like an awl. The strong forecurves of their wings could break a man's arm. Their talons could pierce a wolf's skull.

They were used to *hunt* wolves, or so the twins had heard. Saadet hoped faintly that it was not wolves they would be hunting today.

A clatter of hooves drew the twins' attention as another mare entered the courtyard, bearing Qori Buqa. This one was also a gray, with a bone-white face still dark around the eyes. Tiny freckles of red hair speckled her coat everywhere it showed through crimson and gold, drawing into a mark like a dripped bloodstain down one side of her throat and across one shoulder. Even in close quarters, constrained by the rein and the would-be Khagan on her back, she moved like a falcon's shadow speeding over snow.

Saadet caught her breath to see her.

The twins would have expected the eagles to protest this sudden appearance, but not one bated. Their young handlers deftly hooded each bird, and each bird was handed up to Qori Buqa or one of his falconers. The jesses—soft leather bands attached to the birds' ankles—were made fast to the padded bars of every saddle except the twins'.

With a wave of his hand, Qori Buqa summoned Saadet up beside him. The twins' mare responded to their shift in balance like a soldier to welcome orders. Qori Buqa's eagle mantled as the mare shifted, then balanced itself with a switch of its tail. Up close, they were still impressive—even to one inured to the presence of the rukh and her young.

"Saadet," said Qori Buqa, as the twins fell in beside him. "We are pleased at your companionship."

She nodded, eyes downcast. "Thank you for the loan of the mare."

"You will enjoy her." He laid a hand possessively on the neck of his own mount, just above where the so-called bloodmark began. "When we are out of the city, I would say we should race . . . but it would be unfair to Khongordzol, and she's too good a horse to break her heart running her against Syr."

"Syr," the twins echoed. *Desert.*

"She is of the line of the varnish-colored mare Temurbataar. In her time, there was no fiercer." Lightly, Qori Buqa touched the bright cords knotted into her mane. "She is my heart," he said.

Saadet watched, and steeled her heart against him. He was a tool, no more: a useful contrivance whose proper application would be one of the elements combining to bring the Nameless out of the desert, out of exile and privation, into their rightful place in the world.

She could not like him.

Well, perhaps a little. It would make certain things harder, it was true. But others . . . so much easier.

"What's the eagle's name?" she asked him.

He gave her a strange, wary look. "They have their own names," he said. "They don't tell us, and we don't pretend to know."

Her lips formed an O. He looked at her curiously, but she could not tell him what it was she thought of.

For the Nameless, she told herself, and heard her brother answer:

For the world.

THE EMPRESS WORE GRAY: SILK NOIL, ROUGHLY LUSTROUS, EMBROIDERED with peacocks up the front, their tails sweeping around the extended hem. Her hair was coifed and oiled, the pins pinching her scalp and drawing the skin of her face taut. But as she stood beside her husband in the audience chamber, listening to the pleading of wizards, she felt like a lost child rather than a queen.

She watched Hong-la and Yongten-la kneeling on the carpet before her, as prone as dogs with self-abasement—and all their appeasing could do nothing to lift the chill from her belly. Her kingdom—so hard and so newly won—crumbled in her hands, and there was nothing she could do to fight that dissolution.

"Your august majesty," said the Wizard Hong without raising his eyes, "I must beg you to reflect, to consider . . . is there anything you could have said or offered—in a secret trade agreement, in a letter to a brother king—that might be construed as permission to enter the city? We cannot find a flaw in the wards; they have not been broken. The only other possibility our theorists have been able to offer is that, somehow, inadvertently—"

"Are you suggesting," Songtsan said coldly, "that I am ill-educated enough to have committed such an error? Were my tutors in matters of thaumaturgy and state not wizards of your very own Citadel? Were you yourself not one such?"

Yongten-la shifted on the rug, but it was Hong-la who replied.

"It is as your majesty says," Hong-la agreed silkily. "But if an assassin enters and if the locks were not broken or picked—it must be that someone has thrown a window wide."

"Perhaps it is your own art that is lacking," said Songtsan. "Perhaps you cannot heal the breach because of your own inadequacies." Yangchen thought it was only her own intimate knowledge of the emperor that allowed her to notice the strain in his voice when he said, "Perhaps if I started burning wizards, you might achieve some results."

Yongten-la began to speak now, but Yangchen did not hear beyond the gist that he was arguing—again—for evacuation. She could hear nothing over the howl of her own blood, the sudden wave of miserable certainty. Someone had indeed left the door wide to the demonlings. Someone had indeed invited them within.

She put a small cold hand out to her husband to steady herself; he took it in his large warm one but did not glance at her.

Hong-la, however: Yangchen felt his eyes upon her, although he glanced away before she recovered herself enough to check.

Yongten-la was saying, "Refusing to evacuate undermines your authority with the peasantry, your majesty. Peasants are rioting and sneaking away in the night—even when your soldiers turn them back, it eats away at your appearance of unassailable power."

"My brother!" Songtsan cried, his voice finally rising. "Is it not obvious? My treacherous brother Tsansong is an accomplice of the Sorcerer-Prince. It is he who has made these pacts, he who has taken every possible step to overthrow me, and he who has made vile bargains with dark forces in order to rule in my place. You were there!" His trembling finger indicated Hong-la.

Yangchen swallowed bitterness.

How could he not feel her guilt through her trembling palm, read it in the pinch between her eyes? How was it not blazoned on her face in scarlet, like a whore's cut mouth?

By all the horned kings of the underworld, she thought. *O, not Tsansong. Not Tsansong.*

Me.

EMPEROR AND EMPRESS DINED ALONE THAT NIGHT, SEATED AT A HARDWOOD table on the woven rectangular seats of yoke-backed chairs. The servants who whisked things from sideboard to plate and back again moved like ghosts in the rustle of their livery. It was all Yangchen could do to place each morsel between her lips and chew.

She did not raise her eyes to her husband's face when at last, hesitantly, she said, "I could go among the sick, my emperor. That would be seen as evidence, at least, of our goodwill."

"Can you change a dressing?" he said, after a silence so long she knew mockery would follow. "Can you wield a lancet?"

"I can hold a hand," she said. *Something, anything, to ease the pain I have engendered.*

He shook his head in exhaustion. "I forbid it."

THEY RODE OUT WITHOUT GUARDS, WITHOUT GUIDES, WITHOUT SOLDIERS. Five falconers, a man who would be emperor, and a Rahazeen assassin, all mounted on gray mares. With them ran a dozen milling dogs that dodged expertly around the feet of unperturbed horses. The sun shone on the horses' jingling fittings, on the banners the riders were handed as they passed through the gates of the keep and into the city proper.

The banners insured that people made way before them, and not one made a gesture against the Khagan. On every corner stood men in armor, helms bearing the three-tiered falls that proclaimed their loyalty—but they were on the corners, not surrounding Qori Buqa with their bodies.

It was a grand gesture, Shahruz understood. And in itself it might help build loyalty. The Qersnyk respected a leader who did not give himself airs.

But nothing would silence the little voice that said, with wonder, *It would be as nothing to assassinate this man.*

In the cool of morning, before dust began to rise, the reborn city was different than it had been in the afternoon. The streets were not yet so crowded, and the slanting rays of sun cast deep shadows beneath the awnings of street vendors. It was speedier traveling in the retinue of a man for whom everyone else made way. They reached the edge of the city before the sun had shifted a hand's span up the sky, while apricot color still stained a bright horizon, and they passed through hastily spliced and rehung gates that remained sharp with splinters.

The steppe beyond was gilded, too. Grazed short between the heaps of dead, the clumped grass snagged the light and shredded it.

There was conversation as they rode, jokes and casual banter. The falconers spoke to their lord as if to an equal, and these bare-faced women showed no hesitation in bandying words with the men. The twins did not join in. Saadet could feel Shahruz's stoic disapproval, and while she wondered how she was supposed to win the Khagan's interest by effacing herself, she did not have the strength to disagree with her brother.

At least he was kind enough to keep his distaste at the weakness of her flesh, which he was forced to share, to himself.

Not a hundred cubits from the city wall, they started a hare. The animal bunched and leapt, scattering puffs of dust with every hop. One of the dogs—a lean-barreled thing the color of dust—yipped and gave chase, but a sharp whistle brought it reluctantly to heel. The twins tensed, expecting to see Qori Buqa or one of his attendants unhood an eagle, but though one man half-reached for a bow before thinking better of it, they took no further action.

The twins looked at Qori Buqa curiously. He must have read the glance accurately, because he said, "The eagles are for nobler game."

It was an hour more (and the carnage of the battlefield still spread around them) when the riders fanned out into a broad arc with perhaps five minute's ride between. The dogs wore back and forth before the horses, carving patterns through the grass. The riders could still see each other plainly, horses standing shoulders and neck above the grass as if they swam through it.

The twins, having no hawk of their own, remained with Qori Buqa. He rode silently, gaze fastened on the horizon. Saadet wondered what it was, exactly, that he was looking for.

The falconers had lifted their eagles onto the fist when they commenced to hunt. The twins tried to imagine holding up that stolid, living weight for hours on end. Their arm ached just contemplating it.

On the left, one of the falconers cried out. Turning, the twins saw her unhooding her bird while all the others, even the man who would be Khagan, refrained. So precedence was established by whosoever saw the prey first, and even a king respected that. It was interesting to know.

The falconer held the bird up for a moment, allowing it to orient itself. Saadet saw it raise its wings and lean forward like a racer crouched to start. Then the falconer turned her mare away from the prey—

whatever it was, the twins could see it only as a rippling line crashing through the grass—and into the light wind that lofted the twins' veil and the horses' unbraided tails sideways. She drew her arm back and punched the air, hurling the eagle into flight.

Its wingbeats sounded like the heavy flapping of a banner in a stiff wind. From feathertip to feathertip, the twins thought it spanned the length of a horse, and she was not surprised that at first it struggled to gain altitude. But then it caught the wind and its flight smoothed, dexterous pinions grasping the air to draw it forward. It banked and came around with the breeze at its back now, still climbing. Craning back, the twins could see its head swivel as it sought whatever unfortunate animal it had marked previously.

It mounted the sky, and Saadet could not help herself: she gave a little gasp of fear and wonder as it stooped.

Of course she could not have heard the clap of its wings as it folded them, the rush of wind against its feathered body. But she imagined them, and what she did hear was the thud and crack—quite simultaneous—as the eagle vanished behind the veil of waving grass, striking its prey to earth with all the force of its dive behind it.

Its handler had already kicked her horse into motion. The twins watched as she charged forward, reining up just shy of where the eagle had struck, within the ring of circling dogs. She whistled high and sharp, raising her glove. The twins could see a bloody chunk of meat upon it.

Laboriously, the eagle heaved itself into the air again, settling on the falconer's gauntlet after beating the air with a half-dozen strokes. It pounced on the meat, pinning the meal against the glove with one taloned foot and tearing gobbets free with that hooked beak.

"The eagle would rather have skinned meat than go to the trouble of ripping its own prey apart." Qori Buqa's smile was only in his voice. It did not lift the corners of his moustache at all. "Everything is lazy."

Before the twins could answer, he reined forward—along with all the other falconers (and the twins, who closely followed) closing the gap. One of the others swung down in the saddle—he did not dismount, just hooked a leg over his horse's back and performed a casually acrobatic feat that left the twins blinking—and came up again with a blood-spattered

red fox limp in his hand. He paunched and bled it there on the back of his mare, while the mare appeared unmoved by blood and the presence of a dead carnivore.

"A good omen to start," said Qori Buqa. "The fox is clever and preys on lambs. Now let us see if we can run a wolf to ground."

IT WOULDN'T DO TO SAY REVOLUTION WAS BREWING IN THE STREETS OF TSAR-epheth. Not yet, in any case . . . not quite. But Hong-la was not a naïve man, nor one new to politics. He saw the grainy stares, quickly hidden, when he passed through the streets. He saw the evidence of filth hurled by night against the palace walls and heard of the midnight assemblies that melted into the drifting ash when the emperor's soldiers arrived—or, on a few occasions, were broken up with killings and arrests. Most sa-liently, he saw the graffiti chipped or scribbled on walls and the handbills that younger wizards and novices brought to his attention and that of Yongten-la.

Even the suspicion of sedition would be enough to see the perpetra-tors dismembered or burned, assuming they made it into custody alive. That so many were willing to take that risk so boldly told him how badly Songtsan's authority had slipped.

Rumors of Tsansong's survival abounded, but it was more than that. People believed in princes because princes were magic. They were talis-manic protection against the wolves and wickedness of the untamed world. When the caravans did not arrive, when the demonspawn clawed from your lover's mouth, when the young prince escaped a trumped-up death sentence—or so more and more were whispering—when the Cold Fire was cold no longer: what use were princes then?

Standing over the second flayed corpse of the morning, Hong-la rinsed caked blood from his fingers and implements. Tsering-la rattled her tools in the basin on the other side of the dissecting table. The steam smelled of sulfur—the hot water rose from the depths of the mountain raining ash and cinders over the struggling city—and iron, from a source closer at hand. The reek of bitterness suited Hong-la's mood.

"What use are princes . . ." Hong-la began to ask, and checked him-self.

Tsering did not even glance his way. "What use are princes when the early evidence would suggest that the mountain is cracking open, and the Carrion King stalks the streets of Tsarepheth itself, garbed in the skins of his prey?"

He snorted. It was nearly a laugh. "Something like that, yes."

She shrugged. Her tone without judgment, she said, "Yongten says Songtsan still has not agreed to evacuate—but that sources close to him will argue for it."

And he did not choose to pass along how he knew that. Hong-la wondered if the head of the order was protecting the empress, or someone else. He lifted his dripping hands from the basin and waited until the circulating water ran clean. "The sick can't travel. Does he realize who must stay to nurse them?"

Yongten-la knew that, of course. And so did Tsering, still avoiding his gaze as he turned to her. The dead woman between them stared from lidless eyes, her face rendered forever a mystery.

"Would you desert the Citadel?" she said. "Tse-ten of the Five Eyes did not, in his time."

Hong-la picked up his clean scalpel, steam still rising from it in curls. "The sky was higher in those days," he quoted, "and beneath it giants strode."

"Well, our sky may sag a bit, but that makes up for the difference in height," she said tartly. "Maybe Songtsan thinks a good decimation will teach the rebellious wizards a lesson about not standing up to the Bstangpo?"

"Fear of the wizards is half what's keeping the populace from dragging him and his wives through the streets."

Tsering showed no squeamishness as she began flexing the dead woman's fingers, her wrist joints, examining the degree of rigor. "He's got plenty of guards and soldiers."

"Until the demons claim those too." Hong-la was arguing just to argue, a character trait in which he took no particular pride . . . although that, coupled with the desire to *win*, was probably closely related to his success both as a bureaucrat and as a wizard. At home, and here among these peculiar, wise barbarians of whom he had grown so fond, despite their unnatural attachment to square-hilted sheath knives perpetually stuck through their belts and their tendency to worship rocks. "And more will grow ill on the journey. Will they bring the infestation down on the winter capital, then, like a dog sick with fleas?"

"Tool marks," Tsering said, all weariness and every trace of banter dropping from her tone.

"Excuse me?"

"Tool marks," she repeated. "Tool marks along the bones and in the muscle. The kind you'd get from a skinning knife. Does the Carrion King use a skinning knife?"

"I've never met him," Hong-la admitted. "But to a preliminary approximation . . . no?"

When Tsering looked up, her eyes shone. "So stop grumping, old man, and give me a hand lens."

BY AFTERNOON, THE TWINS AND THE OTHERS HAD LUNCHED IN THE SADDLE on airag and jerky—and each of those saddles had a fox and an antelope or two slung from its bow. They had finally left behind the evidence of recent war and the constant drone of the flies, though the warmth of the sun lay drowsily enough on Saadet's veil to make up for it.

They had glimpsed a great steppe lion, tall at the shoulder as the mares, his matted black mane appearing and disappearing between stems of long grass as he paced them for a little while—but he was too much even for the Qersnyk eagles, and the dogs were adamant in pretending they had seen no such animal passing. As the lion apparently thought discretion the best approach to seven armed riders, they parted ways each unmolested by the other.

Saadet had ceased expecting any wolves. Weren't they night hunters? She found herself trusting Shahruz to handle the reins and trusting the mare to stay with her sisters while Saadet drifted in the welcome quiet.

The wolves must have been denned in the long grass, because when a pair broke away from the riders they started up almost under the hooves of the leftmost mare. The dogs had not even noticed them until they bolted—perhaps they were still too busily engaged in ignoring the lion— but once the wolves broke cover the dogs rounded and fell together in the ragged teardrop shape of a coursing pack.

The wolves—yellow and buff, stippled gray, moth-nibbled and lanky in their summer coats—vanished among the grass. The twins could track them only as a ripple in the grass, which they slipped through with greater facility than did the surging, baying dogs.

Qori Buqa crowed with delight, turning his horse into the wind. The wolves, wise to the hunt, had swung wide to run straight downwind—the most difficult direction for the eagles to fly, as the twins had seen demonstrated again and again that the massive birds' awe-inspiring mastery of the air was dependent upon a stiff headwind.

But now five eagles were airborne, wheeling up on the rising currents of the afternoon, and the sixth was heaving itself into the sky behind them. Where to lesser game the falconers had flown one bird at a time, now they all rose skyward. The twins noticed also that this time the birds flew up, circling overhead like a vortex of vultures, and waited on overhead. They wondered how the trainers kept them from attacking one another—

Qori Buqa sent his bloodmarked mare into a canter, her pale head with its dark-ringed eyes like a bobbing skull. The twins' mount followed, a thunder of hooves to echo the fading thunder of wings, and the falconers fell in behind them.

Three strides, and the pursuit was all. The twins crouched close to Thistle's neck, letting her choose her own path over the unfamiliar terrain. It was easier than riding a rukh; at least a mare was unlikely to eat you. A confused welter of impressions rattled the twins: the hard breaths of the charging mare, the cries of men and hounds, the whip of grass against thighs insufficiently protected by cotton trousers. Ahead, the wolves running flat-out, the pack of dogs strung out in single file behind them. The sudden break in Thistle's stride as she turned aside to follow Qori Buqa's mount.

There was exhilaration in the run, the rush of air through their veils—and yet Saadet could not help but feel a certain kinship for these wolves, harried and hounded.

An eagle yelped. A shadow brushed the twins' face. The twins turned, grabbing at mane as they unbalanced in the saddle, and saw the folded wings, the twist in the air, the dart-sharp projectile of the first eagle strike the trailing wolf.

She cried out as its talons pierced her loins, the force of the blow driving her hindquarters to earth. The twins heard the thud of impact, the snap of shattered bone. She came around, snarling, and her mate whirled, too.

His break in stride saved him. The second eagle missed, striking the earth beyond, a cloud of yellow dust dulling the shining pinions. The dogs circled, bristling, tails low, ears flat, and the male wolf lunged for the grounded eagle.

It fanned its wings, hissing. He jumped back as it struck with its beak. The female screamed as a second eagle—the Khagan's bird, which the twins recognized by the crimson jesses—struck her neck, and the male spun around again. A fourth eagle barreled into his side, clinging with hooked talons and wing-flapping to drag him away from the female, but he was not—this time—distracted. Yellowed teeth, hooked like daggers, latched into the upper part of the Khagan's eagle's wing.

The wolf's head whipped around. The female wolf screamed again as the eagle was torn away from her, and the eagle screamed as the male wolf tossed it against the ground. Qori Buqa and one or two of the falconers shouted—

Saadet could not have said later if it was calculation, reflex, or something else—but one of the twins' pistols was in their hand, the sights lined up slightly above and behind where the male wolf's elbow pressed his rib cage. Past milling dogs, past beating wings—the whole center and attention on the target. A difficult shot. Not impossible.

The trigger press, the click, the scrape of the wheel—the splash of bright sparks as steel scraped pyrite.

The thunder of the gun against their palm . . . the start of the horse, who reared and neighed sharply. War mare or not, she was not hardened to the explosive sounds of such exotic weaponry.

The male wolf fell with a shriek, releasing the eagle as he cried. As if the report of the gun had been permission, the circling dogs lunged in. The she-wolf managed one more cry before she was overwhelmed, and then the falconers were swinging from their horses, wading in among dogs and dying wolves and eagles, separating the combatants. Qori Buqa himself vaulted from his mount with the agility of a younger man and ran to his wounded eagle.

Saadet sat her sidling, snorting, slowly calming mare in a wreath of acrid smoke, watching the falconers drag yapping, frothing dogs out of the fray with heavily gloved hands and felt as if they—as if she—had been party to the murder of a friend.

QORI BUQA CAME TO THE TWINS' CHAMBER THAT EVENING. HE KNOCKED ON the door frame with his own hand, and when she pulled aside the curtain amid a chiming of silver rings, he stood framed in the doorway, alone, dressed in shearling boots and an open-fronted coat trimmed in pewter-brown fur. Somewhere else in the keep, a woman was singing—a throaty, ululating wail from which Saadet could not decipher a single word.

Silently, Qori Buqa held out his hands. Clutched in them, draped over his wrists, was the perfectly tanned hide of a wolf.

Not one from the hunt that day—for those were not yet cured—but the silver-stippled black coat of a winter wolf, deep and soft as snow.

"She will heal," he said. "If she does not take a fever in the wound. She will fly again, thanks to you. She took this prize last winter, and I wish you to have it."

Saadet did not wish the pelt—she did not really *wish* Qori Buqa's *regard*—but she was constrained to seek it. She allowed him to drape the pelt over her shoulders, and likewise allowed him to switch the curtain closed. Shahruz was absent from her head; she was alone now. *I don't want to be here for this any more than you do,* she cursed inwardly, but he was silent.

Men could be so squeamish sometimes.

"Thank you, Khagan," she said. She glanced to the corner where the twins had been practicing their knife drills—Shahruz had certainly had enough to say about that—and then to the samovar heating water on a brazier beside the bed.

"Tea?" she asked him.

He smiled.

IN THE HAUNTED HOURS OF NIGHT, THE TWINS—AWAKE IN THE DARKNESS— heard the man who would be Khagan struggle with a dream. Bound by sleep, his limbs only trembled, and the words that left his throat were converted to a whine and a throaty rumble.

The twins sat up, drawing a veil across their hair and face. They laid three fingers lightly upon Qori Buqa's brow, and Shahruz whispered a swift phrase couched in fluid syllables. Saadet yearned after those words, but they vanished from her ear as quickly as from the air.

Qori Buqa did not quiet, but he turned, questing. He muttered another distorted word or two and one hand clutched at air. He muttered in his dream, a response to Shahruz's spellcasting.

Gently, the twins reached down and shook the Khan's shoulder.

His eyes flew wide. As they focused, he was reaching for a weapon he was not wearing.

"Saadet," he said. And then, "I was dreaming of you."

"My lord," she said through her veil.

"Or of us, rather." He laid his hand over hers on his shoulder. He spoke with fervor, abrupt and impassioned. "The Eternal Sky came to me in my dream," he said. "He said I should be Khagan. He said that there was no difference between the Eternal Sky and the Scholar-God, that they were different ways to address the same God. He said that you and I should be allies, and that the world would long remember our names."

Saadet smiled. "The Scholar-God's caliph would call what you have just said blasphemy."

He hitched himself onto his elbows, half-sitting. "And you?"

She shrugged. "What sky did he address you under, your Eternal Sky?"

"An Uthman—no, a Rahazeen sky."

The twins considered, and replied, "I see no reason your Eternal Sky cannot also be Rahazeen."

Out in the hall, the guard was snoring.

ASHRA'S COUGH WAS NOT IMPROVING. NOT THAT TSERING EXPECTED IMprovement: she had seen this happen too many times, to too many victims. She knew the inevitable end.

Still, Ashra moved among the sick, both Rasan and Qersnyk, coughing into her mask and ministering where she could. She was a competent physicker, and as courageous a healer as any who claimed affiliation with the Citadel. Watching her bend over one dying man or woman after another, Tsering felt a bitterness that pierced even her deadening fatigue.

It was grief, she realized, that she would not get to know this woman better, learn from her, and teach her in return.

The beer was brewing, but no one now sick would live to benefit from it. Ashra had been perfectly plain that if it were drunk before reaching full strength, its only effect might be to strengthen the infection so that a second, full-power infusion would have no power to drive it away. So they waited, and Tsering watched her new friend sicken and minister to others as she did.

The solution that came to her at last was born out of frustration as much as wizardly inspiration. The afternoon of the morning on which the first blood shone on Ashra's lips, Tsering was assisting Anil-la in necropsying yet another demonspawn. She held a steel dissecting pin in her left hand, waiting for him to reach a hand out for it—they were taking turns wielding the scalpel, from one postmortem to the next—and she found herself staring at the wickedly glinting thing, as long as her forearm and as sharp as a skewer.

"Anil-la," she said, holding it up. "Could you make something like this from obsidian?"

He pushed the magnifying lenses from his eyes with the back of his hand. "Well, the demon-ichor wouldn't corrode it, then . . . you're thinking of something else, aren't you?"

"I'm thinking that a fresh obsidian blade makes wounds that heal cleanly and rarely putrefy. And I'm thinking that Hong-la, at least, has the skill to sink a steel pin into a living heart."

It was the last-resort test of death, rarely used. If the pin moved . . . the heart was beating.

Anil-la followed her line of reason as if she'd explained it in detail. "You can't cut open *both* lungs and pull the spawn out. A person might live with one deflated lung. *One.*"

"We don't have to remove the spawn surgically," she said. "Just kill them when they're still small enough that the patient might survive them mortifying in her lungs. With the support of the blue mold, and Ashra's millet brew . . ."

"They'll leak this mess if you puncture them," he reminded, raising a scalpel with its blade already etched by ichor. "Inside the patient."

"Not if one used the process of fire intrinsic in volcanically forged glass to cauterize them. From the inside, so we do not burn the patient, too—which has been the problem with our other attempts."

He stopped, a sharp squint creasing the corners of his eyes. "You know . . . you may be on to something there. And at least we'll be working toward something, rather than sitting on our gold-plated thumbs alongside the blasted emperor."

Men had been burned for saying less condemning things of a ruler. Tsering saw the realization pass Anil's face an instant after his outburst ceased. She held his eye for a moment, and then just nodded and went back to her work.

THE STRANGEST THING WAS WATCHING THE PEOPLE OF TSAREPHETH PACK what they could onto mules and into pony drags—and onto their own backs—while Tsering herself crammed down hasty meals and toiled endlessly over the sick.

There were those who would not leave stricken family members, and most of these found themselves turning their hands to such tasks as were necessary in the field hospital. They replaced Citadel servants who took advantage of the permission they were given to evacuate with *their* families— although a perhaps unsurprising number of the latter chose to put their faith in wizards over princes, and stayed. The spawn still had not managed to penetrate the wards on the Citadel. New infections seemed to be dropping as the populace followed Yongten-la's advice to sleep by day, and in shifts, so that someone was always awake to keep watch.

Now Tsering sat at a makeshift table under the shelter of a makeshift pavilion, eating noodles dressed with ginger and toasted sesame oil so good they made her think somebody's grandmother must be volunteering in the kitchen. It wasn't *her* grandmother: most wizards had been driven to it by some personal tragedy, and Tsering hadn't come to the Citadel because she had any family left to mourn her. But for a moment, in this quiet pocket among the pavilions housing the dead and dying, she felt the warmth of her grandmother's hearth. She wrapped it around herself, mining the memory for peace and strength. The wizardly disciplines of quiet mind were well enough—but they didn't always help remind you what you were fighting for.

When she opened her eyes, Ashra was standing across the trestle, holding a blood-spotted cloth to her lips. The dark tone of her skin was faded to ash. Swollen veins crept through the whites of her eyes like clawing rose-canes. As Tsering's attention settled on her, she wiped her dripping nose on the handkerchief and said, "Hong-la says you are going to be looking for volunteers."

Tsering pushed the bowl of noodles to the side. "Ashra, no. You'll die of gangrene without the beer, and it won't be ready—"

"Until after I am dead." The Aezin woman drew herself up to her small height. "I die either way. This way, maybe you learn something."

This way, I killed you, Tsering thought.

"All right," she said.

THEY DOSED THE PATIENT WITH POPPY WINE TO NUMB THE PAIN, AND THEY bound her to an operating table to help her stay still. Tsering, whose magic had never manifested, could not perform the procedure—but she was there to assist. The surgeon would be Hong-la. There was none better, and it wasn't the surgery that worried Tsering.

It was the aftermath.

In the blue-and-yellow anteroom to the surgery suite, Tsering fluffed Ashra's pillows and held the cup for her to drink between shallow, dry coughs. The opiated wine was bitter no matter how much honey and what spices were steeped in it, but Ashra drank it with barely a grimace, teeth gritted against the evident pain of swallowing. After the first few swallows, that seemed to ease—along with her sad, shallow coughing.

She slipped into a drowsy semiconsciousness. Tsering stood back to allow the novices to disrobe her and carry her into the surgical theater.

It was a chamber chiseled from the warm basalt of the Cold Fire, and Tsering's brow dewed with sweat as she followed the litter bearers in. Hong-la was already there in all of his breadth and height, robed in physician's crimson. The heat was better for the patients, though hard on the surgeons.

Tsering helped fasten Ashra to the stone table with leather restraints—soft, with the buckles turned beneath where she could not cut herself pulling against them—and then stood back to observe.

Hong-la's expertise as a surgeon was in no small part due to his speed. The faster an amputation or a neutering could be performed, the faster the bleeding could be ended, leaving less opportunity for catastrophe. As Tsering watched now, he lifted one of his unorthodox surgical implements from the stone basin where they reposed.

The long obsidian blade glinted from chipped facets. It was more a smoky deep brown than the bottomless black its name would suggest, but even from across the room Tsering could see the vanishing sharpness of the point.

Gently, Hong-la pressed Ashra's breast aside. He measured the small hollows between her ribs with his fingertips and set the point of the blade against her skin. Ashra's eyes were closed, her breathing quick and shallow. Tsering did not think the sweat that dewed Ashra's skin was from the warmth of the room.

"Now, my dear," he said, and pushed down smooth and fast.

She made no outcry, though she tensed against the straps and the long muscles in her legs shivered. The blade slid in as if it found no more resistance in her body than in a ripe fruit. Only a thin line of blood welled around the puncture; Hong-la had chosen his point of entry with skill.

When half the blade was lost within Ashra's chest, Hong-la placed both hands upon the haft. His eyes closed. Tsering felt the sting of her lack of *otherwise* senses as she rarely would acknowledge, because while she knew Hong-la summoned his concentration and directed the process of fire intrinsic in the volcanic glass, she could not *see* it happening.

A small frustration, she told herself. *A small cost for all the recompense.*

She silenced the voice. Her focus needed to be on Ashra now.

Not even a faint curl of steam rose from the wound on Ashra's chest. The heat was all internal. But something heaved within her nonetheless, a sharp and sudden outward push that flexed her rib cage as if her heart were trying to snap itself free.

Now Ashra might have screamed, but there wasn't any air behind it. Her back arched—even the restraints could not hold her against the stone, she flexed so mightily—and the tendons in her throat stood plain as if sculpted there.

Hong-la was already reaching for the second blade. Two novices came forward to hold Ashra in place. Tsering peeled her nails from her palms. If anything, this placement was accomplished more quickly. It was as if his patient's struggles converted Hong-la into a perfectly calibrated engine. With no wasted motion, he slid the other blade into Ashra's body and focused his will within her even as she twisted. It wasn't the surgery hurting her. It was the thrashing of the demonspawn within.

A moment, no longer, and Hong-la slid the blades free again. He laid them carefully in the basin—they were glass, and could chip or shatter—and reached for pine gum and a trimmed section of calf's bladder that he would use to seal the external wounds, so Ashra's lungs would not fail.

Tsering breathed out a sigh. This was routine.

Now it only remained to be seen if Ashra could hold out against the infection long enough for them to produce the cure.

When Ashra awoke from the poppy, she was no worse than when she had been placed under. That was a relief; it suggested that the demonspawn, in dying, had done no further damage to her lungs. Tsering guessed they would have half a day, perhaps a day and a half, before the heat from the decomposing spawn would begin to poison Ashra's body.

In that time, she set out to learn everything she could about the brewing and application of the Aezin beer.

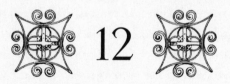

SEVERAL DAYS PASSED WHILE SAMARKAR AND TEMUR WAITED FOR THE CALIPH
to return the countersigned treaty. Temur and Samarkar both thought it
best not to wander about Asitaneh unescorted, but that did not mean
they were idle.

Samarkar took on logistics and provisioning, poring over maps with
Ato Tesefahun and Brother Hsiung. The best route to Ala-Din was by
ship to Asmaracanda—well, the best route to Ala-Din was by ship
directly across the White Sea, but no ship's master would gamble enough
to accept the future regard of a would-be Khan and a defrocked princess
as payment for carrying them to a coast bereft of major ports and in-
fested with pirates and Rahazeen—and no amount of coin was likely to
suffice.

And so by ship to Asmaracanda they would go. They would find
some way to enter the holy city—taxes were prohibitive to anyone not
there on a pilgrimage, and Hrahima had uncovered intelligence suggesting that now that the city rejoiced under Uthman skies again, foreigners
had been lynched in the streets.

"Charming," said Samarkar, when the Cho-tse related that particular
fact.

But Asmaracanda was where they could purchase supplies and mounts for the trip through the Shattered Pillars. And so to Asmaracanda they must.

Temur's bay mare Bansh would be coming with them—after their attempts to leave her in safety on the trip *to* Asitaneh, Samarkar suspected that even if they abandoned her with Ato Tesefahun, she'd just be waiting for them, flicking her ears impatiently, upon the far shore. So there was the issue of what they would do with the mare while they entered the city—or perhaps they wouldn't enter the city at all, but merely visit the caravanserai.

Samarkar had just decided that, yes, that was precisely what they would do, when Ato Tesefahun appeared beside the bench upon which she was drawing up lists of supplies. The Aezin wizard was disheveled, out of breath, a dew of sweat across his forehead.

"Grandfather," she said. "It must be dire news that brings you at a run . . . with a tiger behind you."

For Hrahima had just materialized through the door, her tail lashing.

"There's a skinned corpse in the Convent Marketplace," Ato Tesefahun said. "It fell from a clear sky, they say."

"Skinned?" Samarkar felt like an idiot with her jaw hanging open, and her inability to say anything cleverer than a repetition of Tesefahun's words did not relieve the sensation.

She knew the legends as well as anybody, the stories told to chill one's blood—pleasurably, or to frighten the gullible into obedience to whatever church you preferred. She knew that at least one history of the Citadel claimed it had been erected to keep watch on the Cold Fire and that the Cold Fire had been erected by no less an architect than the Goddess-Mother-of-the-Universe, over the pit that had been left when she hurled the (undying, unkillable) Carrion King from the broken heavens for his arrogance.

She knew that the Carrion King was said to have been able to raise the dead—in a variety of forms—and to have dressed his own raw body in the skins of his victims after an unspeakable accident with the ancient powers of Erem left him flensed alive.

"You don't actually think . . ."

"The Joy-of-Ravens is back?" Ato Tesefahun shrugged. He glanced at Hrahima.

Hrahima steepled her dagger-tipped fingers. "Would it comfort you," she asked, "if I stated categorically that he was not? Someone drove a nail through the bloodstain, however."

Samarkar realized she was still twisting her brush between her fingers, and a haze of ink droplets had spattered her paper. She set it on the pen rest and stopped herself just before pushing her inky fingers against her eyelids as if that could relieve the pressure behind them.

"I don't know my Falzeen folklore that well."

Tesefahun's eyes focused in the distance, the look—Samarkar knew it well—of the scholarly lecturer. He said, "Some hold that the djinn are born from the blood of a murder victim. Driving a new nail through the spilled blood is supposed to stop their manifestation. And there's another tradition, specific to the Joy-of-Ravens, that if you nail the blood to the earth, the Joy-of-Ravens will not be able to walk in that one's skin."

"So someone believes he's back."

"So it would seem," said Ato Tesefahun.

"I'd say the corpse was dropped from rukh-back," said Samarkar. "But on a clear day, you would notice a rukh."

THEY ATE, BECAUSE THAT WAS WHAT YOU DID IN TIMES OF TROUBLE. SAMARKAR was amused to notice that that was no different from Song to Rasa to the Uthman Caliphate. Everywhere in the world, worry could be soothed by food. As the plates were cleared and tea served, she turned to Hrahima and cleared her throat.

Samarkar did the Cho-tse the honor of not pretending she asked an idle question. "I do not know what your tasks have been as you come and go, Hrahima. And I do know it's none of my business. But I also know you hear all, and I must ask—is there any news of my brothers?"

The rings in the tiger's ragged ears jingled. "I have not heard," she said, whiskers flat. Samarkar thought it was irritation at being questioned at all, but who could tell with a cat. Dismissive and very tigery indeed, the Cho-tse continued. "You will forgive me, that that is not the news I have been seeking."

"I did not mean to imply you should," Samarkar said. She was aware of Ato Tesefahun's stare. Definitely time to change the subject.

She hesitated, studying fingernails that had begun to grow longer again after the hardships of the trail. "What if the caliph doesn't sign the treaty? What if he uses it to prove Temur's disloyalty?"

Ato Tesefahun shook his head. "Then you are on the road with a fugitive usurper. And nothing has changed."

WHATEVER THEIR FEARS OF THE CALIPH'S RESPONSE, IN THE MORNING THAT same messenger awaited them beyond the door. In his right hand he carried a copy of Samarkar's caligraphed document. In his left he carried a signet ring.

"From his serene Excellency with his compliments," the messenger said to Temur, having bowed as if before a king.

Not *as if,* Temur reminded himself, accepting the ring and the document. It was not what he would have expected if he had known to expect anything—but an ancient green-and-black jade seal, intaglio of a running horse. The workmanship was Song, but the design was Qersnyk.

"What is this?" he asked. He wanted to be sure.

"A gift," said the messenger. "It is from the Xa-shaol Dynasty."

The last time the ten thousand princes of Song had been united under one supreme ruler, they had conquered the horse clans as far west as the holdfasts of the Lizard Folk—who in those days had mastered great trading cities and a parallel empire.

The ring would have been made by a Qersnyk, in that case, an artisan brought to Song as a slave or hostage. Temur wondered if the Song princes cut off the balls of stonemasons, too, or just bureaucrats—which they did with such abandon that the amazing thing was that there were enough of them left to breed the next generation.

"A prince needs a signet," the messenger said. Temur thought he was quoting his master. "And if you can wear no crown on horseback, you can at least don a ring."

Temur smiled. One could not spend too much time keeping company with Samarkar without picking up some of the nuances of politics, even if you were a second son whose greatest ambition in life had been to serve as one of your older brother's generals. Although Temur supposed upon reflection that being a general demanded a grasp of politics too.

It had been Temur's grandfather, the legendary Great Khagan Temusan for whom Temur was named, who had tossed a lotus-carved crown set with padparadschas and sapphires to the ground and asked dismissively, "Can I wear a crown on horseback? What throne do I need but a mare?"

The crown, gold worked by masters and studded with cerulean and sunset-colored gems, had been proffered to the Great Khagan as a form of appeasement by a prince of Vharathi, one of the Lotus Kingdoms. In respect for their quick and utter capitulation, Temusan had spared the city rapine and plunder—he was not above burning those that fought too hard. A forward-looking leader, he had understood that it helped encourage the next batch to surrender faster—but he had spurned their flattery.

It was from that incident that the Padparadscha Seat, saddle-throne of the Khaganate, took its name.

According to the histories, Temusan had then ridden his horde across the plain where the crown lay, trampling it to pieces. Temur was reasonably confident that in actuality some enterprising Qersnyk had leaned down and scooped the thing up before the sapphires were shattered by pounding hooves.

"Tell his serene Excellency," Temur said, lingering over the words, "that the Khan of Khans meets his consideration with approval. You may withdraw."

He stumbled over that last permission, but imagined Samarkar standing over the messenger's shoulder, mouthing the words to him. It gave him the strength to continue.

"Thank you . . . Khan of Khans," the messenger said to the floor. He scurried backward, withdrawing without raising his head or turning.

If he wore a smile, his stooped head meant it was only for the tiles underfoot—and Temur was just as happy not to know.

He was still feeling chills up his neck from that phrase—"Khan of Khans"—when the explosion shook red dust from the crevices of the walls and rattled his bones one against another so only his flesh bound them together.

THE MESSENGER HAD VANISHED. TEMUR RAN OUT INTO THE STREET, INTO THE cool morning-textured air, not expecting to see his blue-and-crimson livery lingering—but also not expecting the flood of people that surrounded him. Men, even women, some with veils stretched hastily across sacred faces by one hand.

If they were each one and all the image of the Scholar-God, Temur thought at random, the Scholar-God had as many faces as the demon Artiquq.

The commentary floated through his head as strange and aimless as the flakes of ash that settled from the summer sky. Chunks of masonry and hissing-hot, molten glass had already fallen and scattered the street like so many tumbledown stars. Now they were followed by lighter things, which did not fall as fast.

All around him, a press of neighbors—strangers, most of them, people Temur had glimpsed in the street toing and froing or simply never glimpsed at all—rocked and strained together. Their necks craned, their chins uplifted. Some had open mouths—some of the women too, and Temur could see the outline of their gaping jaws even through the fabric when they gasped air in.

A lazy curl of smoke rose from a crater where the glass factory had been.

Temur was not sure how long he had stared—not too long, a hundred fast heartbeats or so—when he became aware of Samarkar standing beside him, tugging his arm. "We have to go."

"Samarkar?"

"We have to leave now," she repeated.

"Why?" Maybe a stupid question, but he was dumbfounded by the

shock, his ears ringing, his eyes stinging with the smallest particles the
hot wind blew.

"The sun," Samarkar said patiently. "It's rising in the west. We are in
the house of the enemy."

His stomach dropped as his chin lifted. He turned, the pain of revelation sharp beneath his chest. The diffuse gray glow of morning, though
dimmed by dust and ash, was giving way to mounting brightness in the
west. And all the shadows—vague still, but blackening—streamed toward morning . . . or where morning should have been.

"That's where we're headed." Temur's voice sounded flat. "Rahazeen
territory."

"There's a lot of desert to seek us in. Here we're hawks on the ground.
The caliph has a document that confirms your location. If the sky has
changed, he is not in control of his own archives anymore. Assuming he's
even still in control of his own head."

Temur tugged against her hand, and realized she was holding him.
There was something he should be doing.

"The glassworks exploded."

"I know."

"There will be wounded."

"I . . . know." She seemed to steel herself. The Wizards of Tsarepheth,
to a greater or lesser degree, were all physicians. Samarkar was not terribly focused on that branch of the arts—but what she knew had saved
Temur's life, once upon a time. He watched her struggle with her own
healer's nature and decided that he would not do more to make her suffer . . . which arguing certainly would. "There will also be revolution,"
she reminded. "And Rahazeen assassins seeking you. And anyone you
care for. We have to go."

Temur shook his head in frustration, and quoted, "He who speaks
truth must have one foot in the stirrup."

"Right," said Samarkar. "Because telling people true things has been
such a priority for the last few days."

He tipped his head to concede the point. "Grandfather can't stay here.
They'll use him as a hostage like Edene. And he can't come with us, not
if we travel at speed."

"We'll think of something," Samarkar said. "Come on, you need to pack. We'll talk about it while we prepare."

"I thought there would be more time."

She nodded, pulling his fingers so his arm stretched out between them. "We always do."

By now, Samarkar could pack almost as well as a Qersnyk woman. Temur had been raised to stay out of the way when the women were working—the plainsmen said, "His herds, her house," and men weren't expected to know their way around the deconstruction of a white-house—but it was easy to see that Samarkar's expectations were different. And it wasn't as if they were packing up a house. Just the gear they had traveled with, the provisions Samarkar had so far collected, and the new desert robes that Ato Tesefahun had given them. It wasn't as if the sun and wind had not already scorched and chafed them . . . but it would be good to have a second set of muffling robes to augment the ones that Nilufer, the Khatun of Stone Steading, had given them.

Temur helped her fold things until she shooed him away. At loose ends, he found himself in the stable, where he tended to withdraw when unhappy or confused. What a strange custom, keeping the horses separate from the men.

Bansh was waiting. Her long neck stretched across the stall door before he came into sight; he guessed she could identify him from his footsteps. The first glimpse of the refined bones of her face made him both want to stop, to appreciate her—and to hurry over and throw his arms around her neck. There were other horses in the stable, but they were simply noise. Bansh was the one that mattered.

His hesitation annoyed her, and with a peremptory whinny she made her irritation known. He came to her, vaulted over the stall door, and landed softly in the sand beside her. She nudged him with a velvet nose, whiskers prickling his neck. He passed an arm around her neck and leaned into her, breathing deeply of the smell of warm horse, hay, and sweets.

Somebody had been bribing her with treats, and somebody had brushed her until her liver-and-black coat shone like watered silk even in the diffused light of the thick stone stables. Temur swallowed jealousy:

he visited every day, but Ato Tesefahun's stable hands took care of her as well. *It is their job,* he told himself.

She had begun to regain some of the flesh she'd lost in their desert trek. And maybe—he ran a hand along her ribs and behind them, judging her belly. Ticklish, she stamped, but he was sure of it now—some of the signs of her thickening girth were due not to better food, but to advancing pregnancy. He ducked down to get a better look at her loins and tuck. Her udder was already taut, but that was from the milk-letting songs he had sung her when they crossed the desert, not her body's preparation for the baby. But still—

He thought a faint shiver of motion ran through her flesh. It could have been his imagination. It could have been the foal kicking.

Bansh showed every sign of being a seasoned mare; this was not her first foal. She would show her pregnancy earlier than a maiden, and while Temur did not know exactly when she had been gotten in foal, he guessed she would drop the filly in no more than four months and possibly as little as three.

In other words, on the way back from Ala-Din.

It couldn't be helped. He'd tried to leave the mare behind once and she had thwarted him. And Qersnyk ponies were often enough born on the run.

He dug in his trousers for scraps of dried fruit and fed them to her one at a time, on a flattened palm. "Good girl," he told her, stroking the warm, silky flesh behind her ears. "Good girl. You'll be seeing more of me again soon."

QORI BUQA, THE MAN WHOM SAADET WOULD MAKE KHAGAN—FOR A while—stood beside the window of the twins' chamber in Qarash, his embroidered silk robe pale against soot marks from the sacking that still licked up the stone wall. Although the sun had set and the evening glowed dull blue outside, he was still careful not to frame himself before the darkness within as he peered out across the square beyond.

"They come," he said. "That's something. I have their confidence at least."

Saadet rose from the bed on which she lay, catching wolf hides about her shoulders as she stood. He had brought her another every time he came to her, and now they hid her body in strips of warmth that stirred as she crossed the room. She was aware that what she did was calculated, and her bare face burned with shame—but she did it anyway. If she must whore herself for the Nameless . . . at least she had no illusions that history would be kind to her because of it. But she did what she did not for history, but for the future.

She paused at Qori Buqa's side, her eyes just cresting his shoulder, and let her breast and hip press his back. Beyond the window, in the forecourt beyond the walls of the keep, men and women sat or lay on scattered blankets, as in an encampment of sorts. Many of them were old; some were not and clutched children in their laps.

"There are so many," Qori Buqa said.

"Who are they?"

"Penitents," he said. "They come to be healed by the touch of the Khagan." He sighed heavily, and whatever he was about to say died on his lips as he glanced at her.

"It's strange, isn't it?" she asked.

"Them?"

"Well, yes, them. Do they really believe your touch can heal them?"

"The Khagan's touch *can* heal them." He pressed the window frame so hard his fingertips paled. "The question is, can mine?"

She paused. She fitted her hand over his, telling herself as she did it that it was manipulation. That his held breath and eventual sigh were the goal. "That's not what I meant."

He leaned back against her, trapping the wolfskins between them. "What do you find strange, Saadet ai-al-Sepehr?"

"That here we are . . . together. And yet politics ensures there is so much we cannot say to one another. There is so much you conceal from me, because of who my father is."

The corner of his moustache twitched as he hid a smile.

"You are the Khagan," she said. "In their eyes you are. Are you so sure you cannot help them, if they believe you can?"

"Not yet," he said. "Not until the clans acknowledge me. Not until—"

"You sit in the Padparadscha Seat," she supplied.

He turned from the window and pulled her into his arms, leaning back against the wall beside it. He tucked her head under his chin. "So you know it's missing?"

She nodded. "If you had it in your possession, would it not be on your mare?"

Silence, though he squeezed her shoulders tight.

"What if I could find it for you? Or my father could?"

"The woman who brought my father's saddle to me?" His breath warmed her hair. "That woman, I would marry."

LATER, WHEN TEMUR HAD BROKEN OUT HIS HARNESS TO CLEAN AND INSPECT it, Samarkar came and folded herself up to sit cross-legged beside him. Silently, with absolutely no ceremony, she held a silver cup of wine up where he could reach it.

He set his needle aside and accepted. "Thank you."

She leaned her shoulder on his. "Sunset?"

"Ato Tesefahun says the tide will be high three hours past. He has secured passage for us."

The streets were not secure—factions still fought house to house. Though the changed sky showed the Rahazeen had carried the day, soldiers and others loyal to the Caliph struggled on as if they could reverse it. Despite this, Hrahima had won through to the docks and handled arrangements.

Once the sun went down, Samarkar and Temur would try to duplicate her feat in order to find and board that one particular vessel that would bear them safe to Asmaracanda, ahead of the Rahazeen revolutionaries. For now, they bided their time and fretted . . . until a scratching at the door heralded Hrahima and Brother Hsiung, both looking defiantly sheepish and toting parcels.

"What are you doing here?" Temur said.

The Cho-tse glanced at Hsiung, who shrugged, and huffed with her whiskers back before answering. "I've always wanted to see relics of ancient Erem-of-the-Pillars. It seems likely your al-Sepehr has a collection."

Hsiung shifted his bundle over one shoulder. When Temur met the mute monk's eye, he merely shrugged. Temur wondered if that meant that he went where Hrahima went, or Samarkar, or that he was pursuing al-Sepehr for reasons of his own.

Samarkar looked up from her own cup of wine. "Well, I can't say I'm sorry you're coming."

"And what about me?"

Temur turned. His grandfather stood dwarfed in one of the other leaf-tipped doorways of the bedroom. He wore desert-traveling robes kilted above the knees of his trousers, and a cowl lay loosely over his shoulders.

"Honored Grandfather," he managed before pausing in confusion.

He wouldn't argue with a Qersnyk man of Ato Tesefahun's age who wanted to embark on a ride of thousands of *yart* across mountains and blasted lands. But Temur's great-grandfather had died in a fall from horseback well past his eightieth summer—he was said to have lost track—and Ato Tesefahun was no Qersnyk man.

"Have no fear, Temur. I'll be traveling, yes—but by ship to Ctesifon. Though it pays tribute to the caliphate, it is by treaty still a free city, and I should be as safe there as anywhere. If your war finds me still, so far away as that . . ." Ato Tesefahun shrugged and smiled. "I am not without friends here, there, in Kyiv, and in Aezin. Word that you mean to challenge your uncle will spread."

He raised his hand and Temur realized he held something in them—a cloth parcel that he had previously held in the folds of his robes.

"You'll need one of these," Ato Tesefahun said.

Temur set his wine down and stood to accept it: silk, heavy, rippling. It snagged on his roughened hands. Samarkar put her cup aside as well and reached up to accept one tasseled end as he backed away.

It was a horse banner, twice as long as Temur was tall and spangled silver-bright on midnight blue. Within an outline of gold thread a bay mare reared, one white foot flashing where it had been embroidered silver.

"Oh," Temur said. It was the most he could manage.

Samarkar looked up at him with eyes jeweled by emotion. Another man—another prince—might have taken their shining for pride or anticipation. Temur knew the once-princess well enough to recognize resignation. *And so it begins.*

"Where will you raise it?" asked Ato Tesefahun.

Temur forced his hands to stay gentle on the stretched cloth. Perhaps some part of him had been considering this, because he knew the answer at once. "Lake of Dragons," he said. "It was my grandfather's summer palace; now it lies in the disputed borderlands near Song. It is in ruins ..."

"You've seen it?"

"It was in lands that once belonged to Song that I honed my craft as a soldier." Temur walked toward Samarkar, folding the banner as he came. "You could say I grew up there, after a fashion."

"Good," said Ato Tesefahun. "In Asmaracanda, there is a friend who can help you, a scholar of the Rahazeen Nameless cult and faith who serves at the Museum of Man. His name is Juvaini Ala-Malik, and if anyone can help you infiltrate the fortress you call Ala-Din, it is he. I shall draw a map of the city, so you may the better find him ..."

EDENE PUSHED HER BELLY OUT BEFORE HER LIKE THE BLADE OF A PLOW PARTing the rich soil of the mountain meadows that were her people's summer range and garden—and as if before a plow, the ghulim parted in its path. She paced their tunnels, knowing the paths in her marrow but driven to walk them still. Besha Ghul—and others, all of whose names she knew, all of whose company chafed her—walked beside her, straightening the braid of beaded red wire that was Erem's crown, offering tidbits of meat she was glad to make no attempt to identify.

Sometimes she still caught that reek of al-Sepehr's attention—but she knew it now, and knew how to push it aside as easily as a curtain. The ring showed her, if she would listen. This was the seat of her power. No Nameless warlock could touch her here.

Here, too, the scorpions followed her—as did other poison creatures. And the ghulim—a gaunt, shadowy horde whose exact numbers were difficult to ascertain, even though it seemed her new knowledge should encompass them. But they bled away at the edges, into the shadows, so Edene felt as if ragged bits of them washed into the mass of the whole and also out again, like foam where a sea pounded against stones. As if they were created and uncreated alike out of the stuff of darkness, perhaps drawn into concrete form and then dissolved by their own will, or some will imposed from without.

Only some time (she could not say exactly) after the image occurred to her did she remember that she—Tsareg Edene, rider of the rose-gray mare Buldshak, lover of Temur of no clan—she had never seen the sea.

In any case, the ghulim came and went around her, sometimes fewer, sometimes more. But Besha Ghul was a constant, until Edene came to rely on her. Besha's cool touch soothed the increasing struggles of Edene's unborn child; it soothed alike the increasing pressure behind Edene's eyes.

The days in Erem were not like other days. The light of the daystars could cook the flesh from unwary bones: human bones. It was not merely the ghulim's essential sympathy with darkness that rendered them vulnerable. Edene knew herself protected by the ring. It whispered its assurances, and the ring would not lie. Could not lie. Not to her who bore it.

The protection extended to her unborn child, but Edene found herself loathe to trust it fully. For herself, she would take any risk at all. For the babe—

—it was different.

Even when the ring whispered, *trust. You must trust us, Edene. You must trust us to rescue your lover, to ride again with your clan. You must trust us to be Queen.*

Gravid as she was, she knew her time was approaching. Her breasts leaked a watery, milky fluid. As she walked she felt sharp spasms through her flanks and back, around the great curve of her belly. Not yet the driving pulse of labor, which she had witnessed many times, but the twinges of her body preparing itself. It didn't seem as if enough time had passed for the pregnancy to be so far advanced—but here she was, and the year not yet turned to autumn. She didn't believe so, anyway. But what was autumn in Erem?

She thought she might have entered myth. She might have been pregnant for a thousand years. She might have become a spirit of eternal bearing, someone expectant mothers and breeding mares might have talismans lashed around their bellies to protect against. She'd met a woman once, a Tashq clanswoman, who had been pregnant for twenty years, her belly taut and hard as a blown-up sheep's bladder.

Someone had told Edene that the child had died, and rather than being expelled as a miscarriage, it had turned to bone or stone in the mother's womb—where it would remain until she died. Song and Rasan wizards were supposed to be able to cut such a child from the mother and leave her alive, at least some of the time. The Qersnyk shaman-rememberers had no such art.

Although she stood under different heavens, Edene prayed to the Eternal Sky that she would not suffer such a fate.

The babe kicked, though. Hard enough that its feet might be stone, and weren't there supposed to be living rocks in the foothills of the Steles of the Sky? Nonetheless, Edene was relatively certain that nothing made of stone could move with such force and decisiveness.

"He has his mother's temperament."

It wasn't a ghulish voice, but it came from directly behind her, where only ghulim should be. She spun around even as her eyes were registering the dancing glow of fire . . . except flames were not blue.

She faced a small man, of Uthman or perhaps Messaline features. He stood on bare feet and wore pantaloons and a vest over an open-collared shirt. His hair was not long, and he would have been of unremarkable appearance had it not been indigo in color and his skin a particularly startling cerulean that echoed the flames dying away beneath his feet.

The ghulim had withdrawn from his presence, crouching on their horny paws, balanced like dogs that do not know yet if a lion plans to attack them.

Djinn, she thought, surprised at how little the recognition perturbed her. Whether it was the confidence and ambition that had come more easily to her since she escaped Ala-Din, or whether she had just seen so many weird and mythic things of late that one more could scarcely break her equilibrium, she could not have said.

She thought of what Altantsetseg would have done, and drew herself up until her spine cracked. The weight of the babe in her womb pulled her off-balance, but she straightened anyway.

She asked, "Who are you?"

The blue man scuffed one bare foot against blinding stone. "If you know not my name, I am not constrained to tell it to you."

"What are you, then?"

"One of the tribes of air and fire," he said. "The desert stone, and the hot wind that blows over. I have come to assist you."

"Who sent you?"

"Perhaps I come on my own behalf; perhaps I am not permitted to say."

"Then why should I keep you?"

He smiled. "Because you cannot make me leave."

THE LAST RED GLOW OF THE SUN PAINTED THE EASTERN HORIZON AS TEMUR swung up into his bay mare's saddle and made sure his bow was strung. The other three were on foot, which would attract less attention—if a Cho-tse could ever be said not to attract attention—but meant also that if they had to make a run for it, their best option was to scatter and try to meet again at the docks. It would have been less obvious to have everyone walk, or perhaps have Bansh pull them in a cart . . . but there was no disguising the mare's breed, stamped in her every elegant bone. And if it came to a fight, Temur would be far more effective on horseback than afoot.

He hoped they could reach the waiting vessel without shed blood, but it was sensible to be prepared for the other options. And so Temur rode, and Samarkar wore her armor—albeit under a concealing robe—even though there were less obvious ways of doing things.

Hrahima knew the ship and the sailor they sought personally, but everyone had been told the slip number of the vessel and for whom to ask when they arrived. Captain Kebede was one of Ato Tesefahun's countrymen—perhaps even a relative.

Though their path was the same as the route that had brought them in, it seemed entirely different in the dusky streets. They were not quite empty—even the specter of a revolution under way was not enough to keep the shopkeepers and water sellers of Asitaneh in their homes, and people were meeting at corner wine shops and coffee bars to huddle together and trade what news they had—but they were emptier than Temur had ever seen them. To Temur's gratitude, they at first met no soldiers other than one company of the caliph's Dead Men jogging at double time in the opposite direction, who seemed to have no pressing interest in them, but the people they did see passing through the streets were most often furtive or armed with cudgels and moving in groups.

The strangest thing was the lack of dust. It never would have even occurred to him to imagine this port city without its red haze—as soon imagine a city without streets, without houses!—but now the air was clear except the smoke of fires, the smells of cooking. And a sound that Temur did not at first recognize, in the unwonted silence of the streets, but which he soon identified as voices, some distant and some nearer, raised in a series of arguments. Normally the sounds of the city would have covered any such shouting match to anyone beyond the immediate neighbors, but in the current hush it carried clearly.

"I don't like this," Samarkar said, her voice hollow and strange within her helm. "This is how massacres start. Too many ethnicities, too many old grudges in a city like this. Somebody thinks to take advantage of the political instability, of the security forces' being busy, to avenge some ancient slight, and the next thing you know there are mobs roaming the city disposing of their hereditary enemies and people are being raped or beheaded or both."

"Go up," Temur said to Hrahima. After their months of traveling together, he knew Samarkar didn't need coddling. He was the more experienced in military matters, and she would understand from his choice of action that he had accepted her counsel and chosen accordingly.

The Cho-tse seemed to trust his decisions too, as she responded without so much as a cough of argument or agreement. She crouched, her heavy tail held out behind her, and when she uncoiled it was into a tiger-colored blur that cleared the wall of the closest building and reached the rooftop in a single prodigious bound.

Brother Hsiung moved up to Bansh's shoulder on the left, Samarkar on her right. Temur sent the mare forward, asking for a trot as his escorts jogged alongside. The less time they were in the streets, the better—and they had to cross almost the entire breadth of Asitaneh to reach the docks. Occasionally, Temur glimpsed the shadow of Hrahima leaping from one rooftop to another, on the left or the right and once directly overhead. He was aware that this was only because she allowed it.

The tension of racing through these strangely vacant streets in the failing light was like the fear before battle. His heart felt as if hung suspended inside an empty cage of his body, swaying to and fro and banging his ribs with every swing.

He had the advantage of the mare's height, and so he was the first to notice that the glow limning the buildings before them was increasing, not fading. The smell of smoke grew stronger. The wind was from off the strait, and Temur didn't need anyone to explain.

"Tell me they're not burning the ships in harbor," Samarkar said.

"That would be stupid," Temur replied. He might not know much about seafaring, but he understood the need for trade as well as any soldier. If you were fighting a war against your own people, destroying their livelihoods was unlikely to make for a long reign for the winner, or to ensure a contented and supporting populace under the new regime.

"People do stupid things," she panted, grasping Bansh's chest strap to hold herself alongside the trotting mare. Brother Hsiung waved agreement from the other side.

"Maybe it's the warehouses," Temur said, aware that he was kidding himself.

"It's a stone city," Samarkar said. "Can it be burning?"

Maybe it's a mob.

Edene, we are coming for you. "We need to be sure."

Samarkar released Bansh's saddle and remained silent, jogging grimly. Asitaneh had grown out from the port like a spiderweb, like the branching of tree limbs from a trunk. Now, as they reversed that ancient expansion, one street emptied out into another like tributaries into a larger river until they found themselves running along the broad boulevard that had been their first glimpse of the city proper on their way in. A group of soldiers wearing the uniform of the regular army were herding any pedestrian they found inside the nearest building, will they or nil they. Down the long street, shops were barred, windows shuttered, lamps within being extinguished so occupied buildings could not be told from vacant ones.

One soldier lunged after Bansh, Samarkar, and Hsiung, shouting "In the name of Mehmed Caliph, stop!" which told Temur everything he needed to know about what was going on in the palace. He lifted his bow and nocked an arrow, but before he could turn in his saddle and loose—he would have aimed it against the stones before the soldier's feet—Samarkar raised one hand and whipped a rising wall of green light around the soldier. He struck it and bounced backward, landing on his ass inside the glowing ring.

"Run for it," Samarkar gasped, breaking from her jog into jarring all-out flight. The hood of her robe fell back. She broke the fastenings at the collar and let it drop away like the cheap disguise it was. Soon it would be dark enough that the black armor itself would hide her—and while they were running, nothing would make them look less suspicious.

Her wizard-wall fell again as promptly as she had raised it, but she cast another behind them, stretching shop to shop across the street's width, which bought them time to vanish into the gloaming and the veils of smoke that began, like mist, to crowd and obscure the dim, unlit road.

A dark shape and then another dropped from the rooftops on either side. "Rahazeen," Temur said, not entirely sure of the identification until one shape reeled backward, Temur's arrow protruding from its chest, and he glimpsed the silhouette of a veiled head outlined against a white lat-ticed shutter.

There were more. Temur felt the cold battle-focus rising up in him, the tattoo of Bansh's hooves punishing his body as her flight became a charge. He rose up from the saddle, crouched above it in the stirrups, and let the mare bring him into the center of the enemy. She left the sprinting monk and wizard behind as she leapt into battle, a furious neigh of her own ringing from close stone walls.

He'd seen two Rahazeen jump from above; at least a half-dozen more barred the road before him. They knelt, couching a row of lances. Temur could have hauled on the reins, pulled his mare around and away from those murderous spear points, but he saw the improvised pike line as if through a haze of blood. It was not merely the mist and the dark clos-ing the edges of his vision in a tunnel.

He loosed twice as Bansh closed the distance. One arrow found its target and a Rahazeen pitched over, leaving a hole in the line. An assassin snatched the other arrow as if plucking a butterfly. He threw it to one side. He and the pike man on the other side of the gap leaned their spears inward, covering as much of the break in the line as possible. And now it was too late to rein Bansh down.

Temur nocked again as Bansh hit the line and—rather than hurling herself upon the lances—hurled herself into the air, up and over, a leap worthy of a horse in a shaman-rememberer's tale. Temur loosed to the other side and took one more Rahazeen assassin through the forearm as he tried to bat the shaft away.

Then Bansh's hooves struck red cobbles again, chips of stone flying, and Temur was hurled forward against her neck. He lost a stirrup; he lost the reins; he nearly lost his bow. But Bansh, as if she understood his danger, kicked up her front feet and tossed him back into the saddle as neatly as flipping an egg.

Now they were beyond the Rahazeen line, and Hsiung and Samarkar were behind it. Bansh, still dangling her knotted reins against her neck, turned her half-rear into a sort of pivot, wheeling on her back legs as neatly as if she were heading cattle, and gave Temur a moment to recover the stirrups and his dignity. She did not shy when something horrible landed at her feet—another Rahazeen, torn open by enormous claws from balls to rib cage, still making faint paddling motions with useless hands after he bounced.

Hrahima would seem to have the rooftops managed.

Temur would have expected any other foe to react to the hurled near-corpse with confusion and failing morale. But the Rahazeen behaved as if they had been reading their own propaganda: they surged forward behind their lances, shrieking. One ran through the pumping blood that spread in a shallow pool all around the first man Temur had shot. The pool gleamed black in the growing brilliance. The Rahazeen assassin's white robe, sodden at the edges, left dark brush marks on the cobbles with every stride.

Running shapes broke from the smoke all around them: men and women, livestock, children—all fleeing the rising flames. A hot wind rasped Temur's face: the fire at his back drew deep breaths, feeding itself, rising against the night. Bansh snorted and shook, fear-sweat lathering beneath Temur's knees.

Temur raised his unready bow, the horn ring slipping around his thumb as he groped for an arrow. There were too many of them, and he was still off-balance—

Brother Hsiung piled into the two on Temur's left with outstretched arms, a simple and inelegant bull's rush that flattened one and left the other spinning away. Meanwhile, a column of viridian light encircled the one in the middle. Its jade-bright glow combined with the flickering orange of flames to create a nauseating, disorienting vortex of shadows. The assassin struck it with his lance and the lance shivered from his hands. Temur clearly saw his green-lit expression of pain and surprise as he glanced down at his palms.

Then the column of light yanked him backward, spinning off down the street like a dust djinn to vanish into the smoky haze.

Two uninjured Rahazeen and two moderately wounded were left of the eight—two jumpers and six others—Temur had glimpsed originally. Hsiung kicked the downed man in the knee and the temple to keep him down, raising his hands to beckon and challenge the one he'd merely knocked staggering. Temur leveled an arrow at the closer of the unhurt two. He thought it was the one who had caught his previous shot, but the veils made it hard to be certain.

The rush of people fleeing the flames had stopped; the few who passed now staggered. Temur thought of other burning cities, of the toll of war. He knew too much of the truth of this, of how many had been trapped behind and burned. He couldn't smell the bodies now, but he could remember the smell, and that was enough to raise his gorge.

He swallowed nausea and opened his hand around his bow, so the shakiness of a tight grip would not rattle his aim.

"We can kill you all," he said, trying to imagine how fierce his uncle Mongke Khagan would have looked and sounded in this moment. "I am Re Temur Khan, and you cannot stop me. Let us pass!"

The Rahazeen paused for half an instant—and then all four of the remaining ones, injured and uninjured alike, threw themselves forward in the kind of ferocious silence that Temur associated with starving wolves, or rabid ones. He loosed, but the arrow went wild as Bansh reared, striking with windmilling fore hooves. A pale-and-dark blur fell from above, Hrahima landing in a tiger's crouch so briefly that Temur's eye had not identified her until she was already leaping again, in among the Rahazeen with disemboweling swipes of her enormous claws. Two went down, Temur thought, before they knew that anything had hit them, let alone what. The third—the one Temur thought had caught the arrow—managed to drop his lance and draw a wickedly back-curved scimitar.

While Temur threw his weight up on Bansh's neck to bring her down, the assassin swung.

The tiger, barehanded, must have parried with her massive forearm. With a snarl more of exertion than rage, Hrahima tore the man in half.

Temur still had no reins. He could have clawed in Bansh's meager mane for them, but she had all four feet on the earth again and was answering his knees. His nocked arrow lost, he didn't trouble with another, just urged the mare forward hard and recklessly fast over cobblestones.

Hsiung's second opponent met the monk in a flurry of blows that Temur could not follow. For the first time, he heard Hsiung's voice—a sharp grunt, as the monk's breath was punched from his lungs by a knee to the sternum. Hsiung had traded it for an uppercut; as he staggered backward, his opponent wavered and shook his veiled head.

The assassin reached for his scimitar. Bansh ran over him without breaking stride, and Temur heard the horrible soft crunching thuds of hooves pounding flesh, breaking bone—and the hollow thump of a skull struck once.

Bansh slowed and wheeled before he could ask for it. Scrabbling in her mane, he found the reins. The man she had trampled lay unmoving. Bansh paused, stamping, her black forelegs splashed shining with gore when he glanced down to check her soundness.

Samarkar arrived at a run, her hands wreathed in blue light, her armor gleaming lurid in reflected colors. "The soldiers are coming and there are more Rahazeen archers on the rooftops—"

"Run," Hrahima said succinctly, pointing forward into the fire.

Into a rising orange hell, they ran.

13

It was bruisingly obvious, once Hong-la thought of it. And once thought, he could not unthink it, though the implications made him wish he had never fallen in love, never fled that love, never chosen the life of a fugitive, exile, and wizard. Made him wish, in fact, that he had stayed a slave in Song.

The emperor wasn't the betrayer of his people, the monster who had invited the demons into his own home. The empress was.

Could not the woman of a house open its door to a killer as easily as the man?

The evidence was there, even the motive. He had seen the horror on her face when he and Yongten-la had accused her husband. Had she not become empress, and first among wives in the time immediately before the arrival of the pestilence? As a wizard, Hong-la knew a little of the ways of demons. As a bureaucrat, he knew a great deal of the ways of contracts. How easy would it be for a young woman, even one raised to the halls of power, to be deluded by something infernally clever?

Hong-la had been floating in the baths, letting the volcano-warmed water ease aching bones, a spine that seemed it might never uncurve itself to stand straight again. It was only when he felt a chill across his shoulders that he realized the revelation had left him standing upright, water dripping from his earlobes, his hands clenching at his hips.

You are about to challenge an empress for treason. When her husband has no love for wizards at all.

THERE WERE THINGS MUCH WORSE THAN FEVER. AND AS ASHRA LAY scarlet-faced and sweating, tossing in incoherence, Tsering contented herself that if this ended in death, it was at least a better death than the slow suffocation and quick mutilation that would have resulted otherwise.

The fever started a day and a half after the surgery. It came in waves and while the soy mold could not break it, it could ameliorate, as could baths in the snowmelt off the Island-in-the-Mists. Some of the time Ashra was aware. By the fifth day, her constant cough was productive, her mouth filling with streaky gobs of greenish-yellow pus.

Tsering had dozens of patients to attend to: she could not stay and nurse Ashra, and her obligations pulled at her, making her heart itchy with anxiety whenever she paused too long. But Ashra herself was an important obligation, a proof of the validity of their approach. And when she lived through the sixth day, Tsering started to feel something she would rather not. The faint tickle of hope.

Hope, that mist-demon leading you into even worse betrayal and despair.

She cupped Ashra's shoulders in her arm as the Aezin woman wracked and retched around the foulness rotting inside her. "You must sit up," she counseled. "Sit up, so it can come out."

She couldn't tell if Ashra heard her, or if she struggled to hold herself upright because it felt slightly less awful. She didn't have the strength to clutch the stained cloth to her lips; Tsering did that for her, while Ashra choked so hard she vomited the froth of an empty stomach.

Tsering caught that in the cloth, too, heat and moisture she'd rather not think about. When Ashra's racking ceased—or rather, abated, because it would not be long before another bout ensued—in heaving gasps, Tsering examined the product. She was hardened—a wizard didn't survive her apprenticeship turning guano piles for saltpeter and dissecting corpses quickly before they could rot too much with a weak stomach.

Her gorge still heaved.

There in the yellow froth of bile, the strings of rot-scented pus, were tiny irregular scarlet shapes that Tsering at first—heart dropping—took for clots of arterial blood. She poked them with a corner of the cloth, though, and found them firm, not jellylike. Rubbing one clean, she amended that opinion. Not just firm. Hard.

Hard like bits of bone. And shaped like bits of bone, moreover—the bones of a mouse or sparrow.

Tsering called a novice over to attend to Ashra and change the dressings on her surgical wounds. "Save all her sputum," she said.

She went to the pump, and there washed her hands and the bits of demon bone three times in lye soap and water. They never came white; they were black and nearly transparent like obsidian. Then she gathered them up in a twist of clean handkerchief and went to look for Hong-la, or for Anil.

Tsering found Anil-la resting after a shift in one of the workrooms where wizards were taking it in turns to restrain the wrath of the mountain. He was slumped against a wall, head on forearms on bent knees. Someone had brought him warmed and honeyed wine. His hands folded around the wooden cup so that it dangled by his shins. He seemed too tired to drink. From the trembling of his hands, even so supported, tiny concentric ripples chased themselves to the walls of the cup and back, seeking a standing pattern.

"That will do you more good on the inside," Tsering said, crouching beside him. She put a hand on the young man's forehead and tilted it up, tugged the cup from his fingers, and brought it to his mouth. He covered her hand with his but let her guide him. The scent of nutmeg rose as he drank, leaving Tsering to wonder how long the stocks would last.

She held it there until he finished and pulled her hand away to set the cup aside. He lifted his head and blinked.

"Ashra?" he asked. Every wizard in the Citadel was aware of the experiment.

Silently, she pulled the handkerchief from her pocket. He opened it with hands that shook a little less now and stirred the damp bones with a fingertip, even as Tsering wanted to catch his hand and jerk it back.

He paused, considering, while Tsering held her breath. Then said, "She might have a chance. If the poison stays out of the blood."

Tsering could tell from the pinch of his forehead that he didn't believe there was that much luck in the world.

"COME WITH ME TO COUNCIL," QORI BUQA HAD SAID. "THAT WAY YOU MAY tell your father that his ally conceals nothing from him."

That his ally has instructed his war-band on what to speak of before me, you mean. But Saadet smiled and raised her veil and went—only to find herself the first, un-agendaed item of business as Hulegu took offense to her covered face.

"She sits there," he said to Qori Buqa, as if she were not in fact sitting there at all, "with no more expression than a serpent! And I must offer counsel in front of her?"

"She is her father's ambassador," Gansukh put in. "Shall we not respect the customs of her tribe?"

But Qori Buqa was regarding her with pursed lips. "Saadet," he said.

She met his gaze—not hard to do, when he stared directly at her with no shame—and saw the command on his face. *Shahruz*—

He would not answer her. She felt his disgust, as she did so often now. Surely he understood that what she did, she did for the Nameless? That she did what he could not?

No. He did not understand. And would not allow himself to.

Saadet steeled herself and lowered her veil. Gansukh set a cup by her hand. She raised it to her lips for something to drink, aware of the unwelcome caress of curious gazes. Gansukh patted her wrist in an avuncular fashion, the tails of his beard snagging on glittering embroidery as he leaned close enough to speak in her ear. She almost snatched her hand back—how dare he offend her sacred modesty so?—but reminded herself that he was a barbarian with no manners and kept her twitching fingers on the arm of her chair.

Saadet knew men thought young women naive, unworldly. Easily swayed. And many of them were.

Whether Gansukh meant her well or not, it would do him no harm if she played to that expectation. So while he explained, she pressed her lips thin and bent them in simulation of a smile.

NEWS FROM OUTSIDE THE SUMMER CAPITAL HAD DRIED UP AS THE USUAL flow of messengers became a stuttering trickle. The roads, the empire's pride and prestige—the roads through which flowed the empire's blood of commerce and communication—were under siege by outlaws, and banditry was the rule of the land. The empire itself was staggering under the weight of plague and the fear engendered by the burning mountain.

Yangchen moved through a nightmare that was nothing like her dreams of royalty. Her house was secure; her child thrived. But outside the palace walls, the world was dying, rotting from the inside. And she knew the truth: it was the chancre, the evil at her own center reflected in the center of the land she ruled.

Were not the lungs the seat of the emotions? Was it not a tightness in the chest that betrayed love or fear? Did they not squeeze in terror, flutter in passion or rage?

Were those not the emotions in which Yangchen-tsa had acted?

She had opened her own body to poison. And because she was empress, and because she was the land, the series of acts that had created her reign had created the weakness in the world's defenses. She did not know the source—although with the awakening of the Cold Fire, she had a sickening suspicion—but she knew the path by which it had oozed into Tsarepheth.

And yet she was empress; and yet she could not betray that knowledge. She could not even betray the haze of horror and self-repugnance in which she moved. She must seem bright—no, more than seem. She must be bright, focused, a bastion of authority, resourcefulness, and calm. Her people needed her. All Rasa needed her. She must be seen to be brave, indomitable. She must by her very spirit and presence inspire courage in the hearts of beggars and soldiers alike. She herself was a display intended to encourage morale, a sort of brave banner snapping in the wind, never permitted to sag for an instant.

An empress had no privacy. An empress was never alone. Her ladies were with her always, her husband often, her courtiers and sycophants interminably. And if Yangchen wept at night under her fine linens, soft to the hand as a baby's skin . . . she did so silently.

While she, brisk and efficient, was fully engaged in arranging logistics that would be necessary should her husband ever accede to the evacuation, the pattering feet of a page heralded the news that Hong-la, the elaborately tall, requested an audience.

At last, she thought, with a kind of sickening relief.

But all she said was, "I shall meet with him in the Elephant Room."

As before, the empress met Hong-la from behind an ancient screen of time-browned ivory. This time, however, she wore mourning white, and her hands were bound with thin ribbons woven in a crisscross pattern to remind her of the dead. She kept them folded before her sash. Hong-la felt a flash of rage at the peculiar peace in her expression, even as the trained political animal that lived in his head recognized the mask any statesman—or stateswoman, for that matter—wore to disguise the strong and vulnerable emotions.

He prostrated himself. Her voice gave him permission to rise. He kept his head lowered and stayed on his knees, a posture of submission still, if not so abject as the belly crawling proper respect demanded. At least the Rasan forms were less elaborate than those of Song and did not vary from principality to principality. *The advantages of a strong central government,* he thought sardonically, and bit his lip against what could easily have become a hysterical giggle.

He said, "Your serene and exalted majestrix, it pains me to approach you on this topic, but as you know from observing my conversations with your royal spouse, my research suggests that there is some imperial . . ."— *don't say negligence*—". . . the possibility that some slight oversight of a member of the imperial household may have provided the chink in our protections that has allowed the demons to enter Rasa and Tsarepheth and prey so terribly on our people. And now the Cold Fire threatens this city . . ."

"My husband fears that if we return to Rasa, we will bring the de-mons with us." She angled her head back. Although her porcelain mask did not change, Hong-la recognized the gesture of a person fighting back tears. "He fears also to be without the shelter of this fortress. There have been no demons within the walls of the Black Palace yet. Should we leave, who is to say what might pursue us?"

"Should you stay, no palace wall will restrain the wrath of the Cold Fire, should it truly awaken."

She had no answer, and she had no expression, though her eyes glis-tened.

"The infected will stay here," said Hong-la. "And the wizards with them."

"What you said to my husband . . . it spoke to my heart," she said softly. "If there were aught in my power—"

She shook her head.

"You are the empress. What is not in your power? Speak to Songtsan-tsa. Plead with him, on behalf of your people, majestrix."

"I *have* pled!"

There was a pause. Then, "Tell me how I may help the afflicted," she said.

"Your husband forbids it."

"So he does," she replied. "Tell me anyway."

AFTER LEAVING ANIL-LA, TSERING CLIMBED THE BATTLEMENTS. NO ONE seemed to know where Hong-la had gone, and though she knew it was selfish, she could not—at least not yet—face the hospital again. Clouds wrapped the heights, catching and reflecting and amplifying the light of the torches and witch-globes of the Citadel into a pervasive rose-colored glow. They stank of sulfur. Through them the fat flakes of ash fell not quite soundlessly, rasping like feathers brushing feathers when they touched one another, or Tsering's cheek, or the white battlements. Now and then, a crack of vivid violet-orange lightning snaked through the smoke belching up from the Cold Fire. She could not see the snaking fork-paths through fog and smoke, but each flash lit the whole world to blind intensity, and each was followed a few heartbeats later by a heart-grinding rumble.

The old stones of the Citadel were worn smooth underfoot, invisible through the fog. Tsering's toes groped over them, careful of their slickness and the occasional lips where they had been laid unevenly. She could not have said what she was doing—looking for Hong-la? Looking for peace?

Neither were to be found here. But there was an eerie dream beauty, alien and strange, in the way the white battlements and the lights loomed from and vanished into the strawberry fog, and there was a certain other-worldly sense to the harsh and sudden shatters of brilliance and noise, as if Tsering had walked from the hard familiar realities of everyday life into a ghost realm unlike any afterlife she'd been raised to anticipate.

Her footsteps stayed hard and plain, boot soles echoing over stone. Yongten-la wouldn't leave the battlements undefended in such a time, and she passed a sentry who had turned at the sound; a full wizard she knew a little, the black skirts of his six-petal coat settling from his sudden movement. He stood well away from the lights, but the radiance trapped by the mist hazily illuminated him. She nodded; he returned it. Neither spoke.

Tsering imagined him watching after her, listening to her footfalls dying. The mist closed between them, so she couldn't turn to see if she was right.

Finally, the dark wall of the Cold Fire, a sheer basalt escarpment that plunged from vanishingly far above, loomed before her. Her path was at an end, and the dying awaited her. Tsering stood for a moment, trying to breathe serenity in, or at least the strength to continue. For that moment, she closed her eyes.

When she opened them, it was not merely the mountain looming over.

Where the mist left off and the beast began, she could not have told. A long neck, heavy with swelling breath; a horned and tendriled head something like a catfish's and something like a horse's, as large as the body of that horse; the whole fog-silver and swirling pearlescent beneath the scales, as if someone had trapped a cloud in a decanter of etched crystal. The nostrils curved like shells and were the faintest blush of shell pink within. The eyes that ran down each side of the beast along its midline would have seemed white and blind, had not moonstone coruscations of lightning blue passed over them with every turn and tip of the long, fanged face.

Tsering froze where she stood. Every nerve, every muscle ached with her body's refusal to move. Mouse before an eagle's stare; rabbit before a wolf. She could not have squeaked, twitched, if her life depended on it.

Maybe it does.

The mist-dragon's slick, skimmed-milk tongue forked out and brushed her face.

"Tsering-la," it said. "Wizard, woman. You have seen in the world a task; you have taken it up with a will. But it is good you take this time to pause. A dragon defends her territory, but recall: she looks to her own life and nest as well."

"I—" Tsering stammered. "That is to say, this humble one is honored by the speech of your magnificence."

The mist-dragon angled its skull like a raven eyeing a bug, pinning her on the gaze of its forwardmost pair of eyes. "Humility ill becomes a warrior, Tsering-la. Where is the dragon in you?"

She tried to find the flowery speech of stories again, but it deserted her under the great cool pressure of the dragon's attention. She spread her hands in resignation.

"I am weary," she said.

"That is when you need the dragon most. And remember, Tsering-la, the greatest dragon of all is the Mother Dragon. She who has guarded Tsarepheth for all time and freely given her sacred waters to sustain. Is she not just yonder? Do you not think if the Cold Fire awakes, so will she?"

Tsering turned to look over her shoulder, following the dragon's gaze—though tearing her eyes from it was the hardest thing she had ever done. Harder than losing her family; harder than lying down under the knife.

She could not see the Island-in-the-Mists, but she knew it was there—the brooding presence of the mountain lost behind the veils of cloud that gave it its name. "What you say is true."

"Of course it is," the dragon snorted. "I am a dragon and I know it. Mind, little wizard, that you know your dragon, too."

She could not think of a retort, or even an answer. And while she was trying . . .

The dragon winked, each great papery eyelid scrolling down in turn along its right side, and vanished as if a strong wind had blown through and scattered it.

Tsering-la stood staring, one hand outstretched, until someone behind her cleared his throat and she almost jumped out of her boots. She spun in place, that hand smacking into the battlement, and clutched it to her chest with a pained—and embarrassed—wince.

"Yongten-la," she said. Of course it would be the elegant little head of her order who stood before her, hands folded inside his threadbare sleeves to ward away the evening chill. "I was just—"

"Talking to Great Compassion Turquoise Stone?"

Tsering forgot the sting of her hand. "You know him? You know his *name?*"

Yongten-la shrugged. "Shall I order you to sleep, Tsering-la? Your eyes rattle in their sockets."

"No," she said. "Not yet. I was looking for Hong-la, to ask his opinion..."

"Will mine do?"

She nodded. How this little man could so intimidate her—

"Ashra, the Aezin and Qersnyk woman...she is not yet dead. And her healing beer will be ready in three days. I was going to ask Hong-la if he thought we should start more surgeries, on the worst affected, the closest to—"

—*hatching*. It stuck in her throat; she couldn't choke it up. Barbed as one of those demonspawn.

His hands emerged from his sleeves; his fingers laced together. "Yes," he said. "Ask for volunteers. I suppose there will be many, so also begin organizing a surgical corps."

He turned away.

"Yongten-la!"

Looked back over his shoulder. "Tsering-la?"

"Me?"

He tipped his head and left words hanging behind him as he walked into the mist again. "Are you not a Wizard of Tsarepheth?"

TSERING'S INITIAL CONTACT WITH THE QERSNYK AND HER FRIENDSHIP WITH Ashra had made her the unofficial liaison between the Citadel and the refugees, so it was no surprise when Tsareg Altantsetseg sent a pony-mounted child to summon her. A Qersnyk never walked where he could ride. Tsering suspected there were some whose feet might never have touched the earth, having gone directly from cradle board to saddle.

She returned with the young messenger, walking while he rode, his feet sticking out as he straddled the pony's roan barrel. The horse betrayed no uncertainty in shuffling across the Wreaking, hoofbeats muffled by the drifts of ash, and the child was as fearless.

Tsering still had to concentrate on the dignity of her black coat and collar to make it across without carefully edging one foot in front of the other—and what she really wanted to do was get down on her hands and knees and crawl.

As they approached the Qersnyk camp, however, she noticed something new: a narrow person on horseback, his saddle decked with eight elaborate blue knots, was riding the edge of the camp. His snowflake-spotted bay was obviously accustomed to the strange pastimes of her human companion. The mare stood solidly as the rider dabbed symbols on rocks, wielding a long pole with a horsehair pad on the tip. Whatever he was using for paint looked like fresh blood and smelled of mare's urine. Each rock he daubed had evidence of previous symbols layered underneath. Judging by the number that had appeared since the last time Tsering visited the camp, he or his coreligionists must have been updating them daily.

Tsering remembered reading that the Qersnyk shamans—they had a different term for them: shaman-rememberer, that was it—were all third-sexed. She glanced with a scientist's curiosity at the person painting what she took to be wards about the camp as she passed, but he looked like any lean, clean-shaven young man to her, eyes already crinkling to a Qersnyk squint against strong sun and far horizons.

He glanced at her—appraisingly, or wondering what she thought of his work. Tsering rapidly jerked her eyes front again. He would not know from her clothing that she had no power and thus no otherwise sight and could not judge the effectiveness of his sorcery. This was intentional—the Wizards of Tsarepheth were careful by no outward design to show which of their number had quickened to their power and which had not.

Though she avoided the shaman-rememberer's gaze, he fell in behind

Tsering and the child and walked wordlessly with them all the way to where Altantsetseg sat beside a fire of animal waste, enthroned on a battered old saddle that was all but hidden in the robes in which the old woman had wrapped herself. An enormous heavy-headed mastiff shaggy as a haycock lay beside her feet, tufts of undercoat fluttering in the breeze. Brief summer was ending in the Steles of the Sky, but it was still not more than cool, and that only at night. Tsareg Altantsetseg's drawn-in posture and evident sense of chill served as a painful reminder that she was old, and that she had endured an arduous journey that many younger women would not have survived.

Altantsetseg summoned the child down from his pony with a wave of her hand and directed Tsering and the shaman-rememberer to sit on rugs by her side. Although they were on the upwind side of the smoky dung fire, eddies of wind blew acrid fumes back in Tsering's face now and again. She accepted the tea Altantsetseg pushed on her and settled herself on her haunches. The shaman-rememberer chose to hunker, buttocks resting on elevated heels, showing boots worn almost through the soles where the stirrups pressed. He too sipped steaming tea without comment.

Altantsetseg passed a few moments fussing with saddle stitchery before aiming her shrewd, bright squint directly at Tsering and saying—through the child, who spoke Uthman very well—"This is the shaman-rememberer Jurchadai. He believes he has developed a ward against the demon-sickness that will prevent new cases. He would like to share it with you, and he would like the opportunity to place wards himself around the city and around the hospital where your sick ones are."

Tsering considered. She might have deferred to Hong-la or Yongten-la: in fact, a part of her was very sure she should. But then she remembered Yongten telling her to take charge, and nodded. Speaking to Altantsetseg while the child translated, she said, "I will speak to the head of my order. I believe what you suggest can be done."

THE PASSAGES OF ANCIENT EREM STRETCHED ENDLESSLY, ITERATIVELY, through the red rocks of the canyon walls. They were not plain hewn rock. Oh, they were hewn rock, indeed, but here there were grand stairs and echoing halls, stone pierced and pieced until it seemed to hover on

moth wings in the vaulted shadows. Shrines and stone chairs lined the
walls, benches carved from the floor of each atrium. Some rooms had
counters, fireplaces. Some had frames that must once have supported
mattresses for the elevated beds that Edene had seen once or twice in the
parlors of rich foreign merchants in Qarash. But now rope and fabric and
ticking had long since rotted away, crumbled to dust in the dry desert air.

As she walked, she talked with the djinn. As good as his word, he
would not tell her from whence he came—but he told her that Temur
lived, that Temur still sought her, that Clan Tsareg had come among the
Steles of the Sky and now bargained for safety there and fought pestilence.
He would not go to do her bidding—she would have sent him with messages, with warnings, with reassurances—but he told her that al-Sepehr
supported Qori Buqa, and he told her that Qori Buqa rebuilt Qarash.

"Djinn," she said. "Would you remove the ring from my hand, if I
asked you to?"

He paused, startle-still, and regarded her with bottomless eyes. "Are
you requiring such a thing of me?"

The ring burned on her hand. "Why would I give it up?" she said.
"That would be foolish."

"So foolish," he agreed, his tone lightly mocking. But then, his tone
usually was.

Edene wasn't sure why she was driven to pace, what she was looking
for. The restlessness seemed to emanate from the taut bulge of her womb,
from the ring on her hand. A shadowy army of ghulim followed and
preceded her, their horny curve-nailed paws clicking and scuffing on
stone. Edene's footsteps did not echo, and neither did the djinn's, though
the twisting light that wreathed him cast her shadow before her, behind
her, and off to every side. It writhed among the silhouettes of the ghulim.

She wondered which was Besha Ghul—they all looked gray and
twisted in these shadows. As she wondered, one ghul detached itself from
the mass and came to stand before her. "My Queen?"

"I want to go outside," said Edene.

"The suns are high," said Besha Ghul. "They will burn you."

The ring pricked on Edene's finger. "They will not harm me." She
stated it with the certainty with which she knew it. "I am the Ruined

Queen. Nothing of Erem can harm me. And we must drill, my soldiers. You must practice for war."

At Edene's right hand, the djinn blazed silently, observing.

"Not in the daysuns of Erem," said Besha Ghul.

Edene raised her hand. She imagined them, thousands of ghulim in ranks, gray-skinned, flews skinned up from yellow teeth and slaver flying when they shook heavy heads. What man would not quail before such an army as that? "No harm will come to you, by my command."

Could a ghul look doubtful? That long dog's face rearranged itself in ways that struck Edene as fraught with doubt. She felt a catch of rage in her throat and swallowed it: did a good master show anger at a hound because the hound was uncertain? Punish a dog or a horse for fear, and they only grew more fearful. Would it be any different with a man—or a ghul, for that matter?

The ring squeezed on her hand. *Punish disrespect, O Queen.*

"You are a thing," she told it. "You do not command one born under the Eternal Sky, one swaddled in the veil of Mother Night."

When she looked up again, both ghul and djinn were observing her with identical quizzical head tilts. They reminded her of her dog, Sube, and a pang of longing for the animal struck her like a blow to the chest. The babe thrashed in response. She felt the pressure of its head against her lower back and winced.

Not long now, said the ring.

No, not long. Soon she would be delivered. Soon she would go to find Temur and bring an unholy army to kneel at the feet of his mare. She imagined him in the Padparadscha Seat and smiled.

"Djinn," she said. "We go to review the troops. Clothe me as befits a queen."

"Silks and satins?" he asked, eyes sparkling like sapphires. "White brocade?"

"Armor," she said. "And flame."

14

SAMARKAR PULLED HARD LIGHT AROUND HERSELF RUNNING, AROUND THE running monk, the running Cho-tse, around the running mare and the would-be Khagan hunched in her saddle. Smoke and flames licked up from the buildings on both sides, groping across the scorched street to stroke the hemispherical shell of clean air Samarkar held close to them. She filtered smoke and the searing toxins from combustion, cooled the air to make it breathable, and made sure all four of them had room to spread out and run.

It was . . . exhausting. Not the hardest thing she had ever done, she who had swum the straits of the White Sea, she who had survived her own neutering, she who had sat three days in the dark and cold to find her power. Not the hardest, perhaps, but one of the most strenuous. She wished she could just uncreate the process of the fire, but there was too much of it: a conflagration of this scale was beyond her abilities to summon or dispel. This azure shell protecting them was the best available compromise.

Her feet dragged. She staggered. Brother Hsiung caught her elbow and hauled her up, giving her one hard shake. *Keep running.*

Nothing would follow them through this fire—nothing sane, anyway, nothing without the peculiar magic of a Wizard of Tsarepheth—

but since it *was* the city that burned, against all odds, they still might beat the flames to the docks. They still might find a ship there, waiting, unless Captain Kebede had done the sane and sensible thing and cut his losses.

Well, if worst came to worst, Samarkar thought, they could swim for it. Between Bansh and herself, they could probably keep Temur's head above water. And did tigers not swim?

She let Brother Hsiung guide her and ran.

The cobbles were searing hot underfoot, and though she bled energy from the superheated surroundings to feed her protective mantle, there was less and less breathable air for her to filter in. The flames consumed it as surely as did she and her friends—and far, far faster.

Bansh charged before them, her hooves clattering wildly on the cobbles, her sparse tail flicking in distress. She respected the wall of light, however, and though Samarkar would have expected any horse to panic amid all that fire, Bansh held her head and kept moving forward.

Well, they had known already she was not like other mares. Samarkar, raised in the land of the Six Thousand, knew how often spirits intervened in human existence. This one, at least, had proved herself uncompromisingly benevolent.

Corpses lay in the gutters, human and animal, charred and curled into flexed positions by the heat. Whether the smoke had killed them or the flames, the result was the same: they cooked on hot stones in the heart of the blaze. Samarkar fixed her eyes on the middle distance and pushed forward.

Bansh's constrained rush was slowing to a stagger as well, her sides swelling and falling like the bladder of a bellows as she fought for breath. Samarkar felt Hsiung's feet dragging. He leaned on her now as much as held her up. Hrahima dropped to all fours, her heavy tail counterbalancing her body, her hands not so much bearing her weight as pushing her forward.

There was nothing but flames before them. Samarkar could not see the end of the blaze.

A black vortex threatened to close around her vision. Wheezing, Samarkar felt her knees under her hands, pushed upward, could not straighten. The safe blue light of her spell wavered, sagged, reformed closer after admitting an eyelash-curling pulse of heat—pushed in upon the little band by her exhaustion, her suffocation, the unbelievable ferocity of the fire.

The idea came to her on a breath that seemed to do her no good at all. The flames were breathing all their air, suffocating her and her little band of allies. But there was heat in the stones beneath her feet, and heat was energy. What the fire could breath, she and the others could breathe as well. And could she not suffocate the flames as surely as the flames suffocated her?

Samarkar reached down into those stones and tapped that strength as a tree grows deep roots to tap water. She still couldn't breathe, but she used the borrowed energy to draw herself up strong, to spread her arms like straining branches. She was dying—dying faster now, as her body used up what reserves it had—but she would meet that eventuality on her feet, as a Wizard of Tsarepheth.

Ancient disciplines of meditation slowed her heart, her breath. She held the emptiness within her, the darkness before her mind's eye. She held her memories of her instruction in patience and silence at the hands of Tsering, of Hong-la, of all her other teachers. At the hands of her father, her brother . . . her husband, of whom she told herself—this once—to feel no wrath and no bitterness and no grief. It had happened. It was done. She had lived and remained Samarkar.

Intention and the lack of intention; mindfulness and no mind at all. Magic lay in the tension between those spaces, in the otherwise senses and the esoteric understanding of two things that did not admit of one another at all.

Air, like fire, was one of the five elemental processes. Of all of them, only earth could not be created by a wizard. Samarkar could make air— but it was a self-limiting process. She was already wretchedly tired. She would exhaust herself before this conflagration did.

And when she failed, they all would die.

She needed a more permanent solution. The heat dried her skin before sweat could form on it. Her throat felt as desiccated as the Great Salt Desert. A voice rang through the emptiness of her awareness, her receptivity. *When a fire burns up air, Samarkar, where does the air go?*

The voice was that of Tsering-la. Samarkar wanted to strain after the answer, but she made herself quiet again. Distantly, she was aware that Temur had circled Bansh around within the hemisphere of hard light she still—somehow—sustained. That the mare had gone to her knees, and that Hrahima had caught Temur's hand when he would have reached for Samarkar.

"She is doing all she can," the tiger gasped.

The flames were mindless, spiritless. Though they roared and crackled like living things, you could not call them hungry: They had no intention, no will. They just were. They consumed to exist, they existed because they consumed. Like any living thing, but they were a mock life at best.

She thought of the delicate work of combining sulfur, saltpeter, and charcoal into black powder with all its potential to burn at a rate ferocious enough to send a rocket into the sky or a flintlock ball through a man's head. But even black powder would not burn under a bell jar, if most of the air were removed by a bellows fitted with a one-way valve.

When a fire burns up air, where does it go? When a lung breathes in air, where does it go?

It wasn't destroyed, because when you breathed in, you breathed out again. But some essence was consumed from it, some vital sustaining component. It combined with something. Air, like fire, was an essential process.

And what was combined, magic could take apart again.

Samarkar reached out through her wards—not into the fire this time, but through it, beneath it, to the char and crumpled ruins. She could feel now that it wasn't the stone houses themselves that burned, but the wooden joists and rafters and furnishings within, roofs thatched with reeds from the silted, marshy mouth of the river that emptied into the Strait of Asitaneh opposite the city. There: the air she needed was there. The process had combined itself with the process of earth, releasing the processes of fire and—Samarkar was surprised to notice—water, and producing as a by-product ash and char.

Samarkar thought she could release the process of air from ash: it was a simple enough procedure to manipulate earth to control the other processes. That was the foundation of most wizardry—that, and the wizard's trade of the ability to generate life for the ability to manipulate it. But she also thought—and this was a new principle, at least to her, though there was no telling what Hong-la and Yongten-la knew and had not yet shared—that she could convert the process of water back into the process of air, at least partially.

Those operations would expend a good deal less of her energy and concentration than creating air. She could sustain them for longer and keep walking the while. She would just have to keep the fire from flaring up in response to the fresh source of air—

It was a chance at survival.

"Guide me," she gasped to Brother Hsiung, groping toward him. She felt his meaty hand on her elbow again, the grip of callused fingers. He stepped forward. He staggered, gasping, but he drew her after.

Samarkar was blind within the glare of her otherwise sight. She groped with senses that weren't, exactly, and felt the process of air trapped within the substance of ash. She took the bonds within fingers that weren't, exactly, and though those linkages resisted at first she inserted her awareness into them and asked them to separate. They snapped as easily as she would have snapped a twig.

The space within her shell of light began to fill with sweet, sweet air. The first breath burned scoured lungs; the second rushed in cool and healing. Strength filled her and purpose came with the strength. Her flagging endurance rekindled and her protective shell of hard light pulsed outward, growing. More, more. She surrounded them all with safety, built a haven, let Hsiung lead her at a sedate walk now. They were no longer running before the flames, under the embrace of the flames.

The flames were dying back. With her otherwise sight, Samarkar could see that they were fading, that the process of fire was returning to a potential.

"Sun Within," Hrahima whispered.

Samarkar had heard the tiger sarcastic, angry, weary, worried. She had never heard her sound overawed before, but she could not allow herself to be distracted. Not now, as the flames flagged, as the path before them opened.

"Go," she whispered. "Just go."

They went, the baked and shattered cobblestones crumbling beneath their feet, heat rising to sear feet in boots. Samarkar leaned heavily on Brother Hsiung; after a little time, Hrahima simply picked her up in arms like young trees and carried her as if she were a tired child—armor and all.

She did not know how long Hrahima bore her up; she did know that she struggled when the tiger would have set her on her feet. But Hrahima soothed her, a rough hand combing her hair, and said "Tcha, Monkey-Wizard, you have done the thing. We are safe. Let it go."

Samarkar opened her eyes and closed them again. The world spun. She leaned heavily, her feet on the stones that were not, now, crumbling. She could not tell if the nausea caused the dizziness or the dizziness the nausea. She could not tell if she was—exactly—conscious. She was determined in the very least that she would not vomit now, and perfectly aware of just how ridiculous that determination was. As if these people would think less of her at this point, just from watching her barfing up her toes.

Surely, they were beyond all that. But she was once-princess, and princesses were not seen to puke.

"See what you have done, Monkey-Wizard," Hrahima said, gentle claws beneath her chin.

Samarkar shook her head gingerly. "Can't." The world behind her eyes spun.

"Samarkar," Temur said. "You have to look."

His encouragement did what Hrahima's touch could not, although Samarkar herself found it ridiculous. Was she a love-struck girl, that something so simple as the fact of a lover could make her step beyond what she thought herself capable of?

She opened her eyes. She blinked. The night above was garish with stars, a half-moon reflecting off the black water of the vacant slips before her. A broad avenue separated the façades of shops and warehouses from the harbor, and through the acrid stink of smoke rose the bitter-sharp tang of the sea.

"Oh," she said, and let the magic splash from around them, its light falling to earth to run in lazy rivulets between cobblestones before dissipating into faintly luminescent curls of mist.

"Not that," Hrahima said, and turned her.

The moonlight fell over a city that was not in flames, over corpses that were still curled in horrid flexion but were not charred, were not blackened into unrecognizable horror. They lay not in drifts of ash and cinder, but in rubble that had fallen under its own weight—and shone clean, whole beams protruded from the collapsed tile roofs.

"You unmade the fire," Temur said. "You put it out. You saved Asitaneh."

Samarkar—wobbling—nonetheless pulled herself from Hrahima's grasp. She crossed to the nearest body—a veiled woman, her black robes reconstructed as surely as her flesh. Samarkar crouched there—more fell to her knees, if she were honest—and placed a hand on her neck beneath the cloth.

The flesh was cool. No pulse beat on her fingertips.

The nausea rose again.

"Can you . . . ?" Hrahima asked.

Samarkar didn't dare shake her head. She lifted her chin. A princess or a wizard was not seen to cry, either.

"A wizard cannot generate life. That is the power we relinquish in order to obtain access to all the others."

It was only when she heard the hollow echo of her own voice that she remembered that her helm would have hidden tears.

"Tomorrow people will stand here," said Hrahima, laying a heavy hand on her shoulder plate. "They will look upon this place as a wonder, and they will say, 'The Wizard Samarkar did this.'"

"Did it too late," Samarkar said.

"Not for everyone," Temur answered. She heard him through the acrid sting of pain, of failure—

"Grieve on the ship," said Hrahima. "Captain Kebede is waiting."

Samarkar looked up, following the line of Hrahima's pointing finger. The docks were deserted, but off the end of the long stone quay a ship waited under oars, sails stripped from skeletal masts. A silhouette raised a lantern at the prow.

Her eyes were so raw with smoke that the tears soothed them rather than stung.

✳　✳　✳

TEMUR KNEW NOTHING OF SHIPS, AND HE LEARNED NOTHING THAT NIGHT. He was too caught up in his pride of Samarkar and his worry over her as he assisted her up the gangplank, then returned for Bansh. The mare took to her second time on a ship with dignity, seeming pleased to be allowed to walk aboard this time rather than being hauled with a band under her belly.

Samarkar had leaned against the side of the ship, watching the mare walk confidently up a plank no wider than Temur's spread arms. She lowered her nose once as if to inspect the footing, then continued on her way, not even shying when he led her through the gap in the rails. Her hooves clopped hollowly on the decking. Temur leaned against her warm side, breathing in the musky sweetness of hot horse that rose from under the reek of filthy smoke from the unburned city. As sailors closed the gap behind them, he dug in his jacket for a few slivers of dried fruit and the mutton-fat sweets he'd had Ato Tesefahun's cooks make up for her. He offered them to Bansh on an open palm.

She whuffled them up, her whiskers tickling.

Samarkar had pulled her helm off once they were safe aboard the ship. Her wizard's collar caught the moonlight, or perhaps Samarkar herself was still emitting a faint residual illumination.

"She's not real," Samarkar said, shaking her head. Her braids had uncoiled from their pins and moved across the shoulders of her armor.

Temur scratched under Bansh's mane, grit and ash wedging beneath his nails. "You're telling me."

Hrahima and Brother Hsiung were helping the crew cast off, although it seemed that the lines had already been untied and were only held in readiness to leave by pairs of sailors. Temur would have moved to assist, but from the muttered instructions of one large, dark man he understood that he would be best disposed managing the horse for now. The mare didn't need much gentling, but after that run through the burning dark Temur was content to stand quietly for a while. Soon enough he'd have to lead her into whatever stall had been provided—he hoped it wasn't in the hold—but for now he could watch limber, half-naked men scramble over the railing and drop into what must be a dinghy below.

Someone threw down a line. Temur watched as it went taut, and the much larger sailing vessel began to edge hesitantly away from the pier, out into the dark water dotted with other vessels. The aftermath of the fire benefited them in this way: it would be no trouble at all to slip from the harbor in this confusion of ships.

He looked up when he felt Samarkar beside him. She let the back of her gauntleted hand brush his naked one and said, "What sort of a vessel is this?"

Temur turned his head to look the length of it. They'd discovered on the brief voyage across the strait that she knew no more about sailing ships than he did, but this one looked large to his uneducated eye. Assuming the crew were all in sight—which seemed likely, the last few scrambling over the rail to come aboard as it moved with majestic slowness from the dock—there might have been as many as thirty men working and living aboard.

The ship rose to ornately carved finials fore and aft. Temur had thought the Aezin folk subject to the Scholar-God, She who could not be represented in art—but this black wood, adorned with beaten gold, showed a dozen or so semihuman faces bearing expressions ranging from a fearful snarl to tragic weeping. As they came through the bobbing vessels that had withdrawn from the quay for fear of flames, the men who had been rowing scrambled aboard and the dinghy itself was hauled up and made fast to the rail.

The ship had three masts, each supporting a long frail-seeming yard rigged parallel to the line of her hull. The mariners—every color of the rainbow, from burnished Aezin copper-black to one who might have been an albino, his light hair shone so in the dark—bustled about unfurling the sharply angled triangular sails. Those of the ship that had brought Temur, Samarkar, and the others to Asitaneh had been off-white, the color of bleached linen. These were painted richly with scenes that rippled and tossed and seemed to come alive in the light from the deck lanterns and those lanterns hauled aloft.

The sails bellied; Bansh snorted as the ship surged beneath them like a startled mare. As easily as that, they were under way north and east, toward the port of Asmaracanda.

Temur was slightly startled to realize that he could still pick out the faintest stain of sunset across the perfectly flat horizon of open water lying east. So little time had passed. Just a lifetime, for those who had not survived the fire. He turned his hand around and slipped his fingers through Samarkar's. Within the prickly carapace of her gauntlet, her palm felt moist and soft. She leaned into him; he leaned into the mare.

The sea was calm and still; the vessel might have been gliding across a black mirror slightly rippled and warped with age. As she gained speed, the frantic activity settled. Some of the men went below; Temur imagined they were off-watch and could take their rest now. A man came toward Samarkar and him, a man no taller than Temur—who was not tall, even by Qersnyk standards—but broad across the shoulders. On black skin sunburned blacker, deep shadows pooled in those places where the sharp valleys defining hard muscle lay.

He stepped into the lamplight. His hair lay braided close to his skull in rows and his features were handsome, fleshy, rounded. He was garishly dressed in a gold-sewn mirrored vest and crimson trousers that bloused to high boots. A dagger's jeweled hilt, the head of a snarling animal rendered in a style Temur did not recognize, protruded from the left one. His ears were full of gold rings, a ruby dangling on a chain from one lobe to tap softly against his bullish neck, another gleaming against the flare of his nostril.

"Kebede," he said, holding out crossed hands. His voice was a rumble nevertheless soft as a catkin. Temur had never seen the Aezin greeting before, but he had heard of it. He grasped Kebede's hands, feeling callused palms and thick fingers, releasing his grip on Samarkar's to do it.

"Re Temur," he said, leaving off any honorific because the captain had. He spoke in his growing-fluent Uthman. "The woman is Samarkar-la, and the mare is Bansh. In the face of the fire, we did not expect you to wait. Thank you."

"You are Tesefahun's grandson," said Captain Kebede, honoring Samarkar with a nod and showing no horror of her uncovered face. "Should I leave a nephew to burn? I would have saved my ship, had it become necessary, but there was not much danger yet."

"You're Ato Tesefahun's son."

"You are my sister-son," Kebede said. "You and your friends are welcome aboard my vessel." His gesture took in the long angled rigging, the black-and-gold prow cutting black water spangled gold with lantern light.

"Captain," said Samarkar. She had turned to follow the arc of his hand. "What sort of boat is this?"

"She's not a boat. She's a dhow," he said. "What they call crab-claw rigged. Come, let me show you where you'll sleep and the stables. We can get to know one another after."

Samarkar followed and Temur went after, still wondering what, exactly, a "crab" might be.

EDENE WANDERED WHERE SHE WOULD AMID THE RUINS OF EREM, UNDER THE moons and nightsun, and under the killing light of the daysuns as well. At night or underground, her ghulim accompanied her in legions; under the burning light of the daysuns, only Besha Ghul and the djinn would walk, and despite Edene's assurances that the ring would protect them both, Besha went swaddled in acres of black cloth.

Now it guided Edene past the conical pit-traps of myrmecoleons, which—if it had been night—might have poked up their shaggy-maned heads to do her homage. As it was, they stayed in their cool burrows in the sand and Edene felt their sleeping breathing like a second pulse beneath her own as she walked over them.

"Just a little farther," said Besha Ghul, mincing as if the sand scorched the pads of its hairy feet.

Edene had asked to be taken to the meeting place of the ghulim, which the ring told her had also been the meeting hall of men, when men still lived here. From the ring, she knew to expect a massive hypostyle that filled a narrow canyon side to side, hunkered in its belly and so doubly protected from the rays of the sun. As they walked, she played games with herself: How much of it would still be standing? What would the ruins look like, and how badly preserved would they be? The sand and heat and general dry lifelessness of this desert tended to preserve buildings, especially when the architecture was of stone. But Erem had been abandoned since the fall of the Sorcerer-Prince, centuries and more ago.

They walked in the firm rubble-dotted sand at the top of a slope beside a tongue of red rock, Besha Ghul patently grateful of the slender shadows. As they came around the tip, Edene's questions were answered.

She looked down along a gentle slope into a narrow cliff-walled valley that lay completely in shadow, though it would not have throughout the whole of the day. Topless pillars forested the lone and level sweep of sand—cracked and crazed, or shattered at sharp angles, or standing inviolate and white as virgin warriors in the violet shade of Erem. Edene had the uncomfortable sensation of *depth*, as if the glade of columns stretched to infinity, rather than being bounded by sheer cliffs in three directions.

Once, she might have said, *Oh.* But that Edene was no queen. Now she bit the tip of her tongue—because you could see someone bite a lip—and started down the slope, leaning backward to counterbalance the belly bobbing before her like a great balloon.

Here in the shadows, ghulim crept from the cliffs and fell in as if they had been there always, and the scorpions and serpents stirred themselves from underground to writhe across the sand before her.

The djinn kept pace, silent as he usually was, and the fires that burned around him cast shadows of the pillars—and of Edene—wriggling on the sand. It was cooler here. The fallen hypostyle had an elegiac air.

"Your master," Edene said to the djinn, in tones of casual conversation. "Is that al-Sepehr?"

"I am forbidden to answer questions about the Nameless."

Edene smiled. "If I am the Mistress of Secrets," she said, "do you think you can keep a secret from me for long?"

"I have been bested," the djinn said. "Until I can return the favor, I must do as I am bid. But I would say I have no master, though there is one who would like to claim that role."

"And you cannot tell me if that one is al-Sepehr?"

He glanced aside, the sharp angle of his jaw stubbornly unmoving.

"Could you tell me that it is not al-Sepehr?"

"I could lie," said the djinn. "But I have not been commanded to do so, and have no reason to do so of my own accord."

He might have been sly. Instead, he was matter-of-fact. What he was not saying—what he was saying by not saying it—lit up in Edene like a torch. "You're constrained to do his bidding. But you are not a willing servant."

"I may not answer," said the djinn, after a moment's furrowed concentration.

"You do not need to," said Edene. "I've seen how he controls the rukh."

She subsided into a considering silence. So she could not send the djinn away, and he was al-Sepehr's agent. But he was an unwilling one.

She might have said more, but a clean, piercing shriek like a glass bell from Song drew her attention skyward. At first the pillars rang with only one note, but in moments another fell between them, and another, until the space among them rang with madhouse, crystalline noise like a storm of wind chimes. Something flitted across the savage sky above, a confused translucence like a shadow beating wings. A half-dozen others followed.

Besha Ghul cried, "Run!"

Easier said than done, when your belly pushed out before you like a wind-billowed tent, but Edene turned and followed the ghul, scrabbling up the slope toward the cliff half on her hands and knees as the chiming grew toward a crescendo.

She did not make it. As the ghulim dissolved away into the shadows at the base of the rocks as if the stones had swallowed them, something struck her across the back. Edene plunged face-first into slipping sand, her lungs convulsing with pain as the breath rushed out of her and would not come in again. She pushed the ground away with strengthless arms and spat grit, trying to tell if the wetness adhering her tunic to her shoulders was sweat or blood.

Within her, a voice like chains over gravel gritted, *A queen does not flee.*

Besha Ghul had not run with the others. Edene had a confused sense of bent knees and hocks pushing the hem of a black robe this way and that. Three fingers and a thumb closed on her upper arm, a horny dog-nailed hand with phalanges pinched slender between swollen knuckles—

Blue brilliance washed Edene's perceptions. For an instant, she thought somehow the light of the daysuns had crashed down into the valley—but then she realized she was bathed in the glow of the djinn's fires. She rolled onto her back, tugging loose from Besha's grip—some queen, if this was her dignity—and shaded her eyes with her hand.

The djinn stood over her, washed in flame, at the center of a storm of wings. The creatures circling him wheeled through the pillars on attack trajectories, too fast for Edene to make more of them than a confused welter of bright pallid sky showing through the gaps in black-transparent rib cages like obsidian, scimitar-pincered heads like those of beetles, bony wings of smoke-colored membrane that chimed and clashed with every stroke. A palpable cold rolled from them as if they were the antithesis of a hearth, even at the distance of a body's length. Edene could feel the burn of it now across her shoulders where one had struck her back.

A queen does not die on her ass.

She took the knotty hand that Besha Ghul held out for her and levered herself to unsteady feet. There was a knife at her belt, some trinket of ancient Erem, no longer than the span of her hand. Just a thing to cut her meat. She slid it from the sheath, the hilt slightly scratchy with decorations and still warm from the sun. A cabochon stone slid against her sweat in the hollow of her palm.

The creatures that had been flocking to attack the djinn must have decided to seek easier prey. As if some signal had gone through them, half the flock wheeled off in pursuit of the few ghulim still straggling for the rocks, and one plunged directly at Edene.

Struggling in the sand, overbalanced by her rigid belly, what should have been a nimble twist became a stagger to the side. She went hard to a knee, tendons in her groin stabbing protest, and felt the cold strike with the force of a shield-wall as the crystal beast swept over. In an instant she memorized it—the grasping black glass talons, the blue glitter of the djinn's fires reflected in a faceted eye, the smoky outline of a pillar through a wing—and in an instant it was upon Besha Ghul.

The ghul whirled, snapping in the face of the beast. Edene caught a glimpse of red maw, flying tongue, fierce jackal-white teeth—and then the winged thing slashed, bowled her over, and would have swept on. But Besha had locked a clawed hand through the thing's empty rib cage, and, as the ghul's arm reached full extension, the creature's own momentum slammed it to earth.

In that instant, Edene was upon it. She dove upon its back, sand-skinned knee pressing it down as she grabbed the base of one flapping wing. An edge of membrane opened her cheek. She saw red spatter but felt no hurt. At the bottom of the pile, Besha Ghul snapped and snarled and slobbered like a rabid thing.

Edene brought the little dagger down like a chisel at the neck below the glass thing's skull. A sharp crack, a shudder: the point went in. She leaned on it, prying, twisting with her grip on the creature's slick wing.

Something shattered, and the creature went not limp, but slack, like a string of jointed bones, in Edene's grasp. It collapsed under her and she rolled away, gasping heavily with the weight of her babe upon her lungs, her knuckles bleeding from a spray of needle-shards of glass.

Besha Ghul shoved the thing off and crouched, its own blood dripping mixed with froth from its jaws. "You could have used the ring—"

But Edene shook her head, timing each word between heaving breaths to make herself understood. "These—are not—beasts—of Erem."

"No," said Besha Ghul, with the air of one who speaks against their better judgment. "They come from somewhere alien. But . . . my brethren are."

THE TWINS KEPT A BRAZIER BESIDE THEIR BED. DESPITE SAADET'S DISAPPOINT-ment in her brother's fastidiousness—at his willingness to let her do this unpleasant work—Shahruz continued to allow her to manage the sexual aspect of their seduction of Qori Buqa. It was bad for Shahruz, trapped in this unfamiliar body—but how, Saadet thought, was it harder for him than for her, or the myriad other women throughout history who had lain with a man, married a man, because they were instructed to?

Now, as the man who would be Khagan lay sprawled snoring beside the wall, Shahruz returned to assume her burdens. Saadet let him—willingly, more willingly than she had lain down for the Qersnyk warlord—and watched as her brother used her small hands to open the packets of incense and spice that she kept in a box beside the bed. He had previously written out a paragraph in tiny, perfect script on a square of rag paper. The cursive letters of the Uthman tongue scribed a spiral, a labyrinth that would trap Qori Buqa's thoughts. Now Shahruz required Saadet to dab a bit of the warlord's slimy spilled semen on the paper. Then he tied it into a scroll with a few strands of the man's coarse hair.

The scrap of spell went into the brazier, along with chips of frankincense to sweeten the mind and exotic rosemary to elevate the thoughts. It all burned quickly, curling around a lick of sun-yellow flame.

Qori Buqa made a sound—a sigh rather than a complaint—as the sweet smoke reached him. He kicked in his sleep, struggling against the furs, and then rolled on his side and was still except for a faint trembling. The twins breathed the smoke too, and though the dream was not for them, they caught the edges of it. A woman veiled in indigo spoke low and sweet, revealing her special love for Qori Buqa, his special place in her design. She might have been Mother Night; she might have been the Scholar-God. She could seem both, with her irises like twilight and the dusky, glowing skin around her eyes.

There is a Dark God rising, Re Qori Buqa, she said. The Sorcerer-Prince has slept long, but sleeps no longer. I am your mother and the mother of the Rahazeen, and all my children together must oppose him.

A horse has four legs, Qori Buqa, and the sky has four pillars. You must unite my children. You and your brother al-Sepehr. I have chosen you.

"I have chosen you," Saadet mouthed mockingly. The stream of incense faded; the woman's soft, persuasive voice as well. Qori Buqa relaxed against her hip.

Gently, she disentangled herself and slipped from the bed. In her trouser pocket was a stone drenched in blood; she could use it to contact al-Sepehr. It was time for her to spend a little time away from Qori Buqa, to allow his desire for her—and his greed and narcissism—to be watered by her absence.

That, and there was word from Asitaneh. The city was Nameless, and Qori Buqa's rival, the man who had killed Shahruz in the body, had escaped . . . and Nameless agents in Asitaneh believed they knew what ship he had taken.

The twins had someplace else to be.

The twins went to the window and leaned out it, into the cool night air, Qori Buqa's snores a reassurance of continued privacy. They drew the blood-caked knot of stone from their pocket and clenched it in a bare fist.

They whispered, "al-Sepehr."

A moment, and he was there before them, as if they saw two realms at once—the night of Qarash, and the ivory stone of an impossibly ornate palace behind al-Sepehr. Both, for the moment, seemed equally, simultaneously real.

"I have learned something interesting, Master," said the twins—very softly. Qori Buqa had a stone of his own; if he should overhear, he would know exactly what was occurring.

"I am alone," said al-Sepehr. "Has Qori Buqa consented to the marriage?"

"He has set a condition," the twins said. "He will marry your adopted daughter, Master, if you can set him in the Padparadscha Seat."

Al-Sepehr's head rose. "The Qersnyk regalia is missing?"

"If he knew where it was," Shahruz said dryly, "you can be sure his fanny would be in it."

The twins reveled in their master's dawning smile. *For the Nameless. For the world.*

"Master, a question?"

"You can ask me nothing it will not be my privilege to explain, my Shahruz."

The veil hid their flattered smile, for which the twins were grateful. "This Qersnyk conceit that a horse has four legs as the sky has four pillars—"

"Yes?"

"The Range of Ghosts, the Shattered Pillars, the Steles of the Sky. All the bastions destroyed when the first Sepehr strove with the gods."

"What is the fourth?"

"What is the fourth, O Master?"

"There is a range near Messaline called the Bitter Root, Shahruz," said al-Sepehr. "Possibly that is the fourth pillar of the sky. Possibly the saying does not refer to mountains at all. Perhaps someday we shall learn the answer and drink what power flows from the knowledge. Or . . . perhaps the Qersnyk mystics are full of shit and obsessed with horseflesh as a metaphor for everything." He shrugged. "The Padparadscha Seat, on the other hand. That *is* real. And I think I have a source that can help us find it . . ."

* * *

OVER THE COURSE OF THE VOYAGE, SAMARKAR, TEMUR, HRAHIMA, AND Brother Hsiung dined with Kebede many times. They learned that the crew called him Ato Kebede; when Samarkar questioned him, he laughed his dragon's deep laugh and said, "Who is more a wizard than a man who can wield compass and sextant to find his way to Song across a trackless sea?"

And in truth, the tools of navigation fascinated Samarkar. She tried not to pester to be taught, but she might as well have tried to rein in a herd of charging horses as her curiosity. Fortunately for her, Kebede seemed to find her enthusiasm engaging, or at least amusing, and he allowed her to spend time with the pilots, although his largesse did not extend to showing her his charts. He did prove a font of information on the natural history of the sea, however. She learned the names of a dozen types of gull, and what a crab was after all, and how unusual it was to see a steppe vulture circling over the ocean, seemingly following the dhow as it beat westward crookedly, often tacking into a wind.

Hrahima, quite shocking everyone, took beautifully to life aboard ship, bending her enormous thews to haul rope and set sail and work winches so great Samarkar would have expected them to require the strength of oxen rather than men. Temur did well enough, once Samarkar convinced him that he could share her cramped bunk. In the tight spaces of the dhow, he had originally offered to sleep in Bansh's stall. Samarkar could imagine too clearly his skull split open by staggering hooves, should the ship pitch in a storm.

Brother Hsiung suffered greatly from seasickness, the more so— Samarkar thought—because he did not complain. She'd have said "could not," but by now she had more than enough experience with the mute monk's communication skills to know that he was perfectly capable of getting his point across as necessary.

So she doctored him, and made herself available to Captain Kebede— whose largesse *did* extend to counseling them on how to enter Asmaracanda.

"It's a controlled city," said he one morning, over a breakfast of salted rice, eggs from the hens that lived in cages near the stern—fresh, and boiled in seawater—pigeon peas, and pickled vegetables that Samarkar was still learning the names of. "Especially given your intelligence that it's returned to the caliph . . ."

"Whoever the caliph may be," Temur supplied.

Kebede flashed them a wide-mouthed grin. His teeth were tortoiseshell-banded like those of Tesefahun. Samarkar had thought it a trait common to all Aezin until she had met Temur, whose teeth were as white and strong as any Qersnyk's.

"It's a holy city," Kebede said. "One sect or another of Father's religion holds it's where their Scholar-God bodily assumed Her Prophet into Heaven."

"I thought Ysmat of the Beads was martyred," Samarkar asked.

Kebede shrugged, charming Samarkar. "Depends on who you ask. Can your priests always get their story straight?"

"In fact, we wizards can't." She scooped up egg diced over rice and peas with her fingers. A bowl of rosewater for rinsing the grease away between mouthfuls sat beside her plate, in a shallow depression carved into the table for that express purpose—lest the ship pitch and roll. "You would think a God who sends out Prophets would have a little more investment in Her worshippers getting their story straight."

She wouldn't have blasphemed so in front of Ato Tesefahun—being polite about other people's deities was a survival skill she'd honed in Song—but it was obvious Kebede was an apostate, if Tesefahun had ever managed to instill belief in him at all.

"Maybe they're all right," Kebede said. "Who's to say only one version of events has the truth in it?"

Samarkar almost choked on her peas. It was a sentiment she might have expected to hear from another wizard, not from a sea captain. But then she remembered that he was Ato Kebede, and swallowed. "As the spirits of Rasa can hold sway in my homeland, and those of Song in the Ten Hundred Kingdoms, you think perhaps all the sects of the Scholar-God are equally valid?"

"The Rahazeen have their own sky," he reminded, gesturing toward a porthole. It was overcast beyond, but Samarkar took his meaning anyway. Somewhere above the clouds, a pale Rahazeen sun moved from west to east across faded heavens.

A frustrated silence dragged until Hrahima—who was not eating, except to pick at eggs—reminded, "Asmaracanda."

"Ah yes," said Kebede. "Whether Ysmat of the Beads was bodily translated into Heaven, or whether she was stoned to death for refusing to remove her veils—it remains a closed city to all but religious pilgrims, scholars in the service of the Scholar-God, and certain dignitaries. It is said to be one of the greatest bastions of learning in the world, but that wisdom is locked away behind white stone walls. It is full of universities and scriptoriums, and only the faithful may enter."

"So how does it manage to be a center of trade?" Temur asked.

Kebede scooped his food up bite by bite in kishme leaves, keeping his own fingers cleaner. He chewed one such morsel thoughtfully while he considered the question. Samarkar, not caring for the kishme's texture, preferred to use her fingers.

"There is a caravanserai without the walls," he said. "And merchants. And a whole trade city, frankly, to support the sacred city within. Are you sure you need to get inside Asmaracanda proper?"

"There is a man there," Samarkar said, "who Tesefahun thought could help us."

"One of the sacred scholars, then."

Samarkar nodded.

Kebede swallowed more rice, another leaf. "Well," he said. "That's simple, if not necessarily inexpensive or easy. Another feature of the sacred city is the crypts. The faithful will pay a heavy tax in order to be buried in Asmaracanda. But spaces are limited, you see, and the waiting list is long—"

"They smuggle in *bodies?*"

"They? I have two in the hold, packed in salt. It's very simple: we dock, I unload, we buy a couple of coffins and bring them aboard under cover of other cargo. Temur and Samarkar can pose as pilgrims once they get inside. They conduct what business they must, and meanwhile Hrahima and Brother Hsiung outfit for the rest of your journey. If we make landfall on a morning tide, you could be ready to set out the following dawn, all your business accomplished."

He smiled, chewing beatifically. Samarkar stared.

"Madam?" he asked, when strong tea had washed down the mouthful.

She shook her head as if to rattle the words loose. "You know a lot about smuggling."

The beatific smile widened. "Hazard of the profession," Kebede said.

I HAVE NO RIGHT, THOUGHT EDENE, AND THE RING WHISPERED, *YOU HAVE the right of queens.*

And there were the ghulim, scattered, crying, being chased down from above by these creatures with the cold of mountain peaks and perhaps even higher places upon their wings. *They come from somewhere alien.*

Beyond the sky? Edene had never before wondered what lay above the canopy of the Eternal Sky, the veil of Mother Night. And she did not have time to wonder now.

The Green Ring of Erem shone chill on her hand as she raised it, a wide band of verdigris-stained gold. She reached out with it, through it, and felt the fear and disarray of the ghulim. How could she ask them—command them—to fight and die?

Because you are their Queen, Mother of Jackals.

They are only dogs. How can they stand against these nightmares from beyond the sky?

Her answer crouched beside her, dripping blood from a lolling tongue. If Besha Ghul could rally on its own, surely these others could rally to a leader.

With a thought, Edene brought her army to heel. With a gesture, she arrayed them and sent them forward.

They could not fly, but the cold enemy must come to them to attack, and when they did, they faced three or four ghulim for every beast. The djinn ripped one from the sky with a gesture; it exploded into raining shards with a sound like crockery thrown on a stone, littering the sky and sand with knives that cut one ghul to ribbons and blinded another.

He held his hand from destroying more. Two more went down to the ghul-pack, at the cost of five ghulim. In the following heartbeat the rest wheeled and withdrew on a shimmer of shadowy, chiming wings.

Her clawed back burning now, Edene stood amid the slaughterhouse reek of spilled bowels and blood curdling on warm sand . . . and found no tears would come.

✳   ✳   ✳

KEBEDE PROVED AS GOOD AS HIS PREDICTION, AND SEVERAL DAYS LATER THEY
came upon Asmaracanda with the dawn. Samarkar joined Temur and
Kebede upon the forecastle to watch as the sun revealed it. The breeze
had freshened; it blew the tendrils of her hair that had escaped her braids
forward into her face, the edges of her mouth and the edges of her eyes.
The dhow slipped up the face of pitching waves and plunged into the
valleys behind them, and each time smacked glittering spray into the sky,
where the wind caught them and tossed them forward. Wet sapphires
gleamed in Temur's wooly hair and splashed his beard. Samarkar knew
herself similarly bejeweled.

Like Asitaneh, Asmaracanda rose from the edge of the sea. Other
than that, Samarkar thought, on superficial acquaintanceship they could
not have been more different.

Where Asitaneh was red stone on humped land, backed by rusty hills,
Asmaracanda rose domed turquoise as peacocks and walled white as
bone from a pale green land. It perched like a fishing bird above the
water. The sea beat against the base of the city's walls, which encircled
the entirety of the headland upon which it rested. From that initial advantage, Asmaracanda mounted a steep hillside until it seemed one single
broad-based tower, incomprehensibly vast, rising toward a shining peak.

The east behind the city glowed azure where the light ran around the
rim of the world; higher, the sky was a blue so dark Samarkar despaired
of finding an enamel to match. The city seemed to hover as if before a
backdrop of some semiprecious stone, painted with an otherworldly
light. Its pale walls reflected gold from the sun rising aft of Kebede's
dhow; its thousand thousand glass windows sparkled.

Samarkar wondered if the city had been so beautiful when Ysmat of
the Beads came here to die, or to be transubstantiated—or if its current
glory was the result of a thriving tourist trade and a good tax base. She
could make an argument for the forbidding loveliness either way, she
supposed: cause, or effect.

"There's no place to land," said Temur. "There are no docks."

"The whole thing is a fortress," Kebede agreed. He stood with them on
the elevated prow, one hand upon the many-mouthed figurehead. "We'll

come around the headland to a harbor in the trade town. The harbor's a good one but the straits are trapped. They'll send out a pilot to guide us, so you'll have to appear to be able seamen if you want to get a look around."

"How do you trap a strait?" Samarkar asked, and then felt self-consciously as if it were the sort of thing a wizard should already know.

But perhaps Kebede forgave her for being an inland wizard, because he said, "Only narrow channels are navigable. Elsewhere, they've hauled out boulders and planted iron spars that would hull this boat faster than you could piss out a match. The caliphs were serious about defending it."

"But surely," Samarkar said, "Once you've sailed in five or ten times . . . ?"

Kebede shook his head. "They come out and move 'em around."

Samarkar swallowed unwilling respect. Indeed, the caliphs had been serious about defending it. And were again, it seemed. "How did your grandfather ever take that?"

Temur gave a funny smile and would not look at her. "Starved them out, as I heard it. Or droughted, more precisely. The city was fed by underground aqueducts—called qanats—and my relatives destroyed them. Now it's probably all hauled water, if you can imagine."

"Well," said Kebede, making a judicious smacking sound with lips that Samarkar found, on due reflection, sensuous. "I think I'm glad he didn't burn it. And those aqueducts are smuggler tunnels now. I'll draw you a map, but you must memorize it. We can't risk the watch finding out what we know about them. They're *your* route back out of the city, too."

IF ASMARACANDA BESTRODE THE WORLD, A REGAL QUEEN OF CITIES, CLOTHED in shining samite and jeweled in blue stones, the trade town that clutched at her hem was a motley procession of beggars. Patchwork roofs shoved for space behind a palisade of mismatched stone. Samarkar identified red clay tile, slates, thatch from the marshes that—once they rounded the headland—spread off to the horizon north of the ragged range of hills that so elevated the city.

On the north end of the harbor, a far more forbidding headland hulked: bronze-black basalt, streaked with rusty color, at its top a fortification clearly manned and bristling with the iron muzzles of cannon.

There was water here, where two great rivers ran together and into the sea, and the hills to the south were thick with orchards and olive trees, vineyards and the white dots of flocks—goats or sheep or some more exotic animal, Samarkar could not determine at this distance.

The piers at least looked as if some central authority maintained them: they were black stone, with bobbing docks defining the slips. Samarkar had changed into men's plain homespun, strapped her breasts, and hidden her hair under a mustard-colored head wrap such as those some of the sailors wore to keep the sun off and the sweat out of their eyes. She played at hauling a line, but mostly watched as a sleek small boat rowed by a dozen slaves came out to meet them. A man dressed in white with a blue head wrap—as if he were an extension of the city himself—sat at the prow in a folding chair like the one the caliph had affected. Even from this distance he looked bored.

He brought his boat alongside Kebede's dhow, and Samarkar saw the captain toss him down a bag that clinked musically when he caught it. She wondered if that was a sanctioned—even demanded—payment of fees, or if it was an illicit bribe. It would tell her something about the culture of the place to know, and she resolved to ask Kebede before she left the vessel.

The pilot brought his boat around and struck back toward the harbor. Kebede followed precisely in his wake. Samarkar leaned over the rail with her knee hooked through it like Temur sideways in a saddle, staring down into the sun-streaked water—and pale and dark shadows beneath it, close enough that she could have spit to them, gave the hints of where those ship-killing traps might be. One vessel—pirates? smugglers? a raiding ship of war?—that had tried to do without a pilot had not been lucky; a sun-silvered hulk lay twisted on rocks she could not see, the waves hissing through its lacework hull.

They must have been through the worst of the traps, because Kebede left his helmsman to the task and walked back to her. When he stood at the rail she had hooked her legs through, he hailed her in a common speaking tone that would not carry. "Come, corpse. Time for your coffin."

Reluctantly, Samarkar cast one more longing look at the dusty corrals of the caravanserais huddled at the base of the hills, the patchwork trading town, the white walls of Asmaracanda rising behind it, the blue water and the western sky lit up pink and gold like a princess's bridal gown. She sighed and pulled herself into the railing, swinging her outside leg over as her inside foot touched the deck. The ship rose and fell beneath her; she wondered how the motion had ever felt alien.

"It's beautiful," she said.

Kebede nodded. "Just remember they'll pull you apart between four camels if they catch you inside, if it helps you stay wary."

Her eyes ached with widening. "What happens if they find the coffins being smuggled in and *don't* open them?"

"They burn them." Kebede gave her a level look. "It's the worst thing that can happen to a body in the Scholar-God's religion—destruction . . . Yes, I thought that might make an impression."

THE COFFIN WAS TIGHT AND HOT IN THE HUMIDITY OF THE DHOW'S HOLD, AND it smelled strongly of salt and faintly of rot. While it lent a certain authenticity to the operation not to use a fresh casket, and while Samarkar's royal fastidiousness had not survived the sometimes revolting toil of her apprenticeship as a wizard, she would have confessed a preference for a box nobody else had already anointed with the products of their decomposition. Salt gritted under her head—gray salt, sea salt, not the purple salt of home—and the coffin bumped in a most disconcerting fashion as it was rolled off the ship—she assumed—and secreted on a cart with the three others; one, like hers, modified with breathing holes, Temur huddled within; two each packed with salt and the mummified corpse of a true believer.

Lying silently in the darkness, listening to the coffin lid being screwed into place and the raggedly accelerating beat of her heart, had required all her discipline. She wore Uthman dress and a Rahazeen man's veil, and the cloth binding her breasts seemed to constrict every breath—or perhaps that was just the anxiety provoked by the closeness and stench of her shipping case.

She had wondered how Temur, already once a survivor of vivisepulture, was bearing it. Perhaps it was better for him, coming as he did from a culture with no tradition of coffins. In Samarkar's experience, they were ritual objects, only briefly used before the fire. She hoped in this case that would not prove prophetic.

Kebede's warnings and her own uncertainties chased each other through her mind. Could they trust the smugglers to whom Kebede had entrusted them?

She had longed fiercely to be going off with Hsiung and Hrahima to the trade town and the caravanserais. And then she had resigned herself, to destiny and to the plans of the Six Thousand. Surely, if she was not dead yet, it was because they had still some uses for her.

I shall build you a shrine in the Shattered Pillars, she promised the small gods of her homeland. For a moment, she wondered if—if she lived to do so—a tiny patch of sky in those uninhabited mountains might change.

Concealed airholes or not, the coffin grew only hotter and more close once the shade of the ship's hold was left behind. They had waited until afternoon to unload, leaving Hsiung and Hrahima plenty of time to begin canvassing the trade town and caravanserais for assistance westward—and also leaving time for the worst heat of midafternoon to begin to fade. Nevertheless, Samarkar was quickly left lying in a puddle of her own sweat. At least the sweat melted the gritty salt, and she supposed if she fainted from heat stress, she—clammy and barely breathing—would make a pretty good impression of a corpse if anybody pried the lid up. Assuming she wasn't already *actually* a corpse by then.

You are a wizard, Samarkar, she told herself. *If cold cannot daunt you, why heat?*

And it was true. She should be able to find the necessary focus to cool herself, to move the heat outside her body and away. It was simply a matter of meditation, of focus, just as when she had found her power.

Simply. While the coffin bumped and rattled and something slid atop it, making the olive-wood top creak. Samarkar paused a moment to wonder that these desert people would inter their dead in boxes made of wood . . . but then she remembered the orchards. There were trees here.

She thought of Temur suffering a few panel-intermediated inches away, and wished she could ease his pain at the oppressive heat also.

Rumble of wheels on packed hardpan; smell of hot dust filtering in, even over the resin and salt and putrescence. It seemed as if they rode that cart for a long time, but it might have been only minutes when somebody stopped them, and there were voices. Samarkar held her breath and either heard or fancied she heard the musical click of coins changing hands.

After the hot, dusty, bumpy portion of the journey came the cool, damp, bumpy portion of the journey. Even within the coffin, Samarkar could hear how the echoes of the bearers' footfalls resonated along endless tunnels, though she lay in a darkness unrelieved even by the flickering lanterns whose burning oil she could faintly smell.

It didn't take as long as she'd expected—even listening to her own heartbeat contained by the coffin's walls—but less long as she had expected turned out to be more than long enough. Her feet were always slightly higher than her head, and her head was to the front, so she knew the abandoned qanat still angled down.

Eventually, the quality of the echoes changed. They had emerged into a larger space, and now a widely spiraled stair bore them upward. Samarkar imagined that this was the dry cistern, and that the stair must wind around the outside edge, intended to give access in order to affect repairs or to draw water—no matter how much or how little water remained. But the engineers had not foreseen that an enemy would sever the qanats and that they would never be repaired.

They didn't climb for long before they entered a close space again: more of the loud, tight sounds of the tunnels. This time, though, they were carried for only a few hundred steps. Some grunting and scraping—and a few hard, painful bangs—indicated that the coffins were being pushed through a close and uneven space. After that, Samarkar thought that ropes were passed through the handles and that the boxes were dragged. It was not the most comfortable of experiences for the passengers.

When that ended, though, the coffins were not lifted again, though Samarkar braced herself against the sides with her hands and winced in anticipation. After a brief pause, she heard the unbelievably welcome sound of screws being backed out of the lid.

Samarkar kept her hands and nose pulled away, counting herself lucky that the men opening her unorthodox mode of transport did not drop the trailing edge of the lid inside the coffin—on top of the occupant—as it scraped off. Blinded, she extended a gloved hand, shielding her eyes with the other. Someone's strong fingers grasped hers. Someone solid and heavy lifted her to her feet.

When she opened her eyes, the first thing she noticed was that they were in another cistern—she presumed another cistern—much like the one she had envisioned from the echoes, complete with the spiraling stair. As her vision cleared with blinking, she found herself looking at a petite Nameless woman whose fragile frame under her masculine robes and indigo veil gave no hint of the unyielding strength Samarkar had just experienced. She was surrounded by a dozen other Nameless warriors, faceless behind veils, swords and long knives ready in their hands.

In her left hand, the woman held a pistol leveled at Samarkar's abdomen.

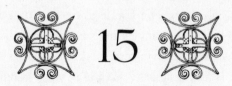

15

EDENE, CLAD IN LONG RED GHUL-WOVEN ROBES, LEANED HER HEAD BACK AND let the light of three suns bathe her face, a sweet searing heat that should have blistered skin and blackened the flesh beneath but only warmed her while she wore the ring. The half-healed gouges on her back stung as she filled her lungs. She could draw a fuller breath, it seemed, than she had been able to in months, as if the baby had finally decided to let her get some air inside her.

Besha Ghul huddled in the shadow of the cliff behind her, a conjured darkness shielding the ghul despite Edene's continuing assurances that in her presence, the sunlight could do the ghulim no harm. Along with Besha stood the three ghul midwives—or perhaps doctors; Edene had not troubled herself to learn their sexes, if they had sexes—who now accompanied Edene everywhere.

At Edene's right hand stood the djinn, wreathed in blue flames and the captured light of the suns. Overhead, the pallid sky was bright enough to blind an unprotected eye, but Edene could make out its graduated tints of dilute, dusty mauve.

"Do you like the fire, my lady?" the djinn asked.

Edene rested a hand on the sun-warmed curve of her belly, feeling her own flesh deform with each of the infant's kicks or punches. Another squeezing pain—tiresome things—tightened her back and belly, followed by a sharp popping sensation as if the babe had coughed.

"There is," she said, "no better thing."

A rush of hot fluid soaked her legs and bare feet and smoked instantly into nothingness against the burning sand.

PHYSICIANS WERE EVERYWHERE THE SAME. THEY MIGHT NOT STEP OUT OF the shadow of the rocks at Edene's suggestion, but the moment her labor came upon her, all three of the cloaked and hooded ghulim surrounded her, their gray hands supporting her elbows, their clawed feet scattering sand in their haste to hurry her within. Once they were in the tunnels of the city, other ghulim surrounded them—offering water, slipping Edene's robes from her shoulders and leading her to a chamber with a bathing pool, a birthing chair, and a pallet padded with woven blankets. She imagined the ghulim must steal the materials for their textiles from the same sources where they stole their food—unless somewhere down their secret ways there were people who traded with ghulim. Even if there were, ancient Erem, blasted and sere, offered little in the way of resources— and yet the ghulim were more than adequately supplied.

The ghulim would have ushered the djinn from the birthing chamber, but they had no power to move him where he did not wish to be moved. And so he stood, arms folded, and said nothing unless Edene addressed him directly. Mostly, she did not wish to speak—to him, to the midwives— unless they were physicians—or even to Besha Ghul, hovering so nervously near.

Now the ghulim made Edene squat and probed inside her body with bony fingers, the hooked nails clipped and filed blunt. They bent their fanged jaws together and murmured things she was not meant to hear. They encouraged her to pace, while Besha Ghul brought cool water flavored with exotic fruits and also cups of a nourishing gruel. The incense in the chamber was cinnamon; the lamps were dimmed by yellow horn shades. Edene walked in circles within the stone, and the water flooded out of her, and she felt mysteriously lighter and stronger with every moment that went by.

She had not allowed herself to think of the child as male or female before this moment. She had forced herself neither to consider names nor to ponder the child's future. Born into such a world, born to such parents—who could tempt fate?

But now, in her labor, feeling the suns wear across the sky outside as surely as if their light shone on her skin, she wondered if perhaps she should have focused her intention, brought her will to bear on her unborn and his or her future. If perhaps she should have tried to shape the child and the world with her will.

And so she wore circles in the stone floor, a round brown ghost that sailed in a fleet of gray and gaunt ones, and she felt the contractions coming faster and sharper, sharper and faster, until the world narrowed to a single perfect goal. She screamed aloud; she crouched down by the bathing pool. The ghulim urged her to the chair, but they were nothing to her. Temur should have been there, and Altantsetseg, and the female elders of the Tsareg clan. Perhaps Temur could have moved her, but these creatures might as well have been water dripping over stone.

Ghulim held her up on either side, supporting her arms and squeezing her hands. She screamed again. She caught her breath and held it, a fuller breath than she'd drawn in months. Blood seeped from the split scabs across her back. The pain was nothing. She felt her body stretch, felt the slip of something hard in blood. A ghul crouched before her, hands outstretched, her blood running over them. Edene shut her eyes, not to block out the sight but to concentrate her strength more fully.

There was the head. And there the rush of release as the tiny body followed. The physician (unless it was a midwife) held the babe up for Edene to see, bloody and trailing the cord still, eyes squinched with rage and throat distended with an unearthly howl.

"A boy," she said, surprised by the rush of disappointment. A boy, another soldier, another pawn for the games of kings—

A strong son. A hero. An heir to the Queen of Erem.

She closed her eyes with another contraction. When she opened them again, panting, disoriented, they were holding up the vein-fretted liverpurple placenta for her inspection. She watched a ghul run hands along the cord as if milking a mare to squeeze the blood from it into the babe, where it could do some good. Another lowered Edene to the floor, allowed her to sit, brought cold, wet cloths to lay between her thighs, towels to dry the sweat from her body, a robe to wrap her shoulders. Not the red one she'd been wearing before—how many hours?—but a blue one, fresh and dry.

She watched lazily as the ghulim cleaned and dried the babe. *A name, he'll need a name.* A call name and a true name, before the suns set that night. *I wonder if Temur will know. I wonder if there will be a moon.*

Her eyes drifted closed, and might have remained so until the babe was brought to her breast, except for the abrupt and enraged skreeling of the ghulim. Edene was on her feet, staggering, forcing herself to stand despite the exhaustion and pain. *Not so much blood lost then, not if I can do this.* But she was staggering, and it struck her that she could stand. That the physicians—unless they were midwives—were not holding her down.

She assessed the situation in an instant. The midwives had tied and cut the cord, and now the djinn held Edene's son in his palms, bent over him with a curious expression. The babe looked up, fascinated, silent, and the ghulim circled just beyond the djinn's reach, shrieking and clicking. As if the physical reach of a djinn's arm meant anything.

"My child," Edene said. She held out her hands, the strength of the ring buoying her. Could she contest a djinn, even so armed?

There is nothing of this world too strong for you, my Queen.

Ah, but was a djinn of *this* world? Even the Sorcerer-Prince had been defeated in the long run, though it had taken all the gods to do so. With a moment's chill, which she did not permit to reach her expression, Edene realized, *he wore this ring as well.*

Well, she would be a craftier queen than he had been prince. For one thing, Edene would arrange not to enrage the gods.

Nor would she trust in the actions of supernatural creatures.

The djinn smiled at her. He held the babe carefully and lifted it to his mouth as if to whisper in its ear. The child remained still, untouched by the fires that haloed the creature, and gurgled fascinatedly at whatever sounds too soft for Edene to hear came from the shapes the djinn's lips formed. The child was too young to smile in reality—she knew that—but still he seemed to smile in response.

"My *child*," she said, imperiously, as if there were not blood crusting on her thighs, as if her hair were not a sweat-drenched mass of tangles.

"Your child," said the djinn. He held his hands out, the babe within them. "I have taken the liberty of giving him a name. But you may call him Rakasa ai-Erem ai-Nar."

Edene looked into her son's indigo infant eyes, calm and dark and endless as the night, and felt as if the world were swept away around her.

HSIUNG AND HRAHIMA ARRIVED AMONG THE CARAVANSERAIS OF THE TRADE town in time for the festival of camels, an event they had not known to anticipate. Not—Hrahima admitted—that it would have changed their decisions. There was a time limit at play. But the presence of so much prey, in such close proximity, was simply . . . distracting.

Hrahima wouldn't eat another sentient creature unless she absolutely had to, of course, but that didn't stop the monkeys from smelling like food. Filthy food, when they gathered in their seething, chattering, poo-flinging tribes, but food nonetheless . . . and that was ignoring their flocks of prey animals, bred so dull and stupid they didn't even know to fight or run. And if human cities teemed with appetizing distractions, how much more so the corrals and picket lines of the caravanserais, where camels and pack mules and ponies of a dozen breeds jostled for hay and for water troughs. There were many of them—too many, suggesting that the caravan masters still felt no desire to risk their stock and lives upon a landscape at war.

The disappointing impression was reinforced by no sign anywhere of loading, or wagons loaded and ready, or camels under packs. No one seemed to be moving—not Qersnyk, not Song, not Aezin—not even the notoriously reckless Messalines, who would take their camel caravans across the Mother Sand itself in the cool season. The tents and clothes were every shade—green and blue, gray and white, dull yellows—and the sounds of voices and music rose on every side. They diced and quarreled; they cooked and fought; and in deference to the pale gray Rahazeen sky overhead many women went veiled, although not the Qersnyk—who did not care if Uthman savages thought them barbarians—and the Song, who considered their own cultural hegemony to extend to any ground upon which they stood.

There was even a group of Kyivvan traders, faces pale as mutton fat, encamped in a circle of their strange drab tents, a few Indrik-zver big as houses on tree-trunk legs picketed with elephant chains within. Even Hrahima could not consider those slope-backed giants dinner—at least, not once they were full grown—but the Kyivvans showed no more interest in leaving than anyone else. Still, Hrahima marked them; if they were to return home, they would at least be traveling in the right direction. If nothing easier presented itself, she would approach them and see if the protection of an Hrr-tchee, a wizard, a horse-lord, and a warrior-monk could help persuade them that it was better to seek a fortune on the road than huddle in a city that might itself trade hands several more times before the fighting was done.

The whole of the trade town sprawled under the scent of dust and dung, the haze of flies and smoke. A dozen languages and a thousand smells assaulted the senses. She caught a glimpse of troops moving through the haze, but either they didn't see her, or they didn't put a random Hrr-tchee together with the missing Qersnyk prince.

And then . . . there were those camels. Hsiung spotted them first, a whooping, shoving crowd surrounding a rope-marked square. Within it paced men leading beasts, both decked in rich finery. The camels had been bathed and perfumed and curried, their long lashes blackened and extended with a mixture of grease and lampblack that left alluring smudges below dewy eyes. Hrahima had seen the like on Rahazeen warriors, who shadowed their eyes in order to protect them from glare—and she had seen it as well on Uthman courtesans. When eyes were the only portion of the body permitted to show, they must be rendered most perfectly expressive.

Monkeys, she thought disgustedly, and then—glancing at stolid, barrel-bodied Brother Hsiung, she felt ashamed of herself. Had not her tendency to judge others harshly led her to where she now stood: alone in a land of soft-handed monsters?

If she had managed to regard others with charity, as illuminated in their own ways by the Sun Within, she might not be a rag-eared exile, wearing earrings she'd bought with mercenary gold to replace the ones that had been earned and given and stripped away again.

She huffed angrily at her own distraction, amused when three by-standers staggered back hastily and Brother Hsiung turned to her, a mild and curious expression decorating his pleasant face.

"A camel beauty contest," she said disingenuously, waving into the corral, the sweep of her gesture taking in gray and blue rags knotted on the rope boundaries and the slow pacing of a white-kaftaned man who—by the way he looked and frowned and looked again at every passing camel—must be the judge. "What will they think of next?"

Brother Hsiung grinned and shook his head, pushing his hood back to let the sunlight fall through the patchy, close-cropped stubble on his skull. His fingers seemed thick and soft for what Hrahima knew they were capable of—poetry, killing—and she took it as a reminder that things were not necessarily as they seemed.

They walked on.

Even in such a relatively cosmopolitan setting as the caravanserai of a city that straddled the Celadon Highway, the presence of a monk of the Wretched Mountain Temple Brotherhood in the company of an Hrr-tchee hunter was uncommon enough to occasion a good deal of comment. Hrahima's ears were keen, and she overheard more than she was intended to.

Ahead, another crowd—glimpsed between tents lining what passed for a thoroughfare—and the milling heads of coffee-gray and tea-golden camels under a pall of dust. Hrahima could pick out the sharp tang of their excitement, the ammonia reek of urine, the baked-grains smell of hunger from the bony children on their backs, starved until they were light as those feathered seeds that are lifted by the wind. Men in concealing dishdashas paced along each side of the road, stringing ropes marked with fluttering rags dyed shades of gray.

Marking the course. Hrahima wondered if there would be some sort of warning before the race began.

She leaned down until her whiskers brushed Brother Hsiung's ear. In a dialect of Song, she said, "People are talking about us."

He nodded, though whether he'd overheard too or he was encouraging her to continue was anyone's guess. But then he made a winding gesture with his hand, as if spooling yarn, and she guessed he wished a fuller explanation.

"That man there," she said, pointing below eye-level with her tail to a desert tribesman whose loose robe and full cowl shaded him from the punishing sun, "is mentioning to his friend that I might be the Cho-tse for whom the priests have offered a reward. Three streets over, a crier is calling Samarkar's and Temur's description through the streets as wanted criminals, and saying that anyone with information should come to Mehmed Caliph's troops for a reward. I'd say the Rahazeen are in town ahead of us again, and this time they have the local authorities in their red-stained palms."

Hsiung nodded. He pointed upward and shrugged.

"True," said Hrahima. "At least they can't rain assassins on us from the rooftops in a tent city." Although many of those tents were more like bannered pavilions. "But I'm beginning to think better of hiring on with a caravan. I think we're better served to buy horses and supplies and go it on our own."

They had come closer to the churning crowd around the camel paddock. Hrahima's ears twitched, her boughten rings jingling, at the rise of wailing music. Criers went out, clearing the road, and Hrahima lifted one of the boundary ropes for Hsiung before herself stepping over it. Hrahima had a clear view over the heads of even the tallest in the human crowd. All those delicious camels were males, jowly and bearded and so racing-fit they had no humps to speak of. They'd be stringy and lean. A pity.

They went from milling to bunched up, their bony-jointed, loincloth-clad jockeys guiding them into a group, shoving and jabbing for position behind a thick white tape. They might be rib-shadow thin and they might be children, but they perched on the rumps of their beasts as if they had been born there. One slashed another rider's camel across the nose with his crop; there were baritone camel squeals and shrill childish curses and when the second rider more or less brought his protesting beast under control, he retaliated against the first rider's flank. The proctors of the race seemed to have no interest in controlling the fights; at the rear of the group, two of the monkey cubs had come to blows. No one intervened, but their competition took the distraction as an opportunity to shove them back from the starting line.

Someone shouted. The whining music ended. A hush fell, and a booming voice counted backward from four. Someone shrilled on an instrument. The tape fell.

The jostling tan-and-gray animals, their woolly heads bobbing, straining on long pipe-curved necks, lunged forward. They did not gallop, but loped awkwardly, big padded feet slapping billows of dust from the road. The monkeys were pressed up against Hrahima in every direction, shoving Brother Hsiung against her. He grasped her wrist, cub-small monkey's fingers not quite closing around the bones, and tugged her back in the crowd, away from the rope. They were trapped here, pinned down; he was right to move them. Shrill screams of excitement and encouragement rose from the crowd. A woman all in black with heavy veils swaddling her head bounced on her toes, waving a fistful of gray and colored betting chits on high.

A bright line of pain wrapped Hrahima's throat, a weight on her back, and she staggered. She opened her mouth to roar. No sound escaped her, not even the hiss of breath, and suddenly her lungs burned with the need to empty. The camels thundered past, choking dust swirling around them. A man pulled a scarf across his face and pushed the veiled gambler aside. She shrieked and would have gone sprawling if the press of crowd had not caught her—but the crowd was rapidly pulling back. As Hsiung spun, reaching for whoever clung to Hrahima's back, the man with the scarf dropped a shining garrote over his head as well.

Hsiung had had warning. Hrahima saw him get a forearm up, between his neck and the wire, and then she was distracted by her own problems as another assassin in street clothes came at her, wielding a leather sack stitched up—she would guess—with sand or shot inside. *They do not mean to kill us.*

It was a small comfort as the wire and her rage dimmed the edges of her vision.

The monkey clinging to her shoulders had thrown his whole weight back on the wire; the one coming at her from the flank was committed. Hrahima somersaulted backward, dropping her hands to the shoulders of the one who had garroted her. She closed her claws and vaulted off again, ripping flesh and yanking her head clear of the wire when his hands jerked wide. The garrote scraped her face, leaving a burning welt and costing her several whiskers. She landed behind him and kicked out, disemboweling the assassin with the sap, but it cost her a blow that numbed her thigh. Better the leg than the skull. She could still force herself to stand on it, though it dragged.

The crowd melted away from her and Hsiung, if frantic pushing and shoving and screaming was melting. A few ranks back, race spectators shouted, irritated, too distracted by the heaving mass of camels surging by to turn and discover why the people behind them were shouting and shoving. The reek of blood and opened bowels rose in the sun—but the crippled and the mortally wounded assassins kept coming. The one Hrahima had gutted pushed slick gray bulges back into his tunic with one hand, a forearm-long knife curving from the other. The other had drawn a wheel-lock pistol and now clutched it low in a hand soaked with his own blood. He probably couldn't raise the arm any further, given the damage to his shoulder.

"So," said Hrahima in Uthman. "So much for nonlethal force, huh?"

Hsiung too had slipped his head from the noose, but it had entangled his fist, and now he and his opponent feinted at one another from opposite ends of the wire like duelists with hands bound together. The crescendoing noise of the crowd and the race tossed and crashed all around. Someone among the tents screamed in pain and surprise, and Hrahima saw more veiled men clad in tunics and loose trousers running from the alleys—running on the heads and shoulders of the crowd as if they skipped over boulders in a stream.

Oh, goat guts, thought Hrahima disgustedly. Her eyes met Hsiung's for a moment as he blocked a blow. A tremor shook the arm of the crippled assassin and his hand whitened with intention and pain. She had to finish this fast, before the ruckus brought Mehmed Caliph's troops of liberation—of occupation—running.

Hrahima dropped to the ground, leg-sweeping, just as Hsiung swung his own partner around and soundly into the back of the man with the gun. She had flattened her ears in exertion and anticipation; even so, the report left her head ringing like a struck bell. Fire lit her already-welted cheek and notched the ragged edge of an ear, but the man she'd disemboweled took the ball in his chest and staggered backward, the thick, glossy black blood pumping from a bubbling hole. White shards glinted in the gray of the flesh.

Hsiung had dispatched his man and the one with the knife, then swung to put his back to hers. Now Hrahima could see assassins coming from every side—except the road become a race track. She glanced at Hsiung.

He was already moving.

She darted after, stumbling on her her numbed leg—toward the rope, toward the road, toward the lashing legs and pounding feet of fifty giant, charging camels.

The boundary rope dipped as she vaulted it, but she was already bounding into the air again. She found herself among the tail end of the pack of stampeding camels, heard one of the child jockeys cry out as she rose up before his beast. Camels were not jumpers, like horses, but Hrahima twisted aside and took the buffet of the beast's impact shoulder to shoulder, rather than trampling feet into her belly, rib cage, head. She leapt, but not far enough—the leg failed her—and found herself perched atop a terrified, plunging animal. She was briefly conscious of soft wool beneath her pads, the surge of muscles. The animal twisted to strike at her, fouled its own legs, began to fall. Somewhere below her, Hsiung spun and dropped and dodged like a bat caught among a flight of arrows, and somehow kept his feet.

Hrahima leapt. Not down, but across, onto the back of another camel while the first collapsed beneath her feet. The child jockey, with more presence of mind than the first, cut at her with his whip. She bore the lash across shoulder and face, leapt again.

Hsiung had found his balance, nearly across the street, and turned now to face the remaining few camels. One bore down on him directly, froth flying from its dangling lip. He glanced right, where three assassins waited with drawn swords—

Hrahima hit the dust beside him with a sharp impact, scooped him into her grip, and leapt again—over the heads of the waiting assassins and into the crowd. She thought of running, but—no.

Spectators were scattering already. The assassins whirled, advancing as a well-drilled unit, and Hrahima was not naive enough to believe they'd left no friends at her flank. Hsiung put his back to hers; she drew one deep breath, her throat burning.

They were on her. Flats of the swords, still fighting to subdue. It was an advantage. She parried a blade with her forearm and broke the wrist of the man who'd dealt her no more than a stinging slap. He cried out when she swung him by that broken wrist into his partner. Behind her, she heard and felt Hsiung engage. Now the camels were past, and more were coming from the other side of the road—skilled, skilled beyond any usual measure, but only monkey-men.

A *lot* of monkey-men.

And the one advancing on her now was better than the rest. She could see it in his stance, in his sidling steps, in the elegant angle of his blades, long and longer.

"Here, puss," he said. "Try those claws on a son of the Scholar-God."

His allies flanked him. She could see that he meant to draw her out, away from Hsiung, to expose and surround her. Even an Hrr-tchee might find herself pulled down under odds such as those. But Hsiung was against her, moving calmly, his shoulders pressed to her back.

"Hsiung," she murmured.

He grunted, which might or might not be a violation of his vow of silence—but under the circumstances, she was willing to give him the benefit of the doubt.

"That caravan thing. I don't think it will work out."

Shift of his weight against her back. Agreement?

"What if we just kill these and take their supplies and horses?"

He rocked away from her, into a fighting crouch. Agreement.

Good enough.

Hrahima lifted one hand and, with a wiggle of her fingers, beckoned the assassin leader in.

SAMARKAR WAS PULLED UPRIGHT INTO A VAST WHITE SPACE THAT SMELLED OF incense and the nervous sweat of a dozen Rahazeen, and Temur's heart squeezed hard.

Temur had faced a pistol before. He hadn't realized there would be a qualitative difference in watching someone point one at Samarkar. On his own behalf, the tunnel vision and humming whiteout of battle mind might have taken him. He might have hurled himself at the woman dressed as a Nameless assassin and trusted his own strength and quickness to outfox hers.

For Samarkar . . . he froze.

Samarkar, standing in her coffin as Temur clambered upright in his, seemed smaller and more vulnerable out of her wizard's weeds. The billowing linen draped in loose folds about her as she withdrew reflexively from the gun muzzle, her hands raised, her body curled as if to protect her chest, throat, abdomen. No simple flesh could stop a bullet, nor any armor of which Temur was aware, but instinct was instinct. He had seen men hunch so from a sword or arrow, too—or a leveled lance. For all the good that it had done them.

Samarkar reached slowly and drew a corner of her veil up to hide her face.

The woman shook her head in—disgust? Though he could only see her eyes, Temur was surprised at how much emotion they revealed. And he was surprised, too, to realize that he recognized them—distinctive variegated hazel irises, with a dark chip out of the bottom of the left-hand one. He'd last seen *those* eyes across the snarling muzzle of a pistol, too—the man's hand darting to the touch-hole with a smoldering bit of slow match clutched between the fingers.

"Impossible," said Temur. "That was a man, and he's dead."

Too late, he realized he'd spoken aloud. But just as he was feeling a wave of relief at the realization that he'd used his own native tongue—and the Qersnyk words were starting to sound strange and clipped to his own ears—the woman with the gun said—also in Qersnyk—"Yes, he is. And soon you shall join him."

Her aim had not wavered from Samarkar's belly. "As if your heathen offenses were not great enough, you must count blasphemy among them? On top of all your other evils, to come into the sacred city, disguised in the garb of the faithful . . . ! Is there no desecration so base you will not undertake it?"

Her voice gave Temur pause. In it he heard not the ranting denuncia-tion of a demagogue—but a blistered, despairing tone. How strange, to find oneself touched by the sorrow and helpless outrage of an enemy. To recognize it—to feel the small chill of it within your breast.

And to know that understanding that grief, apprehending it, even feeling the deepest sympathy for the griever . . . would not stop him from doing whatever must be done to keep safe his women, his tribe . . . and to make himself king.

Around the woman—around the room—the Rahazeen shifted. But for the sound of their breathing—the steady, disciplined regard of their eyes—Temur and Samarkar and the Nameless woman might have been alone in the room. Of the bearers who had carried them into the qanats, there was no sign.

"How did you find us?" Samarkar asked. She stepped carefully over the edge of the coffin, keeping her gloved hands in sight. Temur could tell she was making conversation—stalling for time—and it stunned him that he had come to know her so well already. That she could extemporize—he was sure she had some plan—and trust him to follow without an expla-nation, after only a season or so of association.

If she had hoped to also garner some useful information, she was thwarted—although Temur suspected that the absence of smugglers from the scene was a clue.

"My master," said the woman assassin in Qersnyk, "wants you alive. None of my friends speak your tongue. I say this to you now so you will understand that that is not to be, and I will be making some very pro-found apologies to him I follow. You will not leave this place, Re Temur, who is so bold as to style himself *Khagan*."

"You know," Temur said, "if your brother hadn't spent a quarter-year trying to kill me, he'd be alive today."

Samarkar shifted beside him, her shoulder pressing his as she leaned across the small space between their coffins. He felt the tension in her, though he did not glance at her. If she had a plan, he would do nothing to suggest it to their captor.

He would stall.

Although perhaps, judging by the shaking hands and the narrowed eyes, provoking this woman was not the best way to secure his own safety, or Samarkar's.

He had no bow—not that a bow would have been useful under these circumstances—and the long knife thrust through his sash was not his favorite weapon. But if he could get to it, he stood a chance. The room was large, but even a large room wasn't much space for somebody with a pistol to control somebody with a knife.

"I know you are a wizard, woman," said the assassin. "Rest assured that I am warded against such things."

If the woman assassin's attention were to waver only for an instant, it would be sufficient for Temur to skin his blade. Or perhaps it would be better to go hand to hand, though then he must be confident of his ability to disarm her and turn the weapon on at least one of her supporters.

Through the chill of trained assessment, over the contradictory thunder of his heart, Temur felt the familiar focus of his battle rage rising. He shuddered like a fly-stung mare, a great muscular flinch that jerked his hand toward the hilt of the long knife. He restrained himself a moment before his fingertips brushed the hilt.

The assassin raised her gun. "Try it," she said, "and the wizard dies here as well. I'll shoot her in the gut. You wouldn't like to watch that."

It was a vortex within him as powerful as if he stood at the center of a storm on the steppe and drew all the fury of the lashing rain and thunder down. He saw a world tinged with crimson, felt his lips curl in a grin curved and red as the scar that puckered his throat. His fingers flexed with desire for the knife hilt, frozen in a grasping claw.

He held them still.

"Spare her," he said. "I will go quietly if you do."

"Temur!" Samarkar said, as if shocked. She turned to him; he saw the puff of cloth over her lips, saw one dark eye wink above her veil. Her hand went to her hip, where she wore no weapon beyond the short dagger without which no Uthman man would leave his bedchamber. It replaced her usual square-pommeled Rasan knife. Nevertheless, Temur took her meaning and in that instant skinned his own blade. There was a scraping sound of stone on metal as the Nameless woman pulled her trigger, a reek of gunpowder, and a concussion too sharp to be sound. Temur's head thundered as if lightning had struck beside him; the ground rocked under his feet like an unsteady mount.

The Nameless woman stared down for a moment at the ruined pistol clutched in her bloody hand.

"Good trick!" Temur yelled, leaping from his coffin with a naked blade brandished in his right hand. "Remember that one!"

He didn't imagine Samarkar could hear him. He couldn't hear himself. But she tossed him that short dagger, and now he had a parrying blade in his off hand. He moved forward, the wizard at his back as one of her bulletproof veils of shadowy, flickering green light swept like a curtain all around them. The Nameless collected themselves and rushed; their swords rang off the wards as if from chain mail. Like chain mail, the wards swung and rippled under each blow, and Temur felt Samarkar sway with the battering. This was not a stalemate, then, but a temporary defense.

He stepped to the veil and stabbed through it; it parted for his blade, and an assassin staggered back. Not hit—he hadn't been so lucky—but surprised by the blade's emerging where his own would not penetrate. It made an opening, which Temur—Samarkar sidling backward behind him—rushed to occupy. They were three steps closer to the foot of the stair spiraling up the walls of the chamber. The opening to the aqueducts lay behind them, on the other side of the Rahazeen—and Temur didn't fancy a fight through a maze of tunnels about which he knew less than nothing. If they were as elaborate as he suspected, he and Samarkar might win free only to starve down there.

"How do we get out of here?"

She still couldn't hear. Everything was muted, almost febrile—the rattle of swords, the shouts of Nameless warriors. Temur identified them because he knew they ought to be there, not because he could make out the sounds. He caught a glimpse of the Rahazeen woman. She was pushing forward again, her right hand hanging awkwardly, a scimitar in the left. She pointed it at the wards and muttered—by the moving of her lips—*something.*

A savagely green spark, sun-bright and seeming to drift as slowly, left the tip of her sword and lazily spanned the gap between blade and wards. As it touched the wards it seemed to dissolve, to melt a gap in them, a ring of actinic brilliance washing the darker jade away. Temur felt Samarkar stiffen against his back and the gap slammed closed, but now the whole of the wards seemed thinner and more diffuse.

He felt her voice vibrate her torso, but couldn't make out the words. He knew what the gist of them must be, however—*we can't let them bring the fight to us.*

Those stairs were their way out, and once they were on them—well, they would be exposed to missile weapons from the outside, but Samarkar had just proven definitively that she could deal with guns, and the narrowness of the staircase would keep them from being flanked. It was just a matter of reaching them—

The peal of hooves on stone cut through the cottony hum in Temur's ears as nothing should have. Each footfall rang as those of the Qoroos— that mythic one-horned beast that could walk on water or across grass without bending a blade—were said to, a sound so perfect even the deaf could hear. He glanced up through the veil of Samarkar's ward as another heavy-bellied spark swelled on the Nameless woman's sword tip, and saw—

Bansh, saddled and bridled, wheeling at the top of the steps to— impossibly—descend them. She lowered her head and charged down the spiral staircase at a canter, running as easily as if on level ground. Around them, most of the Rahazeen had whirled, aware now of an impending threat from behind. Samarkar too swung around, the need to watch Temur's back forgotten as the sound of ringing bells swept closer.

"Horses can't climb stairs," said Temur numbly. He glanced at Samarkar in time to read her lips as she answered, *Apparently this one can.*

Two of the Rahazeen unlimbered bows; Temur felt fear swell his throat as one nocked an arrow. He lunged, blade and arm piercing the ward before it caught his body, but came up short. The arrow flew—

—So did Bansh. Her sparse tail snapping behind her, the mare spun on the steps and kicked off, leaping from a height that should have shattered her legs when she landed. Samarkar gasped, her fingers suddenly tight on Temur's elbow as the mare sailed majestically into space. She tucked her legs like a dancer, back arched—and fell like a stone.

Temur was already running toward her when she landed, Samarkar keeping pace and keeping the wards around them. Bansh stumbled as she struck sand-scattered stone, but somehow stayed upright and converted the energy of her leap to a forward gallop. Three strides, four, and she was among the Rahazeen, scattering them as Temur shoved both knives through his sash, then beside Temur and Samarkar as Temur scooped an arm around Samarkar's waist and with the other caught the war saddle's high pommel. He kicked off, feeling the strain as he found a stirrup and slung himself into the saddle, a sharp twinge in one thigh. And then he was up, fumbling for the reins, Samarkar with her arms flung around his waist as she struggled to find her balance on the horse's rump.

"Go!" Temur shouted. "Go! Go!"

Bansh wheeled in one stride, leapt into a Rahazeen brandishing a sword and trampled him underfoot, and charged back toward the steps as Temur grabbed Samarkar's gloved wrists in both hands and held her with all his strength. Arrows shattered on stone around them as Bansh galloped up the stairs. Samarkar seemed to get a better grip on the saddle. Temur hesitantly released her wrists to grab his bow, slung in its usual place by his knee. Red stained his leg, soaking the white cloth of the Uthman trousers he wore, though there was no pain yet. He had stuck himself on the unsheathed dagger still shoved through his sash when he swung into the saddle.

He'd bind it later. It was a stab wound, and oozing more than welling. The danger would be heat in the wound, later on. Now, he found arrows in his quiver, and as Bansh charged up the steps circling the cistern, he returned volley toward the Rahazeen rapidly losing ground as they ran up the staircase behind. Another snort, another surge, and Bansh was over the top, in a vast domed chamber with open, pillared sides. Once it had sheltered the cistern; now it gave shade to a bustling market. The mare darted through the crowd, dodging pedestrians and carts, leaping a laden donkey as easily as if two grown people were not clinging to her back.

Samarkar squeaked and slid as they landed, and Temur clutched her arm again. His hearing was returning; he could make out the cries of those Bansh narrowly missed, the excited yells of the pursuit, the shrieks of children thrilled by the running mare. Many turned to them, a few reached out. One, Temur saw, grabbed after a rope. But the bay was gone before anyone could touch her, pale dust puffing from her hoofbeats, and then they were out in the sun among the glistening blue-and-white buildings of Asmaracanda, lost in the flow of traffic, climbing the spiral city as it rose within its alabaster walls—ascending, ascending, gone.

BANSH DROPPED TO A CANTER AND THEN A LESS CONSPICUOUS TROT A FEW streets on, finally slowing to a walk that would have been entirely unremarkable if it were not for the swelling red patch on Temur's thigh. He dragged a fold of robe across it as Samarkar slid from the horse's rump and came on his left side, standing on tiptoe to see.

"Temur—" she protested, the sickly scent of blood rich in her nose.

"No," he said. He laid a hand on her shoulder and lowered his voice, spoke in Uthman. "It's a scratch. Walk. Like a man, if you can. We can treat it when we're safe inside the museum of Juvaini Ala-Malik."

THE NAMELESS COMMANDER CAME UPON HRAHIMA LIKE A BUTTERFLY MADE of blades, and she felt a moment's respect. She parried—forearm to flat of his longer sword, turned to the side to let the shorter skim her ribs. She would have trapped it with an arm, but the assassin was fast, for monkey-kin, and tried a draw-cut that Hrahima avoided by the narrowest of margins. Another struck at her while she was distracted; she parried with a flat hand and nearly succeeded in putting the offending dagger into one of the man's own compatriots.

At her flank Brother Hsiung was a blur of fists and cropped head and wheat-flour-colored robes, always where the knives weren't. But there were too many, from all directions, and Hrahima and Hsiung no longer had the advantage of ground. Hrahima could leap away, lead them on a chase through flapping tents and corrals of panicked animals—if one did not slaughter her as she turned. She might be able to get an arm around Hsiung's waist and drag him with her—or he might slow her down enough that they would both be cut down in their footsteps.

Another wave of Nameless were arriving behind the first. Hrahima caught their scent, heard the running feet, saw the bob of veiled heads over the welter of combat. The Nameless leader closed again; another passage of arms where his allies covered his flanks and meant she could not use her weight and strength to her advantage.

There was a solution. An option other than death or capture, hers and Hsiung's. An option she should have avoided using . . . one she had, until now, been successful in avoiding using. She could either keep her honor and her anger, her refusal to accept her personal tragedy was a necessary part of the Immanent Destiny—the root of her exile, of her shaming—or she could prove herself a hypocrite and save her own life and the life of an innocent man.

The blades—and the Nameless—came faster now, a whirling storm of knives. For herself, Hrahima wouldn't have done it. But it would be different letting Hsiung die for her pride—and Temur and Samarkar, too, probably, if the means of escape were not ready whenever they came out of the sacred city.

It took a certain courage and a certain bloody-mindedness to turn your back on a god that dwelled within one, that offered strength for the taking if only you acknowledged it. Hrahima knew too well the temptation of that extra strength—

She didn't need to close her eyes to imagine a tom's musty scent filling her senses. She didn't have to cover her ears to hear a cub's laughing snarls as she wrestled with her father.

A blade cut her—not badly, but enough. Another. A soak of blood spotted Hsiung's torn sleeve, spattering her with warmth as he once again parried. More Nameless. More still.

The Sun Within was there, just under Hrahima's breastbone. She felt it burning, bright and strong and full of a power that would let her vanish from the very sight of these monkey-kin, snatch one up with her and draw from him the answers to all her questions—and she could feel, frail as a glass bauble, the barrier of will she had erected around that strength that wanted to flood her, protect her, use her—

So easy to touch. So willing to help. So redolent of capitulation to the ideal of the Immanent Destiny.

No, Hrahima thought. Breath burning her, arms dotted with bruises and slices.

She caught Hsiung around the waist with one arm, the Nameless leader—swords and all—by the wrist with the other—and leapt with everything that was in her. Leapt beyond the capabilities of any of the monkey-kin, and most Hrr-tchee.

And if the Sun Within leant her strength there as well, at least she could pretend to herself for a little while that she had held on to her integrity.

16

TSERING WOULD HAVE LIKED TO HAVE SAT WITH ASHRA WHILE SHE SLID IN and out of fever and ague, but there was no relenting in her duties to all the sick. The empress and her ladies arrived, arrayed like peasants in trousers and aprons, their hair braided up beneath masks—and that alleviated some of the pressure. But the truth was that there were just not enough people to tend all the sick; that more kept sickening despite everything they could do to mend the wards; that Tsarepheth lay so uneasy on the riverbanks that even a wizard hesitated to walk through her streets alone; that the Cold Fire tossed uneasily and would not be coaxed to return to its rest of long centuries; and that Ashra was not getting better.

She was strong, stubbornly healthy and fierce with it. At first, Tsering dared to hope. She saw Ashra rallying, saw the monstrous things she coughed out of her lungs, clutched her moments of lucidity as proof that all the vaunted skill and magic of the Wizards of Tsarepheth could save this one life—and if they could save this one life, they could save more.

But it became obvious that the infection in her lungs was turning into pneumonia, that her moments of lucidity were fewer and briefer, that—as predicted—the healing ale was not maturing fast enough to be of service. Tsering toiled beside the empress and kitchen drudges both, wearying under the burden of service, and saw wizards who had found the fullness of their power as helpless as was she. More died, and more. Pyres could not be constructed to hold them all. And now, even a few of the wizards and the palace staff began to fall ill. Not because of some unanticipated vector—Hong-la and Anil-la were confident that they had correctly identified how the demonlings spawned—but because exhausted people made mistakes, and a wizard who fell asleep outside, away from the wards of the Citadel, was as easy prey for whatever invisible forces laid the demonling eggs as would be any other woman or man. Jurchadai and the other shaman-rememberers were working their own wards around the city, accompanied by younger wizards and men-at-arms, but it was a slow process—especially as Yongten-la had decreed that no wizard go out unaccompanied, or even in small groups, until the civil unrest eased— which it showed no signs of doing, as the Bstangpo kept his royal guards closer and closer to home.

Still, Tsering came back to Ashra when she could. She held her hand, watched her lips split with fever, comforted her. She watched the Aezin woman's eyes grow glassy and the flesh sink over her bones. *Hold on*, she thought. *A few more days now. Hold on harder.*

Somehow she did, when Tsering would have said from the rattle of her breath that every hour might be her last. Until the ale matured, black and pungent. With Hong-la watching, Anil-la holding the beaker, Tser- ing herself dripped the first dose into Ashra's throat from a glass pipette.

It seemed to help. Tsering convinced herself that Ashra rallied, in the hours that came after, that she breathed easier. Or perhaps it was just that she'd grown too exhausted to cough any longer. All those around her, those who had fallen ill at the same time, had long since died and been replaced by the less ill. Ashra, too sick to be moved, lay behind screens to spare the newly infected the sight of what the future held in store for them.

When Tsering, furtively, kissed her forehead, patches of skin adhered to Tsering's lips as if she had kissed sunburn.

The next morning, having snatched a few desperate, desperately needed hours of sleep in the safety of the Citadel, Tsering returned to find Ashra's pallet occupied by a man in his middle years, still well enough to prop himself on his elbows and call for water in a weary tone. Tsering brought him his water, felt his forehead, inspected his chest. When she was done, she found the lay brother who had charge of this ward and asked where the Aezin woman had gone.

She had to ask three times before he understood her.

"To the pits," he said finally, and Tsering's eyes closed. It made no difference, she supposed, if a body went to mass burial. Everyone here dying was someone that somebody had known.

But then the lay brother blinked bleary eyes and said, "No, wait. Hong-la had left a note that if she died, he wished to autopsy her. She's been taken back to his surgery."

"Thank you," she said, turning before the words had quite left her mouth.

She didn't have the strength to run to the pavilion that Hong-la was using for dissections and as a laboratory, but she trudged as fast as her feet would bear her. When she came upon him, Hong-la was laying back the sheet to begin his first incision. He caught her eyes across Ashra's body and frowned.

"I am a wizard," Tsering said, amazed at her own temerity. "I have a right to be here."

Silently, he reached out to the tray his assistant was holding and extended a scalpel to her, handle first. He waited until she accepted it to say, "When we're done, she must be buried with the others. We've not enough wood to burn them all, not if we burned all Tsarepheth."

"What does it matter?" Tsering said. "She's gone on ahead. And she followed the Scholar-God or the Eternal Sky anyway, if she followed anyone. I don't think she'd wish to burn."

TEMUR AND SAMARKAR SOUGHT JUVAINI ALA-MALIK IN THE MUSEUM OF Man. An imposing edifice, it offered a forbidding façade to the street, glittering white and windowless five times Temur's mounted height. Only a grilled gateway broke that expanse between the road and the blue-and-violet tiled roof. Beyond the arch, a long tunneled entryway could be glimpsed, leading to a sort of paradise. A cool draught blew from that inner courtyard, air with enough moisture in it to lay the dust of the street. Green leaves rustled on the other end of the passage and one star-shaped white flower as big as Temur's palm glowed translucent in filtered sun.

Temur felt a painful pang of homesick longing for the lush gardens of Song, where so much of his youth had been spent—fighting, often, but in other pursuits as well—and in the company of his brother, mentor, protector. Their father being dead, Qulan had been more a parent to Temur than any man. And Temur had been able to repay him only with release from a terrible undeath.

It was something, at least, and usually that was a comfort. But at this moment, with the odor of sweet flowers and sweet water heavy on the air, Temur felt a pain in his chest more than the equal of any pain in his leg. *It is for Qulan I do this, as much as anyone.*

Samarkar, without looking at him, laid a hand on his calf above the boot. It still surprised him to find her alert to every nuance of his moods, even when he tried to hide them—but then, he found he could tell a lot from the pinch of her forehead or the smoothness of her cheeks, as well. "Do you need help dismounting?"

He shook his head. The wound would stiffen, and tomorrow he'd be limping—but, for now, the leg would bear his weight. He swung from Bansh's saddle, her reins looped loosely in his hand, and approached the gate.

In Uthman, he called for the porter.

The man who approached was green-eyed above his veil, giving Temur a bad moment, but the veil was white, and the porter was too tall and angular to resemble the Nameless assassin in more than that one detail. He paused within the grille—an arrow would have reached him, but Temur's bow was on the saddle, and a blade would not—and said, "Your business, please?"

"We come with a message from Ato Tesefahun," Temur said, as his grandfather had instructed. "We are to deliver it to Juvaini Ala-Malik and no other. I was told to give you the following words: flame, flame, stone."

"Wait within," said the doorkeeper, stepping forward to slide the bolts that held the grille closed at top and bottom. They were as long as Temur's forearm, as thick as bones. He shared a glance with Samarkar above their veils, wondering what sort of a museum this was that needed a castle's defenses within a walled sacred city where only the faithful were supposed to come and go.

He might have hesitated, but Bansh exhaled softly and stepped forward, lowering her head to enter the tunnel. She seemed to nod to the doorkeeper—standing behind the gate—and surely Temur could show no less courage and no less courtesy than his mare.

He hurried to keep up, and paused beside her before a second gate as the first was closed and bolted behind them. Samarkar stopped right behind him, close against the side of the mare.

"Wait here," the porter said, and disappeared behind a door in one side wall. If he noticed the blood revealed on Temur's trousers when he moved, he gave no sign.

At least they could get out again if they needed, for now they were on the same side as the bolts. And the shade was blessedly cool.

Temur leaned against Bansh's warm side, easing his wounded leg, and let the cool air fill his lungs while he waited. He wanted to sing her a soothing song, but that would have been for him more than her, given how calmly she stood—with relaxed neck and one hoof cocked. And it certainly would have given away his ethnicity to anyone who hadn't already noticed his saddle, his accent, and the distinctive breeding of his mare.

Although it wasn't as if he would be the first Qersnyk to convert to the Falzeen sect.

The wait wasn't long. Just long enough to make it a challenge not to shift and twist with tension while he waited. The quick patter of footsteps heralded the porter's return before the door to the passage opened cautiously—in deference to anyone who might be standing behind it, Temur presumed.

The porter had brought a bucket of water. He set it beside Bansh's head and said, "The mare will be well enough here. Professor Ala-Malik invites you within."

TEMUR DID NOT LIKE LEAVING BANSH, BUT HE SAW LITTLE CHOICE NOW: HE liked even less the idea of letting Samarkar go into the museum without him.

They ascended a stair that turned back on itself every few feet. On every second landing, there was a door, and at the third of these the porter paused. He drew a ring of keys from his belt and unlocked the passageway, then beckoned them onward. Temur shared another glance with Samarkar, who remained silent still—protecting her pose as a man.

Few would guard a place so well unless there were something to guard it from.

This door opened on another white-walled corridor, the stone underfoot grimed with untold centuries of ground-in dirt. They paused before an aged wooden door that had once been painted red, and the porter raised a ringed hand and knocked in the western fashion—with the back. He must have heard something through the thick wood that Temur did not, because a moment later he depressed a brass lever and swung the door open inward, then stepped aside to allow Temur and Samarkar access.

Before Temur even rounded the door, he smelled slightly rotten meat and stale blood. He might have recoiled, but Samarkar was right behind them, and the messengers they were playing—the messengers they were in fact—would not be put off by a sorcerer's experiments.

Or perhaps anyone would have, because when they stepped into the room, the first thing Temur glimpsed was a skinned cadaver laid on its back on a stone-topped table. A round man wearing a butcher's leather apron stood over it, his right hand clutching a pair of heavy secateurs while his left lifted open a plate of the corpse's severed ribs as if it were a trapdoor. Horn windows let the room be bright and yet still cool; a shadowless glow bathed them all as Temur paused within the door.

"I am Temur," he said. "This is Samarkar."

"Ah," the man who must be Juvaini Ala-Malik said. "Come in, come in." He beckoned—unfortunately, with the hand still holding the bone-severing shears. A gobbet of pink flesh flipped off the blades and the man set the shears down hastily. "Shut the door behind you."

Samarkar did, while Temur waited for her. Only when she had returned to his side did he start forward.

She seemed utterly unperturbed by the bloody mess on the dissection table before them. Temur thought he'd seen worse, but only on the battlefield. That was different than this, from a man whose skin had been cleanly and comprehensively peeled from his flesh. Or perhaps it was just that Temur had seen this in his dreams.

"Is that the work of the Sorcerer-Prince?" he asked.

Juvaini laid his shears down and let the chest-plate hinge closed. "It's certainly the work of someone who wants us to *think* of Sepehr. But if anyone is wearing this poor bastard's skin—well, you would think they would have done something else with the corpse other than leave it in a market square. Killing and impersonating a man would be more effective if nobody knew to be on their guard, wouldn't you think?"

Samarkar's shoulders rose and fell under her robes. "It depends," she said, stepping around Temur to get a better look at the corpse. "Who'd want to believe their own loved one had been replaced by a monster?"

"A woman," said Juvaini. "Rasan."

He moved as if to draw a veil across his face, and then seemed to realize both that his hands were daubed with gore and that he was not wearing a head wrap. His thick shock of hair and luxurious goatee had probably been glossy black once. Now they were silver-bright. He seemed to have been composed of fat fruits pushed together on straws—round shoulders and a round body set atop round legs, each joint of his fingers plump as a berry. Nevertheless, he moved lightly on the balls of his feet as he stepped away from the cadaver, stripping his apron off, and crossed to a basin by the wall.

"A wizard," said Samarkar. "And that is why I accompany Re Temur here and we intrude upon your research. Ato Tesefahun told us you might be able to tell us how to breach the defenses of Ala-Din."

"Ah," he said. He paused, frowning at a dry waterspout as Samarkar moved to operate the pump handle for him. She churned it up and down; on the third stroke a spurt of rusty water rewarded her efforts. Professor Ala-Malik dipped a brush into a pot of slimy brownish lye soap and began to scrub the blood from his fingers and arms. As the pink, frothy water ran away, he said, "And you think you can take a stronghold that has withstood the intentions of such conquerors as Temusan Khagan and the first Uthman Caliph?"

"I don't want to take it," Temur said. "I just want to get into it and get something back out again."

The round-bellied scholar considered. "For a friend of Tesefahun—"

Temur lowered his veil. "I am his grandson."

Water splashed his cuffs as Juvaini whirled. Concentration creased his face a moment, and then the man nodded. "Kebede's son?"

"Ashra's," Temur said.

That got a longer, sterner stare, then a curt nod. "Ancient history, then. It'd take a clever swindler to unearth that. Open the second drawer in the map chest, wizard, and remove the bottom map from the tray. My hands are still too moist."

Temur watched as Samarkar stepped up to a chest of drawers marked by wide, shallow apertures and began to do as Juvaini directed. She jerked her gloved hands back as she reached into the drawer, though, and cursed softly.

Wet hands or not, he rushed to her side. For his bulk, he moved as if he weighed no more than an inflated bladder. But she was already waving him back.

"Museum beetles," she said disgustedly. She hovered her hands over the drawer, and Temur saw the blue fire of her craft surround them. Something rustled and clicked within, and a moment later she gingerly insinuated her hands once again. She drew out a ragged-edged sheet of vellum, translucent and mottled in even this indirect light. Temur could see the damage the beetles had done to it, the gnawed channels and nibbled edges. But the ink on its scraped surface was black and fine, the lettering laid on by a certain hand—he could tell that much, even if he could not read it.

Samarkar brushed dead beetles a bit bigger than a grain of barley from the surface and laid the map upon a table that did not currently bear a partially dissected body up.

"You killed the beetles," Juvaini said, drawing back from her.

"Wizardry cannot create or destroy the process of life," Samarkar said primly. "I did, however, evaporate the water from within their bodies. They're quite desiccated now."

Temur limped forward, feeling Juvaini's eyes fasten on his awkward gate. The bloody trousers flashed red beneath the hem of his jacket with each stride. "You should have that seen to," Juvaini said.

"After we look at the map."

"Humor me," said Juvaini. "Tesefahun would hardly forgive me if I let his grandson's wound take a fever while I was standing within arm's reach. Sit on that stool and pull your trousers down. Madam—"

"She stays," said Temur, unwilling to let them be out of each other's sight in this potentially treacherous environment.

"It's all right," said Samarkar. "I am his woman. I've seen that thigh before."

Juvaini paused in his bustling about, silk thread and a pair of forceps balanced in one hand. "A Wizard of Tsarepheth," he said, while Temur was still contemplating how he felt to have her so plainly state the relationship, and in such blatant terms.

"The one does not preclude the other." Samarkar glanced significantly at the wealth of soft flesh ringing Juvaini's wrists. "Do you take an oath of poverty?"

He smiled. "Not as such," he answered. "So. Samarkar. That's the name of the Rasan rogue once-princess, if I have it right."

"I am the once-princess," Samarkar said. "Whether I'm a rogue or not is . . . more a matter of opinion."

"You'll have heard that Prince Tsansong escaped the flames, then—no? Well, then, news of your family. When the emperor made to burn him, a great bird descended from the heavens and snatched him from the flames. Half the world seems to be engaged in making book on where he'll re-emerge, and if he'll have an army at his back. I don't suppose you have any inside information . . . no? Pity."

"It's a greater surprise to me than anyone," Samarkar said. "We've been at sea some time."

Juvaini searched her face, but seemed satisfied with what he found there. He nodded briskly and turned to Temur. "All right. Let's see this wound."

JUVAINI PICKED OVER THE WOUND WHILE SAMARKAR OBSERVED AND HANDED him implements, leaving Temur feeling as much a specimen as the dead man stinking on the next table over. The two or three threads of cloth he retrieved before he stitched it up made Temur feel better about having it done, however. Such foreign matter in a wound could—would—fester, take heat, take poison, and kill.

"A half-moon and you can pull the stitches," said Juvaini to Samarkar when the line was knotted. "You know how to pull a stitch?"

Temur wasn't sure how he could tell so plainly that Samarkar smiled behind her veil—something about the shape of the eyes. "I'm wizard enough to rid you of vermin, *and* Temur of catgut. Now can we look at the map?"

"We can," he said, eyes narrowing as his thick silver forelock fell across them. A disconcerting spatter of blood adhered a half-dozen strands together. "But I'd like something of you in return."

ALA-DIN, DRAWN IN PLAN AND ELEVATIONS ON JUVAINI'S DAMAGED VELLUM by some long-dead architect, was as forbidding as its name—the Rock—suggested. And as lacking in weakness, even to Temur's siege-trained eye. He could see why his grandfather and his uncle had both spurned to conquer it—not only was it nearly unassailable in its fastness, atop a spire surrounded on all sides by many *yart* of barren, broken land, which would make any approach painfully obvious—but there was nothing much there worth having once you got it. The Sorcerer-Prince Sepehr's genius for an unbreakable citadel: put it somewhere nobody would have any interest in taking.

Juvaini noticed the way Temur measured the map with his thumb, figuring crossing times from the nearest terrain that would offer cover, and said, "It's said the al-Sepehrs keep a giant bird captive, a rukh, and use its offspring as spies."

"Funny," said Samarkar. "That's the second time in this conversation that a giant bird has been mentioned."

Juvaini winked. "Care to lay odds on it being a coincidence?"

"It's said," Temur said, "and it's true. The only crossing would be by night."

"Or by magic," said Samarkar. "But once we're there—how do we get *in*?"

"Ahh," said Juvaini. "Here's where I can help a grandson of Tesefahun." Carefully, he shifted the bowls of sand and the ink-pots and the lumpy jade toad that held the map flat, and even more carefully he turned it over. The sketch lines on the rear side were in graphite, faint and thin, and the beetle damage had rendered many of them illegible. Temur bent close, his queue falling over his shoulder beneath the disarrayed veil. He could just make out—

"Tunnels," said Samarkar. "Tunnels in the stone under the Rock."

"Just so!"

"But what's to have kept al-Sepehr from sealing them up?"

Juvaini shrugged. "The grace of the Scholar-God?"

Temur smiled tightly. "In that case, I hope She doesn't like fanatics any more than I do."

HRAHIMA HAD THOUGHT—FOOLISHLY IN RETROSPECT, BUT THE HEAT OF battle was never the best place for careful decisions—that she might induce the Nameless sergeant (or commander or whatever they called their field officers) to reveal where their horses and gear were stowed. Of course it didn't work out that way. He was Nameless, which was to say fanatical, and even a display of Hrr-tchee teeth wasn't likely to convince him. And having escaped reliance on the Sun Within to save Hsiung's life, she was even less inclined to bow her neck to the Immanent Destiny merely to obtain information. She thought she could have overpowered the Rahazeen assassin's will and intellect fairly easily—though it was possible (even likely) that the Nameless had disciplines that would protect them—but . . .

No. It would take more than that to break her convictions.

Also, there was no good place among the caravanserais of the trade town in which to question a detainee quietly. Or rather, there most likely was, but she didn't have access to it, or even the local knowledge to find out where it was. So she did what any sensible Hrr-tchee would have done.

She rather thought Hsiung wouldn't approve of her tearing the Nameless's throat out, so instead she pinched his carotid closed until he fainted, then left him in a heap in the dust and followed her nose. Or, more precisely, her exceptionally keen sense of smell.

Hsiung at her heels, she took off at a fast trot, casting back and forth

through the bazaar until she picked up the scent of the Nameless leader
carried on the dusty air. Hsiung jogged along behind her, nimble on his
feet for all his barrel chest. He tapped her upper arm three times before
she turned to him, dropping to a walk. Her earrings jangled discordantly—
irritatedly—when her ears flipped flat.

He was undaunted. He tapped his chest, tugged his robe. Pointed to
her.

She flipped her tail and turned away. But he wasn't about to let her
brush him off so easily, even when her hackles raised in threat. He did the
same, again—the tug at the sleeve of his robe, the finger jabbed at the
center of her breast. *You're like me. You're a priest.*

"No," she said. The roads—the dusty paths between the blocks of
corrals and tents—forked ahead. A picket line held a dozen horses of
Asmaracandan stock, grays and a chestnut and two bays, their luxurious
manes braided along crested necks to keep them from tangling the picket
lines and everything else in sight. The scent of the Rahazeen leader lingered here, and there were near-black banners strung up around the
site—a warning to anyone with eyes that these animals belonged to the
Nameless. There might be a guard or two anyway, and anything that
looked like a fight would certainly draw the attention of nearby caravan
guards. Their one advantage was that dusk was drawing near—but the
merchants looked out for each other, and Hrahima wasn't ready to take
the chance that anyone would ignore a theft in progress just because the
victims were Rahazeen. Especially when the new caliph's men had liber-
ated the city and could be around any corner—and the Rahazeen sect
appeared to be in favor of the royal court again. Anyway, she didn't want
to be arguing with Hsiung when she walked up to the tent and informed
whoever the Nameless had left in charge that their horses and supplies
belonged to her now.

She stopped hard, so Hsiung overshot her, and stood staring at him,
tail lashing, while he turned back.

He raised his eyebrows.

"No," she said. "I'm not a priest anymore. I lost my faith. Now I just
kill things with my hands."

He held his own hands up, the knuckles split with punching.

Despite her irritation, his persistence made her huff into her whiskers with amusement. Her heavy tail tip slapped the earth painfully as she crouched on her haunches, lowering her hands, retracting her claws. "I don't believe in God. She drops by once in a while and we argue about it. Now can you stop yammering on with your questions long enough for us to steal a few horses?"

THE FAVOR JUVAINI WANTED INVOLVED SAMARKAR'S OPINION OF A FEMALE patient. As a servant of the Scholar-God, he was prohibited from examining women directly, and under Rahazeen rule the city of Asmaracanda was currently not a welcoming environment to the Hasitani—the order of female mendicant scientists and physicians who would normally see to the ills of a woman. But Samarkar—as a woman and a heathen who was still a wizard and a physician of sorts—Samarkar could do something about it. And so, with Temur still unwilling to leave her side, she went with Juvaini down to a room divided by a screen, with a chair on one side and a cot on the other. Temur waited with Juvaini behind the screen while Samarkar went around it.

Juvaini had already sent for the patient. She waited on the edge of the cot, her body tucked together neatly in the encompassing folds of her robe until she took up almost no space at all. She was not just veiled but hooded, her hands gloved, her ankles wrapped with bandages above her shoes.

From behind the screen, Juvaini gave the woman direction, ordering her to remove her glove and show Samarkar the lesions on her skin. Samarkar bridled at his peremptory tone, but the woman obeyed silently, with bowed head. What was revealed beneath the wrappings made Samarkar bite her lip to keep from wincing and withdrawing.

Yellow-white margins of dead, peeling flesh surrounded seeping red lesions. It looked as if someone had burned her with an ember, over and over again, and scoured the resulting charred skin away.

"How did this happen?" Samarkar asked.

The woman startled at her voice, and Samarkar realized that though she'd been told that Samarkar was a woman, she'd believed it was a polite fiction to allow them to be in the same room together. But Samarkar's voice was unambiguously female.

Samarkar stopped herself and went back. "What is your name? I am Samarkar."

"Laili," the woman said, nearly a whisper.

As she peeled Laili's loose sleeve back, Samarkar found herself making horrified little clucking noises with her tongue, as if she—Samarkar—were the wet nurse who had replaced the mother Samarkar had never known. The burns were everywhere. "How did this come about?"

"It just started to happen," Laili said, her voice soft and uncertain. "One day there were blisters, and the next more blisters, and then the skin began to peel. There's pain, but . . . it's not as bad as it looks."

Of course not, Samarkar thought. *The skin is dead.*

"Is there any other pain?"

"My bones," she said. "My knees and hips."

Samarkar would have closed her eyes in pity, but it would have stolen all hope. She kept them open, and dry, and was not sure how. But she suspected she knew the answer.

"Anyone else in your family showing symptoms?"

Laili shook her head.

"Where have you been that they have not?"

"The glass sea," the woman said. "I am a widow, and I walk out to the sea to collect treasures to sell in the market."

"Professor Ala-Malik," Samarkar asked, raising her voice, "what is the glass sea?"

"Do you know the story of Danupati and the dragon?"

"No," she said.

He cleared his throat and spoke through the screen. "There is a place beyond the hills—they say it's where the Emperor Danupati rode out to battle the dragon, under the suns of Erem . . . before they set forever. The sand there is fused into glass. Some people collect 'treasures' there, historical artifacts. Mostly old coins, beads. There is supposed to have been a city there once, before the dragon came."

She described the lesions and said, "Have you heard of such?"

"Seen them often," he said. "Although never to the extent that you describe." He paused, and said in Rasan, "We have no effective treatment."

"I was afraid of that," she answered through the screen. "Neither do we."

Temur asked, "What is wrong with her?"

"We call it dragon-burns," Samarkar said. "There are places in the earth, in the caverns under the Cold Fire, where a man can walk and emerge unscathed . . . until days later, his skin blisters, his teeth fall out, his eyes cloud. It is a poison dragons leave in the earth where they have bled. There is no cure."

"Oh," he said.

A brief silence followed, and then sounds of an argument and a brief, not too strenuous scuffle. Samarkar was on her feet when Temur shoved the screen aside and came in, his veil drawn across his face. Laili pulled back from him, snatching after her glove where it lay on the cot. But he put his hand over it and raised a finger admonishing, and she froze.

"Temur!" Samarkar said, not so much scandalized as worried that he was endangering all three of them—all four, if she counted Juvaini. "What do you think you're doing?"

"You called me Khagan," he said in Qersnyk. "Let's see if you were right."

"By the Six Sacred Vows," Samarkar said, "don't you *promise* her anything—"

Softly, he took Laili's hand, though she froze when he touched her. "Peace," he said to her in his awkward Uthman.

He closed his eyes.

Samarkar saw the strain on his face, the gentleness with which he curled his dark fingers around her sore-spotted, tawny ones. She saw him take a breath and let it go again, the fold deepening between his eyes. The depth of his concentration—and the moment when that concentration folded and his eyes flicked open again, a gasp of effort escaping him.

Laili watched him with concern first, and then consternation. When he released her hand finally, reluctantly, she snatched it back and began working her glove on again, finger by finger, wincing where it rubbed injured skin.

Temur clenched his hand into a fist, then rippled the fingers as if massaging blood back into a limb that had fallen asleep.

"My apologies, madam," he said to Laili, standing from where he had crouched beside her and turning his back. "I am sorry."

"Did you hurt yourself?" Samarkar asked, too bemused for the moment to ask even what he had hoped to accomplish.

"No," he said bitterly. "I didn't feel a thing."

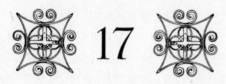

17

ONCE NIGHT FELL, JUVAINI LED SAMARKAR AND TEMUR THROUGH A CITY made wondrous by torches. Flames stained the white stone in shades of gold and orange, so it glowed like amber or carnelian before the sun, and Bansh's hoofbeats echoed in streets that were not deserted but much quieted from the traffic of the day. Samarkar thought of the great university at Rasa, the Citadel of Tsarepheth. This cloistered city of learning had the same hushed air of concentrated scholarship, as if knowledge hung like a pall in the very atmosphere.

They spent no more time in the streets than it would take an egg to boil, but for every step of it, Samarkar was too aware of the high walls surrounding them, the possibility of Nameless around every corner or simply Asmaracandan scholar-priests looking down from their cloistered windows to wonder what two on foot and one mounted on a steppe mare were doing in the street.

She was grateful enough not to have to climb back into a coffin that she was not about to complain. But that did not prevent her from having to force herself to walk normally, eyes front, rather than staring about in all directions for potential threats. The pose of normalcy took all her political experience to maintain.

Juvaini took them not to any of the main gates but to a narrow, iron-strapped portal no wider than the door to a house, close by the Museum of Man. He produced a key as long as a hand from his pocket and fitted it into the lock. "When I have the pins turned, lift the bar and haul the door back. It takes two."

"This place is as secured as a fortress," Temur said.

Juvaini paused long enough to cock a curious eye at him. "Don't academics and academies war upon each other where you're from?"

Samarkar smiled. Temur shrugged, and held his tongue.

Temur was dismounting from Bansh painfully, testing his injured leg—Samarkar eyed the mare and the narrow door dubiously, but she supposed she'd seen this particular horse do weirder things than not shy at close confinement—so Samarkar stepped forward. Juvaini leaned a little away from her, but made no remark.

Samarkar put her shoulder under the bar and heaved.

It was a rod of blackened, iron-shod hardwood as thick as her arm, hinged at one end and sliding through a guide at the other. She pushed hard, finding it as stiff as she'd expected. It showered flakes of rust and withered spider's-egg cases, but at least it gave a little, creaking . . . and then broke loose and jerked up abruptly with a horrible shriek.

"You should get a novice to oil this thing."

Juvaini shook his head amusedly and pushed, the door grating open on hinges that protested as volubly as had the bar. He stepped through, pulling the door wide—

And went to his knees with a crossbow bolt through the throat.

Samarkar swung back through the door, flattening herself against the stone wall beside it. There was no second bolt, though Temur threw himself to the side, dragging Bansh with him. In a few moments, he found his bow and nocked an arrow, but didn't step into the door or draw. He limped. Samarkar pushed down worry, fear, and rage for Juvaini. They would not help her calm the thunder of her pulse. They would not help her concentration as she called the power of her wizardry.

She drew upon her wards again and found them sluggish to respond, patchy and incomplete. She was still tired from earlier, her focus not what it should be. Still, she risked a glance around the doorframe, jerking back as another bolt sizzled past, striking sparks off the stones.

Juvaini was beyond help. He lay facedown across the threshold, just visible in what light fell through the doorway. That light caught on the streaked head of the bolt, protruding from just below his skull—steel-gray amid the silver hair. Blood spread dark from beneath him.

Samarkar caught Temur's eye and shook her head.

"One crossbowman," Temur said. "If that's how long it takes to send a second bolt."

"Or they're shooting staggered."

"The second one would have taken a shot at me or Bansh."

A good argument. She hoped it was also a correct one. "They might not have had enough men to cover every gate," she said. "If so, he's hoping to keep us pinned down until reinforcements arrive."

"So we go now," said Temur. "Mount up."

"The door's too narrow—"

"It is," he said. "We won't be using it."

He stepped into the doorway before she could protest again and sent three arrows singing into the dark. She didn't know if he aimed them, somehow—perhaps back along the trajectory of the one that had killed Juvaini? She just darted across the open space while he filled it, feeling the itch of a bolt that did not strike home between her shoulder blades. A moment, and she was pressed to Bansh's warm barrel while Temur fell back beside her. The mare turned to nose her, seemingly unperturbed. Samarkar stroked the soft nose with gloved fingertips, wishing she could feel the mare's velvety breath.

Temur gave her a leg into the saddle and handed her his bow before swinging up behind. She heard him grunt, felt the unwonted heaviness with which he settled to Bansh's back—but those were the only signs of his injury. That courage would cost him later, she thought.

Then he reached around her for the reins and turned Bansh in a tiny, mincing circle.

"All right, Immortal," he said. "I'm convinced. How are you going to get us out of this?"

The mare straightened her head out and broke into a canter, then a gallop: terrifying in an ill-lit, winding street so narrow Samarkar could have torn her palms on either wall just by holding her arms out straight.

She didn't do that. Instead, she reached around the high pommel in front of her and grabbed on tight.

A wall loomed before them, shadowed by the torches, a turn too sharp for a running horse to navigate. "Oh," Samarkar said, hunching reflexively for the impact—

It never came. With a surge of powerful haunches, the mare kicked off as if running down a hillside with great, sweeping strides. But in this case each leap bore her higher, mounting dark air that rang like solid stone beneath the impact of her hooves until she crested the wall and—still running, shaking her sparse mane—began to descend the other side. Finally, her hooves struck earth again, among the tents of the caravanserai, with men and boys spilling from every doorway to shout and point.

Bansh kept running, and in a moment the commotion had vanished behind. She slowed, snorting, her neck lathered beneath the reins, kicking each foot up like a parade horse as she settled into the trot.

Samarkar leaned back and turned her head to speak in Temur's ear. "Did you expect that?"

"I expected something," he said with a shrug. "You would think I would have caught on sooner, really." Shifting behind the saddle, he patted Bansh's rump with an open palm. Somehow, he'd both stayed on her back and held onto his bow, though Samarkar had the saddle and the stirrups. "I owe Buldshak and Edene an apology. It wasn't exactly fair to ask them to race you, was it, mare?"

Her tail swished, stinging Samarkar's thigh—and Temur's too, by the way he grunted.

"Juvaini," she said, craning backward.

"Nothing we could have done," he said. "Not that that helps."

"It should help," she said. There was a pause as Bansh wove down the narrow thoroughfares. Behind them, she could hear the cries of surprise and excitement dying away. Somebody would be drinking on this story tomorrow, but there didn't seem to be any pursuit. "How do we find Hsiung and Hrahima?"

"I give the pony her head," he said. "She seems to be able to find *me* anywhere."

✳   ✳   ✳

"OUR VERDICT FROM THE AUTOPSY? IT WOULD HAVE WORKED," HONG-LA said, one hand on Tsering's shoulder. "If we had access to the ale a little sooner, if the embryos had not been so developed . . . I believe she would have survived the process."

Across Yongten-la's study, the leader of the order paced slowly beside a shelf, picking objects up, turning them with his fingers, setting them down again. It might have seemed like distraction, unconcern. Hong-la knew Yongten-la well enough to understand that what he was seeing was exhaustion and despair.

He turned an obsidian carving of a contorted warrior over and over, wiping dust from its creases with a damp fingertip. His frown, his hesitancy, hurt Hong-la to see. This was not the master he knew, who led by example, through tireless energy, by doing what needed done and making room for other hands beside his own. This was an old man with a mottled pate, his face creased deep behind the stringy fall of his white moustache.

They were all so very, very tired.

He looked up. "Start with those less than a quarter-moon along the course of the infestation."

And left the rest unsaid. *We can save the most that way.*

TEMUR'S INSTINCTS PROVED GOOD. IN ONLY A FEW MOMENTS, THE MARE HAD brought them to the edge of the caravanserai and into the olive groves beyond. She continued on as unerringly as if she were returning home to a stable, eventually leading them out into a clearing where Hsiung and Hrahima waited, accompanied by three geldings and a mare.

Hrahima was on foot—the only reasonable choice, since she massed half as much as one of the horses, and even a Qersnyk all but born on horseback wouldn't want to try to convince a mare to carry a tiger on her back. Hsiung rode the largest of the geldings awkwardly, legs stuck out to each side. Two of the other horses were laden with gear, the fourth and final one saddled for Samarkar.

She slid from Bansh's back, leaving the saddle free for Temur to heave himself into, and walked across the clearing to the others. "How much did you pay for the horses?" she asked Hrahima, with the air of one accounting necessary supplies for a long journey.

"We couldn't pay for the horses."

"I beg your pardon?"

"The trade town was too hot for shopping and no caravans are moving until the wars are settled. Also, they were looking for us," Hrahima said. "So we stole these from the Nameless. The gear too. Come on; we'd best get as far as possible from Asmaracanda."

"Oh," Samarkar said—as Temur, slowly, began to laugh.

THEIR RIGHT HAND TWISTED IN A CLUB OF BANDAGES, THE TWINS AWAITED their master with bowed head. They had been waiting since sunrise, here out of sight of Asmaracanda, on a cliff overlooking the White Sea. Now the sun was high.

It beat on the veil swaddling the twins' head and cast the racing outline of the rukh's wings into a rippled shadow skimming the wrinkled waves below. Saadet forced herself not to step back as the vast bird plummeted to earth, backwinging at the last moment and landing, light as a ghost, on the cliff edge. The feather tips just brushed the twins' cheek; there was no pain, but a wet trickle told them blood had started below the eye.

They did not flinch. As the rukh settled her wings, the twins walked forward. They grasped the bottom of the knotted rope ladder that allowed access to the stable and steadied it as al-Sepehr descended. Having guided his foot to the ground, they straightened and moved back, only then remembering that, as they were wearing the body of a woman, it was inappropriate to have touched his shoe.

Al-Sepehr tugged his veil up to shade his face from the sun. "So," he said. "They elude you again."

Saadet bowed her head. Was it the frailness of a woman's form that limited her? Had she been mistaken to claim that she could stand in her brother's shoes?

"They have help," she said. "They are aided by a spirit, an afrit or some demon in the form of a horse. It is this beast that killed Shahruz, and it is this beast that foiled us today."

Al-Sepehr folded his hands inside his sleeves. "We must accept that if they still go free, they do so by the will of the Scholar-God. That She has some greater fate in store. Our efforts must be bent elsewhere. Perhaps She knows, as we cannot, that this Re Temur will only sow conflict on the battlefield and help to bring about Her greater glory."

"Master," the twins said. "It is possible that we should not serve you. Not in this . . . body."

Al-Sepehr waited a moment, in silence, while the twins bowed lower and lower before him, until their head nearly brushed their knees.

"Shahruz," he said. "Stand up."

The twins stood. Saadet could not make herself raise her eyes to the master's, though, as he obviously expected. "Master."

"I believe that the Scholar-God has transformed you in this way so that you may better serve Her," al-Sepehr said. "Now come with me. We have an errand to run, and when it is done, you will be ready to rule the Qersnyk tribes and bring them under Her dominion."

THERE WAS SOMETHING DIFFERENT ABOUT THE RELATIONSHIP BETWEEN HSI-ung and Hrahima, and it took several days for Samarkar to distill it down to its essence. Whatever had happened while Samarkar and Temur were in Asmaracanda, it had made Hsiung solicitous of the tiger.

At first they traveled by night, under the light of the moon, camping in draws and the shade of trees by day. But they saw no sign of pursuit, or the rukh, and began to hope that the Nameless had assumed they were making for the steppe again, perhaps to challenge Qori Buqa directly. Then they traveled harder, eating light, living off the land.

At least it was easier terrain than the Great Salt Desert they'd crossed on the way to Asitaneh. The stolen horses were hardy and nimble, and the four of them were well-seasoned to one another's company after previous hard travel, aware of their own capabilities and weaknesses and those of their companions.

Before a ten-day passed, though, Temur was increasingly aware that they hadn't sufficient supplies to take them through the mountains called the Shattered Pillars in safety—and that the season for safe travel was ending, even if they could find a pass. While they had the maps that Juvaini had provided, there was a reason that the Celadon Highway tended to run south of the White Sea and that only the hardy Kyivvans—who hadn't much choice, geographically speaking—used the northern shore. It was true, the Kyivvan traders could have taken riverboats to the White Sea—but river pirates, Rahazeen, and rogues made caravans—large, defended caravans with many Indrik-zver—the safer if more strenuous choice.

Bansh swelled with her foal, and as their supplies dwindled Temur reluctantly shifted one of the pack saddles to her and rode the bay gelding that Hrahima and Hsiung had secured. He was a nice enough horse, but Temur missed a good mare under him—Bansh, or even Edene's rose-gray Buldshak, left behind at Stone Steading for her own safety.

Hrahima supplemented their rations with meat, and the horses—fed from the saddlebags at first—graduated to forage as they climbed into soft alpine meadows. But, working as hard as they were, the horses needed grain. And the humans could not subsist indefinitely on rabbit and antelope.

Normally there would be resupply points along the trade road, other travelers with which to trade—but those had dried up and blown away with the caravans. They had trade goods, but no one to trade with. They had gold, but nothing to buy.

The vulture Temur had begun to think of as *his* bird still circled behind them. More and more, he began to direct his prayers to it—or through it, because though he still stood to pray to the Eternal Sky, the wind pulling tendrils from his queue to whip about his eyes, the sky he saw was someone else's. Not the azure depths of his own sky, but the shallow gray-turquoise of the sky of the Rahazeen. The vulture at least was familiar, sacred, significant. It was a thing of home. It was a messenger that could bear a dead man's soul home.

If that dead man had a name, and someone knew it to whisper it to the birds when they buried him in the sky.

Temur pushed the thought away. Hrahima leapt among the rocks up the trail, seeking their route between the stones and the delicate, curling flowers that grew in their shade. He turned and smiled at Samarkar, leading her gelding as she, too, toiled upward. He had what he had, and it was more than some men—most men—got.

✳　　✳　　✳

IN THE EVENING, TSERING COMBED OUT HER HAIR SO IT LAY IN SLEEK RIPPLES over her shoulders, black as the satin of her best wizard's coat. She closed her collar about her throat because it would force her chin up. She passed through the Citadel and across the Wreaking and presented herself before the fire of Tsareg Altantsetseg as a messenger bearing unpleasant news.

News that would not come as a surprise, she saw, for though Altantsetseg sat, as usual, enthroned on a battered old saddle and swaddled in bear skins, she was surrounded by her clan—the shaman-rememberer Jurchadai, a Tsareg woman with recent scars upon her face and a baby in a cradleboard, and an old man Tsering-la had not seen before. One of the shaggy mastiffs bigger than most men lay at her feet, his coat gray with falling ash.

There were ritual phrases for delivering bad news, portentous circumlocutions steeped in millennia of tradition. They circled in Tsering's brain, studied until they'd become reflexive—and she chose to abandon them all.

She bowed her head, dropped a knee on ground still blurred and gritty with ash despite a recent sweeping, and said, "I'm sorry."

Perhaps there was no need to translate so simple a phrase, because there was no pause before Altantsetseg answered, a string of syllables that banged together so that Tsering could not tell where one word ended and the next began. She waited, and the older man said for her, "Jurchadai informed the clan mother that Ashra died bravely."

"Her sacrifice will save the lives of many," Tsering agreed. "We would like permission to begin treatment of those of your folk who are infect—"

There was no warning. The gray drifts of ash that buried the sky blew in tandem curls as a thing too vast for Tsering to see and comprehend its shape struck the ground before her. The earth jumped up and struck her hands and breast; she had been knocked flat on her face. A great sharp pressure seemed to fill her ears, as it sometimes did when one climbed down from the mountains. It muffled the sound of something that might otherwise have been a thunderclap. She had a brief, blurred impression of scaly gray legs, talons like fishhooks as long as a man—there was another mighty buffet of wind and the enormous bird was gone, sailing down the pass away from Tsarepheth. Bent and reaching feather tips brushed the slopes on either side.

Tsering pushed herself to her knees, pushing gingerly at her scraped face with scraped fingers. She heard nothing but the ringing in her ears—and a keening wail thinned behind that pressure but still audible.

She turned from the waist, supporting herself with one hand.

The woman with the cradleboard knelt, curling Altantsetseg in her arms and wailing, her head thrown back and her throat bent to the sky. Even from here, Tsering could see the dark blood welling thickly from the old woman's nostrils and mouth, the crushed and twisted outline of her lower body.

A wizard should rise, should go to her. Tsering's legs would not bear her weight. She raised her hands to her mouth and moaned behind them.

The saddle Altantsetseg had been seated on was gone.

TEMUR AND THE OTHERS CLIMBED TOWARD WINTER.

The Shattered Pillars had a different character than the Steles of the Sky or even the Range of Ghosts. These were desert mountains, though tall enough to hold ice at the peaks. The slopes of high valleys sustained coniferous cloud forest cut by grassy glades, but the ridges were bare and dry. Water flowed through the passes, clear and sweet as it leapt from stone to stone, melt from the glaciers that glittered between branches every time there was a break in the canopy. The space below the trees was clear of undergrowth, carpeted by thick beds of feathery brown needles, and they slept soft on those at night beneath trees as big around as Temur and Samarkar could have spanned if they linked hands on either side.

The pines smelled of resin and cinnamon, spicy-sweet when you leaned close to their honeycomb-cracked trunks. Hsiung picked the gummy sap to chew and gathered pinecones that they toasted over fires at night for the fat seeds within. Hrahima took to the trees, moving through them as fast as the humans and horses covered the ground below.

Every time they broke out of the canopy, Temur caught himself scanning the sky for evidence of the rukh. It would have been smarter to travel by night, by moonlight. But that would have halved their rate of progress, and they were so close now to Edene—he could feel it. He could taste it in the back of his throat.

They pressed on.

On the thirty-fifth day, Temur slaughtered a gelding whose saddle packs hung empty. He divided the meat between Hrahima and the fire. Cooked, it would keep for several days in the cool of these high altitudes, and the grain they saved could go to the mares.

SLEEP ELUDED TEMUR. HE DOZED IN THE SADDLE BY DAY, THROUGH THE LEVEL parts of the passes where the gelding could bear him. At night, he kept watch while Hrahima disappeared into the darkness and Hsiung snored in the shadows just beyond the glitter of the coals. At first Samarkar came each night to lure him to her blankets, and he went—but once she muttered in dreams, he rose again and went to stare into the embers.

On the forty-fifth day, riding below a forked peak, they crested a pass in starlight and Temur saw no more mountains. The crumpled earth dropped away before him as if here a wave had broken, and the sky fell in lustrous, star-strewn drapes of ebony to a horizon as level and unbroken as the steppe. He drew the first free breath in a season. Though there was no moon, the sky above was big and free enough again, and he realized how much of his anxiety and distress since entering the Shattered Pillars had been the sense that at any moment the weight of the mountains might fall on him from every side.

Hot tears greased wind-chilled cheeks. Temur let them burn.

Beside Temur, Hsiung leaned awkwardly from his saddle—at least he was riding less like a sack of grain with two bolts of cloth stuck out on either side—and laid a hand on Temur's sleeve. Temur turned to see him pointing.

Low on the western horizon, a strange star burned. It flared bright, a sharp blue flicker, then dulled to sullen orange as if a fire guttered before a gust of wind and then flared white-hot again. As Temur watched, it flickered so dim he thought for a moment a cloud had drifted over it, then shaded from violet to brilliant blue once more. Stars twinkled; that would not have been stunning. But this one flashed like a diamond spun before a shaft of sun.

"Oh," Temur said. He looked over at Samarkar, but she was as rapt and—for once—as silent as Hsiung.

"Al-Ghul," said Hrahima. "The Demon Star. We are truly in the lands of the Nameless now."

And having met with winter, they climbed down again before summer was done.

On the fiftieth day, Samarkar came to Temur by the fire while Hsiung practiced his forms—his eyes shining dimly green in that fashion to which they had almost, uneasily, grown accustomed—and while Hrahima did whatever she did out in the darkness. She crouched, elbows draped over her knees, sleeves of her too-big wizard's coat rolled up to show forearms ropy and tough with the hard work of traveling, and said, "I was wrong, Re Temur. You must marry me."

He came close to toppling over into the fire. "Samarkar—"

"*Yes.* Under the customs of your people, you cannot marry. Under the customs of mine, your true name means less than nothing." She breathed deep, bit her lip, and stared into the fire for a moment before shaking her head. "There was news of my family in Asmaracanda."

"Your brother's escape from the fire."

She stared into the fire. He thought it was so she would not have to meet his gaze. "You know what it means."

"Civil war," Temur answered—because he knew his own family; he knew his own people; and he knew that no empire was truly all that different from another.

"One of them will want to use me against the other."

"You are not a princess anymore—"

"Do you really," she said, with such ponderous dignity that he fell silent, abashed, "think that matters in the slightest, Temur Khagan? One of them will use me against the other. Both of them will try. But if I am your wife—"

She sighed. He saw where she was going, but let her work around to it.

"—If I am your wife, then whichever wishes to use me must acknowledge you. Do you see?"

He did. Too clearly. He laid his fingers on her arm. She turned her hand over and captured his.

He said, "The whole world is going to war with itself."

"On Mukhtar ai-Idoj al-Sepehr's bidding. Do you suppose that's an accident?"

He held her hand in the silence, her palm sweating in the warmth between them. She said, "There might be a way to learn your name."

He blinked twice before he believed he'd heard her. He should have turned to her, but felt as if an unyielding giant gripped his skull. He couldn't shift his gaze from the leavened dark above the dying coals. Barely, convulsively, he managed to squeeze her fingers.

She knew him well enough to wait his moment of quiet out before continuing, "Do you suppose it's an accident that a steppe vulture has been following you since—what, Temur? Since Qarash, I would guess? If the souls of your ancestors go back to the Eternal Sky in the bellies of carrion birds, whose soul do you suppose rides in it?"

"No," he said. He couldn't let go of her hand. She didn't try to make him. "No, that's—that's blasphemy, that's an abomination. I could call, yes, but to learn my own name—" He swallowed twice before his voice returned. "If I knew it, what would prevent al-Sepehr or any of his devils from using it to bind me?"

"Temur Khagan." She avoided his gaze as much as he avoided hers. "It is time for you to think like a king."

THE WEATHERED OLD PEACE OF THE MOUNTAINS CALLED HRAHIMA, AND SHE yearned to embrace it. It rang in the empty places inside her and would have filled them if she allowed it to. But she knew what warmth it awoke: the fire of the Sun Within. The power whose purpose was to fulfill the Immanent Destiny.

Whatever you want, I deny it.

So she ran in the night, when she could have stood and nourished that energy, and she killed with her claws, and she did not listen to the wide silence within her breast where peace and certainty reigned. Instead, she embraced the wide, uncertain silence without—the emptiness, the foreign stars, the chill of trees against an uninhabited sky.

The old world hovered on vast indifferent wings above the thrust and intention of new gods. Tigers and men had created them, imbued them with needs and agendas. This night desired nothing; it offered nothing.

Hrahima found it soothing in its apathy.

MOUNTAIN SURRENDERED TO FOOTHILL; FOREST GAVE PLACE TO SCRUB. WHERE a spring bubbled amid the last grassy meadow, Temur slipped Bansh's halter and pulled the pack saddle from her back. Hrahima had made herself wisely scarce by scouting ahead. While Samarkar and Hsiung stood with the two remaining geldings and the silver-muzzled Asitaneh mare, he patted Bansh's swollen belly. The foal pushed sharply against his palm in return.

Hsiung had painted symbols of protection on Bansh's hooves; the ink shone glossier black against the dull surface of the right fore as she pawed a clod from the earth.

Temur straightened her sparse forelock between her eyes. "I'll be back for you. Be safe."

Maybe she understood. Because when he turned away, she dropped her muzzle to the grass and made no move to follow.

Temur rode into the furrowed badlands on a skinny mare he did not expect to ride out again, praying to a sky that was not the one he moved under.

THEY LEFT THE HORSES IN A BLIND CANYON TWO NIGHTS' WALK FROM WHERE the map said Ala-Din should lie. Shade from the canyon walls and a concealed seep meant there was water and grass. They could survive here for the few days it would take Temur and the others to return. And if Temur and the others did not return ... they were Asitaneh-bred. They would last in the desert, or they wouldn't.

Though it pained Temur to admit it, it was out of his hands.

Hrahima moved ahead like a striped ghost in the starlight, a blur to Temur's vision even once it had adapted to the dark. He found himself checking his bow, his knife, the arrows he had brought from Asitaneh and those he had made in the mountains with obsessive little pats. They were still nights from Ala-Din, but his heart sang in his ears as it should before a battle.

You must be calm, he told himself. *Edene needs you to be calm.* But to be so close, after so long—

He almost shrieked aloud when Samarkar laid a gentling hand on his shoulder. Only years of the discipline of raids and military maneuvers stopped his tongue. Then he turned to her, met her shadowy regard, felt the flex of her fingers, and felt the curling tension in his belly ease.

Half a year gone. But he had not failed Edene.

"Right," he said, and hoped she caught the blur of his smile.

THEY FOLLOWED THE BALEFUL WINKING EYE OF THE WESTERN STAR ALL NIGHT and sought shelter when gray washed it out of the sky. They bivouacked in the shade of an overhang bordered by scrub and cactus he did not know the names or uses of. Temur had half-expected the Rahazeen desert stronghold to be a vast sea of sand, a great trackless erg, and he was relieved to find instead a hard, ragged red-and-yellow land, for all its gullies and washes made for rough, unpredictable travel. At least there was water to be found, even here at the end of summer—though Hrahima had to show them how to dig for it in the backs of shallow caves and at the feet of cliffs hung in this season with brown rags of moss. That meant that Samarkar did not need to summon water from the air and could save her strength.

They spent the long day sleeping curled in what shade they could find. It was both a needed rest and a frustration. Temur forced himself to lie on his blanket and sweat and rest tired muscles, even if his mind would find no quiet. Hsiung and Samarkar both resorted to meditation. He was not sure what Hrahima did.

He did see, far overhead, the lazy gyre of the steppe vulture, turning in slow circles upon the foreign sky.

A little before nightfall, they chewed dried rations and washed sparing sips of water around their mouths and began to walk again. It was hard going—loose rocks stubbed Temur's toes and threatened to turn underfoot, and repeatedly he walked into some thorn-guarded shrub that left deep jabs and scratches in his flesh. His feet ached; he knew he would lose toenails to this march.

As they sought shelter in the gray morning that followed, the dawn breaking behind a ridge on the other side of the valley they paused above cast the silhouette of a five-fingered hand against the western skyline. Temur knew from the maps and plans—and poor dead Juvaini's descriptions—what that must be.

He set his gaze upon the curving towers of Ala-Din.

CROUCHED BESIDE A BOULDER UPON A ROCK-STREWN SLOPE IN THE RAHAZEEN wastelands, Samarkar thought, *This is all wrong.*

The stronghold of an evil wizard should be sighted at sunset, not in the rising light. It should not be limned in shades of persimmon and gold upon a clear pale sky, but outlined against black torn clouds in sullen, sepulchral crimson. Honeyed light flared behind the towers as the sun crested the rise, touching the peak behind Samarkar's head and leaving the valley below a well of cool blue shadow.

Hrahima made a questioning noise, as if Samarkar's distress scented the air.

Samarkar said, "It should not be so bright."

"Fear not," said Hrahima. "They'll fix that in the ballads. Besides, the damned thing looks like a talon."

The aspect of a clawed hand was undeniable, and the sort of detail a storyteller could not help but love. Then the wind shifted, bringing the reek of ammonia and rot strongly enough to make Samarkar's eyes burn and tear. A swarm of something indistinguishable with distance churned from the cliffs and towers like banners of smoke, indistinct dots that crawled across the bright horizon in flocks that rose and tore and tattered only to writhe and rejoin as if twisted by the wind.

"Oh, no," said Samarkar under her breath. She darted downslope, out of the shelter of the boulder, and caught Temur's wrist. He had stood rapt, watching the creatures rise, still safe in the well of shadow and lost in his own thoughts. As Samarkar dragged him back beneath the greasy red rock, he seemed as if he would have struggled, but stopped himself out of trust.

"Spies," she said, gesturing upward. "Come on. We have to hide until nightfall."

HIDE, YES, BUT THAT DID NOT STOP THEM FROM LYING IN THE SPARSE SHADE of the boulders, sipping water and studying the passage of the long-necked birds that came and went, memorizing the features of the valley that lay between them and the promontory upon which stood Ala-Din. It was a spare and terrible spire of rock, so stark that Temur could see why generations of Khagans and caliphs had decided to let the Nameless *keep* the blasted thing.

AT SUNSET, THE SWARMS OF CREATURES RETURNED TO ALA-DIN. SHORTLY thereafter, Temur and the others set off down the slope as dusk dimmed to true night and the shadows concealed them. They could risk no light beyond that provided by the stars, and within the valley's walls that was limited. The distance was not great, which proved fortunate, because the going was uneven and slow.

Temur found himself timing each step to the brightest pulse of the Demon Star, which surprised him by offering enough light to make a difference. Its pattern was erratic, so his footsteps grew rhythmless in response. Samarkar and Hsiung fanned out to either side. He could make their shapes out dimly against the lighter-colored earth and hear their occasional curses as they stubbed a toe or slid in sand. The going was particularly hard on Hsiung, with his clouded vision—but, true to his oath, he made no sound. Hrahima had gone on again, vanishing as utterly as if she had turned to a draught of night air, as old stories claimed was possible for the Cho-tse.

Perhaps a memory of those old legends explained how Temur managed to avoid stabbing Hrahima—or at least attempting to—when she appeared before him as suddenly as if she'd stepped out of a rip in the night.

"Guardians ahead," she muttered. "Can you smell them?"

Temur sniffed, but got nothing above the pooling smell of ammonia and corruption. It seemed to rest stronger here in the valley.

"I smell something dead," he said. "And the biggest bird cage the Sky has ever seen."

"They're not dead, exactly," Hrahima muttered. "And the chains are quite long. Have a care as you advance."

He would have asked, but she was off to warn Hsiung. Anyway, he could guess: his stomach lurched as he remembered they were dealing with a thearchate of necromantic cultists of the Scholar-God. The Rasani called the historic Sepehr al-Rachīd the Carrion King. Temur's own experience with the blood ghosts summoned by the modern necromancer-priest who styled himself *the* Sepehr suggested that the epithet had been well-earned.

He drew his long knife from his belt and reached for the soft-leather, folded packet of violet salt he'd taken to keeping always at hand. He spat down the fuller on each face of the blade and sprinkled gritty crystals down it. To either side he could hear Hsiung and Samarkar making their own preparations.

Then, without a glance or a signal beyond the understanding of long familiarity and close journeying, they collapsed into a knot and moved forward—Hrahima leading, Samarkar at the center.

Temur had rarely been grateful for the time he'd spent on battlefields, but he was grateful now. A slither of metal chinking against stone warned him a moment before the guardians of the valley lurched out of the dark, preceded by a wave of eye-watering rankness. He swung, aware of Hrahima to his right side picking something only dimly seen up and hurling it to the ground with bone-shattering force. The thing stabbed for him with a straight, wickedly tapered dagger and Temur's blade struck its arm as he riposted.

It was like striking bamboo or some other soft wood. The blade sank in but stuck, and Temur had to twist it loose again, one boot against the thing's chest for purchase while he dodged its other claws.

When he raised his eyes from its weapon, he dimly made out a humanlike shape clothed in rags. Al-Ghul flared on the horizon, low beside the jutting stone tower upon which stood Ala-Din. In its dim blue glow Temur glimpsed the face of a dead man.

The hardest shadows he had ever seen filled empty sockets, lay below the gaunt promontory of cheekbones that glimmered pale in the gaps through stretched, leathery skin. The cheeks had cracked apart; the mouth gaped like a snake's, showing snapping teeth nearly back to the mummified ears. He recoiled, and as the thing lurched after him he saw the steel chain—scoured shining by constant dragging—fastened around its waist and snaking behind it into the dark. Another mummified swordsman lurched up behind it, armed with sword and shield and dragging another bright chain ...

Someone had set these men here as defenders, and chained them so they could never retreat. And had left them, shackled in place, until they died of thirst or exposure—then kept fighting beyond what should have been the grave. Pity nauseated him—or perhaps that was the stench—but Temur hewed again, this time as if chopping wood. The night was a chaos of shadowy limbs and thrusting blades, but he felt his long knife crunch into a neck and danced aside as the dead man stabbed at him in return. Hsiung moved on the far side. Temur heard a brittle thud as the monk engaged and then the stick-snap fracture of dry bones.

Nothing mummified should smell like this. There were no soft organs left; the eyes had long since shriveled and the flesh dried. He heard Hrahima make a thick, choking noise like any disgusted cat as she tore an arm from the poor creature she was ripping apart, and he decided that the miasma was as much in his mind as in his nostrils.

There was a peal like thunder and something cracked off stone by Temur's foot, sending sparks and chips flying. Behind him, he heard Samarkar curse.

"Carbines?!" she demanded of the night. Temur felt her outrage as his own; as if reeking undead weren't bad enough, some had guns?

"Wards?" Temur suggested, ducking a swishing blow of the mummy's blade. The second one was catching up to the first. They weren't fast or nimble, but they were aggressive and seemingly nearly indestructible. Unless you were a Cho-tse and could just disassemble them—

He heard Hsiung grunt in pain, the rattle of more shaken chains in the dark. At least two more were coming at Hrahima, and he couldn't see what lay in the other direction.

"Wards glow," she answered, and he knew she was thinking of observers on the parapets of Ala-Din. "And I am not a strong enough wizard just to set the stones themselves against them. But wait, if these things aren't alive—"

A faint azure light swirled about her hands, as if she had coated them in mica dust and waved them in a shaft of sun. And that easily, on every side, the dead men—they didn't stiffen, because they were already stiff—*ceased*, one and all, between a moment and the next. They tottered and collapsed, the momentum of their attacks pulling them over when they no longer controlled it.

"—then my magic can touch them directly," Samarkar said, and even the light dripped away and dried up as she lowered her hands.

"Was that all of them?" Hrahima asked, dropping a dismembered arm.

A rattle of chain in the night answered before Samarkar could. Temur's ears ached with listening for the scrape of a ramrod, the click of a hammer being cocked.

"Just these," she said. "Let's hurry, and hope that one missed because they can't aim well in the dark."

HSIUNG LIMPED WITH A GASHED THIGH. SAMARKAR WORRIED ABOUT POISON in the wound but couldn't clean and bind it until they found a place to hide a light. Fortunately, they reached the bottom of the spire of stone without further interference. While Hrahima set about looking for the entrance to the promised tunnels, Samarkar pulled Hsiung into the shelter of a tumble of boulders and made a small witchlight. Fortunately, the wound was open, and, though she removed a few shreds of foreign matter, it seemed mostly clean. While they waited and Temur stood uneasy guard, she stitched it, wondering if it were some sort of portent that they had left Asmaracanda with Temur being wounded, only to arrive here and have Hsiung take a similar injury. At least she had sense enough to keep the question to herself.

When she was done with the leg, she cut the string, then handed Hsiung the needle and let him stitch up his trousers himself.

Hrahima returned before he was quite finished, sliding down rocks like a spill of oil. She crouched in their makeshift shelter and said, "At least they don't seem to have heard, or if they heard they don't seem to have thought much of the gunshots. There's activity on the parapets, but no more than last night."

She pointed with a pink-palmed hand, the claw fully retracted. "I found a tunnel. It's protected by a steel door and a lock."

"A padlock?" Samarkar asked.

"Self-lock. Looks like a big bolt, too."

Samarkar's belly clenched on anticipation. "My turn."

✳   ✳   ✳

TEMUR WATCHED AS SAMARKAR CROUCHED BEFORE A HANDLELESS BLACK door that could have guarded a king's vault or dungeon, a blue spark shaped like a miniature firework floating before her finger within the cavernous space of the keyhole. She could have poked her entire finger into the gap, but instead she just leaned her forehead against the steel straps and peered within.

"Stand back," she said at last. Temur withdrew a few more steps as Samarkar leaned to the side and stretched her arm out, keeping her face well clear and her fingers more than a hand span back from the lock, outlined in the sickly blue glow. She pinched air as if she held the head of a key, and Temur saw her eyes close in concentration.

The witchlight blinked out, leaving him dazzled in the darkness— but he saw Samarkar's hand rotate and heard a click exactly as if she had turned a key.

"Heh," she said. "Thought so."

The light shimmered into existence again, this time slightly larger and off to the side. Its drooping fronds were made of thousands of softly colored sparks, just as if scraps of something hung and burned in the sky after a rocket's explosion.

What it revealed was less beautiful: a glistening needle as long as a finger protruding from the lock. Its filament-fine tip—greased with some thick, translucent substance—had stopped a fingernail's width from Samarkar's hand. She smiled at it quite smugly.

"This wasn't meant to be opened from without," she said. "But the lock and hinges are well-maintained. I'd say we should be alert for guards within."

She stood, and with a wave of her hand gestured the door—too thick for Temur to have grasped the edge of—silently open.

18

Beyond the black door lay a winding stair.

Temur might have expected rough-hewn steps, or slabs laid unevenly to make a terrace up which one could scramble. But this was a grand flight, polished shining, the sweep of its curve echoed up ochre stone walls by fluted banisters of mahogany-veined red marble made violet by the light. The glow from Samarkar's witchmote spilled up it as she sent it high, revealing work that would have seemed rich in a Song prince's palace.

Samarkar turned over her shoulder so Temur saw the light shining sideways through her irises, remaking their near-black in gold and warm brown. "Step inside," she said. "I guess we'd better close the door."

Their footsteps did not echo as they climbed, for they took care. Hsiung went barefoot, and Temur and Samarkar each swaddled their boots in a layer of felt from the leg of Temur's well-worn trousers. It made the slick stairs treacherous, but their footfalls soft.

Hrahima's footfalls were—of course—as silent as any cat's. She bounded past Samarkar and led them, pushing the edge of Samarkar's light. Though the stairs were clean and dusted, fresh unlit torches set in the sconces that lined hewn walls, there was no sign of anyone—not even guards. Emptiness and perfect order gave the place an air of eeriness subtler and deeper than the horror of the dead men guarding it.

"Wasn't this supposed to be a labyrinth?" Temur asked at one point, in a whisper that nevertheless carried.

Hsiung shot him an aggrieved look, but Hrahima answered. "I think we've left the maps behind, Re Temur."

They came at last to a chamber—a landing, really, as it was no more than twice the diameter of the stair—from which there seemed no exit. Temur turned in place, fretting with the string of the bow slung across his back. "Have we been decoyed through the wrong door?"

"I can ask the stones—" Samarkar began hesitantly, but Hrahima raised a paw. "There's scent this way."

The chamber was round; it had no corners. Temur followed the Cho-tse to a wall and paused as she cast high and low. Finally, she extended the claw of one thumb and scratched lightly at the stone with it.

Something curled away, leaving a level-edged gouge at eye level. "Putty," said Hrahima. "Colored to match the stone." Quickly, she sketched out a shape less tall than Temur, and no more than half again his width.

Temur looked from it to the massive Cho-tse dubiously. "Hrahima—"

"A cat can fit through anything that will admit its head," she said carelessly. "Though for my dignity I beg you allow me to go last."

"Has it a lock like the other?" said Temur, looking at Samarkar.

She shook her head. "There are no mechanisms within. But there is magic." Lightly, she touched the groove that Hrahima had cleaned. "I wish Juvaini were here now."

"To complain about his map?"

She smiled, though it looked like an effort. "He might know what the pass phrase is."

"Sepehr al-Rachīd?" Temur said hopefully. But the stone sat in place, obdurate, leaving Temur to frown back just as stubbornly.

Samarkar laid her fingers against the stone and said, in the Rahazeen dialect of Uthman, "For the Nameless. For the—ow!"

She snatched her hand back. When she raised it to inspect, it dripped red from the fingertips. A tiny perfect lozenge shape of pinpricks marred each one, as if a minuscule snake had bitten her. "Not that," she said disgustedly.

Hsiung touched Temur's sleeve. Startled, he looked at the mute monk, struck by the way his blue-clouded eyes shimmered like milky moonstones in the inconstant light. Hsiung mimed covering ears and moving back. When Temur cocked his head at him, the monk did it again, more emphatically.

Temur glanced at Samarkar and Hrahima. "He wants us to move back."

Hsiung patted his arm, and again placed his palms over his ears and squinched his face to close his eyes.

"Move back," said Hrahima. "And make ourselves deaf and blind."

THEY CROUCHED AROUND THE TOP CURVE OF THE STAIR, HANDS OVER EARS, hunkered together as if expecting an explosion. And perhaps it was like that—whatever happened, even through blocked ears there was a sound like a human voice, like a tolling bell, like a braid of hot barbed wire drawn through Temur's head by way of his ears. He gasped aloud and regretted it: the sound got into his mouth and scorched his tongue like lye—bitter, burning, while he struggled to spit it out again. It faded fast, though when he pulled his hands from his ears he felt as if the skin on their backs was blistered by the sun.

They climbed up the stairs to find Hsiung before a stone block that had moved into the chamber and slid aside, his eyes glowing green as he spat a tooth onto the floor. His lips were blistered; he probed them gently with his tongue.

"The tongue of Erem," Samarkar said. "I am sorry."

He shrugged, and did not speak again.

NOW THE STAIR GAVE WAY TO A CORRIDOR CROSSED AT REGULAR INTERVALS by other corridors, this one constructed of mortared boulders rather than hewn from the earth's old stones. Hrahima led them again, whiskers flicking as she sniffed and listened. "Women this way," she murmured at last. "Do you suppose he would have put her in his harem?"

"I do not pretend to understand him," Temur whispered. "We will go first where there are many women, and then we will see what other women there are—in cells, I imagine, or the high places of the tower. I assume you cannot tell a Qersnyk woman from a Rahazeen?"

"In the field?" Hrahima asked. "Of course. Here, where they eat the same meals strewn with the same spices?" She shook her head, her heavy ruff rippling, disturbing the order of her stripes until she stopped and they lay sleek again. "Your flesh stinks the same."

THE EMPTINESS OF THE CORRIDORS MADE THEIR TASK EASIER, BUT TEMUR's skin shuddered with every step. Once, Hrahima pulled them into a side room to avoid two old men in white robes who laughed and argued in Rahazeen accents as they walked, their indigo veils draped loosely about their necks here in this their stronghold. Other than that, they saw no one.

"This place should be crawling," Temur said at last, when he could stand it no longer.

"It was," said Hrahima. "By the scent of things."

"Where are all the Rahazeen?"

She looked at him sadly. "Asitaneh, Temur Khagan. Asmaracanda."

THEY HAD LEFT THEIR OLD AND THEIR WOMEN BEHIND, THOUGH. HRAHIMA led them down a polished corridor, along the margins of a courtyard shadowed by night, and at last over a wall into a thorny garden. She leapt the roses that lined the stone fence easily, as did Hsiung; they snagged on Temur's tunic and the hem of Samarkar's black coat. She—Samarkar— reached out to him while he was disentangling himself, silently and in haste, and squeezed his shoulder softly.

It was all she offered.

It was enough.

The garden and its wall ringed and shielded a long room pierced by airy windows. There were arches without glass or paper, pieced and pierced and open to the cool air of the night. Long drapes in pastel shades hung before them, a few pulled to one side, all lit like jewels from behind with the light of lanterns. Music in quarter tones floated limpidly from within, but there was no singing, although Temur glimpsed the sleek dark heads of unveiled women seated amid cushions.

Paths sealed with pale stones led to several of the windows, which were tall as Hrahima—and reached almost to the ground so there was only a low sill to step over. Temur felt his hands shaking as Hrahima allowed him the lead. But so many of their backs were to the windows. They faced a slender girl who bowed over the bent neck of an oud, her fingers moving effortlessly as she played within the veil of her unbound hair.

He could wait, observe. See if he spotted her. Surely these women would raise the alarm if they noticed him. These were likely to be wives, here in this open gallery, and not captives. He *should* wait. But the night was wasting, and he could not leave and seek Edene elsewhere in the compound until he was sure.

The lutenist came to the end of her song.

While Hsiung and Samarkar remained flanking him, Hrahima vanished to the roof of the gallery. Temur stepped up into the window and crouched upon the frame. "Edene," he called.

His voice was too soft. He drew a breath and yelled, "Edene!"

Forty faces turned to him, women as young as Edene—as the lutenist—women older than Samarkar, with gray streaks in their hair. They pivoted in place, from the waist, without moving their hips. They did not reach out their hands.

Every one of them stared at him with blue-white, unblinking eyes. The lutenist, her hands tightening on the neck of her instrument, opened her mouth and made a garbled, inchoate noise.

Temur stood frozen, the window frame biting his fingers, as her china-blind eyes began to flare with the crawling green glow they had seen so many times in Hsiung's. Hers, and those of every other woman in the room.

Temur fell backward from the window frame, recoiling as he scrambled to get away. Samarkar was beside him, hauling him to his feet. Hsiung stood behind her, his eyes too blazing with that unholy light. Something. Something the al-Sepehr was doing *caused* that glow.

Temur turned to Samarkar; even night-blinded by the brightness within, he could make out her stricken face. She had seen what he had seen.

She jerked his arm as if it was his fault.

"They read to him," Samarkar said fiercely. "Don't you understand? They read the books of Erem to him, and they wither *and go dumb and blind.*"

He might have remained there, horrorstruck, forever—except from the roof behind them, Hrahima said, "This way. Climb. Run."

TEMUR SCUTTLED OVER ROOF TILES ON ALL FOURS, GRATEFUL HE'D PAUSED to kick the scraps of felt from his boots. Samarkar, raised to a childhood scrambling over cliffs and among river stones, was considerably more nimble, but at least he had the advantage of balance developed over years in the saddle. Unsurprisingly, Hrahima moved like mist over stones. Hsiung kept up surprisingly well for such a barrel-bodied man, leaving Temur wondering not for the first time what the training of a Song monk entailed. He'd seen a few in court or along roadsides; even fought them, when he and his brother were serving as his uncle Mongke Khagan's daggered hand in the south and east. He had never before *known* one. It seemed to him a great loss.

He wondered briefly, bitterly, how many people at the borders of his grandfather's empire he would be able to say the same of before all his killing was done and the Eternal Sky turned his nameless soul away to drift aimlessly, ineffectually through the world.

"This way," Hrahima whispered. "There are windows up the tower here. The scent is cold, but these rooms have had two women within."

The terraced roofs brought them within thrice Temur's height of the window she indicated. Samarkar seemed willing to climb it, testing the crevices between the stones with fingertips and toes—but Hrahima simply jumped up, and a moment later a thin rope slithered down. It was a simple enough matter for Temur to climb up, feet on the wall and hands on the knotted line, while Samarkar and Hsiung remained behind to guard their escape. The last grab and heave over the ledge taxed him, but not so badly that he made a sound.

For the second time that night he crouched in a window frame, but this time the room he faced was dark and stale. He knelt, rubbing life back into his forearms, aware that he was silhouetted against the star-strewn sky—but if there had been an enemy in this room, Hrahima would have already dealt with it.

He hopped down when his eyes had adjusted and he could be sure of not landing on any furniture. A moment later and with a chinking sound light flared, dazzling him again. Hrahima had kindled a small oil lamp with flint and pyrite. He turned in place as the yellow light spilled across the floor, a dim glow but sufficient.

"A woman stayed here," Hrahima said. "Another visited her from time to time. The scent is cold. Since then, the room has been uninhabited."

"How long?" Temur asked.

"Months," said Hrahima. She went to a chest beside the bed and knelt, and opened it, and began removing things. Women's Uthman veils, and desert robes . . . and folded at the bottom, a pair of Qersnyk trousers and a patchwork, skirted coat, mostly in shades of green and ivory. Temur came to her—even hunkered on her heels, she was nearly as tall as he—and touched the braid at the standing collar.

"Hers," he said.

Hrahima's whiskers smoothed back against her face. "I cannot smell her blood."

"You would, if she had died here?"

"If she had died in Ala-Din," Hrahima said. "And not in some sealed place. And in such a manner as to spill her blood."

"She is nowhere, then."

"She is not in Ala-Din."

He nodded. "There would be no tracking her across the sand after so long?"

"I am sorry," said the tiger.

He touched her shoulder, her fur slick and dense and soft. Her earrings chimed with the distressed flicker of her ragged ears.

"There's something else," Hrahima said. "She was with child."

Temur flinched.

Hrahima rose from her crouch with effortless power. He did not move away from her, though the rise and fall of her breathing brushed their arms together and she loomed over him, even stooping so the tall ceiling did not brush her head. Hesitantly, as if offering a gift she thought unwanted, she said, "I know what it is to lose a mate and child, Temur Khagan."

His eyes burned; he let the tears flow. There was no shame for a man in weeping for lost family. He had seen his brother weep so, for a father Temur had not known. He turned his face to the window so the night breeze could cool his cheeks.

"His name was Feroushi. Hers . . ." Tigers did not cry, so that grunt could not be a sob. "Hers was Khraveh."

He had no answer, so he paused to let her know he had heard. What did you say? *I'm sorry? I am honored by your trust? So much is suddenly made clear?*

All of it, inadequate as the rain that fell in droughts and evaporated before reaching and quenching the thirsty earth.

He touched Hrahima's hand with the back of his own. "She escaped," he said. "She is a Qersnyk woman. I will go home and raise my banner, and she will find me."

"Temur—"

He raised his hand to silence the Cho-tse. "She will find me. She is Edene."

THE WOMEN THEY HAD DISTURBED DID NOT SEEM TO HAVE RAISED THE alarm. But then, Samarkar thought, sliding her hands fretfully across roof tiles in the dark, how could they?

She and Hsiung hunkered like gargoyles near the wall of the upper story, where they would not be silhouetted against the sky or easily visible from below. They crouched back-to-back, keeping watch in opposite directions while they waited for Hrahima and Temur to return—but Samarkar found even the sound of his breathing comforting.

She had lain enough nights awake in a virgin princess's broad empty bed—hostage to a foreign kingdom, wondering if the morning would bring her husband-in-name's wrath—to appreciate the simple presence of an ally. It was something not to be alone in the dark.

The compound spread out around them, still nerve-wrackingly empty. A few lights burned here and there, but there were none in the long building she presumed to be the barracks and only a few glowing warm

and dim in the various high rooms of the five towers. A guard walked a
desultory circuit around the parapets of the turrets, each in turn, gleams
of his lantern flashing this way and that. She watched him scurrying
across the courtyard as he moved from one tower to the next, his silhouette craning its head from side to side. Conscientious as he was, that light
would blind him to anything outside its beam.

That he was needed made her realize that all the Nameless assassins
were busy elsewhere. She wondered how many of the ones she and the
others had been meeting were sell-swords playing a part in blue veils, like
the mercenary actors they had killed in the high passes of the Steles of
the Sky when they escaped Tsarepheth.

She supposed it should be a comfort that the Nameless resources were
drawn so thin . . . but the small size of this stronghold instead filled her
with wonder. Samarkar had some experience estimating the size of a
force from the quarters available in which to garrison. That this man,
this al-Sepehr, had created so much chaos, so many dead, with only these
resources at his command—

We have killed a significant fraction of his men.

And yet he—he and his sorcery, he and his cat's-paws—had destroyed
two cities and conquered at least two more, and all through manipulation, indirection, and bloody magics. It was an evil kind of statecraft, but
wickedly effectual.

We might come back here. It would be good to have a better idea of the lay of the land.

She paused in the midst of shifting her weight.

I wonder if I can find this sorcerer's library.

There, at the center of the compound, was something that looked like
a chapel—but it was the brightest place in Ala-Din. It glowed with a
steady light as if a thousand lamps burned within, and Samarkar did not
feel up to taking on however many Nameless might be attending services
within. But books . . .

A wizard should be able to find a shelf of books anywhere, Samarkar.

She reached behind her, touching Hsiung's bare foot to let him know
she was edging away. He turned and caught her eye, made sure he had her
attention before he nodded. The green flicker in his gaze unnerved her
and she quickly averted her eyes. Slowly, testing each step, she moved away.

What was a book? Not just ink and fiber and stitchery: a series of processes. To a wizard, it was not a static object—but human thought caught and bound, made concrete through a sacred technology. Magic, then, and a deep form of it.

Gently, Samarkar reached out with *otherwise* perceptions, all too aware of the possibilities of arcane traps left waiting for the blundering of an unsuspecting wizard. She found the edges of a few, but since she wasn't launching an attack, she skirted the defenses rather than attempting to undo them.

Books. Somewhere here there should be rather a lot of them. The Nameless might be a cult, but they were a cult of the *Scholar-God*, with all the implied worship of knowledge. Oh, of course; the long hall so lit up would be the scriptorium, and any actual monks of the Nameless would be involved in their prayer rituals of copying books out by hand. So that was one thing, and there *were* books there. And the whole stronghold reeked of dire old magics. She sensed something in another tower: a brooding, leaden presence with no pretense of humanity . . . and everywhere the *otherwise* world hung moss-heavy with the sense of lives incomplete and bound to remain uncompleted. Deaths in abeyance; quietus withheld.

Samarkar thought of what Temur had told her of the blood ghosts. Perhaps when they found Edene, she could free them. Except, not knowing their names . . . what would freeing them do? It would prevent al-Sepehr from using them as a weapon (she thought of the sucked bones of Kashe, piled in meticulous pyramids), but it would not prevent them from ravaging anything they came into contact with, simply because they were blood ghosts and the hungry dead.

Somewhere in the darkness, she heard the rustle of great wings.

The rukh. But if it knew she was there, it made no sound of alarm. Perhaps like other birds it slept in the dark. Perhaps—

The blood ghosts. The dead men chained in the valley.

Perhaps the rukh was not a willing ally to the Nameless after all.

She found the library. And blinked a moment in surprise: it was immediately on her left, within the tower.

Just above the women's quarters. Of course.

Hsiung was still glancing at her occasionally. The next time he did, she gestured to the windows. These were of a casement type, definitely added since the ancient construction of Ala-Din. Though they latched and were glazed, they were no trouble for a wizard to open from without. She worked the lock by magic, pivoted the sash, and slipped within.

The room was dark and still and sweet with the smell of old paper. Taking a breath, Samarkar summoned a small witchlight low above her hand. It took a little extra effort, but she shaded the color to gold: more like a lamp. Less likely, she hoped, to draw the attention of a casual observer.

The walls were covered in bloody, severed hands.

She didn't scream because her breath stopped. When it started again, she had had a moment to observe and realize that what she was looking at was not hands . . . exactly. It was just the skin, dissected and tanned and hung in frames so that anyone who cared to could read the verses of Ysmat of the Beads tattooed upon them in inks of black and red.

Between the macabre wall hangings, the long room was full of cases of books and racks of scrolls, stretching the length of the tower. Samarkar fixed her eyes on those. How hard would it be to start a fire here? Paper harbored the process of flame . . .

But something damped her attempt. She reached for the fire, encouraged it—and there was a brief flickering sense of smoke, then nothing more. As if she attempted to burn wet rags.

"There are books of Erem in this library," Hrahima said from the window behind her. "They protect themselves. You will burn nothing here."

Samarkar turned. "We could burn the compound—"

"If it were as easy as that to destroy the writings of Erem," said Hrahima, "do you think any of it would have endured this long?"

Samarkar thought about it. "The blind women are innocents. And the ones we wish to destroy are not here. But I thought I could take their weapons from them—"

The tiger's head filled the whole of the window. "Are you ready to go, Wizard Samarkar?"

"Did you find Edene?"

The tiger's earrings jingled. *No.* She held out her hand through the window frame.

Samarkar let Hrahima lift her from the library to the roof. Temur was just behind her, back against the wall, arms folded across his chest. Samarkar touched him in passing.

He raised his head and looked at her. "Come on," he said. "Let's go raise an army."

THE SURGERY—AND ASHRA'S BREW—WORKED. THEY COULD NOT SAVE everyone, but nearly half was more than none. And as Jurchadai and the other shaman-rememberers taught the wizards their new wards, the rate of infection slowed.

And yet Tsering found herself no better rested. Without Altantsetseg to lead them, the few young men among the Qersnyk refugees often found their way into the city even though it was forbidden, either out of curiosity or the daring of adolescence. She heard rumors that they were mingling with the revolutionaries.

Meanwhile, Songtsan-tsa still refused to evacuate the city, although Hong-la said the empress too was working toward that solution. Song-tsan seemed sunk in a hysterical denial of the necessary, as if by refusing to admit the danger he could by sheer force of will make it not be. Tsering would have bet on Yangchen-tsa's ability to move her husband to any decision . . . but on this he seemed obdurate, and Hong-la said that even appeals to the safety of their son accomplished nothing.

Tsering found herself unable to do much to help the wizards involved in placating the Cold Fire. They needed magic to draw down its strength and energy, to siphon off the tensions in the earth that made it shift and crack. And magic . . . was the thing Tsering did not have.

She had been a peasant woman once, though, and there was use in seeming so again. She let her grief for Ashra and for Altantsetseg line her face. She dressed in ragged woolens. She went out among the people of Tsarepheth as one of their own, and she *listened.*

She was not the only one. Other, younger wizards and novices risked themselves in gathering intelligence: Anil-la, Elevarasan-la, others she did not know so well.

The teahouses and the noodle shops and the wine sellers were supposed to be closed by order of the Bstangpo, but Tsering—with her hair braided plainly down her back and her throat feeling naked and soft without its collar—found many a narrow room with sealed windows where *rakshi* could be bought or bartered. And in most of those rooms she found young men and a few older men and women who were scarred by imperial justice, and who were drinking. And talking about how the emperor would seal them all up in this city to die of the plague or the smoking mountain.

It might be a boy with one hand here; a woman with a slit nose there. But every one of them had anger, and a story.

And Tsering... Tsering found that she kept their names to herself, even as she visited them more and more.

The *RAKSHI* BAR SERVED WINE AS WELL, AND MILLET BEER, AND SOMETHING that might have been tea after a few less steepings. Whatever—it was really just to water and warm the *rakshi.* The bar was close and noisy and it stank of urine. Tsering sat with her back propped in the half corner between the wall—which was swaddled with quilts on the inside to absorb light and sound—and one of the ribs supporting the wall and the ceiling.

Tsering held a warmed cup of millet whiskey in her hands and made a show of nodding as she listened to men spread rumors about the return of Prince Tsansong and how the Bstangpo was in league with the Carrion-King. Over the past month, she'd been easing into the regular haunts of the disaffected, and she thought now they accepted her as part of the scene. At least, if they were censoring themselves in her presence, she couldn't imagine what they were not saying.

Then her eyes fastened on a young man slipping in through the door, and she felt the wrongness of his presence like the stab of a knife. He wore the clothing of a farmer or journeyman, and his hair was bound back in an unprepossessing queue—but he moved with a warrior's grace and ease and the rolling gait of someone who had spent his life in the saddle.

Qersnyk.

The tavern didn't hush as he entered, and his boots made no sound on the mixed sawdust and sand of the floor. But he crossed to one of the older, quieter men who was always sitting near the outspoken firebrands calling for revolution, and Tsering felt a chill radiate from her center.

She drank her *rakshi* down in a swallow and stood, dropping the bowl under the server's table as she passed. A brisk wind pricked her cheeks as she passed through the door into evening; autumn was settling over the mountains.

Head down, walking like a woman on an irritating errand, she passed a dozen of the emperor's men moving in formation. A flock of some ill or dead herder's tooth-birds, left unattended, scattered in all directions before their boots, clawed fingers scrabbling on the ends of brightly feathered arms.

She heard the cries of alarm, the violence beginning behind her as she lengthened her stride for the Citadel.

THE TWINS' HAND HEALED WITHOUT DISABILITY, IN LARGE PART DUE TO THE intervention of al-Sepehr. He had brought them to the ghost city of Qeshqer and made a nest there, refusing to allow Saadet and Shahruz to return to Qori Buqa until they were again strong, and he had sent one of the young rukhs bearing messages to inform Qori Buqa that Saadet had been needed by her father but would be returning soon.

Saadet herself wrote notes—or dictated them at first, until her fingers could crimp together to hold a pen—and was surprised to receive replies. Unsentimental replies—but the ones she sent were businesslike as well. She could not bring herself to flirt in front of her father, even *if* flirting had been an art at which she excelled.

When she rode back into the keep at Qarash, it was through the front gate, mounted on a fat dish-nosed Song mare. The saddle for which she and the Master had gone into the Steles of the Sky was on the back of a pack pony behind her, hidden under blanket rolls and sacks of grain. She wasn't sure that was entirely necessary—the Padparadscha Seat, it turned out, was a battered old war saddle, blackened with age and sweat, sword-cuts lovingly repaired across its skirts. But she still found herself running her hands across it wonderingly every time she dismounted to sleep or urinate.

The depths of the Qersnyk sky spread over her, heavy and oppressively blue. She longed for her own horizons, but kept the homesickness to herself. Shahruz, increasingly withdrawn and sharp as the days progressed, would only have mocked her for it. She was aware enough of her womanish weakness without him to remind her.

When she brought her animals to the corral, she simply lifted the saddle down from the pack pony and gave instruction that the blankets and gear were to be taken to her room.

The twins had ridden a week from the border farm where their Master had bought the ponies for them. They were dusty and road-stained, face bare as a Qersnyk woman, hair braided about their throat to keep the wind off. It was the end of summer, and the skies were growing torn.

"Where is the Khagan?" Saadet asked a Qersnyk man without lowering her eyes. Her arms were full of saddle; he neither rushed to take her burden from her nor looked away from her naked face. Shahruz frowned inside her, but if she were going to live among barbarians—if she were going to play their Khatun—it was as well she learned their ways.

Having received enlightenment—at least in regard to her lover's whereabouts—Saadet bore her saddle into the hall and from thence to a council chamber. She did not knock, but entered.

Qori Buqa sat behind a knee-height table that supported a sprawling heap of maps. On his right was a shaman-rememberer in its layers of bright blue silks; arrayed around the rest of the table were four of the Khagan's war-band. They leaned forward in Song-style ox-yoke chairs designed so one could lift them by the back and they would fold together. A filigree screen of dark wood stood behind Qori Buqa, supporting a streaky panel of gray and amber agate that framed his head.

He started to his feet as Shahruz thrust aside the beaded curtain that filled the doorway. He entered the room on two big strides and stopped there.

It was Saadet who bowed her head, extended the saddle across her arms—above the young curve of her pregnant belly—and said, "As you bid. I have fetched your throne, my husband."

IT WAS EASIER GETTING OUT OF ALA-DIN THAN IT HAD BEEN GETTING IN. THE dead men didn't seem to be ensorcelled to stop anyone leaving, and the interlopers were out of the valley by dawn. This time, they just kept walking while the sun was low enough to permit it, eager to get as much clean earth between themselves and Ala-Din as possible.

Temur had planned to make sure they found shelter before noon, when the sun would be at its fiercest. They could sleep, ration out some of their water, and—he hoped—be back to the canyon where they had cached the horses by the following morning. Then they faced the challenge of the mountains, and the impending winter, and the steppe. If he meant to raise his banner at his grandfather's former summer palace at Dragon Lake in the spring—as he had told Ato Tesefahun—they would have to ride hard and find remounts.

But as the pale Rahazeen sun climbed the sky, both sun and sky began to vanish behind a gold-lit pall. The wind freshened, rising dry and hot from the west, and each breath Temur drew frosted his throat with grit.

When he looked back over his shoulder, he saw a wall of yellow ochre like a bellying sail rising to the drape of heaven behind them. The leading edge groped across the earth as lightning crackled through and around it, lacing the atmosphere with blue-and-violet fire.

"What," said Samarkar, eyes wide, "on earth is *that*?"

"Haboob," Hrahima muttered, as Temur said, "Devil wind. A dust storm. We need to find shelter now."

But they were halfway up the bowl-shaped slope of a baked plateau as featureless as—if considerably smaller than—any stretch of the steppe. The storm didn't appear to be moving quickly until Temur glanced at its bottom edge and saw how it consumed standing rocks and thorn trees as quickly as a good mare could run. They had no canvas with which to make shelters, only the thin blankets in which they had shivered each night and the coil of rope at Hrahima's hip.

She pulled that loose and began linking them together, belt to belt. "We stay upright; we stay together; we keep moving. Maybe the afrit is just passing."

Temur bit his lip. "Afrit?" He was afraid he knew before he asked. There were storm-demons that rode such winds when they came across the steppe. Of course, the desert people would have their own name for them.

"Like a djinn," the Cho-tse said, snugging the last coil of rope around her own midsection and winding the tail over her shoulder to keep it out from underfoot. "But air rather than fire."

"That's an *afrit*?" Samarkar asked.

Hrahima shook her head and started walking. "It's an afrit's chariot. Pray it rolls us by."

"What do you suppose the odds are that it has no connection to al-Sepehr's magic, and this is just a coincidence?" Samarkar said.

"No bet," Temur answered, a moment before Hsiung's deep brown eyes began to glare and coruscate jade-green.

IN THE MORNING, SAADET STOOD IN THE WINDOW OF HER BEDCHAMBER, both hands resting on the slight curve of her abdomen, and watched her husband to be go out among the afflicted on his blood-shouldered mare with only two of his war-band beside him. The ill and infirm came to their Khagan, clustering at his stirrup.

Saadet smiled as Qori Buqa leaned down from his battered saddle and—one by one—pressed their foreheads with his hands.

Shahruz shuddered from his citadel of loathing within her. She leaned her forehead on the windowsill and thought, *I have borne all this, brother dear. You may concern yourself with the next part.*

Gladly will I redeem your whoredom, he answered.

ON THROUGH THE DUST, THROUGH THE BLINDNESS. THEY MUFFLED THEIR mouths and noses in folds of their desert robes and breathed through cloth. Their eyes they wrapped as well, groping their way often on all fours, by means of Samarkar's arcane senses and Hrahima's inhuman ones. Even if the dust had permitted them to open their eyes without agony, its pall would have utterly blinded them. They lost nothing through binding their faces, and at least they could breathe.

Temur tapped the ground ahead with his fingers and toes, wishing his midnight encounters with the local vegetation had better inured him to the barbed and prickly flora of the Rahazeen wastes. Apparently no matter how many times you got stabbed by a thorn tree, it still hurt. He heard Samarkar exclaim occasionally too, and could only assume that Hrahima and Hsiung suffered in silence.

His hand found warm hide, a long hard cannon bone, the unmistakable leg of a mare. She snorted and stamped; her tail smacked the side of his head. The hard-muscled curve of her rump was familiar, and so was the throaty whinny with which she greeted him.

"Oh, Dumpling," he said. "Have you come to lead us out of this?"

"Temur?" asked Samarkar.

"The mare is here," said Hrahima. Which was good, because Temur's throat was too full of emotion for words to squeeze through it.

He ran his hand up her side while the others gathered behind him, keeping the ropes from tangling. When he touched Bansh's belly, it felt taut as a bow. A great shudder ran through her, the ripple of muscular contraction.

She was in labor, though not yet straining hard.

She stepped forward. Temur walked beside her, one hand hooked in the girth of the saddle she was—inexplicably, yet again—wearing. As the ropes tugged, the others came with him. "We follow the mare," he said.

Through a world of close air, of filtered darkness, of the rasp of breath through breath-wet cloth, Temur followed Bansh and the others followed Temur. She moved purposefully, and even when the contractions took her she did not stop. One foot lifted, slid forward, came down. Another. Another. A hesitation-march as slow as if she bore her rider in his funeral parade.

No, thought Temur. *She's leading him out of it again.*

The storm had a sound, a kind of sighing hiss. Though what hung on the air was dust and not sand—it was not whipped by wind but hung in the air like smoke, and it felt like silk where it coated one's fingers—still, there was a soughing noise where so many tiny particles brushed against one another. It infiltrated into all the gaps of Temur's clothing, worked into the creases of his armpits and his groin, chafed and rubbed him red with every step. But the mare walked on and so did he, and so did those who followed.

He only knew from the silence that they had come out of the storm.

There was no shifting hiss, no scour of dust soft against his hands. Bansh stopped, groaning like a bellows at the strongest contraction yet.

Samarkar walked into Temur. He staggered, caught himself, and realized that layers of dust were not dragging his feet. Hesitantly, he touched the wrappings across his face. There was light beyond them; despite the still air, she had not brought them to a cave.

Ochre scales cracked away as he unwound the bandages, ready at any instant to snatch them closed again. A crack of light came through his gritty, clotted eyelashes. It was clean light, bright as many moons, white and pure.

"The storm is done."

He pulled his crusted wraps and over-robes away, drawing a full breath through lips smeared with mud that tasted of iron and salt. It was night, but no night such as he had ever seen; the sky was deep violet between stars as thick as seeds strewn on a cake. A vast moon as black as his bay mare's mane floated half-occluded by a shattered horizon, and two other moons gleamed the colors of rust and ivory. Directly overhead one star shone so bright and white that it would have been no challenge to read by its light.

Mountains rose on every side of them, green and forested at the base, stark white at the peaks. One forked summit seemed familiar but strange, as if Temur had seen it from a different angle. The season was mild and moist, and between the stones of the road they strode upon, thick moss dimpled underfoot.

They stood at the mouth of a valley flanked by two trees as great as any of the forest giants of Song—except the trees were long dead, bark peeled back almost to the spreading, knotted roots to leave their trunks and their wandering tributary branches bare. Their lowest boughs meet to form a great peaked arch above a stone-paved road that led deeper into the valley beyond them. Something was carved on the foremost branch— a word in twisting letters that glowed with their own viridian light. They made Temur ill. He glanced away, and realized that the trees were grown not of wood, but white stone.

Beyond the trees, the ruins of a shattered city stretched as far as the eye could see, twisted with vines and ferns and shining in the glow of that brilliant star and the two moons that gave light.

"I do not know how we've come here, but this is the sky of ancient Erem," Hrahima said. "We must find shelter before the daystars rise."

Hsiung's eyes still flickered with a changeable light. His desert veils hanging about his neck in limp, stained coils, he looked up at the word that Temur could not abide and then glanced away and crouched down on the stones. With one thick finger he began to write in the syllabary tongue of Song. His finger trailed a wet stain.

Temur looked down at his own hands and realized that—scoured by the dust until there was not a finger width of intact skin left on them—they too were bleeding.

Samarkar bent over Hsiung, to read what he wrote in the light of his eyes and of the moons.

"*Reason*," she said. "Is that this place's name?"

The mute monk nodded. Something welled in Temur—grief, exhaustion, the relief of survival, and the numb discomfort that was all he could muster. He had reached the end of his endurance.

Temur stepped past Samarkar and Hsiung, brushing Samarkar's elbow with his own. He put his arms around the neck of his laboring mare, pressed his face to the velvet skin there, and—for Bansh, for Edene, for everything brave and indomitable—he wept.

Bansh's flanks shuddered again. She snaked her head around and snapped irritably at his shoulder as if to say, *I have no time for your histrionics, inconvenient man. I have a foal to get born.*

19

Temur and the others walked through the bright night into reason, following a laboring mare. Bansh's tail swung, knotted and matted with ochre dust. Temur's raw fingers itched with frustration. He should have braided it for her before the birth pangs started. He should have—

He had done what he could to keep her safe. Perhaps there was still time. And she had come back to him, had she not? And led him to a place of safety as well.

Well, safety of a sort. Ruins of any sort had a nasty tendency to harbor ancient magics and forgotten monsters. And he could not ignore Hrahima—*Hrahima!*—and her nervous glances at the sky. *We must find shelter,* she had said.

Bansh would not have brought them here if there were not a place of safety. Two and two abreast, they trailed her down the stone-flagged road that hugged one edge of the fern-hung valley. Great trees such as Temur had never seen—like massive ferns themselves—bowered crack-faced, roofless dwellings that stared with empty eyes. Here and there, where a wall had fallen recently, he could see that they were built of white and peach and golden stone, but elsewhere the moss and heavy-flowered vines had covered every inch.

On the right, a drop continued down to a stream that danced from stone to stone, but the valley was narrow enough, the light of the sky bright enough, that Temur could clearly see more ruins on the other side. Bridges, arched and golden, had once spanned the stream. Now their stubs branched off from the road he and the others followed—and then crumbled away into empty air.

"Who do you suppose keeps the road clear?" Samarkar asked.

No one answered.

The scent of flowers and fruit saturated moist air, and great blooms like pale trumpets competed for space with tiny sprays of delicate petals as red as the heart's own tide. Tiny frogs in all the colors of embroidery silks hopped amid stones and ferns, and birds flickered among the tree fronds. One bough drooped ahead of them, bobbing under a moving weight. Temur caught a glimpse of a climbing serpent, thick as his wrist and green as jade, so brightly colored that even in the dim light it seemed translucent. It paused to flick a wax-pale tongue at Bansh, eyes catching light as if it were some jeweled automaton with garnets set in their place. Picked out in scales along its length were elegant, intricate black interlocking cursive symbols Temur knew must be calligraphy—though in no tongue he'd ever learned.

"Can you read those?" he asked Hsiung.

The monk, squinting through what must for him have been tremendous gloom, bit his lip and shook his head.

The snake slipped away, its course visible for some time by the bobbing of tree fronds. Samarkar strained after it, but said nothing and followed thoughtfully when Bansh and the others walked on. The moss breathed out a sweet moisture Temur had not known since Song. Banners of mist, opalescent in the starlight, draped like a dancer's veils through the forest, the reclaimed city, and the night.

Something Temur had taken for a shaggy boulder in the stream below shifted, lifted, streaming water from a mossy, saturated algal beard.

It was the head of an enormous turtle.

The thing's shell was big as a trade wagon, each plate rising to a dull spike as if someone had dipped a rod in molten glass and drawn it up. Like a baby bird's mouth—but big enough to snap Bansh in half—the beak gaped shockingly wide, revealing a pale-pink gullet as the only softness in an armor-plated skull. The skin was gray-green, corrugated, festooned with tags and growths and verdant with water slime; the eyes were flat black beads behind gray lids creased like folded rice paper.

The turtle's back half seemed partially buried in the opposite bank, but it rocked one foot like a pillar out of the stones of the stream and strained up the ferny steepness toward them. Bansh flicked her grotty tail and snorted, stalking past with a fine display of unconcern.

Well, if she wasn't worried, Temur could pretend not to be. He noticed, though, that even though the turtle's own length separated it from the road, they all fell into single file against the far slope. Even Hrahima gave the thing the respect of distance.

The sky above might have been brightening as the valley widened before them, or perhaps it was just that they came out of the shade of quite so many trees. Temur didn't miss Hrahima's lashing tail. But here the ground was more level, and the overgrown buildings stood in better repair and greater profusion. Bansh moved forward smartly, seeming to direct herself to one in particular—a low structure breathing moist air from a black doorway that suggested an intact roof under the weight of its vines.

As they approached, a rustle like a gust of wind spread through the vegetation, though Temur felt no breeze. He turned his head; on every side the ferns and fern trees were folding up their fronds and fans and drawing the glistening dark-green spears that resulted into armored, squatly conical trunks. The vines rolled their leaves up in lances and swallowed them in fat winding stems, leaving the valley looking as if someone had stacked rank upon rank of odd-sized terra cotta beehives haphazardly everywhere.

The sky was definitely brighter.

Bansh vanished into the dark doorway. Hsiung jerked his foot up and half-skipped as he stepped over a centipede as long as Temur's forearm. It whipped out of sight, but not before giving Temur an unfortunate, stomach-clenching memory of the gut-worm he'd fought in the lands of the woman-king Tzitzak. He eyed the close space ahead and hesitated. *Trapped in the dark again.*

Samarkar touched his wrist, slid her fingers through his. She stepped forward. He followed, half-sideways. Together, they went through the door.

THE LIGHT OUTSIDE LAY SAVAGE OVER A BARREN LANDSCAPE, SO SCORCHED and sere that Temur could hardly credit the verdant jungle they'd walked through, so bright that he avoided even looking at the door. He wished for water—for Bansh and for himself and his companions—and there was a leathern bucket with Bansh's gear, where he had heaped it in the corner. But Hrahima would permit no one to risk those suns. And so the others took it in turns to sleep while Temur kept watch beside his mare—with time to braid her tail after all.

Now that it was upon them, he could not help but wonder what she would give him: colt or filly? The foal would have a steppe horse's unique light-catching coat, but in what shade? Blood-bay, liver-bay, black, or sorrel? The black-maned mirror-gold called phantom, so highly prized for its beauty? A marmot-colored roan? Not knowing the stud at all—or the mare's lineage—he had only Bansh's liver-bay color to be his guide. And bay was a color that could overshadow others—with a few exceptions, the foal could be any shade from the dove-colored dun to silver, depending on the stallion.

Let it be born easily, Temur prayed as her water broke, trying not to think that he stood under a roof and the wrong sky lay above it. *Let mare and foal be well.*

In the meantime, he cared for the mare and Samarkar cared for him.

The mare went down on her side in a drift of dead leaves and Temur crouched behind her. But when the foal's long legs, like curved sticks, emerged from the birth canal, he could not believe his eyes. The hooves with their protective overgrowth seemed weirdly long and ragged, just as they should—but the legs themselves looked white in the shadows; when at his request Samarkar sent a witchlight close and tuned its color to match the daylight of the steppe, he saw that they were splashed with white to the knee, and the color above that—even darkened by the womb's wetness—was a pale and glistering shade of electrum: silver tinged with yellow. One could not even call it gold.

The nose breached, and it was pink as a pig's snout, a white streak wide as a finger dipping between the nostrils. The hair above it was shone that same pale gleaming color.

Temur's mouth opened. With the next heave, the foal's entire head emerged. It laid as flat upon the forelegs as if it were a leaping hunter depicted in some stylized art of the Lotus Kingdoms. The membrane about its head was tearing, and Temur found himself meeting the gaze of one wet-lashed eye, as white-blue as a hazy sky, the pupil a black horizontal bar amid a streaky, brighter halo.

"Impossible," said Temur.

Samarkar materialized beside him as if *that* were her magic. "What's wrong?"

"She can't be that color." He crouched beside Bansh's hindquarters. The foal's forelegs kicked sheaves of dead foliage this way and that as she scrabbled at the ground. Temur's voice shook, but his hands were steady as he tore the white, slimy veil of the membrane away from the foal's nostrils. Bansh heaved again: a gush of hot fluid followed, and the foal was pushed from the birth canal as far as the shoulders but slipped back in again.

"The shoulders are the hard part," Temur said.

"What do you mean, she can't be? She is—" Samarkar shook her head. "I ride well enough."

He knew that. He also knew Samarkar well enough to understand that it was a qualification to whatever she would say next, and waited. Another push brought the foal out to mid-body. Bansh craned her head around to look, and Temur touched her rump. "Almost," he told her. "One more good one." He could drag the foal free at this point, but it was better if the mare did it herself, and she did not seem tired yet.

"I've never bred horses. She can't *be* that color?"

"She's a ghost sorrel. She should only be that color if Bansh were phantom-colored, or mirror. You have to breed phantom or mirror to each other, or to ghost, to get this color. And no one would allow that breeding."

He looked up, spreading blood-and-mucus-slimed hands helplessly. "It's an unlucky color."

She put a hand on his shoulder. "You know it's a filly already?"

"I hope." Mares were worth more than stud horses or geldings. Mares were milk and foals—

Even a ghost sorrel.

But Bansh heaved up suddenly, leaving Temur scrambling into a squat to support the foal, and it slid into his arms in an awkward mess of kicking limbs and slime. He caught it and eased it down—but he'd felt the foal's testicles when his arm went between its legs and stood up disappointed. The cord had broken. Temur prayed for an intact afterbirth, quickly to follow.

"Colt," he said. *Unlucky colt.* Still, healthy. Already raising his head and blinking around with those blue demon eyes as Temur bent over to help peel the rest of the membrane away. As he did, an idea struck him.

"Take his bad luck away," he said to Samarkar. "Name him."

She stopped as if struck, eyes wide as if he had given her a tremendous gift. Which, after a fashion, was true.

"Afrit," she said, with a glance at Hrahima. "For the time of his birth. And for blue eyes."

Temur touched the colt between the ears, noticing that the white stripe on his nose ran up to a ragged white pattern between the eyes as well. "Your name is Afrit," he said.

The foal blinked at him with lush eyelashes, just beginning to feather and dry. Beside him, Bansh heaved again, beginning the process of getting the afterbirth out.

HONG-LA ROSE FROM HIS READING TABLE AT THE SCRATCHING BESIDE HIS door. He expected the opened panel to reveal a novice. What he found was two women he did not expect to see together, each dressed in clothing so foreign to their usual habits that he blinked and rocked back, too stunned to gesture them inside.

In the leathers and wool of a farmer, Tsering took the empress—dressed as a lesser courtier, a baby in a sling across her chest and her face plain of its usual varnish—by the elbow and pulled her across the threshold. Yangchen-tsa's eyes widened that anyone would so mishandle her. Hong-la was more shocked that Tsering would come in without an explicit invitation. He was even more startled to realize that the fussing baby whose cries pierced his ears was the heir to all of Rasa—here alone, with no protection except his mother.

Whatever might have driven her to such risk—he felt the cringe start at the nape of his neck, run between his shoulders.

Tsering released the empress, shut the door, and bowed low, an apology for her abruptness. Hong-la noticed that her gesture was in no way aimed at Yangchen.

"Fear not, Wizard Tsering," he said. "I know one of my peers would not barge in without reason. Especially not dragging a queen."

Tsering flinched, a lowered gaze brushing Yangchen's shoes. She pointed to the window and said, "Revolution."

Hong-la's split-toed shoes squeaked on the floor as he pivoted. Forgetting himself, black coat flapping about him, he crossed the room in three strides and grasped the window frame in both hands.

Hong-la's window faced Tsarepheth. He could see the sharp red roofs, the beige-and-white walls, the towers of the Black Palace in the distance. Thin lines of smoke always rose from the cookfires and chimneys of the city—but now he saw a heavy pall, billows, and—here and there—the vermilion toss of flames.

"Shit," said the Wizard Hong.

It could be dealt with—it was only flame. A process, and wizards were nothing if not experts at controlling processes.

There was a speaking-tube beside the hearth. He uncapped it and called down. "This is Hong-la. Please request Yongten-la come to my chamber in haste. This is an emergency."

The echo of his own voice down the tube was followed by the echo of a novice repeating the message. When Hong-la had confirmed it, he capped the tube again and turned to the women. "That does not explain why the empress is here, dressed as one of her maids."

"It was the only way I could escape the palace," she said. "My husband ordered me to my rooms." One arm curved protectively around her son's back. He burrowed against her breast, wailing as he snuffled for the nipple. Yangchen-tsa turned away, self-consciously tugging the wrapped collar of her dress aside.

"Never mind," Hong-la said. "I'm a eunuch, and I have seen a breast before, and frankly I prefer the male variety. Please continue, majestrix."

"The guards did not know me bare-faced," she said. "I took my son for a rest, I said. By now they will have found us not in my room. I came to tell you . . ."

She pressed her nose to her son's head. He did not seem contented with the breast, but she breathed deep anyway. Hong-la fought back a surge of irritation—not that she needed to draw strength from the child to speak, but that now—*now*, after the infestation had come under control, after so many lives had been lost—her conscience would drive her to speak.

She surprised him.

"I have come to evacuate the city," she said. "Whether my husband wills it or not. It is time for the empress to stand for her people."

"But will the people stand for the empress?" Hong-la asked.

There was another scratch upon the door. "Come!" he said, unsurprised when it opened only wide enough for narrow-shouldered Yongten-la to slip through.

"I guess you've looked outside?" said Yongten.

"We need a corps of wizards to fight the fire," said Hong-la. "Or the whole city may burn."

Yangchen-tsa put her hands to her mouth. "Why would they burn their own houses?"

You *ask that?*

"They can reach them," Tsering said. "And they have to burn something."

"A corps is assembling," said Yongten-la. "We will join them in a few moments."

Tsering held up her hand. "Yongten-la, I believe the riots were triggered . . . that is to say, today when I was in the city, I saw three of our own disaffected youth and a Qersnyk lad dragged through the streets by the emperor's militia."

The ends of his moustache shivered as his creased lips pursed. "You believe the refugees may join the rioting?"

"There are some young women and men—"

"I will close the Citadel Gates."

While he went to the speaking tube to give the order, Hong-la quickly explained that the empress had come to offer them aid in evacuating the city. "I'm not sure how that would work," Yongten-la said. "Without your husband's troops to maintain order and carry the word—"

"There will be those fleeing the burning," said Tsering. "They will follow an authority figure, especially one who is telling them what they want to hear. If we can get her to where they gather, we will save lives."

"A train of refugees," said Hong-la, with the sickening certainty of remembrance. "Turned out into the fields without preparation. Not enough food, not enough water, not enough warm bedding or clothes . . ."

Tsering nodded. "And how would we get her through a burning, rioting city?"

"We send her with the wizard corps," said the Wizard Yongten. "You, Tsering, have a special relationship with the Qersnyk refugees. You will go to them and explain why the gates are sealed."

Thin-lipped, Tsering nodded. But Yongten-la had focused his attention on the queen. "What do you say, Empress? It will require a great deal of physical courage on your part."

She looked down, but nodded. "It is the least—"

Her words were lost in the shattering of a tremendous wall of sound. The floor jumped; dust sifted from the gaps between the white stones of the wall. For a moment, Hong-la thought the Cold Fire had erupted, and this had all become abruptly academic.

But he would have *felt* that, *otherwise.*

They stood stunned for a moment. Yongten-la was the first to recover, Tsering-la at his heels as he made for the window. When Hong-la joined them, he saw a huge billow of dust rising from the direction of the Black Palace.

A long section of its façade was cracked and fallen.

"Black powder," said Tsering, her voice level and plain. "A wizard made that happen."

TEMUR HAD SAID HE MEANT TO FETCH WATER AS SOON AS THE DAYSUNS SET, but when the daysuns set and the whole soft forest rustling unveiled itself once more, Temur lay finally sleeping. It was Samarkar who picked up the leathern folding bucket from beside where he slumped against the wall, picked her way past the exhausted bay mare (nearly invisible in the gloom) and her pale colt (already standing and nursing, his stubby tail working like a pump handle), and borrowed Hrahima's rope.

The Cho-tse was standing just within the door. Samarkar would have expected her to be looking out at the night, but instead she stood watching the foal. He did look like a ghost; a stark reverse silhouette that seemed to gather what little light there was until he shimmered. It was the steppe-pony coat, of course, with its strange reflective shine. Knowing that didn't make looking at him any less spooky.

Hrahima handed her the rope and said, "Afrit? Do you really think that was such a good idea?"

"It was the one I had," said Samarkar.

She picked her way to the riverbank. It was not such a steep drop here, but she went carefully even in the bright moon- and star-light. She was not unmindful of the dragon-turtle . . . not that she'd ever seen one before, but what else could it possibly have been? It hadn't seemed likely that that one was going anywhere . . . but where there was one, there might be many.

The water was cold and clear and smelled fresh. More of those jewel-toned frogs hopped along the margins, leading Samarkar to wonder if they hid themselves in the mud when the daystars rose.

Well, she had to test it on somebody: she bowed her head and drank her fill. It did not seem to hurt her, beyond the ache of the cold across her teeth.

As she climbed back up the bank with a brimming bucket, a sound reached her that did not seem to belong to the jungle night. There were birdcalls, of course; frog croaks; the droning of insects. But above them, a faint silvery jingle, regular and repetitive.

It sounded like bells.

Careful not to spill the water, she trotted back to the others. Hrahima was outside, ears pricked, staring into the night.

"You hear that?"

"Hoofbeats," said Hrahima, which Samarkar had not detected. "And harness bells."

A STEADY WIND BLEW THE COLD FIRE'S SMOKE BACK THROUGH THE PASS ABOVE the Citadel, behind the mountains and north toward the Range of Ghosts. Hong-la could not remember the last time he'd seen so much of the sky.

A ripple spread across it, and Hong-la turned his head. It had no color of its own, but behind it the color of the sky was not the same.

The empress walked beside him, head down, anonymous in ill-fitting, borrowed wizard's weeds. All around them, Citadel guardsmen protected a dozen wizards, and the flames of a burning city flickered and died away.

Hong-la cleared his throat. Were she dressed as a colleague or not, he could not bring himself to touch an empress's shoulder.

She looked up slowly, as if she must winch herself up to the effort. She squinted when she saw the flat expanse of turquoise overhead, the broad pale circle of the sun. She did not raise a hand to shield her eyes.

"So," said the Dowager Empress Yangchen, first such of that name. "Tsarepheth has fallen."

She hid her face again.

TEMUR AWAKENED IN A FIGHTING CROUCH WITH HIS KNIFE IN HIS RIGHT hand, with Hsiung pitching pebbles at his boots.

"Sorry," he said, and made to sheathe the blade, but Hsiung stopped him with a gesture. Their gazes met through the filtered night light, just within the doorway. Hsiung jerked his chin. *Outside.*

But not an immediate threat of, say, archers, because Samarkar and Hrahima were standing on either side of the door. Temur went to join them, the monk at his heels.

"Someone is coming," Samarkar said when Temur came to stand beside her. "And is not trying to hide."

Temur strained through the noise of the night. Yes, the clop of hooves on a stone road, and the familiar shimmer of bells. As he listened, the cries and rushings of the night creatures died away. Against a brightening sky came the hushed brushing sounds of the forest furling itself against the suns of day.

What would a shaman-rememberer be doing here?

A moment more, Temur thought, and he could ask for himself. Because there came a mouse-colored mare with a face splashed white from ears to lip, bearing a saddle with eight blue knots hung on it, wearing reins and other trappings strung with tiny bells. And on her back was— yes, a shaman-rememberer, dressed for ceremony or parade in a tall, brimless felt hat and an embroidered coat that covered him to his calves.

He stopped before Temur and bowed from the saddle as prettily as Temur had ever seen.

"Re Temur Khagan," he said, in a high and musical voice. "Raise your banner for me."

My banner was left in the desert, cached near the horses we had to abandon. But it was ridiculous to raise such arguments with a shaman-rememberer. They all knew what any of them knew, and each of them knew whatever the Eternal Sky chose to share with him. Temur turned to duck back inside only to find Samarkar standing behind him. She held out her hands. A length of silk draped over them.

"It was in Bansh's things."

Of course it had been. Temur turned back to the shaman-rememberer; the shaman-rememberer held out a lance.

"The suns—" said Hrahima.

"Are the Khan of Khans' to command." Temur had heard that voice before—in a dream, a fever dream, in an iced-over slab cave in a pass through the Range of Ghosts. He stopped and squinted; the shaman-rememberer smiled encouragement, cheeks smooth and youthful where they bent around the grin.

Temur hadn't seen the goddess's face. Mother Night wore a veil.

But he knew that voice. He would have sworn.

Hands shaking, Temur grasped the lance around the smooth shaft, behind the iron barbs, and drew it to him. With Samarkar's help, it was easy enough to thread the loops of the banner around the shaft and fix it there.

When he raised it and shook out its folds, the dawn breeze lifted and rippled the shape of a running mare.

Light touched the top of the slope overhead, but it seemed mellower than Temur had expected. More golden. "Bring your mare inside," he urged the shaman-rememberer. "The light in this place kills."

"Stand fast, Khan of Khans," the shaman replied. "The kings that claimed this place are dead. Your sun rises."

Temur tilted his head back, heart lifting as the familiar dawn of the steppe limned the eastern rim of the valley lavender and silver. He glanced over his shoulder, alerted by the creeping sensation of being watched.

Brother Hsiung's eyes burned with a smoky green light as they followed him.

Edene was Queen, and her commands were obeyed without hesitation. By the ghulim, by the djinn.

All her commands except one.

She could not bid the djinn to go against his master's word. She could not bid him to leave. She could not bid him to tell her what he had named her son. Well—she could bid him any of those things, and all. And she did—but he only smiled and glanced aside like a shy maiden.

It would have been easy to direct her wrath against him. But the djinn was as bound by circumstance as she was—and more, bound against his will. He came and went—she assumed al-Sepehr summoned him— and while he never showed her frustration, she imagined she could sense it in him.

They hated the same man. While she could not trust him, that made him an ally.

Her son at her breast, wrapped within the violet folds of her ghul-woven robe, she stood overlooking the sands of Erem where they glowed softly under its brilliant night. She was watching her soldiers drill upon the slopes of the ancient city. The rattle of their spears comforted her.

She had made Besha Ghul her general. There were scrolls in the lost libraries of Erem on military things, tactics and strategy and provisioning. As a daughter of the Tsareg clan, Edene already knew many of these things—and the ring knew more. The ghulim proved quick studies. She could have ordered them, commanded them—as she had when the glass demons attacked. Instead, she made them promises: *love me, serve me willingly, and when we are free I will give this ring to Besha Ghul.*

The scent of al-Sepehr troubled her no longer.

Soon she would find a way to free the djinn, too, or at least twist his bonds of service. Soon she would bring the ghulim to Temur, the finest betrothal gift a queen could offer her warlord bridegroom: an army of loyal monsters.

IN THE QERSNYK CAMP, BENEATH THE PALL OF THE COLD FIRE'S FOUL BREATH, Tsering resigned herself to wandering. She was hoping for someone to recognize the black coat she'd changed back into and to come up to offer assistance. Since Altantsetseg's death, the meticulous maintenance had fallen off somewhat, and Tsering found herself kicking through drifts of ash as she meandered aimlessly between tents.

The problem was, she decided, that the refugees were used to seeing her. Except every other time when they'd been seeing her, she'd had someplace to go.

She'd just resigned herself to collaring people at random until she found someone who spoke enough Uthman or Rasan to take her to a leader when someone she recognized stepped up. A blue coat thrown loosely over his shirt, his collar untied, it was the shaman-rememberer Jurchadai.

She opened her mouth to explain that he and his people needed to evacuate, that except for the few who stayed behind to mind the Citadel, the wizards were surrendering Tsarepheth to the volcano. He spoke before she could shape the words.

"Re Temur is Khagan."

She choked; swallowed the words she had meant to say; spat out the ones that formed in their place. "Qori Buqa is Khagan."

"He is," said Jurchadai.

"How can that be?" Tsering asked, uneasily certain that she already knew the answer. "That two men may be Khagan?"

"Two men may call themselves Khagan," the shaman-rememberer said. "Until one of them is dead."

IT HAD BEEN A BEAUTIFUL WEDDING. ALL THE MORE SO BECAUSE AL-SEPEHR had planned it himself. Oh, not the ceremony, carried out at the hands of one of the Qersnyk she-male monstrosities they called priests. And not the horse races, the archery competition, the lancers on galloping mares tilting at rings and each other. Not the endless ritual exchange of gifts between the bride's family—in this case al-Sepehr—and the groom's family and war-band... although al-Sepehr could not deny the bride-wealth would be usefully deployed to hire more disposable mercenaries.

Certainly not the food. Or the rotten mare's milk served as a beverage. And al-Sepehr found himself wincing a little when the groom lifted his new bride over the withers of a blood-shouldered gray—carefully, with respect for her gravid state, for all it was in its early stages. Bitterly, he wished that Shahruz were there beside him, to share his discomfort in this barbaric ceremony with its bare-faced, swollen-bellied "bride."

Amid a great deal of whooping and protests—both from al-Sepehr's chosen escort of Nameless and from the war band of the new Khagan, Qori Buqa rode off with the twins into the distance, leading a dappled mare who would serve as the twins' mount once they were a discrete distance away.

There were protests but no whooping when the twins rode back the next day, leading Qori Buqa's mare. She was burdened with the body of Saadet's husband, draped flaccidly across the Padparadscha Seat.

He had fallen racing his new wife, she said. Like his father, and broken his neck in the slide from a running mare.

"MY DAUGHTER'S SON WILL BE QORI BUQA'S HEIR," said al-Sepehr, dropping a hand upon the twins' shoulder. Saadet kept her head down demurely, her hands hidden in a fold of cloth in her lap. Al-Sepehr thought he was the only one who could see that she was picking at the edge of her nail. "My daughter is his regent. That is how it shall be."

The war-band in the council chamber did not like it. They shifted in their yoke-backed chairs, and one with gray streaks in his hair—al-Sepehr wondered if he should have bothered to learn the man's name—stood up. He said, "Qori Buqa has other sons. Your daughter's child may be a girl, yet—"

They had argued the night through. The sky was silvering. Soon the sun would rise. "Qori Buqa had no other sons in wedlock."

The gray-haired man slammed his hand down on the table. *Barbaric children.* "As if your bizarre prejudices matter!"

But another man, this one with a forked beard and a high forehead, put a hand on his war-band brother's arm. "The girl has spirit," he said. "And sense. If she accepts our counsel, why not? We will need united tribes, if Otgonbayar's son Temur is raising an army. Do you think he'd let a one of us live, *forgive* a one of us, if he came to power?"

The gray-haired man frowned. But they all knew—word had come through the shaman-rememberers—that Re Temur had raised his banner.

The Scholar-God did indeed have a reason for letting him live, al-Sepehr thought. *His existence drives them into my hands.*

"Come outside with me," said al-Sepehr, and before they could protest that too, he went to the door. "I want to show you something."

IN THE GRAY MORNING, LIKE A FOG ROLLING OVER THE BATTLEMENTS OF the keep, like a breaking wave, the blood ghosts came. Al-Sepehr stood unmoved, Shahruz at his right hand, and kept his eyes open and unfocused until they had finished feeding on the last of Qori Buqa's men.

The exhaustion of the summoning made him want to stagger. It made his boots feel heavy as if caked with mud. But he went to the gate, still sealed for the night. When he struggled with the massive bolt, Shahruz intervened and threw it for al-Sepehr.

Before him, new light was spilling over the half-rebuilt city. The first tradesmen and merchants in the streets paused and turned; the gates of the keep were not usually thrown wide by a pregnant girl.

Saadet clung to the bolt as if that were all that held her upright. She raised her voice; she raised her unveiled face and cried, "Blood ghosts! Blood ghosts within the keep! Loyal men of Qarash, to me! To the son of Qori Buqa!"

Merchants and tradesmen, they came. They *ran.*

Behind al-Sepehr, there was blood. There was dust. Before him, Saadet disappeared into a swirl of embroidered coats and drawn knives.

Against a turquoise sky, a hot pale sun rolled up the western horizon to shine on a land that had not seen it before.